Finding Felicity

By
Monica Marlowe

Eternal Press
A division of Damnation Books, LLC.
P.O. Box 3931
Santa Rosa, CA 95402-9998
www.eternalpress.biz

Finding Felicity
by Monica Marlowe

Digital ISBN: 978-1-61572-447-5
Print ISBN: 978-1-61572-448-2

Cover art by: Amanda Kelsey
Edited by: Kim Richards

For Mom.

Acknowledgements:
This novel could not have been written without the support of the Noel Hynd workshop in Los Angeles; a huge "thank you" to Noel Hynd and Desiree Coderre, who always believed in me.

To Steve, who inspired the story in so many ways. And to all my friends and family who always offered their unwavering support of my dream to be an author—you know who you are!

My heartfelt appreciation goes to the staff at Eternal Press for the hard work that goes into turning a manuscript into a finished novel. And last of all, to my Mom, who taught me that God is everywhere.

“We believe that the divine presence is everywhere.”
—The Rule of Benedict 19:1

Beryl,
To your felicity!
In Love
Monica

Part I

1943

At seventeen, Marco was too young to know that what was about to happen would change his life forever. He shook his head and hurried through Venice's narrow streets, his monk's robe billowing about his feet. He had enough of war. Germans did not belong in Italy. Hitler's military machine ravaged Europe and soon the German army would be here. In his beloved Venezia.

Marco came to Venice for the summer to serve at the Order of Saint Peter and continue his monastic studies. He intended to eventually become a priest. The war was not going to change that. It ruined enough lives. It was not going to take any more from him than it already had. He lost his brother to the war. Arturo. As he walked, Marco remembered for the thousandth time the promise he made the last time they saw each other: he would become a novice at the monastery instead of becoming a soldier. He would serve God's will, not the political will. And when it was over, he would fulfill his mission. He would find a way. Make his way. Nothing would stop him. Of that he was certain. He knew how he would spend the rest of his life. So it would be. And had to be.

To Marco, all that mattered was God, and serving God. His sole purpose in life now was to turn the minds and hearts of humanity to the Holy Spirit. To peace.

On this bright summer morning, though, his mission was less exalted. He was running an ordinary errand, returning candelabra borrowed from a small nearby abbey. With his destination in sight, he quickened his pace.

Ascending the front steps two at a time, he reached the unlocked door and let himself in the chapel. Inside, the darkness brought a quiet stillness, a sanctuary from what ailed the world. It took a moment for his blue eyes to adjust, and when they finally did, he saw her for the first time. He stopped, motionless. His breath held.

She stood on the far side of the altar facing him, but she did not notice his arrival, so focused she was on lighting candles. There were dozens of ivory pillars laid out before her. One by one, she lit them with delicate hands and concentrated movement. Her face was luminous, her dark hair and thoughtful eyes in sharp contrast to her creamy complexion. Hers was the most beautiful face Marco had ever seen. He wondered how old she was. Sixteen? Seventeen?

For a moment, he stood mesmerized. His pulse quickened. Passion, hot and unfamiliar, inflamed his blood. His body.

Who was this girl?

What was this feeling that overtook him?

Aware suddenly of someone else in the chapel, she lifted her gaze from the candles and looked at Marco.

Their eyes held in a moment of wondrous discovery.

Lost in the dark depths of her eyes, Marco ached to know her. Spontaneous desire struck his body with a jolt. His hand released its grip on the candelabra and it crashed to the floor.

The moment was broken.

"Are you all right?" Even in its urgency her voice had a soothing softness that echoed through the chapel. She hastened toward Marco, the sound of her footsteps reminding him of the gentle patter of a ballerina's slippers. He watched her body move beneath her plain black dress, graceful even in her haste. The fullness of her breasts rose and fell with each step and he felt his body catch fire at the sight of her.

Shaken, scared by these unfamiliar feelings, Marco turned and began to hurry out of the chapel.

"No! Wait!" she pleaded.

He glanced back at her as she rushed to follow him, her long dark hair flowing with every movement. He wanted to stop and pull her into his arms. To kiss the lips that had just spoken.

At her pursuit, he lengthened his stride and reached the door. He opened it quickly and stepped into the glaring daylight. He ran for blocks before stopping to catch his breath.

Finally, he stood on an ancient bridge overlooking the sparkling Grand Canal and took a deep breath. *I cannot ever go back there*, he thought. *I must never see her again!*

* * * *

Present Day

The only sound in the empty Art Deco lobby of the Empire State Building was the click of Madeline O'Connor's designer heels. She hurried toward the elevator banks, in a rush, as always, to her office. The sun was just beginning to rise over Manhattan and the city was only now blinking awake. Madeline had been up since five a.m. She already had answered email and completed conference calls with staff in Paris and London from her office at home. She loved the quiet of the early morning. The way it whispered about fresh possibilities. New beginnings. It was her favorite time of day.

"Good morning, Miss O'Connor." It was Sam at the security desk, a serious and handsome African-American. He was in charge of security at the building and, like Madeline, enjoyed arriving early.

"Good morning, Sam," Madeline smiled. The sight of him always made her feel better. Safer. "When will you start calling me Madeline?" He called her Miss O'Connor and whenever he did, she admonished him. For years, it had been a ritual for both of them; something that never changed in a constantly changing world. She relished it, and so did Sam.

"You look especially lovely this morning ... Miss Madeline," he said. He smiled broadly, as if calling her Miss Madeline was a concession.

And he was right. Madeline was lovely as she strode through the lobby. She carried her slender five foot six inch frame with a confidence perfected by her exquisitely tailored pale green suit. The color set off her flawless ivory complexion, sparkling jade eyes, and long glossy auburn hair. Men were drawn to her and Sam, too, admired her beauty. What struck him more was the down-to-Earth kindness she always displayed.

She laughed easily. "Thank you, Sam."

He bowed his head slightly, straight-faced, his eyes returning to the monitors on the console before him.

"You have a good day, Miss O'Connor."

She laughed again, shaking her head, and continued into the elevator.

Madeline's position as Chief Executive Officer of Felicity International required her to dress in the latest styles. What started as a single high fashion lingerie boutique in Beverly Hills had grown into a worldwide chain of stores with a successful catalog division and corporate headquarters in Manhattan. In rare quiet moments, Madeline missed the early days of the business when Felicity was a fledgling company. Those days were long gone.

Arriving at Felicity's offices on the 49th floor, she glanced at her watch. Six-thirty. She had an hour and a half before her weekly Monday morning management meetings. First marketing.

Then operations. Finally legal. There would be the inevitable interruptions. Another Monday morning and, as always, excitement stirred in Madeline's blood as she contemplated her day. The elevator doors parted and she stepped into the world of Felicity. Her world.

This early, the offices were empty and quiet. By eight, the receptionist would be at the front desk and the phones would be ringing. People would be at their desks or in meetings. The suite would be buzzing with designers, executives, and office staff. Madeline continued to her office where her assistant, Eric, was already placing some reports and folders on her desk. He was in his late twenties and, with black hair and cornflower blue eyes, more handsome than a man had a right to be. He glanced up as Madeline entered the office.

"Good morning, Eric. You're here early. Good weekend?"

"Yes. Too short, though." He grinned slyly. "I won't even ask about yours. I know you worked all weekend."

She shrugged. He was right. She *had* worked all weekend. "So what's that?"

"Sales reports. Mail from Saturday's delivery."

"Anything interesting?"

She set her attaché down and slipped into her ivory leather chair, glancing at her computer screen, which displayed a dozen or more emails which arrived during her commute. She turned her attention back to her young assistant.

"Just the usual junk. There was one letter marked personal so I didn't open it. From Italy. Is there something you're keeping from me?" Eric teased, ever curious about Madeline's personal life. Even though he worked for Madeline for almost five years, she kept her private life just that. Private. Curiosity gnawed at him and he dangled the letter out to her.

"You know all you need to know," she winked at him but at the sight of the letter, her stomach contracted. "I'll get to it later. Thanks." She reached into her handbag and pulled out a pair of black-framed eyeglasses, slid them on, and turned again to her computer screen and clicked open an email.

Recognizing his cue, Eric propped the letter up against the vase of flowers on her desk and turned to leave.

"Oh, Eric?"

"Yes?"

"Leave early today, okay?"

"Thanks. I planned to." He smiled and walked out the door.

She rolled her eyes in mock frustration and laughed. Her phone rang. Madeline's eyes darted to the envelope that stared at her. She pulled her eyes away and answered the phone. "Madeline O'Connor."

"Madeline. Tyler Reed."

Oh, not him again.

She sighed impatiently. She knew what this was about.

"Tyler."

"I'm glad I caught you. Listen–"

She cut him off. "I've gotten your messages. I know you have a buyer for Felicity. How many times do I have to tell you? The company is not for sale. You know that."

"Aren't you at least interested in hearing the offer? Let's have dinner to talk about it."

"No."

"Just to hear—"

"Sell a company that is my life? Never."

"It's a good offer, Madeline. I feel obligated to ask you to consider it."

"Not to mention obligated to think about the fees for your firm," Madeline quipped.

"I'm not going to give up that easily. Neither is the buyer."

Her other line rang. "I've got to go. Good-bye, Tyler."

"Madeline–"

"Good-bye." She shook her head impatiently and disconnected him by picking up the other line. "Madeline O'Connor."

With this interruption, her nonstop morning was underway.

* * * *

Two weeks prior to its arrival in Manhattan, Anthony Lamberti held the same letter in one hand while slipping his simple tortoiseshell glasses onto the bridge of his nose with the other. He stood on a terrace overlooking a serene green valley. The twilight sun cast just enough light on the Italian countryside for him to read the neatly handwritten words that Jonathan Brown spent the entire day composing. The letter almost glowed.

"Please read it aloud for me," Jonathan respectfully asked the older man.

Anthony's deep melodic voice began.

"Dear Aunt Maddie," he paused at the endearing salutation and wondered again about his young protégé's aunt. He continued, his

Italian accent transforming the words into near poetry.

This letter must come as a surprise. I hope and pray that it will be a welcome one, although I wish it were being written under more favorable circumstances. Oh, Aunt Maddie, how I have missed you over the years. I have wanted to write to you many times but I didn't know how to begin. There is much to tell you, and I fear that I may reveal too much or too little in this long overdue correspondence. How can I possibly update you on the last seven years? How can I possibly hope that you will be willing to hear what I have to say?

Where to start? I suppose the best place would be with the most important news. Mom has cancer. Treatment isn't working, and the doctors are not at all hopeful. Aunt Maddie, Mom is dying. She only has a few months to live. Dad left her, us, shortly after we arrived in Italy. For a young model in Milan. They got divorced and so Mom raised me by herself. I can only tell you how very sorry I am that you and Mom have spent so much time apart. She very much regrets the pain her actions caused you. I hope you can believe that.

As to what became of me. I'm seventeen now, and a novice at Monastero de Saint Valentine. Eventually, I will be a monk. Can you imagine having a monk as a nephew? While my decision to travel this path was an easy one, it has not been easy to explain to those closest to me. Least of all, Dad. I hope to have the opportunity to explain it to you.

And now for the real purpose of this letter. In short, Mom needs you. She would never dream of contacting you herself, and asking you to come to Italy, and neither has she asked me to contact you. I know that seeing you would mean everything to her. I know it is a lot to ask. I fear I would not be able to live with myself if I had not reached out on Mom's behalf. And on my own behalf. You are my family and I have missed you. I, too, would love to see you and have my Aunt back in my life.

Please consider this note an olive branch. Come to Italy.

Anthony swallowed. He wondered what could have happened to keep sisters apart for so long. What could Madeline have done? He was too private, too respectful of others' privacy, to ask.

"Well?" Jonathan looked every bit the vulnerable young man he was.

"It is a good letter. Come. Let's post it." Anthony placed a fatherly hand on Jonathan's shoulder and guided him inside.

* * * *

Madeline's meetings ran late. Through lunch and dry take-out sandwiches. Then more conference calls. Her marketing team was brainstorming ideas for a line of cosmetics. The company took on a life of its own and Madeline tried desperately to keep sight of the business' long-term strategy. She was not entirely sure that make-up was a direction she wanted to take. Too regulated. Too bureaucratic. Too competitive. Yet she always encouraged her staff to run with their creativity. Sometimes it worked, sometimes not. There were always risks in business and she thrived on them. Business was, after all, where risk-taking belonged.

When is Heather getting back from Paris?

Heather Clark was Madeline's executive vice president, chief financial officer, and best friend. They went to business school together at a time when women were still rare in MBA programs. Heather. Pretty, smart, brunette Heather had always been there for her. Always. Personally and professionally. She was in Paris for the *Pret à Porter*, followed by a couple of well-deserved days off in the South of France.

At five-thirty, Madeline left the conference room and hurried to her office. There was a deluge of email waiting for her. Eric was still there, on the phone, taking yet another message. So much for his leaving early. She made a note to give him an extra day off.

Two hours later Madeline responded to the last of her email. It was thirteen hours after she arrived at the office and she felt tired. Accomplished, but tired. Everyone was gone for the day and the office was quiet again. Jonathan's letter rested, still sealed, on her desk.

She picked it up, gently brushing the Italian postage stamp with her fingertips. Slowly, she opened the envelope, withdrew the letter, and started reading. She read it through once, quickly. Then again, more slowly. After the third read, she set it down. Taking off her glasses and rubbing her eyes, she walked over to the window and stood gazing out onto the Hudson River as the sun slipped away.

As though it were yesterday, the memory of seven years earlier returned to Madeline. Her sister's secret had been revealed innocently enough, delivered in one sweeping statement that sliced through the lives of an entire family and irreparably severed its fragile relationships. It was a day that changed all their lives, and Madeline had tried to put it behind her. Tried to forget what had happened. But holding the letter from Italy and gazing at her nephew's handwriting, all Madeline could do was remember.

It all came back to her. The antiseptic smell of the hospital. The good doctor. The nurses rushing about silently with their rubber soled feet. The fear for Jonathan's life. She loved her nephew as though he were her own son, and the news of the car accident had terrified her. She could not lose her nephew. He was just ten years old. So young. Too young. And what of her sister, Carrie?

My God, poor Carrie! Madeline remembered thinking. *My poor sister.*

With the news of the crash, she had rushed out of a strategy meeting—they had been discussing the idea of launching a perfume under the Felicity brand—and gone directly over to the hospital where Carrie waited. It struck Madeline as odd to see that her own husband, David, was already there with Carrie. She dismissed the feeling as she had so many times before. Bobby, Carrie's husband, was on his way and they expected him at any moment. Madeline had an arm around her sister, comforting her, when the harried young doctor approached them.

"Jonathan's legs are badly injured. We're going to need to get him into surgery. I can't perform the repairs to the ligaments myself. I don't have the expertise. We've already contacted a surgeon and he's on his way. Jonathan will be in excellent hands."

Bobby was just arriving and pulled Carrie to his side.

"This is Jonathan's father," Carrie explained to the doctor, who nodded in acknowledgment. "Jonathan's going to need surgery. His legs are all..." she could not finish her sentence.

"We have a surgeon on the way. I expect Jonathan to be fine," the doctor explained to Bobby. He turned as if to leave but then added, as an afterthought, "By the way, you do know that your son has type O negative blood, don't you? That's highly uncommon. We're short on it right now and have coordinated some blood donor drives in the next week. Please think about donating to help replenish our supply."

"I don't understand," Bobby said, confused.

"Type O negative is highly compatible, meaning that most other blood types can receive it in a transfusion. So it gets used often. An O negative recipient, like Jonathan, can only receive O negative blood. Since we're short on it, you might consider donating sometime during the next week. That's all." The doctor smiled in an awkward attempt to comfort Carrie and Bobby. It was obviously not the right time to raise this matter.

"Oh, we'd be happy to donate blood. Anything we can do to help," Carrie interjected uncomfortably.

"But I have Type AB blood," Bobby persisted, still confused. He looked at Carrie. "You're Type A."

Madeline's mind snapped the look David and Carrie exchanged in that instant like a perpetual photograph. Over the years, she replayed that look again and again. Again and again and again. Until it became a worn out video. Here it was in her mind yet once more, the fleeting exchange between them that said everything. A look between two people who had a secret. A quick cast of the eyes between two people who loved each other and had a secret. A pregnant glance between her sister and her husband.

My sister and my husband! The small voice that Madeline had silenced so many times before screamed at her. *I've known this all along.*

"That's strange. It's not usually possible for Type A and AB parents to produce a Type O child," the doctor explained, confused himself now. "Did you adopt Jonathan?"

"No! We did not adopt Jonathan!" Bobby was distressed. "What exactly are you saying?"

"If you have Type AB blood, I don't understand how you could possibly be Jonathan's biological father." In a flash of understanding, the young doctor's eyes fell to the floor. Medical school failed to prepare him for the intricate tapestry of human relationships and he thought aloud without fully realizing the impact of his words.

"I'm so sorry," he said, embarrassed. He glanced at Carrie, then turned and left.

Madeline, David, Carrie, and Bobby stood silently in the waiting room as the lives of everyone else around them continued on as before.

"David, your blood type is O negative, isn't it?" After eleven years of marriage, it was a statement more than a question.

The implication of her words hung in the air. Bobby, shocked, collapsed into a chair, his face in his hands. Carrie and David stood speechless, neither able to think of anything to say.

"I'm going to find out if I can see Jonathan," Madeline said slowly. She walked away. From her husband. Her sister. Her family.

It was the last time Madeline saw any of them. The nurses had not allowed her to see Jonathan before his surgery, but she had called the hospital and learned that he was expected to make a full recovery. She had gone home that day, packed a small bag with some clothes and other personal belongings, and stayed with Heather.

She refused calls from David and Carrie. Within a few days, Bobby filed for divorce and called Madeline to commiserate. His attorney insisted on immediate DNA testing which confirmed that David was indeed Jonathan's father. She spoke with Bobby briefly, but found that even the mention of Carrie and David's names was too heartbreaking. She learned from him that Carrie and David were planning to go to Italy; a business opportunity arose there for David that he had never mentioned to her.

Italy, she remembered thinking. The news had been a surprise and she remembered thinking how little she had really known her husband. Really *known* him.

Eventually, David served her with divorce papers. Although she initially resisted the idea, she found herself feeling grateful that David had insisted on a prenuptial agreement prior to their marriage. Now her earnings from Felicity were hers alone.

The divorce was quick and relatively effortless.

Strange, Madeline thought to herself at the time, *that you get married in church and divorced in court.* How was it that those vows exchanged before God were undone with lawyers' keystrokes and a signature or two? She resumed using her maiden name and decided that Felicity would be her legacy. And her family. She would treat her employees well. Support charities. Create a company that would better people's lives and the world. Yes. Felicity. That would be enough, she had decided.

And it had been enough.

Hadn't it?

She glanced around at her office. At the walls decorated with photos of her with staff and models. At awards and certificates she received over the years for good corporate citizenship and as honors for women in business. Covers of prestigious business magazines featuring her perfectly photographed face.

Now, seven years after that life-changing day, in her luxuriously appointed offices forty-nine stories above New York, Madeline held Jonathan's letter in her hands.

And cried.

* * * *

It was daybreak in Italy and the bells of Santuario di Saint Valentine rang throughout the hillside overlooking a lush tranquil valley. Dew kissed olive trees and vineyards that were scattered here and there shimmered in the rising sun while the countryside yawned and slowly stretched itself awake.

An ancient spiritual center, Santuario di Saint Valentine was one of the most famous European buildings of the Middle Ages and, due to several restorations, remained much as it was when originally built. The monastery, situated just fifty kilometers from Rome in the small town of Farfa, was a world unto itself. Perched high in the hills, the buildings housed a small beautiful chapel, adorned with stained glass windows depicting biblical scenes and a dramatic domed ceiling painted with breathtaking frescos. A spectacular library stored thousands of preserved documents. In keeping with the Benedictine tradition of hospitality, Saint Valentine's also maintained guest quarters where tourists or those seeking spiritual respite could lodge during the summer months.

Brother Anthony Lamberti stood silently on the historic terrace and watched as the morning began to unfold. Dawn was his favorite time of day and he inhaled deeply, breathing in the peacefulness of the moment. The bells ceased. He was late. Again. With a sigh, he pulled himself away from the beckoning morning and walked quickly but deliberately to the chapel to commence Morning Prayer.

"What has come over me?" he asked aloud, distressed by his tardiness.

When he arrived in the ancient chapel, the others were already immersed in prayer. Anthony was quick to observe that Jonathan, always an eager and conscientious novice, did not notice his late arrival.

Grazie a Dio! Thank God, Anthony thought, pursing his lips to keep from smiling at the irony. It was Anthony's intention, and indeed, his duty, to set an example for the novices. And in particular for Jonathan. He felt the two of them were kindred spirits and often wondered what it would be like to have a son like Jonathan. But that was not meant to be.

Less serendipitous was the feeling of Father Marco's gaze. As he took his place in the pews, Anthony lifted his eyes to meet Father Marco's. The kind older gentleman raised an eyebrow ever so slightly and instantly returned his attention to his worn book of prayers. Then, seamlessly, Anthony's voice joined in unison with his brothers' voices and he prayed.

* * * *

1943

Marco read the same paragraph of The Rule of Saint Benedict a dozen times, one after the other. It was Chapter 19: "We believe that the divine presence is everywhere." He read the passage again and again. He sighed heavily, his concentration lost.

He had already been in the library for over an hour, passing his time sketching or gazing out the window at the sparkling Grand Canal. Or reading. Or, more accurately, not reading. His ability to focus had completely escaped him. Where was his mind? His heart? Had he left it at the abbey with–

He looked down at his rough penciling of her face. Her eyes stared back at him as they had in the abbey. He did not even know her name. Yet he felt as though his heart knew hers. As though in that brief exchange of looks, they had exchanged whispered promises of what would be. What could be.

And yet could not be.

What was he thinking?

Of her. Of nothing but her. He chastised himself for it. Yet he loved her. He loved her the moment he had seen her. It was beyond understanding or explanation. Yet, she inspired feelings in him that he had never known before. He wanted to be with her. To know her mind and her heart. And her body. He had not even taken his vows and yet felt he was betraying God for wanting her, for thinking the impure thoughts that constantly barraged him. But they did not feel impure. They felt real and true and alive.

And loving.

"Wonderful drawing. Who is she?" It was Marco's friend, Lorenzo. He and Marco grew up together, their families neighbors. Lorenzo had always been different from the other boys. He always knew he wanted to be a priest.

"No one." He hated that he lied to his friend. How could he tell the truth? How could he tell Lorenzo that she was everyone and everything.

"No one?"

Marco would not add to the deception and glared up at his friend in silent response. Guilt gripped his heart just as his feelings for the mysterious girl had opened it.

Lorenzo shrugged. "She's a beautiful no one." He walked to the next desk and sat down, his back to Marco.

Marco returned his gaze to his sketchpad. To her. Could she be his destiny or was she testing his destiny?

He slammed his book shut with a loud thud and stood, scraping his chair loudly on the polished wood floor.

"Marco!" Lorenzo shouted.

He ignored his friend, gathered his books and papers, and swept out of the library in a blur of flowing black fabric.

There was only one way to find out.

* * * *

Present Day

Upon his arrival at the office on Tuesday, Eric found Madeline hunched over on her desk, her head with its spray of auburn hair resting on her folded arms. Her glasses were buried underneath some open reports, and crumpled tissues were strewn about. He stood in the doorway looking at her, unsure of what to do, when Heather joined him.

"Has she been here all night?" Heather asked him.

"I guess," he said. "She must have been. She's wearing the same suit as yesterday. This is a first. And aren't you supposed to be in Paris?" he asked, trying to sort out the sudden chaos.

"I was. I decided to just come straight back instead of taking a few days off."

"You can't stay away, can you?"

"Well, look at what happens when I leave!" Heather was joking. "Let me see what's going on."

Eric nodded and returned to his desk and Heather entered

Madeline's office, closing the door. She walked over to Madeline and gently placed her hands on her friend's shoulder, softly nudging her awake.

A small moan escaped Madeline and she began moving, raising her head slowly and getting her bearings.

"Madeline?"

Madeline turned around to find Heather's familiar comforting face.

"What are you doing here?" Madeline asked.

"I work here, remember? What are you doing here?" Heather was smiling.

They laughed and embraced.

"I'm glad you're back. How was the Pret?"

"Actually, it was great. You missed some really good parties." Madeline rolled her eyes. She had been there. Done the parties. But after a while, they all started to feel the same. The people. The conversations. All that changed was the clothes.

"I know. I know ... you hate it. That's why you send me. But it would do you good to get out and have some fun every now and again. Maybe get laid," she teased, then softened. "Oh, hon' come on. You look terrible. Have you been here all night?"

Madeline sighed a long heavy sigh, "I must have fallen asleep reading some reports."

Heather stood listening, knowing there was more to it, and waited for Madeline to continue.

"I got a letter yesterday. From Italy. From Jonathan, actually." Madeline handed Heather the letter. She read it quickly and sat down on the luxurious ivory leather sofa.

"Want to talk about it?" Heather motioned to Madeline to join her but Madeline stayed at her desk.

"Heather, there's nothing to talk about. I am not going to Italy now. I can't. There's too much going on. The new catalog is being shot and -"

Heather cut her off. "Hon' you have go to Italy."

"No, Heather, I don't have to go to Italy. And I won't. Why should I?"

"It sounds like Carrie needs you."

"How can you take her side like that?! All these years I needed her and where was she? Halfway across the planet. With David. With *my* husband! I don't care if she needs me now. I just don't care." Tears were brimming in Madeline's eyes again even after spending hours crying the night before.

Heather got up and went to Madeline, kneeled before her and handed her friend a tissue.

"Madeline, go to Italy. Not for Carrie, not for Jonathan, but for yourself."

The intercom rang and Eric's voice came over the speaker. "Sorry to interrupt, but Heather, I have marketing in Paris on the line for you. A follow up from the Pret."

"Have them hold. I'll take it in my office in a minute. Thanks." Then, continuing to Madeline. "I really have to take that call. You'll regret it if you don't go, you know."

Madeline crossed her arms. "I know," she said quietly and watched Heather leave.

She would not decide now. Work pressed. She looked for her glasses but had somehow misplaced them. Feverishly, she searched her desk, lifting reports and moving files. She finally found them underneath a pile of work and slid them on. Picking up the report, she began reading but found her mind was not on the numbers.

It was already four thousand miles away.

* * * *

Carrie's eyes brightened as Jonathan entered her hospital room. She sat in a chair in the corner, a small bag packed. Out of her hospital gown and dressed in a yellow silk blouse and khaki capri pants, she was slim and pretty. Her complexion was brighter today than it had been of late. Her most recent round of treatment had gone surprisingly well and the doctors were sending her home. Despite her illness, she remained an attractive woman. She wore her chestnut hair cropped short with wispy bangs accenting her delicately featured face. Her eyes were green, like Madeline's, and she had taken the time to apply some make-up. Today she did not look sick. Today she did not feel sick.

"Jonathan, you're here!" Carrie's face brightened at the sight of her son. Seeing him always reminded her of her reason for living.

"Hello Mom," Jonathan replied. "You look great!" He was relieved and wondered for the millionth time how his mother would receive his news.

"I'm having a good day and I just want to get out of here. Let's take a drive. Is Anthony with you?" She liked Anthony and felt grateful to him for taking Jonathan under his wing, especially so since the onset of her illness.

"No. He's having lunch with one of the nuns from Convento Santa Maria. The abbey is having some financial troubles and they're going to talk about some ways to try to raise money."
"So he's at the convent?" Carrie asked.

"Um hm. I'll be picking him up there later tonight."

"So we have the whole day to ourselves then?" she asked hopefully. Time with her son was more precious now and she wanted as much of it as possible.

"We sure do. Mom–there's something I want to tell you." He wanted to get this over with and now was as good a time as any.

"Oh, suddenly so serious." She was immediately worried. "What is it sweetheart?" She got up and sat on the bed, patting the mattress beside her for him to sit at her side.

Sitting down, he began. "I know how much you've missed Aunt Maddie over the years."

The color drained from her face and her eyes lowered to the floor, the pain in them concealed by her feathery dark lashes. "I–"

He interrupted her, "No, Mom, let me."

She wrung her hands in her lap and stared at the tile floor.

"I wrote to Aunt Maddie and asked her to come see us."

"What?!" her voice was a high-pitched shriek that echoed into the corridor of the hospital.

"Mom, I had to. It was the right thing to do. You need to see her now more than ever. Before –" he instantly regretted his last word.

"Jesus Christ!" Then realizing the inappropriateness of that phrase, "Oh God, I'm so sorry!"

They looked at each other now. Communication between them was so awkward sometimes. The young man before her was her son, yet in his monk's habit, he looked like someone else altogether. His green eyes pleaded with her.

"I *had* to contact her! You never would. Don't you think it's time the two of you at least tried to come to some sort of peace!" He was pleading, not asking.

His wisdom belied his years and he was indeed right. Carrie dreamed of the day she would see Madeline again.

My sister.

Carrie had needed Madeline so much over the years. So had Jonathan. Life had been so difficult on their own. Yet, in her heart, Carrie knew she lacked the fortitude of spirit it would have taken to contact Madeline and she hated herself for it. She had picked up the phone to call her sister hundreds of times over the years, but each time, slammed it down in shame and cowardice. Carrie had not forgiven herself for what she had done to Madeline. How could she ever expect Madeline to forgive her?

Yet, here, in this moment, looking at Jonathan, she did not regret what she had done. Jonathan had been borne of her relationship with David and she marveled as she had many times at the mysterious design of life's twists and turns. Jonathan knew how she felt and that was why he wrote to his Aunt. For the first time it occurred to Carrie that Jonathan needed Madeline as much as she did.

I'll be gone soon and it would be good for Jonathan to have Madeline back in his life. I'll be gone soon...

"Has she responded?" Carrie's voice was quiet.

"I got an email from her a few days ago. She's arriving today and is planning to drive up to Saint Valentine's tomorrow to see me."

Suddenly tears sprang to Carrie's eyes. Jonathan took his mother's small frame into his arms.

"Oh, Jonathan!"

She pulled back then, her arms still on his shoulders. With her right hand she reached up to stroke his cheek. "My dear, dear Jonathan." She let out a long sigh and then her lips parted into a smile. Standing, she said, "Shall we, then?" She bent to pick up her bag, but felt an unexpected rush of weakness. Swaying a bit, she dropped back down with a heavy breath.

"Mom?" Jonathan rose from the bed and stepped to his mother's side.

"It's okay. I'm okay," she said, upright again. "I just need a minute."

Jonathan nodded and turned his face away from his mother. He did not want her to see the tears brewing in his eyes like watery clouds, ready to burst into a heavy downpour. They were both quiet. After a minute, Carrie smoothed the creases in her pants and stood up, steadily this time. Jonathan picked up her bag. Carrie started toward the door with him at her heels.

"Monks with email. How about that?" She shook her head and laughed.

Jonathan laughed too. Mother and son left the hospital to spend the day together, while at Rome's Leonardo DaVinci Airport, Madeline's plane landed.

* * * *

Madeline decided to spend her first day in Italy in the heart of the Eternal City at the Hotel de Russie on the Via del Babuino. Within walking distance of Rome's fashion houses, she had stayed at this hotel twice before on business and for a personal trip she wanted to be somewhere familiar. She needed time to recuperate from the long flight, and now craved a brief respite before driving to Saint Valentine's the next day to see Jonathan. As the handsome young bellman opened the door to her luxuriously appointed room, she felt pleased with her decision.

He set down her bags and she tipped him generously.

"*Grazie,*" he said.

"You're welcome."

He bowed his head slightly and left. Madeline looked out the windows at the sunny Rome morning.

Walking directly over to the balcony, she opened the doors and was welcomed by buildings that dated back to the thirteenth century. Immediately catching her eye at the northern end of the piazza was the Gothic church of San Francesco, built by a brotherhood of Franciscan monks in 1258. Madeline marveled at its beauty and at Rome. It was a city of contradictions. Modern in many ways, it was steeped in history, unforgettable monuments, and exquisite art. She felt herself swept away by the current of the past.

Rome, she thought to herself. It had been several years since she was here and she remembered how much she enjoyed it.

Maybe I'll take a little walk later and see some sights, she pondered. Taking in the city, she wondered what Carrie's life had been like here.

Carrie.

What is it going to be like to see Carrie?

At the thought, Madeline suddenly felt tired and wanted to rest. She quickly unpacked a few things, undressed, and slipped into one of her favorite Felicity nightgowns for a nap. When she awoke a few hours later she was hungry. It was time for lunch.

* * * *

"*Ciao bella*!" A pair of young handsome Italians were watching Madeline as she walked along one of Rome's narrow cobbled side streets.

It was a beautiful warm September day. Madeline donned a pretty flowing summer dress and sandals with a matching sweater loosely strewn over her shoulders.

She laughed aloud, having forgotten how ardently admiring Italian men could be. She knew they would say the very same thing to the next pretty woman who crossed their path. It was harmless fun and Madeline found herself enjoying the attention.

It had been a long time since a man approached her on the basis of just being a woman. Usually, men would know who she was either by acquaintance or reputation. They wanted to meet her. She was beautiful. Rich. Madeline knew her money made her that much more attractive. She had earned it by working very hard. Sometimes she felt she needed a wife, not a husband. Over the years she learned men were not willing to put up with Felicity's demands. So over the years she thought about men less and less, until she hardly thought about them at all.

But here, in Rome, romance surrounded Madeline. Songs of *amore* whispered to her from intimate sidewalk cafes. The language serenaded her. Warm breezes beckoned. Felt like silk against her bare skin. She was immersed in Italy's raw sensuality. The encounter with the young men reawakened a part of her that felt foreign.

How long had it been since she found herself enveloped in someone's arms? She could not recall.

Her last relationship ended when she discovered her lover had been sleeping with someone else. Maybe she had neglected him. Too many meetings. Too many business trips. Of course she had many offers from men. Some of them married. Some of them just out of a relationship and needing a therapist more than a girlfriend. She'd dated here and there but nothing, no one, compared to her passion for Felicity.

Now ceaseless inward questions that had long been buried in Madeline's heart rose up, unbidden. Questions she not dared ask herself in the years since her breakup with David.

Are there men who understand the preciousness of love? Who want to create a glorious and wonderful relationship with one woman? With me?

Sadness stroked her heart, strangely comforting in its far away familiarity. Questions raced across her mind uncontrollably. *What happened between men and women? What is it that makes men feel trapped by love instead of feeling reverence for the gift, the honor, of loving? Were all men alike? Is there someone out there–some one–who can love me? God, I'm an utterly hopeless –*

Her thoughts were interrupted when she rounded a corner and

found her destination. Trattoria Franco. She had been delighted when the hotel's concierge told her the restaurant remained unchanged since her last visit. A business associate introduced her to it and she had enjoyed her meal there immensely. Just a few blocks away from the usual tourist spots, it was the kind of place locals frequented. She was already looking forward to having some refreshing Italian gelato; nowhere on earth was ice cream as good as in Rome. And she needed a simple pleasure.

"*Buon giorno*!" her host greeted her.

"Hello."

"How may I help you?" He switched to thickly accented English.

"A table for one please."

His dark eyes assessed her for a moment and he simply said, "Of course. Would you prefer the patio?"

Madeline nodded.

"Follow, please."

He led her through the restaurant with its tables dressed in crisp white tablecloths and flower filled vases. Laughter, conversation, and food surrounded Madeline. She was hungry. A delicious meal and a glass of fine Italian wine would do her good.

The table he selected was perfectly situated to the outside of the patio in a quiet corner. He graciously pulled out her chair and she sat down.

"I am Franco. It is a pleasure to have you join us, *Signorina*–"

"Madeline." She smiled at him.

"Madeline." He bowed his head slightly. "A beautiful name. Your waiter is Giuseppe. He will be right with you." He handed her a menu and wine list. "If you need anything, please let me know."

"Thank you, Franco."

Alone – again – Madeline surveyed her surroundings. A young French speaking couple were seated beside her, clearly enjoying each other as much as their meal. People milled about on the street. Pretty young mothers strolled with their children. Two elderly women in black dresses and hose stood bickering. The occasional teenager rode by on a bicycle. Four nuns dressed in full habit walked briskly along.

"*Buon giorno*." It was Giuseppe.

"Hello." Madeline smiled.

"May I offer you something to drink?"

"Yes. A glass of red wine please. Could you suggest something?"

"Oh! *Sì*! We just received a wonderful Brunello. From Tuscany," he said.

"Sounds perfect." Madeline nodded. Not that she knew one wine from another, but it sounded good. She had never found the time to truly educate herself about wine.

"Right away. Have you decided on lunch?"

"Not yet. What's good today?"

"Well, of course, antipasti to begin, and we have a special – grilled lamb chops served with a roasted tomato and vegetable sauce. *Delicioso."*

"Sounds wonderful."

"Grazie," Giuseppe said and left.

Madeline relaxed. Italian service was charmingly slow and eventually Giuseppe served her the wine and, as promised, a delicious lamb entrée. With a free afternoon ahead, she indulged in another glass of wine and finished her meal. Then she paid her bill. Standing to leave, she felt light-headed.

Oooh. Shouldn't have had that second glass.

She decided to stop at the ladies' room to freshen up and made her way through the rows of tables. A man seated with his back to her was in the midst of an argument with the man across from him. As Madeline approached, he gestured wildly and she jumped back to avoid being struck. She lost her balance and tripped, landing in someone's lap.

Strong arms held her tightly. She felt her body against a man's firm chest. Her hands grasped clumsily at the table, catapulting dishes and flatware noisily to the floor. She watched as wineglasses, as if in slow motion, sailed into the air. Still floundering, she turned to see whom she had fallen upon.

Her breath caught.

Here was the handsomest man she had ever seen. He was so extraordinary and somehow so – familiar. His salt and pepper hair was cropped short, any shorter and it would have been shaved. Deep brown eyes studied her face. The hands holding her were warm against her body. His face was lined and Madeline guessed him to be in his mid-to-late forties. He was elegantly but casually dressed in a black polo shirt and khakis. Beyond his appearance, there was something about him, a feeling, a calmness, that instilled in Madeline a sense of strength and comfort.

He seemed equally enthralled and the two of them, for a timeless moment, remained as they were. His hands on her. Her hands on him. Looking into each other's eyes.

"I'm so sorry!" Madeline finally managed.

"Not to worry. Are you all right?" His voice was soothing and melodic. His English was laced with a sexy Italian accent.

"Yes. Yes... I'm fine."

Franco arrived. "Madeline. Here ..." He graciously helped her to her feet.

"*Grazie*," she said and tried to collect herself.

For the first time, she noticed the woman seated at the table. A pretty young brunette with a shocked expression and an enormous red wine stain across her white blouse.

"Is okay, no?" Franco asked.

"Yes. *Sì*. It's okay. It's all okay." Madeline was still disoriented. "I'm fine. I was just leaving."

Franco nodded. "Okay."

"I'm so sorry," Madeline said again to the man who a moment ago held her. She glanced at the young woman who was watching her intently. "I'm so sorry."

"Really. It's fine." He smiled broadly. "No harm done."

God he's exquisite. "Well ... good-bye then."

"*Arrivederci*."

"This way," Franco said.

Madeline nodded and followed him. As she walked, she had the feeling the handsome Italian was watching. She glanced back and her suspicions were confirmed. The handsome Italian *was* staring at her. Their eyes met and held. She quickly looked away and continued out of the restaurant.

She struggled to think of a time when she last felt that way about a man. When *had* she last met someone who quickened her pulse?

Nothing, no one, came to mind.

It's probably just Rome, she thought. *Or the wine*. She pushed the handsome Italian's face out of her mind.

* * * *

1943

Sister Francesca's voice rang out like a mission bell. "Marco! *Ciao*!"

Marco turned in the abbey's courtyard to face the elderly nun. Marco knew her from having assisted with several community projects that Saint Peter's had worked on together with the convent. Although she was in her seventies, she had endless energy.

"*Ciao*, Sister Francesca."

"Is there a meeting today?"

Marco shook his head. "No."

The sister looked confused. "Then what brings you?"

"I'm looking for a young woman," Marco said to the aging nun, restraining his excitement at the thought of seeing her again.

She cast her eyes downward and was smiling when she looked back up at him. "Marco, we have many young girls here."

"I saw her the other day... in the chapel...she was lighting candles. She had dark hair, and dark eyes."

The old woman's eyes narrowed. "Dark hair? She wasn't wearing anything on her head?" She tugged at her own habit's headpiece.

Now that the nun mentioned it, Marco remembered that the young woman had not worn a habit. Then he remembered his sketch.

He pulled it from his pocket and held it out to the nun.

"Here."

She took the rendering, looked at it, and raised her eyes to Marco's intently. "What is your interest in this girl?"

"I–she– " he stammered, unprepared for the question.

"I do not know her." Sister Francesca set her jaw. "No such girl is here."

"But I saw her–just the other day," Marco said.

"That is not possible. I'm sorry." Sister Francesca walked away.

Marco followed her. He reached for her arm and stopped her. She turned to him, her eyes steady.

He was insistent. "I know what I saw, Sister Francesca. I did not imagine it. She is here. And I want to see her."

The old woman held her ground. "There is no such girl, Marco."

"You're lying." The accusation hung in the air between them.

Marco's heart raced. He had not intended to show such disrespect but it was the truth. The old woman was lying and they both knew it.

Sister Francesca set her jaw. "She was just here for a few days. She left yesterday."

She left yesterday! Marco's heart contracted with the news. How could she possibly be gone?

He bit his lower lip. Another lie. "I see. *Grazie.*"

Sister Francesca nodded and turned, leaving young Marco to himself in the abbey's small courtyard. He sighed and made his way over to a small meditation bench. His body and heart ponderous, he sat down.

What would cause such a aching in his chest? The pain he felt confused him. He did not even know her. And yet–

And yet-

Prompted by a small inner voice, Marco lifted his gaze up to the centuries old stone building. There she was, looking down at him from one of the windows with those eyes he had come to know as his own.

She smiled. A slow dreamy smile and stepped back into the shadows and out of view.

Marco rose to stand, as if somehow that would bring him closer to her. His mind raced with questions. Who was she? Why was she here if she wasn't a nun? Why had Sister Francesca lied?

Even though it was wrong for him to want to, seeing her again was suddenly all that mattered.

* * * *

Present Day

The phone was ringing as Madeline opened the door to her room. She rushed to pick it up.

"Hello."

"Aunt Maddie?" Jonathan's voice was tentative.

"Yes Jonathan, it's me." Madeline sat on the bed, taking off her sandals and rubbing her feet.

"*Come lei sono*? How are you? How was your trip?"

"It was good," she answered. "The flight was long, but it was fine. I'm settled in and looking forward to a good night's rest."

"I can't believe you're really here."

Madeline smiled. "I know. Your voice – you sound so grown up."

You sound so much like your father, she thought.

Jonathan laughed. "I guess I've changed in the last seven years."

So had Madeline.

"I can't wait to see you tomorrow," she said.

"So you're definitely coming, then. You haven't changed your mind or anything? I mean, you're really here."

"I'm really here. I'll be at Saint Valentine's in the morning. Any particular time?"

"Not really no. Unless you want to come for breakfast. That's at seven-thirty. Actually, maybe that's not such a good idea–we eat breakfast in silence. Other than that, just come and tell someone you're looking for me."

"Great. Jonathan?"

"Yes, Aunt Maddie?"

"How's Carrie?" Her voice was quiet.

"She's right here if–"

Carrie leaned forward on her chair, hopeful.

Madeline interrupted, "No! I mean–not just yet."

Disappointment tinged Jonathan's voice. "It's okay. We'll catch up on things tomorrow."

"Okay then. Tomorrow it is. Oh, Jonathan, one more thing?"

"What is it?"

"Will I have Internet access in my room at Saint Valentine's? I'll have to check email."

"Not in your room," Jonathan answered. "But we do have one computer with a dial-up connection."

A dial-up connection! "Okay. Yeah. That'll work." Madeline frowned.

"Okay. *A domani.*"

"*A domani?*"

"Until tomorrow."

Until tomorrow. "Oh! *A domani.*" Madeline hung up the phone.

A domani. Until tomorrow. Is everything about Italy romantic?

She was tired. She curled up on the bed. The trip and the time difference were catching up with her. Not to mention the wine and that embarrassing scene at the restaurant. Her thoughts were scattered.

How will I face Carrie? Why is Jonathan becoming a monk? What's happening at the office? With the new catalog?

Unbeckoned, the image of a handsome face returned. Had it ever really left? *Who was that man?* Again, she felt the touch of his hands on her waist. Saw the look in his eye. Had she imagined the flicker of attraction? Or was it amusement? He and his date must have shared a laugh or two at her expense.

He probably thought she had a little too much wine. He was so handsome. Yummy, as Heather would have said. But what did it matter?

I'll never see him again anyway, Madeline thought with a deep sigh. *So why am I even thinking about him?*

She turned out the lamp and rested her head on the plump down pillow. A moment later she was asleep.

* * * *

The stranger pressed his hard naked body against Madeline's bare skin. White satin sheets caressed her, cool in contrast to the heat of him. Madeline's nipples grew hard as he gently suckled her. She stroked his hair, not wanting to miss a strand of him. He raised his dark eyes to meet hers. Like smoky mirrors they reflected her pleasure.

"I love you," he said quietly into her ear. The warmth of his breath breezed through her. His voice familiar from a long ago time and place.

Then gently, lovingly, he pressed his lips to hers and kissed her tenderly. Then more passionately. His tongue circled hers and she moaned. A stream of heat spiraled its way to her core and demanded release. She pressed her hips to his. Felt his hardness. He understood her need and lifted his body to enter her, gazing into Carrie's eyes.

Carrie's eyes.

He was making love to – her sister. Madeline was confused. They both looked at her, standing naked in her office. They were laughing now. Loud cackling laughs.

David appeared, dressed in the tuxedo he wore on their wedding day. He walked toward her.

"You're so beautiful," he said. His eyes traveled up and down her exposed body. Then he reached out to embrace her. "I'm so sorry."

"No!" Madeline sat up in bed. Awake now. Disoriented. Alone. "I'll never forgive you." Anger rushed through her and she shivered as though a cold wind had blown. "Either of you."

I can't do this, she thought.

I shouldn't have come.

"Please, God, give me strength," she said and wondered if anyone heard.

Unable to get back to sleep, she got out of bed and plugged her laptop into the hotel's port.

Felicity. She hadn't thought of the company in hours. Now, staring at her computer's glowing screen, it was difficult to concentrate on work. Her thoughts kept floating to the man in the restaurant. The man in her dream who kissed her oh so tenderly. Held her, and said, "I love you."

* * * *

Anthony had never seen Jonathan so full of energy and

excitement. The young novice was barely able to restrain himself during Morning Prayer. Now, at breakfast, he managed to eat in silence but constantly glanced at the doorway, obviously hoping his Aunt Maddie would arrive.

Aunt Maddie. Anthony wondered what she would be like. All he knew was that she was Carrie's younger sister and she ran a clothing business of some kind. He imagined she and Carrie would be alike. They were sisters, after all.

Carrie was soft-spoken. Nurturing. A loving mother. He came to know her more closely since the doctors diagnosed her cancer. His heart went out to her. It could not have been easy raising Jonathan alone. What would cause a man to leave his wife and family?

What kept Madeline and Carrie apart all these years? He had always been curious, but, in service to Carrie's privacy, never asked. Still, he wondered again what it was that Madeline did to have kept them apart for so many years.

He found that he was playing with his food. Not eating. Women were such a mystery. Even the nuns he knew communicated amongst themselves in the secret language women had with each other. Life was simpler without women. Less confusing. There was no decoding to do.

"Brother Anthony," Father Marco spoke. The silence was broken and so breakfast was officially over.

"Father Marco," Anthony nodded.

"Not hungry this morning?" the older priest's eyes were inquiring but kind.

"No. I guess I'm not."

"I'd like for us to talk. You haven't been yourself. Why don't you stop by my office later this afternoon?"

Anthony had no choice. "Of course."

Father Marco smiled, "I'm concerned about you, Brother Anthony."

"Thank you, Father."

"Hmmmm." With that, Father Marco was off to tend to his duties for the day.

Anthony watched as Jonathan and the others left. Alone in the austere dining room, he stood and began clearing the dishes.

* * * *

The lane to Saint Valentine's was lined with stately cypress trees. As she approached the old buildings, Madeline stopped her rented black Mercedes for a moment and rolled down her window. he The fresh country air was still and she listened to the silence. She was completely unprepared for the monastery's beauty. For its serenity.

For its divinity.

"God is everywhere, Madeline." Her mother's words came back to her.

God certainly is here, she thought. She was struck by how little time she spent contemplating God. Had she even thought of God at all?

She inhaled deeply. Here, for the first time in a long time, she could breathe.

Starting the engine again, she proceeded slowly along the drive and parked in the small lot for visitors. It hadn't occurred to her that there would be other guests. Then she remembered. Jonathan mentioned the monastery offered lodging to tourists or people needing a place for spiritual renewal.

With fewer and fewer novices, monasteries needed to find ways to earn money and providing accommodations was one of them. The guests enjoyed affordable lodging and the monasteries enjoyed the income.

A proverbial win-win, Madeline thought. She wondered what kind of people stayed here.

Emerging from the car, she noticed there was no one about. Then it greeted her. The gentle ethereal sound of Gregorian chant.

It soared from the chapel behind the main building where Madeline stood listening. She felt her heart, her soul, begin to melt. Never had she heard such beauty.

It's beautiful. So... so... beautiful. Almost too beautiful to bear.

The voices beckoned. Madeline made her way around the main building with its ancient carvings and columns. Beautifully landscaped gardens embraced her. Birds sang sweetly. The air swelled with peace and tranquility.

Something tells me I'm not in Kansas anymore. She smiled.

The door to the chapel stood before her. She hesitated. It had been years since Madeline had attended services other than a wedding or a funeral. The door was slightly ajar so she opened it and quietly sat down in the last pew. The monks carried on, taking no notice of her.

She surveyed the group, looking for Jonathan. Madeline felt sure she would still recognize him. Row by row, one by one she assessed the faces. Some old. Some young. Some, surprisingly, in secular clothes.

Madeline glanced around. Beautiful stained glass windows were alive with sunlight and magnificent murals blanketed the domed ceilings. The floor gleamed beneath her feet. She noticed her open sandals and red painted toes and a shock of self-consciousness coursed through her. Red toenails! The haunting melancholy rhythm of the chant worked its way to her heart and-homesickness set in. She ached for New York and Felicity. Her office. Her apartment. Her bed. A wireless Internet connection. Heather, Eric, and Sam. She belonged in Manhattan and despised traveling. She hadn't wanted to come to Italy but this was one trip she couldn't delegate to Heather.

Madeline wondered if she might feel more at ease at the hotel instead of staying at Saint Valentine's. Yes. She would return to the hotel. It was closer to the hospital. To Carrie. Somehow that didn't feel right, either.

Confused, she stood quietly and left the chapel.

Where could Jonathan be?

She set out to explore. Maybe find an office and call the hotel to make arrangements for a room. Glancing around, she noticed someone standing on the terrace. A man. He leaned against the railing admiring the view. Probably one of the guests.

Walking toward him, Madeline's heart quickened.

"Excuse me," Madeline said.

Her breath caught.

Standing before her was the stranger from the restaurant, as handsome as the first moment she saw him.

No, even more handsome.

Today he wore a crisp white shirt that set off his olive complexion and slim fitting jeans. His eyes seemed darker. Pools of sweet dark chocolate. Bitter-sweet dark chocolate.

His eyes widened at the sight of her.

"Oh! Hello." Madeline was at a loss for words. Her cheeks burned at the memory of their first meeting.

"*Buon giorno.*" He pursed his lips, trying to conceal amusement at her obvious embarrassment.

"Well, this is quite a coincidence, isn't it?" Madeline was beginning to recover. Maybe staying at the monastery was not such a bad idea after all. Casually her eyes glanced at his left hand. No wedding ring. Perhaps there was a God.

"Yes. It most certainly is." He smiled. A broad handsome smile.

"If you believe in coincidences."

If you believe in coincidences. God, he's handsome. And that accent.

"I'm so embarrassed about yesterday. Nothing like that has ever happened to me."

He laughed easily. "Or to me. Don't give it another thought. It was an accident. It's forgotten," he said.

How could it be forgotten?

"So, you're staying here?" Madeline continued, nervous, not letting him answer. "Maybe you can help me. Is there an office or something? I need to check in."

"Oh, yes. There is. Here. I'll walk you there." He started to walk in the direction of the main building.

Madeline walked alongside him. She noticed he adjusted his stride to match hers. "Oh, thank you. This is a new experience for me. I've never stayed at a monastery before. It's so peaceful. I'm from New York. I'm not sure I'll be able to stand it. How's the food?" She struggled to make conversation.

He smiled again. "Actually, it's very good."

"Hmm. By tonight, I'm sure I'll be bored."

His expression changed. He looked almost amused.

He's flirting, Madeline thought. "Maybe we could have a drink?" The words were out before Madeline could stop herself. "I mean–if you're not here with someone."

What has come over me?

They rounded a corner around the main building.

His expression changed again and he looked almost startled. Taken aback. Madeline regretted being so forward.

"No. I'm not with anyone." He trailed off at the sight of the approaching novice.

"Good then." Madeline smiled, relieved. A drink with a handsome man in Italy.

"Aunt Maddie?" His voice was a whisper. Madeline was so focused on her companion that she had not seen the young monk.

Walking toward her was an intense young man dressed in a black religious habit with its hood and long flowing sleeves. A younger version of David.

Tears appeared from nowhere. She blinked them back.

"Jonathan?" she asked.

He pulled her to him in a warm embrace.

"I can't believe it's really you. You're really here."

"You're so tall."

"You're so beautiful."

She pulled affectionately at his sleeve. "Just look at you."

His resemblance to David was striking. The dark hair. His nose. Cheekbones. Strong jaw. The cleft in his chin was identical to his father's. Yet his green eyes were Carrie's. They mirrored her own. He could have chosen anything, but here he was at Saint Valentine's. A novice.

He smiled shyly. "There's so much to tell you. I don't even know where to begin."

"It's okay. We'll have lots of time." She smiled at him.

He grinned broadly. "So why don't I show you around. Get you settled in your room."

"Perfect. And the computer."

Jonathan laughed. "And the computer."

"Oh–I'm so sorry," he said. He turned to the man who stood watching their reunion.

"Aunt Maddie. This is Brother Anthony Lamberti. He's teaching me everything he knows. This is my Aunt Madeline." He smiled in obvious delight. "From New York."

"It's a pleasure to meet you. Jonathan has spoken of little else since learning you would come." Anthony extended his hand. "A most anticipated arrival." He bowed his head. Smiled. That same disarming smile he had worn at the restaurant.

Brother Anthony Lamberti. My God! He's a monk!

Madeline swallowed. Her stomach churned.

She was at a loss for words–again–so she clasped his outstretched hand. His fingers wrapped around hers firmly. His hand was large and strong while hers was smaller, more delicate. With red nails. She hated to let go but he quickly released his grip. Too quickly. Rejection and humiliation swept through her.

"It's a pleasure to meet you too." She managed the words.

"Aunt Maddie," Jonathan took her arm in his. "I'm so glad you're here. Let me show you to your room. Then I'm afraid I'll have to go." He shrugged. "Chores." Jonathan was dedicated. "But we'll all have dinner together tonight."

Smiling, Jonathan led his aunt through the lovingly landscaped grounds to her room.

* * * *

Father Marco was sitting at his cluttered desk when Anthony arrived.

"Anthony. Come in." He waved to the guest chair opposite him.

"Thank you, Father."

Anthony had known Father Marco all his life. He was a compassionate, fair man. But he could be demanding, commanding even, at times. More so with Anthony than the other brothers.

Father Marco raised Anthony ever since his mother left him at the monastery's doorsteps as an infant. The priest treated Anthony like a son and was very proud of the excellent work he did at the monastery. Anthony was always on top of things. He was learning about business management and marketing so one day people from all over the world would learn about Saint Valentine's and the Rule of Saint Benedict.

Lately, though, Anthony seemed distracted. Less involved than usual.

"How are you? We missed you at Afternoon Prayer today. You haven't been yourself."

"I suppose I could say that I don't know what you mean, but that would not be honest." Anthony sighed. "I don't really know what it is."

Father Marco looked thoughtfully at Anthony. "You've become very attached to Jonathan. How is his mother doing?"

"She continues with her treatment. Some days she feels well– considering. Other days she is hardly able to get out of bed. The doctors are doing their best, but the cancer is very advanced. It's very serious."

"How is Jonathan dealing with it?"

"He's being brave. Looking to God."

"And the young woman who arrived today? Who was that?"

Nothing that happened at Saint Valentine's escaped Father Marco's notice.

"Jonathan's Aunt Madeline. From New York."

"An American," he raised his eyebrows. "She'll be staying with us?"

"Yes. Jonathan thought–"

Farther Marco interrupted, "It will be good for Jonathan to have her here. And for her. It is very painful to lose a sibling."

Anthony took in a deep breath as though the idea had not occurred to him either. "Other than his mother, she's all that Jonathan has."

"He has us, Anthony. You. He's become very fond of you."

"And I of him, Father."

Father Marco leaned back in his chair and carefully studied

Anthony. "So, why don't you go and check in on Jonathan and his Aunt – what did you say her name was?"

"Maddie. Madeline."

Anthony shrugged his shoulders too casually. Shook his head.

"Madeline. What is she like?"

"I didn't really have the chance to talk much with her. She's very..."

Father Marco watched Anthony struggle to find the right word. "Beautiful," he offered.

"Not at all how I imagined her." Anthony's eyes brightened as he spoke.

"And how is it you imagined her?"

Anthony shook his head. "I don't know. Plain. Reserved. There's something about her that's so –"

Father Marco pursed his lips and interrupted Anthony. "See how she's settling in. Welcome her to Saint Valentine's. I'm sure it would mean a lot to Jonathan. Take her this." He reached for a book. An introduction to the Rule of Saint Benedict. "It might interest her to know what her nephew is up to."

Anthony took the small volume. "You're absolutely right, Father."

"Good." With that, Father Marco picked up some of the papers on his desk. Anthony was dismissed.

"*Grazie.*" Anthony replied.

Anthony slowly got up and left Father Marco's office. With a few strides he stepped out into the sunny afternoon in search of Jonathan and the unexpectedly beautiful Madeline.

* * * *

1943

Lorenzo had to stop himself from steaming the envelope open. Tasked with delivering the mail, he was familiar with the patterns of who received what and from where. This was Marco's first letter in the five weeks he had been at the Order of Saint Peter's. There was no return address. So, instead of resorting to less than honorable devices to find out who had penned the note, Lorenzo hurried to Marco's room to deliver it personally. He did not knock, but simply opened the door and let himself in.

"Lorenzo!" Marco looked up from his book and smiled at his friend.

"This came for you today," Lorenzo held out the note.

Marco's brows squeezed together. "For me?" He reached for the envelope while Lorenzo settled onto a chair and waited.

Marco's hands began trembling and he was filled with the idea that the letter was from her. He felt it. The essence of her on the paper. On the ink of the lettering. In the feminine style of the penmanship. How she had written his name.

"So...open it," Lorenzo urged.

With trembling fingers, he did.

* * * *

Present Day

Madeline had not slept in a twin bed since her college dorm room. She was so focused on seeing Jonathan and Carrie again that she had not considered the amenities at Saint Valentine's or rather the lack of them. This was not the five-star hotel she was accustomed to.

The room was Spartan. A simple hunter green bedspread covered the small bed. There was no phone. The door did not lock. There was a small desk. A dresser. Closet.

"It's perfect!" she said to Jonathan, a wide smile on her face.

"This is one of our best rooms. Look. You have a view of the valley and a private bath. Most of the other rooms have to share."

Madeline glanced out the window at the peaceful green countryside, "Yes, it is beautiful here. I'll be very comfortable."

Jonathan beamed. "Okay. I'll leave you to unpack and get settled. I've been completely neglecting my chores so I need to get to it. Dinner's at seven. You will join us, won't you?"

She had not given the matter of dinner any thought. "Yes. Yes, of course."

Jonathan was just turning to leave when Anthony appeared in the doorway with a small worn book in his hands.

"Hello," his voice was deep and quiet.

Madeline found that all she could do was look at him. Just look at him. As if just looking at him could be enough.

It has to be.

"Hi Anthony. I was just leaving–I need to get to some things," Jonathan turned to Madeline. "I'll see you later, then."

Madeline nodded. Anthony stepped into the small room to let Jonathan pass.

"I wanted to see how you're settling in." He looked at her attentively.

"It's fine." Madeline felt awkward. She never had a monk in her bedroom before. A handsome monk, at that.

"How long will you be in Italy?"

"I'm not sure yet. I..." she hadn't thought about how long she might stay. A week, maybe two. Until Carrie – "I'll be visiting with Jonathan's mother."

"Your sister, Carrie."

"You know her?" Madeline was surprised.

"Yes. I've taken Jonathan to see her a number of times. She's a lovely woman."

She's a lovely woman.

Madeline felt anger rise from long ago. Everyone always loved Carrie more, even their parents. As children, Madeline's friends became Carrie's friends. All Carrie had to do was bat an eyelash or crack a joke and she got everyone's attention.

"I'm so sorry..." Anthony continued.

And now Carrie was dying. Madeline felt ashamed at her petty jealousy. "Thank you."

"Jonathan tells me you haven't seen Carrie in quite some time."

"What else has Jonathan told you?" Madeline's voice was edgy. How was it that this man – this monk – knew so much about her life? None of it was any of his business.

"Nothing. I only meant– "

Madeline interrupted, "Look. I'm tired." She just wanted him to leave. She couldn't stand the nearness of him. The farness of him.

"Of course. I'm sure none of this is very easy for any of you. If there's anything I can do, please .. well, I'm here."

"That's very kind of you."

She looked at him now.

His expression was kind. Compassionate. Handsome. Too handsome. She just wanted him to stay.

"I'll leave you to yourself then. Oh, Father Marco asked me to give you this. A kind of welcome and introduction to the monastery."

He held the book out to her. She reached for it but he let it go before she had a firm grasp. The book fell to the floor with a loud thud. Anthony stepped forward but she reached down for it first.

Madeline picked up the book and stood slowly, the length of Anthony's body in full view. She was entranced by the details of him. Of his legs pressed against his jeans. His thighs. His chest strong underneath the crisp white shirt.

Upright now, he stood inches from her. His face was so close to hers she felt his breath warm across her cheek. His eyes reached into hers. "I'll see you at dinner," he added quietly.

Madeline didn't respond but watched him walk away. In the doorway he stopped, turned, and looked at her.

"You know, Madeline, you're not alone." He said quietly and gently closed the door behind him.

"Could have fooled me," Madeline said. "You will not see me at dinner."

Yet Anthony's words rang in her ears.

You're not alone. You're not alone.

What did he mean? What was he trying to tell her? That *God* is with her? *Easy for him to say. He's hidden himself away from the real world here. He has no idea what my life is like.*

"God and I went our separate ways a long time ago," she told herself, a sadness flowing into her heart. "A long time ago." She unpacked her expensive silk lingerie. In the drawers of the simple pine dresser, it looked as out of place as she felt.

* * * *

The library was deserted. Quiet. Anthony slipped his glasses on and sat at the computer. He typed in, "Madeline O'Connor". Within two clicks of his mouse, he found Felicity's Web site. Images of beautiful lingerie clad models leapt off the monitor. Lacy bras. Panties. Garters. Tasteful for Madison Avenue but sexy. Very sexy.

He shifted uncomfortably in his chair.

A few more clicks and he found information about Felicity International and its Chief Executive Officer.

The black and white photo of Madeline was elegant and businesslike. Anthony read the story of how Madeline started Felicity with a single Beverly Hills store and how the business grew to become a lingerie brand recognized worldwide. He learned how the company contributed to causes that its employees cared about. Battered womens' shelters. Literacy. Initiatives for women-owned businesses. How Madeline had been listed as one of the top one hundred women in business earlier that year. She was savvy, successful, and educated. He spent several minutes reading.

"Find what you're looking for?" Madeline's voice echoed in the library.

"Madeline!" Anthony's face turned scarlet. He had not heard

her walk up behind him.

"I suppose you disapprove," she said. Self-consciousness struck again. She tried to hide her red nails.

"What is there to disapprove of?"

"I guess–I mean–you're a monk and I–" Madeline felt grateful none of her employees could hear her stammering.

He spoke in a tone filled with awe and respect. "You run a very successful company. Create jobs for people." He looked at her. Took off his glasses in one slow deliberate motion and placed them gently on the desk. "It's not for me to judge you, Madeline."

The tone of his voice as he said her name was a song to her soul. Still, Madeline judged herself. What was it about Anthony that made her feel uneasy about Felicity? About the choices she had made?

Here, at Saint Valentine's, her life in New York seemed unreal, as though it did not even exist. She glanced at her picture on the computer screen. The polished composed woman she saw there was a world away. And reminded Madeline of who she was. Or thought she was.

"I was hoping to use the computer to check email. But if you're using it–" She turned to leave.

He reached out and caught her arm. Held it. Held her eyes with his.

She reminded herself that he was a monk and refrained from flirting. One does not flirt with monks. What if it was the monk who did the flirting?

Was he flirting? *Was* that a glimmer of male interest in his eyes?

"No. No. It's okay. Please." He stood up, still holding her arm. Not letting her go. "You go right ahead. You're a guest here, and hospitality is a Benedictine tradition."

"Speaking of tradition, why don't you wear a robe?" *Instead of looking like someone right out of a magazine ad,* she thought. She pulled her arm from his grasp.

"It's not a rule that we wear a robe, and I just prefer to wear clothes more often than not. I mean-" He blushed again.

She laughed. The image of his body without clothes was enticing. His blush endearing.

He blushed more and looked to the floor.

God he's charming! He doesn't even have to try.

She contemplated him. She wondered if he had ever been with a woman. Had sex with a woman. The idea of him being a virgin aroused her. What if he wasn't? She heard stories of nuns and priests who broke their vows.

She hated herself for what she was thinking.

"I'm sorry. I guess I have all these preconceived ideas about monks. Jonathan looked so elegant wearing his robe." She hoped that talking about Jonathan would ease the sudden tension between them.

"Novices tend to be very enthusiastic. I've been around much longer, so am less ardent." He seemed apologetic. "We really are just people, you know."

"I know, it's just that you've chosen this way of life. Given up so much."

"I wouldn't know .. I've lived here all my life." He said, his tone melancholy.

"All your life!" The idea shocked Madeline.

Anthony's face was serious. "*Sì*..."

Too close, too soon, Madeline thought.

He regained himself. "Here. Please. Sit." He motioned to the chair and changed the subject. "Your company's web site is very well done."

She followed his lead.

"Thank you. We worked hard on it." Madeline sat at the computer now and clicked away Felicity's web site. The computer was slow and it took a moment for her email screen to appear.

"I'm working on a site for Saint Valentine's. One day I'd like for us to be able to take reservations on line. Sell our wine."

"Sell your wine?" She turned to look at him.

"We have a small winery."

"Really? I'd love to see it while I'm here. I like wine, but don't know much about it."

"Yes... I know you like wine." He was smiling. His eyes twinkled.

Was she imagining the sexy lilt in his voice as he spoke? He *had* noticed she drank too much wine at the restaurant. She swore he was flirting.

Flirting with a monk would be harmless, she supposed.

Wouldn't it? It's like flirting with someone who's married. Nothing can come of it. Nothing at all.

She turned to face him, her lips curving into a grin. "I don't go around falling into men's laps, you know."

"Having a beautiful woman fall into my lap hasn't happened to me before." His eyes shined. "It wasn't altogether unpleasant."

Damn him! He *was* flirting. Madeline recognized flirting when she saw it. Or did she? Anthony was not a man who was sophisticated in the ways of the world. In the ways between men and women. Perhaps he was being friendly. Perhaps she just *wanted* him to flirt.

Have I been so starved for attention that I'm imagining his interest? The question rushed into Madeline's mind.

"*There* you are." A woman's voice beckoned from the entrance.

Madeline turned to see an attractive woman, smartly but simply dressed in a white shirt and black skirt walking toward them. She immediately recognized the young brunette as the same woman who had been with Anthony at the restaurant. Her shiny dark hair was cut short. She wore a sprinkling of makeup, enough to subtly enhance her pretty eyes and smile. She looked at Madeline briefly, then directed her sparkling eyes at Anthony.

"I've been looking for you. You didn't forget that I was coming, did you?"

The expression on his face told Madeline he *had* forgotten. "*Scusi*," he said to Madeline. He turned and walked toward the younger woman.

Madeline watched as Anthony and the brunette shared an embrace in greeting. Too long an embrace. Too close an embrace. When they finally separated, he placed a hand on the small of her back. The gesture struck Madeline as intimate. Too intimate. Together they walked toward the exit, Anthony's hand slipping easily around his companion's small waist.

Madeline's teeth clenched. She struggled to wrench her gaze from Anthony's hand pressed against the woman's body. Who was this woman? What was her relationship with him?

Why do I care?

Abruptly, Anthony stopped. He whispered something to the other woman and walked back to Madeline.

Warm melted chocolate, his eyes poured into hers. Madeline felt the sultriness of his body as he stood close and reached around her shoulders. What was only a few seconds extended across lifetimes.

"My glasses." He picked the frames up and fanned them in the air. The skin around his eyes creased as he winced. "I'm always losing them."

Before Madeline could say, "Me too," he was gone.

* * * *

Carrie knelt in front of the toilet, her body spent from retching. Today was not a good day. Today she felt sick.

"One day at a time," she sighed. She pulled herself to stand up. "Just where have you been?"

Truffles, a cream colored cat with alert aquamarine eyes, rubbed her soft warm body against Carrie's legs.

"I suppose it's food you want," Carrie said.

The cat had just appeared one day and for the last two months, Carrie adopted her. As much as a person can adopt a cat. Truffles came and went as she pleased. For Carrie, her visits were a special treat. A truffle.

Carrie walked down the small hallway of her apartment to the kitchen. The cat trotted gingerly after her, meowing as if to say "hurry up", tail waving in the air.

"Sì! Sì!"

On the counter, several cans of cat food were awaiting Truffles' arrival. Carrie reached for one. Tuna dinner with chunks of cheese. Carrie punctured the tin with a can opener.

Truffles' meowing grew more insistent while Carrie scraped the food from the can into a bowl. She bent down and placed it on the floor for the cat, who began devouring the meal.

At once Carrie's nostrils were assaulted by the sickening smell of the food. Her empty stomach wretched violently. Then stopped.

Carrie dragged herself to a chair and sat. Spent. She watched Truffles finish her food. Feline etiquette demanded that the cat lick her lips and wash her face with a ladylike paw. The ritual brought a small smile to Carrie's face. There was something so precious about the little pink pads of the cat's paw.

Satiated, Truffles sauntered over to Carrie and launched into her lap. She stroked the cat's head. "Oh Truffles. You won't like it as much but I think we'll have to switch to dry food."

Truffles purred contentedly and Carrie's eyes filled with tears. Her cancer touched everyone's life. Even a stray cat's.

There was a knock at the door.

"Who could that be?" Carrie asked the cat.

She rubbed the back of her hand against her eyes to stop her tears. Standing slowly, she walked to the door and opened it.

"Hello Carrie." Madeline spoke quietly and looked straight into her sister's eyes.

Carrie's face was pale.

"I'm sorry. I should have called first. But..."

Silently the two women assessed each other. Finally, Carrie

managed, "No. It's all right. Please. Come in."

It had been seven years. Seven long years. Now, Carrie stepped aside and held the door open for her sister.

"*Grazie*," Madeline said, and stepped through.

* * * *

1943

Marco could not remember another time in his life when he felt so alive. He sat in the convent's chapel, waiting for her. For Isabella. He knew her name now. Isabella was such a beautiful name–lyrical, the way it floated from his lips when he repeated it over and over. Her note said to meet him there at three o'clock, and, just now, the tower bells began to toll. The sound vibrated through his body. Once. Twice. Thrice. He held his breath in a failed attempt to slow his runaway heart. She would arrive at any second.

Even the silence in the ancient chapel could not calm young Marco's nerves as he waited. He knew he should pray. But for what? He no longer knew what to pray for. He already prayed to know God. For peace. For the insanity of the war to end. None of his prayers, it seemed, had been answered. Yet. He wondered, as he sat in the mahogany pew with his hands folded motionless in his lap, if they ever would be.

"Marco!"

Isabella's voice echoed in the chapel. Marco... Marco... Marco. He wanted to turn around but found he could not. Instead, he sat, closed eyed and motionless, listening to her approaching footsteps. He felt the warmth of her body as she sat next to him, the place where her thigh pressed against his burning through the fabric of his robe. Without a sound, she took his hand in hers. Her skin was soft, smooth.

"Isabella," he said.

"I was afraid you wouldn't come," she said.

He opened his eyes then and looked at her. She was just as he remembered. Her beautiful face with those dark eyes that smiled to belie the sadness just underneath.

"I got your note. How did you know where to find me?"

"I told Sister Francesca I'd seen you in the chapel. That you had returned the candelabra. She told me you were a novice at Saint Peter's. I'm glad you came."

"How could I not?"

He watched her lips curve upward into a small smile.

"Thank you," she whispered and squeezed his hand.

He gazed down at her and felt his heart expand with indescribable warmth, as if a large and beautiful rose was blossoming inside his chest. *This feeling*, he thought, *it must be love.*

He struggled for something to say. "Sister Francesca. She said you had left."

Isabella looked down, her long black eyelashes a sharp contrast to her pale skin.

"I cannot leave," she said.

He looked at her, a question in his eyes.

She answered simply. "I am a Jew. My parents –"

"Isabella!"

Before they both turned to see who was speaking, they both knew it was Sister Francesca.

"Marco!"

She gathered the skirt of her habit and hurried to them. "Isabella, go to your room immediately."

With tear-filled eyes, Isabella cast a quick look toward Marco, got up and hastened out of the chapel.

Marco sat silently, staring into a nothingness that he longed to feel. But he did not feel nothing. He felt everything. He felt as if all the injustices of the world were colliding with the love that had somehow been planted in his heart.

"Marco. You mustn't speak of this to anyone. It would put all of us in grievous danger. I fear the Germans will be here any time and no one must know that she is here –"

"Speak of what, Sister Francesca?"

The old nun and the young novice looked at each other long and hard.

"The situation is dangerous, young Marco. It is not just the Nazis I'm afraid of. If others in the Church found out –"

"Others in the Church?" He squinted as if the sun had blinded him.

The old woman sighed. "Not everyone would approve of Catholic nuns harboring a Jew."

Marco shook his head in naïve protest. "I don't understand."

The old woman sighed. "You are young and the Church is not always what it is supposed to be. Well, now that you know she is here, you may come back and visit. She is lonely. It would be good for her to have a friend from outside the abbey. But she isn't one of us, you know. " Sister Francesca rose and left young Marco sitting in the chapel, alone with a smile on his face and wings on his soaring heart.

* * * *

Present Day

Anthony had known Veronica Bocelli for over ten years, ever since her arrival as a young nun in Rome. She watched as he surveyed the rows of grapes that would become the red wine they had enjoyed together many times.

"The stain will never come out of my blouse," Veronica said. "That poor woman... she was so embarrassed." She was referring to Madeline and how she had fallen on Anthony.

Anthony turned to look at Veronica. "Yes... she certainly was," he laughed. Then turned his attention back to the grapes.

"I love these vineyards," she said.

"So do I."

"Anthony, please, let's sit. I have something important to tell you."

His face registered concern. "What is it?"

Veronica nodded toward a small bench and, silently, they walked to it and sat down.

Anthony looked expectantly at her and waited.

"This isn't easy to tell you." Her voice was soft. Her expression serious. "I'm leaving the order."

"What? Leaving the abbey? Veronica! But why?" Stunned, he took her hand in his, holding it tenderly.

"I don't want to be a nun anymore."

"What!" His face was incredulous.

"I know this comes as a shock to you."

"A shock! To say the very least. What has happened? Why didn't you talk about this with me?" He raised his voice and stood up.

"I didn't think you'd understand. You've always been so dedicated to Saint Valentine's." She shook her head and shrugged her shoulders. "Nothing in particular happened. It just started slowly. A kind of restlessness or discontent that settled in my soul."

"Questioning your faith," he said.

"No. Although at first that's what I thought, too. But it went much deeper. Mother Superior and I have discussed it over and over. I've realized there are many ways to serve God."

They looked deeply into each other's eyes.

"Anthony, I don't want to die not having lived."

"Not having lived? You don't feel as though you're living?"

She sighed. "It's hard to describe in words, Anthony. But this life, my life, doesn't fit anymore. It just feels – small. Like there has to be more."

"I see. Will you be staying in Rome?"

She shook her head.

"Where then?"

"New York." Her face brightened. "My parents are thrilled and they need me. I can help them with the restaurants until I decide what else to do."

He sat back down beside her and pulled her into his arms. Held her tenderly. Closely.

"Oh, my brave Veronica. Whatever will I do without you?" He whispered into her ears. "You're sure about this?"

She pulled away to look at him.

"No." She laughed nervously. "Is anybody ever really sure about anything? But it's what I'm doing. It feels right. I trust that God's grace will be with me–wherever I go."

Anthony gazed at her, deep in thought. "Maybe leaving takes more faith than staying."

Veronica considered his words for a moment and glanced down at her watch. It was time for her to go. "Walk me back? I need to catch a train into the city."

"Of course my dear, dear Veronica." Anthony stood and took her hand in his again.

Together the two friends walked through the sunny Italian countryside accompanied by a fleeting summer's end breeze. All the while Veronica chatted excitedly about her new life in America.

All the while Anthony quietly listened.

* * * *

Madeline glanced around Carrie's small apartment. It was tastefully decorated in antiques. Floral tapestries. Fresh flowers. Little piles of clutter here and there took away from the sense of order and made the rooms look lived in.

Carrie led Madeline to the pale rose sofa and motioned for her to sit down.

Madeline sat, then looked closely at her sister. Carrie moved slowly to the floral chintz wing chair across from the sofa and eased into it. Without make up, Carrie was pale and looked weak. She seemed to Madeline a faded photograph that captured the memory of what once had been.

What once had been.

Sitting across from Madeline now was the sister who had slept with her husband. Given birth to his child. To Jonathan.

Madeline had imagined Carrie's life in Italy completely differently.

She had imagined her own life completely differently. If only–

If only -

Carrie interrupted her thoughts. "You look beautiful, Madeline."

Not beautiful enough for David, Madeline thought. "Thank you." She managed a smile. "Your apartment is lovely."

"Thank you. I haven't been here that long. Moved in after Jonathan went to Saint Valentine's. I'm happy here. It's home."

The phone rang.

"Oh. Excuse me, would you?" Carrie stood slowly.

"Of course."

Carrie walked down the hallway and answered the phone in another room. "*Pronti.*"

Madeline stood and walked about the living room. She crossed the floor to a bookshelf where photographs were displayed.

Sitting on the shelf was a picture of their parents departing for an anniversary cruise. They were waving. Smiling. Madeline smiled. The same photo hung on a wall in her New York study although she seldom really looked at it.

Their parents died when Madeline was in her late twenties. Their mother of breast cancer. Their father had died the following year in a car accident. Yet here they were. In Italy. Smiling and waving. About to embark on an anniversary cruise.

There were photographs of Jonathan. Jonathan skiing. Jonathan in Paris. Jonathan as a baby.

Jonathan with his father.

Madeline's gaze hung on her ex-husband's face. He was smiling the handsome smile that first captured her heart. His arm was around Jonathan.

From the corner of her eye she saw it. Another photograph. Carrie radiant in a wedding dress. David with that smile beside her. The image violently assaulted every cell in Madeline's body. The old familiar ache in her heart swelled again in her chest. Yet David and Carrie, too, had divorced. Were all marriages doomed?

"Madeline?" Carrie stood in the hallway.

Madeline turned to face her sister.

"That was the hospital. Some of my results are in. I'm afraid I have to go."

Madeline felt weak. She sighed. "I'll come with you."

"You will?" Carrie's face brightened.

Madeline nodded. "No one should hear test results alone. Let's go."

Carrie's expression fell. She nodded. "You didn't come here because you thought I'm going to die, did you? Because I'm not. I'm going to get through this."

Madeline looked at her sister. The one who always got her own way. Always got what she wanted. Ever since they were children Madeline resented that about Carrie.

But this was different. This was the first time Madeline wanted for Carrie what she wanted for herself. How many times had she wished her sister ill? Fleetingly wished her sister were dead. Guilt throbbed painfully in Madeline's head.

"Yes, Carrie. You will get through this."

You have to. For both of us.

* * * *

Anthony sat on the edge of his bed, alone in his room. The news that Veronica was leaving the abbey barraged him. How could he not have seen it coming? He shook his head, mystified that he missed some of the signs. Her restlessness. Her lack of interest in the usual things – long contemplative conversations, meetings about the abbey's financial affairs, twilight walks. He wondered what was wrong. Yet how was it possible that he could have known Veronica so well, for so long, and yet have been completely unmindful of her innermost thoughts? What was it that had kept him from asking?

Perhaps the questions I'm not asking myself?

Uncomfortable with the thought, he got up and walked over to his small closet, filled with the sudden urge to put on his monk's robe. He sifted though his clothes–the shirts and slacks and sweaters and jackets he collected over the years —and found it hanging at the back. As he started to pull it off the hanger, something else caught his eye and a thin golden cord that tied his heart to his past tugged, gently.

What is coming over me?

Surrendering to a tide of sentimentality, he reached for a small box tucked into a corner on the top shelf and pulled it out. He carried it carefully, as if it contained a great treasure, and returned to sit on the edge of his bed.

He opened the box. In it was a baby blanket, hand knit in pale shades of pink and blue. He pulled it out and pressed its softness against his cheek. Closing his eyes, he inhaled its mustiness.

Was it knit by my mother?

A part of him wanted to believe that it had. Yet, a part of him would not believe it. Could not believe it. It was the blanket he had been wrapped in when the monks at Saint Valentine's found him all those years ago. The blanket that sealed his fate and set him on the path to a monastic life.

Who had his mother been? What happened that she had abandoned him? Simply left him at the monastery to be cared for by the monks. And what of his father?

Such thoughts and questions had fermented and blended in his mind over the years, aging in the chambers of his heart like a fine vintage in the cool dark stillness of a cellar.

He told himself again and again that the answers did not matter. The mysteries of his past could rest in peace, forever unanswered. God's will directed the course of his life and he was exactly where he was supposed to be.

God's will...but what of free will?

And what is my will?

A quiet rapping at the door drew him out of his thoughts.

"Anthony?" It was Jonathan.

With haste, Anthony returned the blanket to its box. "Just a minute." With two long strides, he was back at the closet, sliding the package back into its appointed spot on the shelf. He glanced at his monk's robe still suspended on the hanger and slid it, too, back into its place. There was no time to change now.

"Come in," he said to the young novice who waited in the hall.

The door opened and Jonathan entered the room, a serious expression on his face.

"What is it?"

"I think I may have been wrong to ask Aunt Maddie to come here."

"Wrong? What do you mean?"

The novice held out a Felicity catalog to the monk. "I found this in her room. I wanted to surprise her by leaving some flowers and it was lying on her bed." Tears were bright in his eyes. "I looked at it. I've never seen anything like it before. Those women are–I got so–"

Anthony leafed though the glossy pages filled with voluptuous vixens clad in the latest lingerie from Madeline's company. His own blood stirred and he could understand Jonathan's reaction to the images. The boy was, after all, just seventeen.

"Come. Sit down," Anthony sat on a pine chair, indicated the bed to Jonathan.

Tears were streaming openly down the novice's face. "I'm so confused. How could I feel such things? It was like my body had a mind of its own. I just–I had to–"

Anthony raised an open hand to stop Jonathan's outburst. "It's all right, Jonathan."

"What do you mean, it's all right! I'm in training to be a monk. I'm not supposed to be thinking about sss-" he stammered.

"Sex. It's okay to say it," Anthony pursed his lips.

Jonathan looked at his friend with wide eyes.

"This is a matter that we have all been dealing with for centuries. We are human, not saints. We live in these bodies that have physical wants. It's how we deal with them that matters. In every situation, we have a choice."

"So, I wasn't wrong to feel what I felt?" Jonathan started to calm down.

"No. It wasn't wrong at all. You do have to understand that if you choose this way of life, you will need to learn to deal with your desires. Rechannel them."

"How do you do that?" Jonathan asked.

Avoid them. Shut them out. Deny them.

"I pray." It was a lie and the truth at the same time. "Everyone has their own way. You'll find your own."

Jonathan considered his older friend's words. "Thank you."

Anthony nodded and held the catalog back out to Jonathan. "Here. Put this back where you found it."

Jonathan nodded and Anthony watched the young man leave. He sighed a long slow sigh.

An image of Madeline face came to mind. How she looked at him. Had somehow looked through him. How she felt beneath his hands.

A twinge of envy for Jonathan coursed through him. Jonathan was making a decision to become a monk. It was a life he had chosen or had chosen him. But Anthony had been raised at Saint Valentine's. He led a cloistered life. Had he ever been free to choose?

If I had, would I have chosen differently?

* * * *

Madeline hated hospitals. Despised everything about them. The smell. The pace. Every memory she had of time spent in them was painful. Her parents' deaths. Jonathan's accident.

The heartbreaking scene in the waiting room where David and Carrie's affair was exposed.

Now here she was again, in a hospital with her sister. Except this time, it was Carrie's life, not Jonathan's, that was in danger.

The two sisters sat together in a small office, waiting for Carrie's physician, Doctor Adam Ferguson.

"You'll love my doctor," Carrie said in an attempt to fill the silence. "He's originally from England. He fell in love with an Italian psychologist and moved to Rome. They're married now."

Madeline ignored her sister's small talk. "I can't imagine what you're going through Carrie. The chemotherapy must be..." she trailed off.

"I'm not having chemotherapy. I tried that. It was unbearable. I'm not going through it anymore," Carrie said.

Madeline furrowed her brows. "What do you mean – not having chemotherapy? What kind of treatment are you getting?"

Carrie looked down at the floor. "It's an experimental therapy called the Di Bella Method. It's a combination of vitamins, hormones, and drugs."

An experimental therapy! Vitamins, hormones and drugs! Sounds like Bela Lagosi.

"But Carrie. Does it work?"

"There have been cases where people have recovered."

"How many cases?"

Carrie looked up directly into Madeline's eyes. "I thought you wanted to be here to support me."

"I am. I do. But –"

Carrie interrupted her sister. "Well, it doesn't feel like it to me."

"Carrie, I just want you to get better."

I don't want you to die.

Doctor Ferguson arrived. "Carrie, *ciao!*" He looked at Madeline.

"Hi Adam. This is my sister. Madeline. She's here from New York."

Madeline quickly surveyed the doctor. He was young, probably in his forties. Attractive. He wore a wedding ring and glasses.

He extended a hand toward Madeline. "It's a pleasure to meet you," he said with an English accent.

Madeline shook his hand. "Doctor Ferguson. Hello."

"Please. Call me Adam." He perched himself on top of the desk across from Madeline and Carrie. "Well. I've got some news. It's not good or bad, really. Then again, in a way it's good. Your tumor has not grown. Neither has it diminished. For now, nothing's changed. How are you feeling?"

"Good actually. I'm not as tired as I have been. The chemotherapy was dreadful. This is much–"

Madeline interrupted. "What, exactly, are you treating my sister with?" Madeline asked the doctor.

He looked at Madeline, carefully assessing her, then replied. "With a combination of somatostatin, melatonin, bromocriptine, beta-carotene, alpha-tocopherol, vitamin D, ascorbic acid, retinoic acid and cyclophosphamide. Drugs. Vitamins. Hormones. The treatment is known as the Di Bella Method. It's experimental, controversial, and unorthodox. Carrie came to me demanding it. While I don't endorse it, I feel I must offer it to people who have tried everything else. Like your sister."

Madeline swallowed. "I see," she said. "Is it effective?"

Out of the corner of her eye, Madeline noticed Carrie fold her arms across her chest. Set her jaw. It was a pose Madeline herself adopted during tense business negotiations.

"Doctor Di Bella has treated more than 10,000 patients over the past twenty years."

"Successfully?"

"It depends on your definition of success," he said.

"Meaning?"

He glanced at Carrie. Then replied, "This is a treatment. Not a cure. Above all its purpose is to give patients a more dignified quality of life. Making them more self-sufficient, limiting their physical suffering and prolonging their life as much as possible. It's more about learning to live with the disease than trying to cure it. In some situations, we do see a disappearance of the disease. In that case, the recovery has to be followed by a use of drugs and by regular diagnosis controls."

A treatment. Not a cure.

Silence settled into the small room in a failed attempt at comfort.

It was Carrie who spoke first. She turned and looked at her sister. "Madeline, you haven't been here. You have no idea what I've gone through. I can't go through with any more chemotherapy. It wasn't working. This is my last hope. I have to believe it will work. I need you to believe it, too."

Madeline sighed, reached over and squeezed her sister's hand.

"I do, Carrie. I do," she lied for her sister's sake. *Please don't die.*

* * * *

Madeline sobbed into her pillow. Deep heavy sobs that rose from the caverns of her soul. Her whole body shook with each new wave of tears.

"Madeline?" It was Anthony's voice, barely audible in the darkness of the small room.

She froze.

"Madeline?" he asked again.

She sat up on the edge of the bed. Moonlight danced on her glossy hair, shimmered on the black satin of her nightgown, and illuminated her skin.

"What are you doing here?" Her words were loud in surprise.

"Shhhh. We're not supposed to be talking." His voice was a whisper as he knelt before her. "I was hungry—on my way to the kitchen–and I heard you crying. Are you all right?"

Madeline was not sure if she believed him. "Yes. No. I–" Everything was a blur. "I saw Carrie today. She looked awful. Not at all the way I remembered her. I wasn't prepared. I didn't know."

"Of course you didn't. How could you?" Anthony knelt before her, listened, and waited for her to continue.

"Anthony, I don't know how to deal with any of this. I hate hospitals. And the doctors. They seem like they know what they're doing. But they don't. Not really."

"What did they say?"

"I don't know. I don't know what to think. They said the tumor's the same. No bigger. No smaller."

"That's good news."

"I know, but they said that about our mother, too. She died. And what about this Di Bella treatment? I looked it up on the Internet. It's so– so–"

"Oh, Madeline."

She looked at him through tear filled eyes. His face was so handsome in the shadows cast by the midnight light. His expression was tender. Compassionate.

"I don't want her to die. I don't want her to leave." A single luminous tear trailed down her face.

Anthony moved and sat on the bed beside her. She felt the bed shift under the weight of him. He took her delicate right hand in his and glided the tip of his thumb slowly across the skin on the back of her hand. A hot chill coursed through her and she trembled under his touch.

"Of course you don't," he said.

She found herself falling into his arms. Into the warmth of his embrace. His body. She felt him breathe her in. Fully. Deeply. He held her. Stroked her hair. Her muscles tensed. Then surrendered.

The world became him. Her breasts pressed against the firmness of his chest. She nuzzled against his neck and breathed in the smell of him. The scent of a man. His skin was warm and she wanted to taste it. She parted her lips in a breathless sigh.

In an instant, she felt him tense. Freeze.

The abrupt cold made her senses swirl and collide with the sharp edges of her mind. *Anthony is a monk. Anthony is a monk.* From somewhere a voice repeated the mantra.

Willfully she peeled herself away from his body. She felt the heat of his hands still resting on her waist, searing her body through her filmy garment. Their eyes met. Their mouths were separated by a veil of cool night air. His breath was warm on her lips.

Then he bolted. Sharply. Painfully. The moment evaporated. With two silent strides he was at the door.

"*Buona sera,*" he said. *Good night.* And then was gone.

Madeline fought to regain her composure but it was hopeless. She fell back on the bed and surrendered to herself now. To the rich sorrow that welled from the infinite depths of her soul.

She cried. Wept. For her mother and father. For her marriage. For Carrie.

For herself. For the Madeline she left behind. For the Madeline she no longer knew. And for the Madeline who could love a man like Anthony and yet knew would never have him. Finally, emotionally and physically spent, she slept.

* * * *

1943

Isabella was not allowed to leave the abbey. All the nuns knew she was there, and each one had tacitly agreed to keep her presence a secret, even if they did not agree with her asylum. To report

Isabella to the German authorities would mean betraying the order, and so long as Isabella was not found, everyone was safe. So, in an odd way, the situation instilled a bond among them, a silent conspiracy that became the undercurrent of their daily lives. To Isabella, the abbey came to feel like a prison, albeit a caring one. Her only crime was that she had been born a Jew.

At the first murmurings of war, Isabella's father fled to Africa and had planned to send for she and her mother as soon as he settled somewhere. But days of no word from him turned into weeks. Then months. When it became clear that something had happened and he was not coming for them, Isabella's mother begged the nuns to take fifteen year old Isabella in, fearing that she would not be able to protect her daughter from the inevitable German onslaught. She, too, promised to return for Isabella. As soon as she could.

Now the German army occupied Italy. Nazi commandos had rescued Mussolini and the Allies were advancing. All of Italy held its breath.

All Isabella could do was wait. For the war to be over. For her mother to return. And for Marco to come to see her.

As summer faded into autumn, he did. As often as he could. Two or three times a week. Sometimes four. It was never often enough. They would meet in the chapel and talk for hours. About her life. About his life at the monastery. He would read to her. Books that he was studying or sometimes stories. She hung on his every word.

Today, he read from The Rule of Saint Benedict.

"And, we believe the divine presence is everywhere." It had become his favorite quote. He looked at Isabella, her face radiant in the twilight sun that filtered through the stained glass windows.

"Everywhere?" she asked, her voice small.

He nodded. "Everywhere."

"If only everyone believed that. If we could all see the divinity in each one of us. There would be no war. How could anyone kill something divine?"

Marco thought of the way priests blessed missiles intended to kill the enemy. The divine enemy. Created by the same God. He sighed in resigned anger at the senselessness of it all, not sure if he was angry with man or with God.

"I know. I know just what you mean." He marveled constantly at how they looked at things the same way, as though they gazed out at the world through the same pair of eyes.

"It isn't fair," she said.

"No. It isn't," he said.

He fought, as he had many times, the urge to pull her into his arms and hold her. Just hold her. To feel the weight of her, the breath of her, against him. To stroke her glossy dark hair.

"Marco?"

"Yes?"

"Would it be all right if you hugged me?"

There it was again. That feeling of an enormous flower blossoming in his chest, basking toward the sun, glowing with its life and warmth.

He could no longer resist. He gathered her into his arms and closed his eyes. All there was, was Isabella. Her body pressed against his. The skin of her cheek warm against his neck. The scent of her hair. The gentle rise and fall of her breath. He lay back against the bench and she followed, the length of her lying on top of him. Her head resting on his chest.

"I can feel the beating of your heart," she whispered.

He smiled, and stroked her hair, overcome by a feeling of peace, a sense that he was exactly where he was supposed to be. With her. They lay that way for a few minutes, until they fell asleep with the sun setting over Venice.

Hours later, they were still lying together in the chapel. But now it was past curfew. Marco could not leave until morning.

* * * *

Present Day

The morning bells sang throughout the dawning valley and coaxed Madeline awake. Birds chimed in and she reveled in a dreamy peaceful moment before full consciousness jolted her awake and reminded her of the night's events.

Had it been real? A dream?

Or a nightmare?

How could she be falling for Anthony Lamberti? A monk! It was an impossible situation yet she could not help herself. Somehow she had to. She would face him in the light of day and things would be different. Feel different.

She got out of bed. After a long soothing shower she felt more like herself. More like the in-control and in-charge chief executive officer she was. Naked, she walked over to the dresser and pulled open a drawer filled with lingerie.

Felicity!

Panic surged through her as she realized she had not responded to her email the previous day.

What was happening to her?

Am I losing my mind?

She slipped on a bra and panties and dressed in a flowing blue knit dress. Sliding on her sandals, she saw her nail polish had chipped.

"Damn it!"

Madeline rummaged through her cosmetics case and found a small bottle of nail polish remover and cotton balls. Within a minute she whisked off the red paint and tossed the stained balls into the wastebasket. How odd they looked. The blood red fluffy little balls were out of place here in a stark guest room at Saint Valentine's. Her bare nails looked even odder. When was the last time she had gone without polish?

She grabbed her bag and hurried out of the room. Breakfast was ready in the dining room and she wanted to face Anthony. To set things right. Act as though nothing had happened.

Nothing *had* happened, she told herself.

She breezed through the ancient courtyard and into the dining room. Jonathan and Anthony were seated with Father Marco. Facing Anthony was the best thing to do. She wanted to deal with him sooner rather than later. Show him that their exchange the previous night had not affected her. That it had not touched her at all.

With feigned confidence she walked to the table, pulled out an empty chair beside Jonathan, and sat directly across from Anthony.

"Good morning." Her voice was loud. Clear. It echoed throughout the dining room. She smiled broadly.

Six eyes stared up at her.

Il silenzio. Silence was observed through breakfast.

Oh my God! Her cheeks burned.

Jonathan reached over and placed his hand upon hers. Squeezed. She looked at her nephew helplessly. He smiled and gently squeezed her hand again. Reassured her. She let out a long slow breath and glanced up at Anthony.

He peered at her from over the edge of a coffee mug. He winked.

He winked!

Her eyes widened in disbelief. Had she imagined it?

"Madeline!" Father Marco's voice was a firm gentle whisper.

His Italian accent thick. "While you are a guest here at Saint Valentine's, please observe our practices. Just eat and breathe." He smiled.

His words flowed through her. Eat and breathe. Eat and breathe.

Multi-tasking, she thought. *I can do that.* She pressed her lips together to avoid smiling at the thought.

Eat...

Breathe...

Life at Saint Valentine's was a world away from life in New York. From *her* life in New York. She pictured her assistant Eric juggling phones, messages, email, regular mail, ordering lunch while wolfing down breakfast. Coordinating meetings. Remembered the many working lunches. Dinners with Heather discussing nothing but financial statements. Budgets. Profits.

There are so many different realities. All going on at the same time. Everywhere. For everyone.

Which reality is the real reality?

What holds it all together?

Where are these thoughts coming from?

She rose from the table and walked slowly over to the simple buffet of rolls, jams, and fruit. She reached slowly for a plate, watched her hand as it moved. Watched her fingers clasp the plain white porcelain. She felt her own heart beat rapidly in her chest.

An awareness of her own self settled over her.

What is my reality?

The question jolted her. Her fingers lost their grip on the plate and it crashed to the floor. Shattered.

She stared at the fragments of porcelain lying at her feet, pieces, that only a moment ago, had been a whole she held in her hand.

Father Marco and the other monks turned abruptly to see what had happened.

Anthony appeared before her.

Tears–how could there be any left after last night–welled up in her eyes. She opened her mouth to speak.

Anthony shook his head and in a single smooth motion reached for one of her hands. Held it. Pressed his index finger softly on her lips and silenced her. Steadied her. She quivered.

For a moment they stood there. Held each other's eyes. Each other's hearts. An indefinable, indescribable – oneness – passed between them. Connected them. For the moment and for forever.

Anthony slowly released her, bent down and picked up the

pieces of the broken plate while Madeline watched, mesmerized by the slow and deliberate movement of his hands.

Her attention turned to Father Marco who stood and walked toward her.

"Come with me," he said.

She glanced down at Anthony and turned to follow Father Marco out of the dining room. She watched as the fabric of his long black gown floated about his feet with each assertive step.

Her stomach grumbled and it occurred to Madeline that she had not eaten.

Too late for food, she thought.

Breakfast was obviously over.

* * * *

Father Marco silently walked through Saint Valentine's courtyard and onto the terrace while Madeline's mind raced. She hurried to keep up with him.

Madeline could not remember if she had ever spoken with a priest. Her mind scanned memories from childhood, but aside from services on Christmas or Easter, church had not been an important part of the O'Connor family's life.

"God is everywhere," her mother used to say. Madeline left it at that and had never given the matter much thought. Felicity always kept her busy. Too busy, even, for God.

Finally reaching the bench that was his destination, Father Marco sat down. Feeling like a delinquent teenager in the principal's office, Madeline joined him. Together they looked out at the verdant sun washed hillside.

"I'm afraid I haven't properly introduced myself. I'm Father Marco." He extended a hand to Madeline.

Relieved at the break in the silence, she shook it. "I'm Madeline O'Connor."

"You are Jonathan's..."

"Aunt."

"Aunt. And you will be staying with us. I understand your sister is not well."

"Carrie. No. She's very ill. After her most recent tests, the doctors are hopeful."

"It is not an easy thing."

Madeline watched as a small flock of birds flew across the valley and momentarily interrupted its stillness.

A respectful silence passed between them and Madeline's eyes turned to the tranquil green hills that reclined before them.

"No. No it isn't. I really want to apologize for my behavior at breakfast. I—"

Father Marco reassuringly placed his age worn hand on Madeline's.

"It's quite all right," he said. "Staying at a monastery is a new experience for most people. It's a much different pace from living in America, I imagine."

"Especially New York," Madeline turned and smiled at him.

"Jonathan is a fine young man. He'll make a good monk one day." *Just like Anthony,* she thought.

"How, Father, does someone become a monk?"

"Well, it's a different process for everyone. Some men come at a young age, like Jonathan. Others join the Order after having careers. After having seen the ordinary world and deciding it didn't fit for them. They start out as a novice like Jonathan. It takes years."

"Do monks eventually become priests?"

"Some do. But not always."

"Jonathan seems very close to Brother Anthony."

Brother Anthony. The words felt strange on Madeline's lips.

"Yes, they are very close. Anthony is very special to me. He arrived here when he was an infant. His mother just left him here. The orphanage that was in town at the time – it's gone now – was full. We decided to keep him here and raise him ourselves. He's like a son to me."

"He never left the monastery?"

Father Marco shook his head slowly. "No. We're very lucky to have him. Which, actually, brings me to what I want to discuss with you." His face was serious.

Oh no! He knows about me and Anthony.

But what is there to know?

"I think that while you're here, you might want to occupy yourself in the winery. Anthony can always use some help there. It occurred to me that it might interest you. You seem like someone who is used to being busy. I understand you run a successful company. You might have some ideas for selling our wine."

Madeline was mortified. She did not want to be around Anthony any more than she needed. But how could she say no to Father Marco?

"I don't know anything about wine. Other than, you know, a

merlot is red. Chardonnay is white. Just basic things."

"Business is business, isn't it? The principles are the same, aren't they?" he smiled at her.

"Well, yes. I suppose if you put it that way, I don't see how I can refuse. He mentioned something about creating a website... been such a help to Jonathan and my sister..." She was confounded. "Maybe there is something I can do."

"Good. Thank you. I'll speak to Anthony. We'll talk again soon." Father Marco stood and walked away.

Madeline looked after him and wondered how her life had spun so out of control.

She rose and stood at the terrace wall. The expanse of Farfa's valley, with its fertile olive groves and gently sloping hillsides, lay outstretched before her. She gazed into its stillness and its beauty embraced her. Comforted her.

Breathe...

Father Marco's words rippled through her and she took in a long slow breath. Slowly, she exhaled.

Her eyes fell upon two figures as they walked toward Saint Valentine's. Madeline watched as they approached. She recognized the couple as Anthony and the woman from the library. They were holding hands. Holding hands! Nausea gushed through Madeline. Weak legs gave out from under her and she leaned more heavily onto the terrace wall. *Who is that woman?*

Anthony looked up at Madeline. He stopped and released the woman's hand.

Guilty, Madeline thought. Caught in the act. Just like David. Her eyes filled with tears of fury at Anthony. At David. At Carrie. And at herself. For allowing herself to feel again.

She turned and ran from the terrace all the way back to her room. She wanted to be alone. To be done with the pain but she had no idea where or how to start.

There in her room the memory of Anthony holding her on the bed rushed back. She felt him there with her. His body warm and comforting. She remembered the loving compassion in his face and she wanted him. Wanted to be in his arms again.

But he was with someone else. The confusion was unbearable. She stood and gazed out the window trying to slow her thoughts.

The door opened and Anthony walked in.

She spun around.

"Don't you knock!" Madeline accused.

"I'm sorry. I–"

She interrupted him. "How dare you come in here like this? And last night?"

"As I told you. I heard you crying."

"You took advantage of that and just walked into my room in the middle of the night."

"That isn't true, Madeline. And you know it." His voice was rich. Resonant. Soothing.

"I don't know anything."

"It isn't how it looked, Madeline," he insisted.

Her eyes narrowed. "Isn't it?" She spoke through clenched teeth.

"Veronica is a friend."

"A friend. Seems to me you should be explaining that to God. Not to me."

"I'm explaining it to you."

"Why?"

"Why are you so upset?"

Chess. *I've had it with men who play games,* she thought. Men who answer questions with questions. Who talk in riddles instead of truths. Her anger ignited into adrenaline.

She crossed the room. Wrapped her arms around the back of his neck. Pressed her lips to his. His lips opened to hers. Her tongue found his and encircled it. Slowly at first. Then more fervently. He responded and they kissed deeply. Passionately. He pulled her to him and she felt him grow hard against her body.

Checkmate. He wants me, she thought. She *knew.*

They kissed long and tenderly. Reached into each other.

He pulled his face away slowly and gazed into her eyes. His look caressed her. Balmed her raw emotions.

Somehow he excavated her anger, dug beneath its surface, and uncovered the love that swelled, unbidden, in her heart.

"That's why," she said quietly.

"You've been through so much." He took her face in his hands. "I must go."

Madeline was exhausted by the roller coaster ride her feelings had taken. She was drained by all the ups and downs of the anger, confusion, and even the love she felt.

He is a monk.

She nodded, "Yes, it would be best if you leave."

He turned and walked out the door. Madeline sat down on the bed.

"Now what have I done?" she said aloud.

Then she remembered how perfectly Anthony's body felt pressed hard against hers.

"He does want me. I know he does."

She had to admit the truth.

I want him too, she thought. *Tomorrow, I'll get a room in Rome. It'll be best. It'll be...safer.*

She looked around the small room. Her eye caught the book Anthony had given her. *The Rule of Saint Benedict.*

She picked it up and started reading. Started learning about Anthony Lamberti and the rules by which he lived.

Or strived to.

"God help us," she said. "God help us both."

* * * *

1943

"Marco!" Isabella elbowed his side gently. "Marco! Wake up!"

"Mmmm?"

"Wake up!"

Marco groaned and rubbed his eyes. "What is it?" He opened his eyes and, in the darkness, struggled to focus them on her face.

"It's late. You're not going to be able to get back to the monastery. Oh Marco, what are we going to do?"

She was still lying on top of him, his body warmed by hers. He smiled. "It's fine. I can stay here until morning." Her face was mere inches from his, her breath a gentle breeze across his cheek.

"In the chapel?"

"Why not?"

"Alone?"

"With God." He smiled and wondered what it would be like to sleep next to Isabella. In her bed. For an entire night. He wondered what kind of a God would demand that he not love her. That he not touch her. That he not kiss her. "You are so beautiful," he said.

"So are you," she said, her eyes searching his.

He reached up and cupped her face with his hand. Slipped it behind her neck. Pulled her to him. And they kissed. There in the small chapel. His first kiss. Her first kiss. Their first kiss. It started with a simple brush of his lips against hers. Then became more daring, more passionate. She pulled away, her eyes floating in a teary sea.

"Stay with me tonight, Marco."

He wanted to say yes and he knew he should say no. When he looked at her, in her eyes and into her soul, he knew something had begun that was more powerful than him. Than her. Together, they created something which demanded its own way. To it, he could not say no. He would not say no.

He nodded and said, "Let's go."

* * * *

Present Day

Madeline stood at the registration desk in the lobby of the Hotel de Russie.

"What do you mean the hotel is booked? That can't be possible!"

The clerk behind the counter maintained her composure. "I'm sorry, *Signorina* O'Connor. There is a conference. All the guest-rooms are occupied. Many of the local hotels are sold out as well."

"A conference! Great. How long does this conference last?"

"Four more days."

"You're saying there are no rooms available until then?"

The pretty young clerk typed a few keystrokes into her computer.

"I'm sorry, but that is correct. Do you want me to reserve a room for you then?"

"No. Forget it." Madeline was furious with the clerk and with herself. How could she have just assumed a room would be available? Now what would she do?

"Madeline. I thought that was you." The man's voice was shockingly familiar, but completely out of place.

Madeline turned to see Tyler Reed's smiling handsome face. It had been weeks since the investment banker spoke with her about selling Felicity.

"Tyler! Hi. What a surprise. What are you doing here?"

"A conference. You know, the annual obligatory global investment banking summit." He grimaced. "Thank God I've done my presentation .. so now I'm home free."

Madeline smiled and nodded. A conference. That explained the sudden onslaught of professional men in the hotel. The testosterone in the lobby was almost tangible and Madeline was well aware of admiring looks from several businessmen. These men were not monks. They were not Anthony.

"I know how you feel. I hate conferences."

"So, you never returned my calls. I managed to talk to Heather and she told me I might find you here. I've been looking for you." His blonde hair and blue eyes appeared more so because of his tan.

She ignored him. "Summer at Martha's Vineyard again this year?"

He smiled broadly at her. "Madeline! You're impossible!"

They both laughed and started to walk through the lobby. Tyler was right beside her. "And you are relentless. Felicity can't be bought, Tyler. It's not for sale."

Madeline enjoyed the game he played. Tyler reminded her of New York and Felicity and business and of who she was. She felt like herself for the first time in days.

And yet–

"Okay. Just checking. Again. I can't believe you're not even interested in looking at this deal." He ran a hand through his hair in frustration and genuine bewilderment.

She stopped and looked at him. He was good looking, well dressed, a Harvard Business School graduate. Late thirties. As one of the few unmarried Vice Presidents at one of the world's most prestigious investment banks he was the eternally eligible bachelor. Madeline often wondered why some socialite's young daughter had not yet snared him.

She sighed. "Look, Tyler. The truth of it is, I wouldn't have a clue what to do with myself if I sold Felicity. It's not just a company, Tyler. It's my family. Let it go, okay?"

Who said that? She had not meant to be so honest. So vulnerable.

He seemed taken aback, as if he was as surprised by the statement as Madeline. "The rumors are true, then."

"What do you mean? What rumors?"

"That Madeline O'Connor is all work and no play." He smiled but the look in his eyes was serious.

Madeline noticed the absence of – something. Still, she liked Tyler. He was everything a woman in her right mind would want.

But what about a woman in her right heart?

"Is that what they say? It isn't true." She backpedaled.

"Oh, it isn't? Well then—have dinner with me tonight."

"No, I–"

He interrupted her. "So, they are true." He raised his eyebrows flirtatiously.

Her eyes dropped to the gleaming marble floor.

He stepped closer and spoke softly. Seductively. "Madeline. We're here. In Rome. Please...save me from having dinner with a bunch of boring bankers. You don't already have other plans, do you?"

Slowly she lifted her eyes to meet his. She thought of Anthony.

Pure celibate Anthony. Who she could never have.

"No, I don't have other plans at all. I'd love to have dinner with you."

"Great!" He trailed his fingertips smoothly down the side of her arm. Squeezed her wrist. "I'll see you tonight."

"Okay. Are you staying here?"

"Yes. Are you?"

"No. I'll meet you here. Seven thirty?"

"Perfect. Until then."

Until then. Italy and its romance has gotten to him, too.

Madeline nodded and watched Tyler walk away and join a few colleagues. Leaving the hotel, he glanced back at her and they shared a parting smile. Biting her lip, she looked away and wondered what was beneath the perfectly polished and pressed surface of Tyler Reed as he disappeared. He was brilliant and obviously loved his work. What else did he love? Or who else? There must be plenty of women vying for his affections. Not to mention his money.

She dismissed the questions as quickly as they arose. What she did know was that as successful as Tyler was, he would not succeed in persuading her to sell Felicity.

With that, her mind turned to business and she walked over to the lobby phones. It was six a.m. in New York. She picked up the phone and dialed. Madeline listened impatiently as the phone rang twice. Three times. Four.

"Hello?" Heather's voice was familiar and comforting, and, as usual, she sounded wide awake in spite of the early hour.

"Heather. It's me." Madeline smiled into the phone.

"Hon'!. How are you? Fill me in."

"You'll never guess who I just ran into."

"Oh, let's see—"

"Oh, Heather! You spoke to Tyler Reed."

Madeline heard Heather let out an exaggerated wistful sigh. It made her smile and miss her friend. "What I wouldn't give to be in Italy with Tyler Reed. What's he doing there?"

"Some investment banking conference."

"Well, that's a happy coincidence. Has he convinced you to sell the company yet?" Heather had been approached by Tyler many times about Felicity's availability.

"Heather!" She ignored the question. "I'm having dinner with him tonight."

"You're kidding! Business or–?"

Madeline interrupted. "How are things?" She listened while Heather laughed at the evasion.

"Everything's great. We got the proofs from the Paris shoot for the catalog. We have a set of prints on their way to you by Fedex to St. Valentine's. Hey–maybe we should do a Valentine's day shoot there! Ah–*Vogue* would love it!" Heather cackled. "Huh. Maybe we could even get some of the monks to model with the girls!" More laughter.

Madeline was shocked into silence by Heather's surprising lack of good taste. She imagined models with silicone implants jiggling around in bras, stockings, garters, and too high heels at Saint Valentine's. Two weeks ago she, too, would have found the image hilarious. Now it revolted her.

Madeline's tone was cool. "It's hardly appropriate."

There was an awkward pause before Heather replied. "I'm only joking, Madeline. What's gotten into you?"

What has gotten into me?

Madeline pushed the question away and told her friend about the turn her life had taken in the past few days. About how her sister was fighting the cancer that threatened her life. About how Jonathan was on his way to becoming a monk. It felt foreign to talk with Heather about such things instead of reports and deadlines and new nightgown designs.

"In the middle of all of this you're having dinner with Tyler. Go girl."

"Oh, Heather! Don't be ridiculous."

"Oh, go on, hon'. Live a little. Tyler's positively gorgeous. Eligible. Successful. There's not a woman in New York who wouldn't want to be in your Gucci's right now. Including me. Just go for it."

Images of Anthony and moonlight and entwined bodies swirled like fog in Madeline's mind. She felt him around her. In her. His presence was palpable. He was there, and then gone.

"I don't know. Something about Tyler seems so...so–"

"What?"

"Superficial."

"Superficial? Since when are we so...deep? Honey, look again.

He's fabulous! Give him a chance."

It occurred to Madeline that even if she tried to explain, Heather would never understand. She thought of Anthony again. Of his quiet strength. His wisdom. No. Heather could never understand.

Maybe Carrie would. Her sister. The thought surprised her.

"I don't know –forget it. Look, I've got to go."

"Well, I'll expect a full report."

"Don't hold your breath." Madeline laughed stiffly.

"Oh, come on. Things here are on autopilot. Just try and have a good time. Okay?" Heather sounded more like the best friend she was.

"*Ciao.*"

Madeline hung up the phone and looked around the hotel's bustling lobby. She picked up the phone again.

"Carrie, it's Madeline."

"Hi!" Her sister sounded pleasantly surprised.

"Would it be all right if I came over?"

There was a slight pause. "Of course. Of course it's all right."

"I'll be right over." Madeline hung up the phone and smiled.

* * * *

1943

By the time they reached Isabella's room, they were both out of breath. They made their way quickly and, with a close call or two, managed not to be seen. Isabella hurried to open the door and they both slipped through.

They were alone now, and stood looking at each other, both unsure of what would happen next. What to do, or not to do. Marco was certain she could hear his pounding heart.

I should not be here, he thought. *But I cannot leave. I would not want to leave even if I could.*

Isabella's soft voice broke into his thoughts. "We don't have to do anything, you know," she said.

Her saying it made him want her more.

"No, we don't-"

"Marco, I love you." Her young eyes told him it was true.

He stepped toward her and they clung to each other. "I love you too, Isabella. I love you too."

They kissed. A long slow tender kiss that ignited his deepest yearning for her. He reached for her breast, firm yet soft. She moaned, the sound urging him for more. His hand slid down to her waist, lifting her shirt from underneath her skirt. The bare skin of his palms pressed her back closer to him, breast to chest.

His whole body quivered. He would have her. With a single step back, he was able to undo the delicate buttons of her shirt. He gasped when he slid the simple cotton garment from her shoulders and saw her breasts, round and firm and rising and falling with her quick breaths. It was madness, how much he wanted her.

"Oh Marco, I've never–"

He laughed, relieved. "Me either."

She laughed too, took his hands and placed them on her eager breasts. He closed his eyes at the feel of them, their round fullness. The firm peak of her hardened nipples. She slipped off her skirt and her panties. She smiled and pulled quickly away from him to lie down on the bed.

"I want to see you," she said.

He nodded. "I want to look at you first." He smiled and allowed his eyes to linger over her body, softly illuminated by the light of the half-moon. "You are so beautiful."

With one sweeping movement, he slipped out of his robe. His underclothing. And went to her, his body hard and eager to be inside her. They were lying together now, kissing. Moaning. Smiling at the pleasure their bodies gave to each other. At the love their eyes mirrored to each other's. At this wonderful initiation they were sharing.

How easy it was for Marco to surrender to the forces of nature, to his body's natural understanding of what to do. She was ready for him, and he entered her, gasping in almost unbearable ecstasy at the warm wetness that welcomed him.

"Oh, God," he moaned, and moved deeper into her. It was the first time they made love that night. It would not be the last. Each time, Marco found himself amazed that a woman could and would give herself to him in such a profound and sacred way. That two people, two souls could connect so deeply with their hearts and bodies.

"I love you, Isabella," he said with all his heart.

He waited for her reply. For her to say, 'I love you too'. But there was only the gentle whisper of her breath. He closed his eyes and smiled, filled with a deep peaceful content. Then he joined her in the sweetness of slumber.

* * * *

Present day

A kettle of water boiled on Carrie's stove. A plate of biscuits was set out on the table. Truffles sprawled out, basking in a patch of fading sun, her fluffy stomach rising and falling as she inhaled and exhaled.

Breathe.

Madeline watched the cat and remembered how as a young girl she had always wanted a dog.

Madeline's mother's voice rang in her ears. "Dogs are too much trouble. They need walking. Training. And more walking. We are not getting a dog. Cats are so much more...they're just simpler."

It had been an ongoing losing battle against her mother and her sister. One dog little girl against one cat little girl and one cat mother. Two cat people against one dog person. Her father, a man who chose his battles very strategically, stayed out of it. So, Madeline never had a dog.

How was it that a bruise of resentment remained on her heart after all these years?

Watching Truffles, she thought to herself that one day she would get a dog. A big dog. A big beautiful collie. Like Lassie. Yes, just like Lassie. Maybe even two Lassies. She smiled.

"She's adorable, isn't she?" Carrie said smiling. She had taken the kettle from the stove and poured steaming water into a teapot.

Typical Carrie, Madeline thought. Her sister had no idea what she had been thinking and it made Madeline smile even more broadly. She surrendered. "Adorable."

Madeline wondered why she called Carrie. Why had she reached out to her sister?

She watched as Carrie bustled about the kitchen, setting small plates and teacups on the table. Carrie never understood Madeline. Never had. Never would.

Madeline sighed quietly.

"How do you take your tea?" Carrie asked.

My own sister does not know how I drink my tea, Madeline thought. *My assistant does, but not my sister.* She missed New York.

She missed...someone.

"Just a little milk, please." Madeline said. "Just a little milk."

* * * *

Tyler Reed had a puzzled expression on his face as he watched

Madeline from across the candlelit table. Her glowing auburn hair was swept up into a loose twist. She wore a dress with a revealing halter cut of forest green crepe accessorized with simple drop earrings.

"You look stunning," he finally said.

"Thank you." Madeline met his eyes and they gazed at each other for a moment.

The waiter poured a sample from a bottle of premium Italian merlot into Tyler's crystal wineglass, then stood for a moment.

"Sir." The waiter waited.

"Ah yes." Tyler dragged his gaze from Madeline and picked up the glass. He inhaled deeply from the wine glass, then swirled the red velvet liquid and sipped.

Madeline watched Tyler with interest, the candlelight transforming her eyes into sparkling aquamarines. There was something sexy about a man who appreciated fine wine. Something arousing about the way he inhaled its bouquet. Allowed the liquid to slip across his lips and then played with it in his mouth. It was sensual. Evocative. Provacative.

Unbidden, Madeline's imagination conjured up a picture of Anthony in the vineyard. She saw his face against a backdrop of fruit-laden vines, his eyes intent on the grapes that he would magically transform into wine. An alchemist. She pictured him breathing in his latest vintage. Breathing in her.

She ached to feel the closeness of him. Wanted his hands touching her skin. Longed for his lips to consume hers. Heat stirred in the fathoms of her body.

"It's wonderful." Tyler announced finally, his eyes on Madeline.

The sound of Tyler's voice extinguished her reverie. She lifted her gaze to meet his.

"Very good." On cue, the waiter poured wine for Madeline and then Tyler.

Tyler raised his glass. "To a perfect evening in Rome...with you."

Madeline could not help but be charmed. She laughed and raised her glass to his. Nodded. Sipped.

"And to breakfast." Tyler smiled easily.

Shock spread across Madeline's face. She was too startled by his suggestion to object.

He burst into a fit of laughter at his own joke and her expression. In spite of herself, Madeline joined him. Slowly he reached over and tenderly took her hand, an apology of sorts.

"I would never presume," Tyler said sincerely.

They settled into smiling at each other and Madeline relaxed into the moment.

"So, what brings you to Rome? Business or pleasure?" Tyler asked.

Madeline cast her eyes downward and looked at the way his hand rested upon hers. "Neither, really." She raised her eyes to his. "My sister is very ill. Cancer."

"Oh, I had no idea." He squeezed her hand. "I'm so sorry. Are the two of you close?"

Madeline considered the question for a moment. What were the degrees of closeness between sisters? Between mothers? Husbands? Wives? What was it that defined closeness?

She doesn't know that I take milk in my tea.

Finally, her reply. "I suppose we're as close as possible. It's a long story."

Tyler held her eyes. "I understand. Family stories almost always are."

"What's your story, Tyler?" Madeline challenged.

"Oh..." He shook his head.

"Come on..."

"Okay. Well." He thought a moment. "Let's put it this way. I come from a successful family. Success is the only acceptable thing. If you're not successful, not perfect...well...that just isn't an option." He shrugged and took a sip of wine.

His honesty caught Madeline off guard. Perhaps there was more to him than Madeline thought. He had not once raised the question of selling Felicity. Yet. He turned out to be surprisingly good company and Madeline found that she liked him. She liked him very much. Suddenly, the suggestion of breakfast with Tyler intrigued her.

Maybe it wasn't such a bad idea after all.

* * * *

Madeline fell onto the bed laughing. Tyler laughed too and slid beside her. She was in his arms now and he held her. Then stood up and slowly pulled her to him. He reached behind her neck and untied the back of the halter. The dress cascaded from Madeline, exposed her breasts. Under his teasing caress, her nipples hardened.

He ran his hands smoothly along her shoulders, down her arms, to her waist and slipped the dress off entirely. A quiet moan escaped him as he kneeled before her and gently slid off her red satin underwear. He pressed his cheek against her navel and pulled her close to him. He ran a finger ever so delicately between her legs. She moaned now and pulled him up to stand before her.

She laid back down on the bed and watched as he undressed. His body was powerful. Tanned. Firm and athletic. He joined her on the bed. Kissed her. His tongue teased hers playfully. Then he stopped and pulled away, letting the wetness of their kiss trail from his tongue along her neck and down to her nipple. He sucked her. Delicately at first, then harder. Slowly he traveled down her abdomen and opened her legs, exposing her fully to him. He tasted her. Expertly.

He's well-practiced, she thought lucidly. The idea was repulsive, but her body betrayed her and responded.

He stopped and collected himself. Found his wallet and pulled out a small silver packet.

Very well practiced, Madeline thought again. *But considerate. He gets points for that.* "Thank you," she whispered.

He paused for a moment and slipped on the condom. "Now, where were we?"

She laughed and pulled him to her. They kissed deeply. Hungrily. It had been too long for Madeline.

How long has it been for Tyler?

She forced the question from her mind.

Half an hour later, Tyler was asleep. He snored. Loudly.

Madeline lay awake and stared at the ceiling.

She wondered if Anthony snored.

Probably not, she thought. *How could I have let this happen? My God! I'm living an episode of Sex and the City.*

She dreaded the idea of waking up in the morning with Tyler. Making awkward small talk over breakfast. In her heart, she knew the truth. It was Anthony she wanted to see in the morning. Anthony she wanted to be with.

Quietly, Madeline got out of bed and dressed. She gathered her purse, slipped on her shoes, and left Tyler as he slept.

It was two a.m. She made her way through the quiet hotel and to her rented Mercedes. All she wanted now was to sleep in her small twin bed at Saint Valentine's. To wake up and eat breakfast in silent intimacy with Anthony.

* * * *

1943

It was not until the next morning when young Marco was putting on his shoes that he understood–*really realized*–what he had done. What did it mean that he and Isabella made love? To be sure, he violated the rules of the Order and if that were found out, he could certainly be expelled. Yet, he was still a young student and had not taken his vows. What had he done that was wrong? Fallen in love? Confusion overwhelmed him and he felt Isabella's eyes watching him as he dressed.

"Are you sorry?" she asked from where she sat on the bed. She wore only a tattered peach colored bathrobe and was stunningly radiant with the afterglow of their lovemaking.

"No. Not at all." Marco's reply was immediate and genuine.

Too many thoughts bombarded him too quickly. He was not sorry he made love to her. He was only sorry there were rules against it and that now he had to ask himself whether or not he could devote himself to a way of life he was no longer sure he believed in. If his was a God who judged people by their religion and made loving a woman a sin, then his was not a God he could honor. Marco was not sorry he made love to Isabella. Looking at her, he could not deny that he already wanted her again. That he loved her. How could it be that a war and a young Jewish woman could make him question everything he had once been so certain of?

"I do have to go," Marco told her. "I will come back tomorrow."

"Do you promise?"

"I do. The day after that. And the day after that."

Isabella leapt from the bed and threw her arms around him.

"Oh, Marco. I do love you." She drew away and looked at him, serious. "I don't know how much longer I will be here. When the war is over, my mother will be coming back for me, and after that–"

"Shh." He pressed an index finger to her lips. "We'll deal with that when it happens. You'll always know how to find me." He kissed her on the forehead. "Let's just wait for the war to be over."

"I feel like I will go crazy until then, locked away here."

"You will not go crazy. You are safe here and you must never leave. I'll be back. It will be all right."

She nodded and lifted her face to kiss him. It was wrong, this war. That someone like Isabella had to hide away because she was a Jew. Because Hitler had a horrendous notion that Jews were inferior and somehow managed to convince others to believe him. God did not make Jews or Christians or Buddhists or Hindus. People did that. Classified themselves. A seed planted itself in

Marco's mind that religion had very little to do with God.

He sighed. The sun was rising over the red rooftops of Venice and it was time for him to leave Isabella. But the departing Marco was not the same young man who had arrived just the previous afternoon. He found himself wondering, now, who he had become. In one night and because of one young Jewish woman, Marco had become a stranger to himself. Everything had changed. He no longer had any idea what his future would hold or what would happen next.

* * * *

Present Day

Anthony's place at the breakfast table was empty. Disappointed, Madeline ate breakfast silently with Father Marco and Jonathan.

Where was Anthony?

She counted on seeing him. Depended on him to be there.

Madeline looked around at the other monks. She felt a gentle tug of attachment to them. A reverence for their quiet strength and loving discipline with themselves and others.

With a start Madeline realized that she had sex the previous night with someone she barely knew and was now eating breakfast with men who had chosen to forego sex altogether. These were men who strived to love God. Who made love with God.

She spread orange marmalade on her toast and contemplated God.

If it is true that God is everywhere, then God resides within me. Then to make love to me, is to make love to God. I am a home for God.

Tyler Reed had not made love to God. The memory of their exchange the previous night filled Madeline with emptiness. She appreciated Tyler's technical expertise. He knew all the right things to do. Technically. It had been fun. In spite of herself, Madeline thought it had been just what she needed. It was good to have someone next to her, skin to skin, holding her. Physically, she felt satisfied. Emotionally, she was bereft.

She had not felt a connection with Tyler. Perhaps she had not allowed it. Whatever the reason, there had been no sweet whispering to her soul, telling her how much she was loved. How much she mattered. And yet, he had given her a physical experience that Anthony would never be able to provide. Yes. There was something about Tyler. *Something.*

But there was something about Anthony, too. He gave her an experience of her own heart, her own soul, that she had not had in years.

Or ever?

She frowned and took a sip of coffee and wondered if Tyler wanted to see her as a way of accessing Felicity. Would he call her when she returned to New York? She decided he would. If for no other reason than to convince her to sell Felicity. Which, of course, was out of the question.

When *would* she return to New York?

She sighed, unsure of the answer. Everything was uncertain. Nothing seemed to make any sense. She wondered what Anthony would tell her. Something true and wise that would bring her comfort, no doubt.

Where was Anthony? It was another unanswered question that hung in the quiet that wrapped itself around Madeline.

She found she liked the silence. There was space now for her thoughts to flutter across her mind. They were butterflies, her thoughts. Floating. Drifting. Like monarchs flitting about a meadow.

Who observed these thoughts as they dashed and darted about?

She raised her eyes and found Father Marco gazing at her. She smiled. He smiled back. For a moment, Madeline felt a genuine affection pass between them.

When she glanced over at Jonathan, he smiled at her too. Her heart opened in a rush of love for her nephew.

She returned to her toast and finished the last few bites. Sipped the remainder of her coffee.

Where was Anthony?

* * * *

Carrie rested on the sofa when she heard the knock at the door. Slowly, she forced herself up and crossed the room to answer it.

"Anthony! Is everything all right? Is Jonathan all right?" She looked panicked.

"*Sì. Sì.* I'm sorry. I didn't mean to scare you like that. I should have called." Anthony was awkward. Jonathan usually visited Carrie with Anthony along as a companion. A friend. He had never even been alone with Carrie.

"No, it's fine. Please come in." She opened the door and stepped aside. Her face gave away her confusion.

Anthony entered the familiar apartment. "How are you feeling?"

"I'm a little tired today. But overall I'm doing better. I know I'm getting better." Carried smiled. "Please. Sit down. May I get you anything? Coffee. Tea."

Anthony shook his head. "No, thank you." He sat down.

"So...is Jonathan with you?" Carrie's confusion over Anthony's uncharacteristic visit was evident.

"No. He's at Saint Valentine's."

"And he's all right?"

"Yes. He's just fine. I guess I'm here because I'm concerned about Madeline."

"Madeline?" Carrie blinked.

"She didn't get into Saint Valentine's until almost three in the morning last night. Completely disregarded curfew," he said, his voice disapproving.

"Oh." Carrie laughed and sighed at once. "She was just on a date, that's all."

"A date?"

Carrie nodded. "Yeah. Someone she knew from New York was in town. They went out for dinner. I guess you could call that a date." She was matter-of-fact.

"Until three in the morning?"

Carrie smiled at Anthony. "Yes. Until three in the morning. I hope they had a good time."

"A good time? What exactly does that mean?" Anthony was distraught. It was unlike him.

"What exactly is your interest in Madeline?" Carrie's eyes were narrow. Amused. Fixed on Anthony.

"She's Jonathan's aunt. I'm concerned for him. He thinks the world of her and she should set a better example. She stays out until all hours. She abandoned you for almost a decade. Obviously her character is–"

Carrie interrupted him tersely. "Madeline's character is untarnished."

Anthony regarded Carrie. "You're a very forgiving person, Carrie. I can see where Jonathan inherited his virtue."

"I'm not so forgiving. I have nothing to forgive Madeline for." Carrie's eyes welled up with tears. "If anything, it is me who needs to be forgiven."

"I don't understand."

Quiet tears streamed down Carrie's face. "Then let me explain."

Anthony sat quietly and waited.

"Madeline and David were college sweethearts. They got married right away–it was crazy, really. But love does that, doesn't it? Then Madeline went to business school and David, he floundered for a while. So, six months after their wedding, while Madeline was in classes, David and I–we fell in love." She shrugged. "I was married to Bobby but things were rocky and we were separated. I got pregnant and thought that David would leave Madeline and I could leave Bobby. But David said he wouldn't. Couldn't. That he wasn't ready to be a father. So, I got back together with Bobby and had the baby. I had Jonathan. I knew he was David's but I lied to Bobby. I lied to Bobby and to Madeline," she sobbed.

Anthony sighed.

Carrie continued. She confessed to the monk in her living room about the day at the hospital seven years prior when Madeline's world collapsed. When she had learned of the affair.

Finally, Carrie broke into sobs. "I don't know how Madeline could ever forgive me. Oh, Anthony. I've been carrying this guilt around with me all these years." Her sobs continued.

Anthony stood from the chair and found a box of tissues. He held them out to Carrie. She plucked one from the box and wiped her face. Blew her nose.

"I'm sorry. I didn't mean to–"

It was Anthony's turn to interrupt Carrie. "It's all right. I'm the one who should apologize. I had no right to-"

"No. No. You have every right. You're doing so much for Jonathan. I'm happy to have told you. I've wanted to tell you for some time but I was too ashamed. So, I just let you believe I was a struggling single mother. Now you know the truth about Jonathan. It explains a lot about him."

Anthony nodded. "Yes, it does."

"So, you see. Madeline deserves some happiness. I don't think she's ever recovered. Maybe she'll find it with the man from last night. Or with someone else. I just hope she does, that's all." Her tears resumed. "I only hope that she'll be able to forgive me. Someday."

Anthony went to Carrie and sat at her side. He pulled her to him and she dropped her head to his shoulder. She cried.

"You must forgive yourself, Carrie. You must forgive yourself."

"How can I Anthony? How can I forgive myself? I deserve to be sick. I deserve to die."

Carrie erupted into convulsive sobs. Anthony held her. Just held her.

And time passed.

Eventually an exhausted Carrie fell asleep on Anthony's shoulder. He gently slid out from underneath her and covered her with a blanket, letting her rest on the sofa. For a time, he knelt down beside her, his hand across his mouth. Thinking. Watching her sleep. Thinking.

He had known Carrie and Jonathan for years. *Thought* he had known them. But their lives had, in fact, been a mystery to him. Until now.

He rose slowly and walked across the room. Glanced back at Carrie. At Madeline's sister. He had been wrong about Madeline. With her money and jet-setting lifestyle, it had been easy to misjudge her. He sighed.

"God bless you. God bless you both," he whispered. Then opened the door and left Carrie sleeping, alone, on the couch.

* * * *

Madeline was on the phone with Heather in New York when Jonathan arrived in Saint Valentine's small office.

"No. I just don't like it. Something about it doesn't work. I want it to be a little more...a little more...virginal. It's not crazy. I just want it to look a little more pure. A little less vampy." Madeline was waving an ad mock-up in the air. "Have them re-shoot it. That's all."

Jonathan pointed at his watch.

"Look, I've gotta go. Heather. Just do it. Okay? Bye."

Madeline sighed loudly and hung up the phone.

"Hanging around all us virgins is having an effect on you, isn't it?"

"Jonathan!" Madeline was shocked.

The young novice threw his head back and laughed aloud. "Let me see." He reached playfully for the ad.

"No!" Madeline yanked it out of reach. Flushed.

Jonathan howled even more loudly. "You're hilarious. You're actually blushing."

Madeline's face was scarlet.

"We need to get going."

They had planned an evening in the city together. Dinner and the symphony. Madeline was delighted when she discovered

Jonathan shared her love of classical music. The program was Mozart, one of her favorite composers, and she was excited that she could share it with her nephew.

"You're right. We need to be sure to be back by eleven." Jonathan seemed concerned.

"Or what?"

"Or...nothing. We have an eleven o'clock curfew, that's all. Just a courtesy."

"Oh!"

"I should have told you." Jonathan smiled knowingly at his aunt.

Madeline blushed again at her latest breach of monastery etiquette. She wondered if Anthony had also noticed her middle of the night return to Saint Valentine's.

"Don't worry. You only woke a few of us up."

"I'm so sorry."

"It's all right. I should have told you. I just didn't expect–"

"Well, how could you have expected that your aunt would come traipsing into Saint Valentine's at all hours of the night?"

Jonathan smiled and shrugged. He extended an arm for her to take. "Come on. Let's go."

Madeline sheepishly slipped her arm through her nephew's and together they walked out into the golden Italian twilight.

"There's something else I should tell you." Jonathan's expression was serious.

"Another rule?"

"No." He smiled. "Not another rule."

They reached Madeline's Mercedes and got in.

"What is it then? Something about Carrie?"

"No."

"Well?" Madeline started the engine.

"I wrote to my Dad."

"To David?"

Jonathan nodded. "He'll be here tomorrow."

"Here? Tomorrow?"

The news was beyond belief. Madeline's past collided with itself again. Images of Carrie and David together hurled themselves across her mind. She felt her heartbeat quicken as shock turned to anger.

"I didn't want it to be another surprise for you." Jonathan's voice was quiet. "I thought he and Mom should..." He trailed off.

"Should what?" Madeline stared at her nephew incredulously.

"Make amends. You know. Forgive each other."

"Forgive each other! What on Earth for?" Madeline gasped. "You don't think your parents will get back together?" Madeline's head started throbbing.

"No. Not at all. They were miserable together. Their divorce was more miserable still. Mom's been carrying around all this pain and anger. She should forgive him. Not for him. But for herself." He hesitated but then added quietly, "Just the way you should forgive her for *yourself*."

Madeline glanced at him and put the car into gear.

Madeline's anger surrendered. Imploded into itself.

Forgive Carrie. Forgive David. Where would she start?

She pulled out of the parking lot.

Carrie and David had been unhappy.

Then what had been the point of it all? All of Madeline's pain. All the tears she had cried. How could she ever forgive them?

If they'd only been happy together, then maybe, just maybe, all my pain would have been worth it.

But their marriage had fallen apart, too.

We would have been happy if we'd stayed together, she thought.

She looked over at Jonathan again. He was silent and pensive, staring out the window at the passing countryside.

Jonathan. How selfish she had been. Jonathan had lost his father. Not once, but twice. First Bobby, who vanished from his life after that day in the hospital. Then David. Now he could be losing his mother. It was no wonder he sought safety and refuge behind the ancient walls of Saint Valentine's.

She wondered about her ex-husband, Jonathan's father. How would he look? How had he changed? Had he remarried after leaving Carrie? How would she feel when she saw him?

What kind of a man was David? Leaving one sister for another? Then leaving again. Did his vows of marriage mean nothing?

An image of Anthony leapt into her mind. Kind compassionate Anthony.

She remembered the kiss they shared.

Maybe David and I would not have been happy together after all. The thought came as a surprise.

Jonathan's voice broke into Madeline's deliberations. "Aunt Maddie?"

"Hmmm?"

"Did I mention that Anthony and Veronica will be joining us for dinner?"

Madeline shook her head slightly and blinked. "No. You did not mention that. You're full of surprises tonight."

"It came up at the last minute. Anthony was in Rome today and called me. I told him about our plans and he, well, he invited himself along. Veronica too."

Invited himself along. Veronica, too.

"Who is Veronica?" Madeline wondered if it was the woman from the library. The same one whose hand Anthony had been holding.

"She's a nun from an abbey in Rome. She and Anthony have been friends for a long time. Ten years or so, I think."

Friends. Men and women cannot really be friends, Madeline thought to herself with disdain. *Sex always–*

She caught herself. These were not ordinary people. Anthony was a monk. Veronica was a nun. Of course there would be nothing more than friendship between them. Friendship. What if there was more between them? She hated herself for asking the question.

There has to be some virtue left in the world. Honor. Somewhere. Still, with all the stories she had heard in the news about priests, it didn't seem to be in the church.

It can be such a lonely world, Madeline thought.

"What were you thinking about just now? You looked so...sad," Jonathan asked.

"I was just wondering if Anthony and Veronica ever had sex," Madeline had to smile at how she sounded.

Jonathan roared with laughter. "You're outrageous, Aunt Maddie. My glamorous Aunt from New York. I'm glad you're here."

Madeline glanced at her young nephew. "Me too." She paused. "Now answer my question."

"No! That's ridiculous," Jonathan, serious, insisted. "Anthony would never have sex with anyone. Neither would Veronica. They've taken vows, Aunt Maddie. Sacred vows. That means something."

Madeline was alone with her thoughts.

Vows. How often are they broken? Vows between priests and God. Between husbands and wives. Between doctors and patients.

"Okay," she finally said. Her eyes returned to the road ahead.

Outrageous...we'll see.

The idea of dinner with Anthony and Veronica seemed, all of a sudden, more appealing, and perhaps less ridiculous than

Jonathan thought.

For the moment, Madeline forgot all about David's impending arrival.

* * * *

Madeline felt Anthony's eyes on her as she took a sip of wine. She looked into them, those eyes.

Those bittersweet chocolate eyes that beckoned her to–what?

Where?

"How is it?" Anthony, seated beside Madeline, leaned toward her, his arm on the table. She felt the warmth of his arm as it pressed almost against hers and a tingle floated through her body.

Earlier, Anthony declined his role as taster and approver of the wine so the task fell to Madeline. The waiter looked expectantly at her. So did Jonathan and Veronica.

"It's quite good." Madeline smiled weakly, hoping this was the correct response.

"Is it?" Anthony raised a brow and smiled. She noticed his eyes were twinkling from their brown depths. Mocking. Flirting. Or was it the reflection of the candlelight?

"What, exactly, about it is good?" Anthony's expression was expectant.

Madeline felt her face flush. Men always selected the wine. She found herself helpless, completely unable to articulate what it was about this wine that she thought was good. Was it mossy? Or grassy? Or were those white wine terms?

The nearness of Anthony flustered Madeline. She stammered, "It's just–"

He interrupted. "No. *Cui.*" He glanced at the waiter and pointed at his empty glass. The rich Tuscan red glistened as the waiter poured a small sample for Anthony.

Madeline was surprised at Anthony's almost impolite demeanor with the middle-aged Italian man as he poured. It was not that he was rude. It was a gesture more characteristic of the men she encountered in her business life.

For an instant, Anthony seemed like an executive and not a monk. Like a man in charge of the moment, in charge of himself.

*He has–power–*Madeline thought. But not power based on wealth or accomplishment. No. Anthony's power was based on something else.

But what?

She watched him nod as the waiter finished pouring and she knew in that instant what it was about Anthony that reached into her heart.

He was his own man. He answered only to himself.

And to God.

He was free to be completely–to completely *be.*

Madeline held her breath as she watched Anthony lift the glass to his nose and deeply inhale the wine's bouquet.

"Come on," he gazed at Madeline.

Jonathan and Veronica watched the exchange with interest.

It took Madeline a moment to understand that he wanted her to follow his lead. To breathe in the wine. She raised her glass and took in a long slow breath.

"Close your eyes," Anthony instructed in a quiet voice, his accent sexy.

Their eyes locked for a moment and then Madeline drew her eyelids down, slowly, as if they were shades. Distractions gone, her senses sharpened and she inhaled the wine's seductive bouquet.

"Now, what do you smell?"

Madeline struggled to find words to describe the wine's aroma and how she was feeling.

Anthony leaned closer to her.

She took another breath and opened her eyes.

He whispered into her ear. "Breathe. Just breathe."

Veronica and Jonathan looked on with interest and exchanged a quizzical look.

In a ritual that spanned thousands of years, Madeline closed her eyelids, breathed in the wine's bouquet, and experienced wine for the first time. She found herself initiated into a symphony of intoxicating aromas. Cherry. Oak. Could that be vanilla? She inhaled again. Yes. It was definitely vanilla.

Had it been there all along?

Behind closed eyelids, Madeline felt tears smoldering in a bittersweet clash of emotions. How was it that until now, she had experienced wine but never the cherries, oaks, and vanillas?

How much vanilla had she missed?

Madeline's heart broke open with regret that collided into joy. Regret for the wonderful discovery of how much she had missed. And joy–for the wonderful discovery of how much she had missed.

A veil of gratitude slowly floated over her like a downy feather drifting on spring's first warm breeze. Things would be different now. She could live life differently.

But how? What would that look like? She felt overwhelmed by a new world of choices.

I'll definitely drink better wine.

She smiled and slowly opened her eyes to find Anthony looking at her, a knowing expression on his face. Madeline wondered if Anthony could read her mind.

Or maybe he just understands. Isn't that what we all want? To just be understood?

Madeline dropped her eyes to the glass of wine she held. Veronica and Jonathan shared a look.

Jonathan's voice sliced through the air. "So, Veronica, are you excited about moving to New York?"

The mention of home broke the moment's spell. "New York?" Madeline asked, her eyes shifting to Veronica.

The table was unexpectedly quiet and Madeline felt like a schoolgirl left out of the latest gossip.

"I'm leaving the abbey," Veronica volunteered.

"What do you mean, leaving the abbey?" Madeline squeezed her brows together.

"I don't want to be a nun anymore, so I'm leaving the abbey. I'm going to stay with my parents in New York," Veronica smiled as she spoke, pretty in the candlelight.

"You can just do that? Just pack up and go?"

"It's not quite that easy. It was a difficult decision. But, in some ways, it's been the easiest decision I've ever made. Knowing what the right thing to do is the easy part. It's acting on it that's difficult."

Madeline sighed her agreement.

"I guess sometimes things just change." Jonathan sounded wiser than his seventeen years.

"You're right about that, Jonathan." Madeline glanced over at her nephew and they exchanged a smile.

"I'll drink to that," Veronica said animatedly and raised her glass.

Madeline watched Veronica and Anthony exchange a glance. A smile. Anthony raised his glass.

"*Salute*," he said.

"*Salute,*" everyone said in chorus, their glasses clinking.

Madeline took a sip of wine.

"You know, a monk left Saint Valentine's a couple of years ago," Jonathan casually piped in.

"Really?" Madeline was interested in what her nephew had to

say. She felt Anthony's arm move ever so slightly away from hers. Felt the sudden coolness of the air as it drifted and floated between them.

"Yeah. Monastic life didn't suit him anymore, so he left." Jonathan plopped a piece of bread into his mouth.

Madeline and Veronica exchanged a look, and, for a moment, Madeline wondered again if Veronica and Anthony had been more than friends.

"Do you like New York?" Veronica's eyes were wondrous.

Madeline nodded. "Yes, I do. Maybe when I get back, we can get together. Have dinner. Maybe do a little shopping."

"I would love that!" Veronica answered.

Madeline smiled and became pensive.

"Don't you think you'll miss the abbey? The other sisters?"

Veronica looked down at the table. "Of course I will. But that isn't really reason enough to stay, now, is it?" Veronica's voice was steady, certain. She looked back up at Madeline.

"No. No. I suppose not."

"Did you grow up in New York?" Madeline asked.

"No. I grew up in Rome. My parents had restaurants here. But my mother is American. My father is Italian and they lived here for years. But eventually, my mother missed the States. Her family. She made sure we learned English ... I guess it made her less homesick."

"We?"

"My brother and I," Veronica replied.

Madeline nodded. "What made you become a nun?"

"I went to Catholic schools all my life, and when my parents left Italy, I wanted to stay." She paused and thought for a moment. "Looking back, I guess it was the safest choice to make."

Madeline turned her face to look at Anthony who had been quiet during Madeline and Veronica's exchange. He was staring thoughtfully at his glass of wine, fascinated by the glistening ruby fluid. He pondered private thoughts, his face sober.

Madeline longed to know his mind.

Maybe he's thinking about leaving Saint Valentine's. Maybe he'll move to New York, too. Then we could–

"When are you planning to return to America?" Veronica's voice was grey velvet.

Maybe he'll move to New York to be with Veronica.

The thought sent nausea rushing over Madeline. "I don't really know," she said.

Frankly, I don't really care.

* * * *

Madeline fell into her small bed at Saint Valentine's. Weary and exhausted, she felt overwhelmed with a foreign helplessness—a sense of being out of control.

How could Veronica be moving to New York? Of all places! Madeline imagined herself running into Veronica at Bettie's, her favorite coffee shop. Or newspaper stand. Everywhere. What exactly do ex-nuns do? Do they even go to newsstands and drink coffee?

She tried to imagine Anthony in New York but could not. The idea was unthinkable. He would not survive it. The city would chew him up and spit him out. He would be absolutely miserable. New Yorkers would wear on him, erode his spirit until it finally disappeared.

Could his spirit disappear? *Can anyone's spirit disappear? Be broken?* Maybe Anthony was stronger than that.

Maybe we all are. Maybe I am.

No. Anthony could never go to New York. Certainly not to be with Veronica. He could go, but he would never be happy.

That is, if he even left Saint Valentine's.

The thought consumed Madeline ever since it had sparked. Now, it simmered like hot lava and bubbled up, unbidden and uncontrolled, from the depths of her vast imagination.

Anthony leaving Saint Valentine's!

If Veronica were leaving her order, then it was not impossible that Anthony could leave his.

Perhaps marriages, even to God, were doomed to fail right from the beginning. What if a lifelong commitment of any kind was simply too much to ask?

Madeline's thoughts turned to David.

It occurred to her that they had both been too young to marry. Too young to fully understand the ramifications of that level of agreement.

For the first time, Madeline understood that marriage was not a promise you made to someone else.

It is a promise you make to yourself. And then to someone else. Yes...instead of having a husband or wife, like a possession, the promise is to BE a husband or wife. Just be that. Know yourself that well, with all your flaws and imperfections, and expand past them. So maybe I didn't fail at marriage after all. Maybe David just wanted to be someone else. Instead of my husband. Or anyone's husband. He hadn't lied to me when we got married. He had lied to himself. About what he wanted. And what and who he wanted to be.

She took in a deep breath. Let it go. Felt lighter. Her thoughts were a reminder that David was en route to Saint Valentine's. He would arrive the following morning.

David. After seven long years they would see each other again. She had never thought it would happen. Her heart raced at the thought.

* * * *

1943

In October 1943, Sister Francesca's deepest fears materialized. Nazis occupied Venice. Now, it was more important than ever for Isabella to stay safely inside the abbey. Marco had to be much more careful in his visits to see her, which grew less frequent because of the Germans' arrival.

"How could this have happened?" Marco asked Lorenzo. "Nazis here in Venice?"

The pair of friends stood on the tower of San Giorgio Maggiore and marveled at its all-embracing panorama of the city floating in the shimmering lagoon. Venice had survived so much. Famines. Plagues. Fires. Floods. Yet miraculously the city survived, somehow managing to remain afloat.

"From up here, it doesn't even seem real, does it?" Lorenzo asked in reply.

"But is it real." Marco knew only too well how real the occupation was, and how much more danger Isabella was in because of it.

"Marco?"

Something in the tone of Lorenzo's voice made a shiver creep its way up Marco's spine. He looked at his friend, whose face wore a serious expression. "What is it?" Marco asked.

"There's someone at the abbey, isn't there?"

Marco narrowed his eyes. "Someone at the abbey?"

"The girl in your sketchbook. You've been spending so much time over there. I know you say it's because you're helping out... fixing little things that need it. But –"

"That is what I'm doing there, Lorenzo."

"I know, but–"

"There is no but." Marco tilted his head in disbelie friend was saying. But Lorenzo was right. "Are you liar?"

"Marco! No! But it's me you're talking to, rem known each other all our lives." He nudged Marco's shoul maybe–maybe you just don't know what you want, is all. Why do you want to be a priest? Really."

It was a question Marco had been asking himself. More and more, the answer that he had promised Arturo was not enough. He wondered what kind of a God could allow such a war. And yet knew it was not a choice that God had made. But one that man had made. The mind of God, he thought, could not conceive of war. Not the kind of God he could devote his life to, that is. "Don't you ever question whether or not God exists?" Marco asked his friend.

"No."

"Never?"

"Never. God is as real as the earth and the sea and the sky. God is everywhere and in everything. I know it."

Marco thought of the war and the men dying and heinous acts that they had committed.

"I'm not so sure, anymore, Lorenzo."

"Wars don't happen because God forgets about man, Marco. Wars happen because man forgets about God."

"I wish I had your faith, Lorenzo."

"Maybe it isn't about faith. Maybe yours is just a different path, is all."

Marco's reply was a whisper. "Maybe."

"Do you love her?"

"Yes."

Lorenzo put a hand on Marco's shoulder. Together they gazed out at the glittering water and stood for a while in silent companionship, until it was time to leave for afternoon prayer.

* * * *

Present Day

Carrie sat in front of Doctor Ferguson as she had many times before. The office was small. Books and medical journals in English and Italian were neatly arranged on floor-to-ceiling walnut bookshelves. A charcoal sports jacket hung carefully on a hook on the door. Patients' charts for the day were filed neatly in a shiny chrome stand on his desk like soldiers on a morning drill.

am's round silver-framed glasses balanced on his nose and his yes were intent on the chart before him. Carrie's chart.

She watched him. And admired him. He was English. Educated at Cambridge and had attended medical school at the University of Rome. He had decided to specialize in the treatment of cancer after losing both parents to the ravages of the disease. He was intelligent. Funny. And had a heart of gold. He was also controversial. Disillusioned by the conventional treatments of chemotherapy and radiation, he had started to treat cancer patients with the controversial drug-and-vitamin method of Italian doctor Luigi Di Bella. The decision had cost him credibility in many ways, but patients, like Carrie, had demanded it. He felt compelled to offer it to them.

If he were single, Carrie would have fallen in love with him. But he was married to a psychologist whose practice specialized in oncology psychology. His wife had amazed him with her belief in the healing power of the mind. And the healing power of prayer.

"If a patient really wants to live, with her whole heart and mind, she will. Until it's really her time. And that, I'm afraid, isn't up to you," she had told him on their first date. He had fallen in love with her on the spot. They lived happily together in Rome. Carrie looked at the wedding picture he kept on the credenza behind his desk. Beside several photos of two smiling young girls. He was a good doctor and a good man.

He glanced up at Carrie from her file. "I want you to see something." He stood up and walked over to the panel of slides that hung on his wall. With a flick of his finger, the pictures were illuminated by a crisp white light. Adam pointed to the nearest slide.

"This was your tumor three months ago." He indicated the next slide. "And this," he paused for emphasis. "Is your tumor now."

Carrie's eyes widened. The tumor was noticeably smaller. She laughed, then cried a little, then laughed again a lot.

Doctor Ferguson smiled and knelt beside Carrie.

"We're beating this, aren't we?" Carrie's eyes were bright with tears of joy.

"Yes, Carrie." The doctor placed his hand over hers. "I think we are."

* * * *

The battery on Madeline's laptop blinked, telling her it was running low. She had been editing a report for over two hours and now she, as well as the laptop, needed recharging.

She sighed. "I guess that's it, then," she said to her computer and shut it down.

Madeline sat back in her chair and surveyed the view from Saint Valentine's terrace. The valley was quiet in the midday sun and, although the trees were still green, the air smelled of autumn. She longed to see the gold and crimson mosaic of Central Park.

In spite of herself, a small smile flowed from Madeline's lips as she remembered the day David proposed. They had been walking through the Park on a cool fall day. Leaves were scattered everywhere. David had scooped up a handful and tossed them high into the air, yelling at the top of his lungs "I love you, Madeline O'Connor." He picked her up and swung her around as leaves drifted around them like confetti.

When she touched ground, she noticed onlookers' reactions were mixed. Some, most, were nonplussed; anything could and did happen in New York. Others, mostly women, were discreetly amused. Others, mostly men, were obviously annoyed. Madeline had laughed and David cupped her face in both his hands and said quietly, "I love you, Madeline O'Connor. Marry me."

How happy she had been in that moment.

When–*how*–had things changed?

"*Bon giorno.*" It was Anthony. Madeline had not heard him approach.

"*Bon giorno,*" Madeline echoed. She looked up at him and smiled.

Anthony smiled back. "May I?" He put a hand on the back of an empty chair.

"Yes. Please do."

He pulled out the chair and sat down. "You looked so, so ..." he hesitated a moment to grasp the perfect word. "Pensive. Are you all right?"

Madeline nodded. *No, I'm not all right. I'm falling in love with you.* "I'm fine."

"You did not look fine." He grinned. Coaxed.

"Well, okay. Maybe I'm a little homesick."

"Homesick?" He seemed surprised.

"I guess I miss New York a little." She shrugged sheepishly, as though she had just confessed.

"Are you planning to go back soon?"

"Oh, I couldn't possibly. Not while things are so...so uncertain with Carrie."

Anthony nodded while a serious expression slid over his face.

"You know, Carrie loves you very much." Anthony's voice was quiet.

"Hmmph," Madeline crossed her arms and sunk more deeply into her chair in a childlike gesture.

Anthony's eyes stayed on her while she stared at the ground and watched leaves as they drifted and danced with the gentle breeze.

"You do not think Carrie loves you?"

"Anthony, Carrie doesn't even know me." Madeline looked straight up at him to emphasize her point.

"Maybe it is time she did."

"What do you mean?"

"What would happen if you gave her the chance to get to know you?" Anthony pressed.

Madeline hesitated. "She'll die. And leave me."

Silence interrupted them.

Anthony lowered his eyes. "Have you ever really let anyone get to know you, Madeline? Get close to you?"

"Oh, come on, Anthony. How well does anyone ever really know anyone? I mean, you, for instance. I'll bet you thought you knew Veronica, and yet it surprised you that she's leaving the abbey. How well did you really know her?"

"People change, Madeline. They evolve. Grow."

"If you were that close to Veronica, you would have known."

"I had my suspicions. Veronica and I are good friends. Have you ever had a good friend? Were you friends with your husband?"

Madeline felt anger begin to burrow in her stomach. She stood. "What do you want, Anthony? Are you saying you want to be my friend?"

She studied Anthony as he considered her question. Watched as he rose from his chair and stepped in front of her. Held her breath as he reached for one of her hands and took it in his.

"Don't underestimate the bond of friendship, Madeline."

She took a step closer to Anthony. Leaned forward so her cheek almost touched his and whispered into his ear. "Don't underestimate the bond of sex, Anthony."

He stepped back. Looked at her. "Hearts bond, Madeline. Bodies do not."

The sting of rejection made Madeline's blood run cold. Her voice was colder. "How would you know?" She regretted her words even as she spoke.

Anthony's eyes met hers. He paused. Bowed to her slightly. Graciously. "Forgive me, Madeline, for my obvious shortcomings."

Madeline groped for words, struggling to find some way to convey the regret that immediately consumed her.

But Anthony simply raised a hand, turned, and left Madeline standing there, her mouth gaping open and the stab of fresh tears in her eyes.

She watched him leave and her heart ached. Her mind raced.

How could I have been so cruel?

Was friendship all he really wanted? Maybe that was enough. But what if there could be more? What if it was possible to be friends and lovers?

Wouldn't that be more than what most people have?

Anthony was right. She and David had never been friends.

I was never friends with my husband. Never truly close to him. Or any man.

She started to run after Anthony. She hurried around the old buildings. Turned corners that had been turned a thousand times. Passed through gardens that had been planted by hands long since gone.

How had Anthony gone so far so quickly?

"Anthony, please–wait!" Madeline shouted as she hurried to catch up with him.

She rounded a corner and stopped. Abruptly.

Anthony stood on the path. With David.

They both turned and looked at her.

David!

In a split second, Madeline took him in. He was handsomer than ever. Tall. Dark hair. Blue eyes. Impeccably dressed in an expensive black jacket, jeans, and black loafers.

The last time she had seen him was that day at the hospital.

Seven years ago! It feels like yesterday.

"Madeline!" David was clearly surprised to see her. "My God! What are you doing here?"

God, I'm a mess.

"Hello, David." She struggled to keep her composure. She had been expecting David but anticipated his arrival later in the day. Her nails were not even polished.

David had always loved red nails.

He walked toward her like an old friend. "It's good to see you."

Was it her imagination or was there mocking in his voice?

Madeline forced a smile at David and turned to Anthony. "I–"

He interrupted her. "I'm sure the two of you have a lot of catching up to do. Excuse me." He started away.

As she watched Anthony leave Madeline, it struck her. *He knows. He knows that David and I were married. Knows about David and Carrie. That David is Jonathan's father. He knows everything. Everything!*

And now he wanted to be her friend.

He probably thinks I need one, she thought. *And I do.*

"How have you been?" David asked, breaking into her thoughts.

"Great! Everything's been great!"

"Felicity has done well."

"Yes. Yes it has." She nodded.

He narrowed his eyes. Studied her for a moment.

"Are you okay? You look...tired."

I am tired. I've been tired for a long long time. I'm tired of red nails and men like you. You were never there. Never there! Not even to rub my shoulders. You were too busy with my sister.

Long-buried anger burrowed in Madeline's gut. It scratched and clawed at her like a cornered cat.

The scene at the hospital seven years ago flashed in her mind. She saw David as he had been then. A coward. Guilty. Ashamed.

"You know, David. The truth is, I am tired. And I'm not okay." The floodgates opened. "I had a husband who screwed my sister. Now she's dying. And-"

He cut her off. "Madeline, please." David's embarrassment was obvious.

"Please what? Please quiet down?"

"Quiet was really never your style. I would have thought that by now-"

She interrupted him. "What is that supposed to mean? Oh, I get it. I actually asked something of you, didn't I? And you weren't up to it. All you were up to was screwing my sister. I'm sure Carrie was much easier. Much much easier. My sister for Christ's sake. My sister!"

"You know what? I don't need this. This is ancient history." His tone was cold. "Good seeing you, Madeline."

He walked past her, toward Saint Valentine's courtyard.

Ancient history! How could it be ancient history when it still hurts this much?

"God damn you!" Her anger turned to tears. "God damn you."

"Madeline!" Anthony's voice boomed. His hands wrapped around her shoulders and spun her around.

His harsh expression softened. The afternoon sun glistened on the moist trail tears had left behind on Madeline's cheeks. She looked up at Anthony. Shaken. Shaking. Vulnerable. The soft green of her eyes was set off by the redness of crying.

Confusion overtook her.

"Oh, Madeline." Her name fell smoothly from his lips.

"I'm so sorry." She was childlike. "I didn't mean to..." She shook her head, not knowing what to say.

"I know, Madeline. I know." He pulled her into his arms and held her. "Don't think for a minute that I don't want you. Because I do."

She felt him draw her closer to him. Their bodies pressed against each other. Here, in this world that was Anthony's arms and chest and shoulders, Madeline was home. Safe. Protected.

The undeniable unbiddable awareness washed over her as she surrendered to the moment. This was where she belonged. Here, with Anthony.

Anywhere. With Anthony.

They stood there. Enfolded in each other's arms. Cradling each other. For what seemed to Madeline like too long.

And then again, not nearly long enough.

Slowly, she pulled away from him and looked up at him. She had come to know each line, each curve, each nuance of that face.

She struggled to speak. "So, where does that leave us, then?"

"I don't know, Madeline. I just don't know."

"*Scusi.*" It was David.

The moment vanished.

Had it been real?

Yes, Madeline thought. *As real as anything I've ever known.*

Madeline and Anthony awkwardly stepped apart while David regarded them with idle curiosity. He addressed Anthony. "Jonathan doesn't seem to be in his room."

"Well, he might be running an errand. Something." Anthony's hands waved about as he spoke. "He'll be at dinner. Perhaps you'd like to stay and join us."

"Join you for dinner?" David's surprise was evident. He glanced at Madeline.

In spite of herself, Madeline's heart warmed at the idea of Jonathan and David together. It would mean so much to Jonathan.

"Why don't you? I'm sure Jonathan would like that very much," she said.

"And that would be all right with you?" David asked.

The thoughtfulness underlying the question surprised Madeline. Then again, it was probably just guilt. "I think we can manage civility."

Anthony suppressed a smile. He clasped his hands together and announced, "Well then, it's settled. We'll all have dinner together tonight. Seven o'clock. Dining room."

"Thank you." David smiled but looked lost.

"Here. Let me show you to a room. Will you be staying with us for the night?"

"I hadn't planned on it."

"You're welcome to if you like. You might want to spend a little time with Jonathan." Anthony looked pleased with the idea.

The muffled sound of a car entering the parking lot cut their conversation short.

"Who could that be?" Madeline asked no one in particular.

The click and thud of doors opening drifted through the air. In an instant, Carrie and Jonathan appeared on the path.

Madeline had never seen Carrie look more vivacious. She wore a flattering red dress and her short chestnut hair was luminescent in the golden Italian twilight. Her skin glowed. Strappy red sandals with a perfectly feminine little heel adorned her perfectly pedicured petite feet.

Her nails were polished red.

Red!

"Carrie!" David rushed forward and embraced Madeline's sister while Jonathan looked on. He stood back, holding both her hands, to look at her. "You look fabulous. *Bellissimo*!" He gathered her into his arms again and she squealed in delight.

Madeline looked on, eyes wide in utter bewilderment at the unfolding scene. Unable to keep watching, her eyes darted to Jonathan. How happy he was to see his mother and father together.

Her head throbbed.

Madeline was so caught up in the strange reunion that she almost failed to notice that Anthony had walked up behind her. He was inches away. He stood there, a quiet pillar of strength that bolstered and supported simply by being.

Madeline inhaled deeply and slowly exhaled. Finally, she thought, someone understood.

"Thank you, Anthony," she said.

"For what?" His words were barely audible.

"Just being here."

His smile, which she knew intuitively had appeared, warmed

Madeline. She watched, an outsider, as Jonathan walked to his parents and joined in on their hug.

"Madeline!" Father Marco's voice echoed from the courtyard. Out of breath, he walked toward her.

"Father Marco, what is it?"

"This just arrived for you. From New York. I thought it might be important."

He handed her a medium Federal Express box. She scanned the computer-generated label for the sender's name.

Tyler Reed. She had not thought of him in days.

"Aren't you going to open it?" Anthony looked curiously at the package.

"No. Not now. It's just work. I'll open it later."

His eyes met hers. She knew, that he knew, she had lied. Not lied, exactly, but withheld the truth.

It's the same thing, isn't it? She thought. *Withholding the truth and lying. At least that's how someone like Anthony would see it.*

She felt Father Marco's eyes on her. "I thought you loved what you do," he said.

She was taken aback. "I do love what I do." She defended.

He smiled and looked down at the ancient cobblestone pathway.

"What?" She asked.

He looked up at her. "If you really loved what you do, my dear, it wouldn't be work."

Madeline stared into the challenging depths of Father Marco's blue eyes. What was it with these monks? Priests. Whatever.

Who were they to always be making these kinds of wild pronouncements?

A part of Madeline collapsed–surrendered–under the weight of his gaze.

A small voice, long buried in the caverns of her consciousness, screamed, as loudly as it could, *they're right.*

* * * *

1943

For Marco and Isabella, the days rolled on and fall turned into winter. Marco had no desire to return to Saint Valentine's and, with the occupation, it seemed safer to stay in Venice. So they made love as often as the stars allowed, Marco sneaking into her room when the nuns were in services or prayer or choir rehearsal. Once, in their fervor for each other, they made love in the chapel, on the floor in between a row of pews. Other times, they simply read together or talked.

A light snow had fallen overnight and this morning, Venice slumbered beneath the glistening white. Marco hurried toward a waiting water taxi, his breath visible in the cold. He paid his fare for the crossing from San Giorgio Maggiore and boarded the small craft. Too restless to sit, he stood tall and savored the brisk wind as it combed through his hair. His mind wandered while he watched the water sparkle in the early morning sun and he felt a sudden thrill at being alive on such a glorious morning. Or was it that he was on his way to see Isabella?

He wanted to think what they were doing was wrong and a part of him knew it was. But everything between them felt so perfect. So right. Isabella needed him. How else would she survive the insanity of being locked away, a Jew in a Catholic abbey? And he loved her. Her quick mind and wit never failed to delight him. She always managed to bring a smile to his face and his heart. With her, he felt more alive than at any other time. How could it possibly be wrong?

Marco had been so immersed in his thoughts about Isabella that the trip across the shimmering lagoon was lost upon him. He alighted from the craft and hurried along Venice's cobbled streets and narrow bridges to the abbey. By seven, the nuns would be at morning prayer and he and Isabella could be alone.

Just as he approached the abbey, the bell in the tower began to toll. His arrival was perfectly timed. He watched, impatient, from behind the gate as the sisters began making their way through the courtyard to the chapel. When the last nun had disappeared behind the chapel door, Marco slipped into the courtyard and into the residence.

He took the stairs up to Isabella's floor two at a time. Rounding the corner, he collided into Sister Francesca, almost knocking the old woman down.

"Good Lord!" Sister Francesca's hand flew to her chest and she fell against a wall for support. "Marco!"

"Oh! Sister Francesca! I'm so sorry!" Marco's eyes were wide. "Are you all right?"

"Yes. No thanks to you. What on earth are you doing here at this hour?"

"I came to see Isabella. I thought I might help her with–"

"I'm afraid you won't be of much help to Isabella this morning."

"What do you mean?"

"I mean she's not well. The flu. She's been sick to her stomach all morning."

"Oh no!" Marco wanted nothing more than to see her. "Is there anything I can do? Take her some tea?"

Sister Francesca shook her head. "No, dear. She just needs to rest."

Marco nodded.

"But if you want to be of some use, help in the kitchen with breakfast. Join us if you like."

"Of course, Sister Francesca." Marco just wanted to stay at the abbey as long as possible. Maybe he could see Isabella later.

"Come on, then." Sister Francesca led the way back down the stairs.

Before Marco knew it, instead of making love to Isabella, he found himself setting tables in the dining room. As he placed the forks and knives down one by one, he longed to see her.

* * * *

Present Day

Madeline rummaged through the small closet in her sparse room at Saint Valentine's.

I don't have a thing to wear! She laughed at herself.

Five dresses hung in the tiny closet. None of them were red, like Carrie's. It seemed odd that a few weeks ago, she would have been frustrated, angered even, by this meager wardrobe.

But instead of frustration, freedom enveloped Madeline. Lifted her heart and her spirit. For the first time Madeline could remember, she had no one to impress. At least, not with a dress. No. Anthony was not that easy. It would take more than a plunging neckline and red nail polish to get *his* attention.

Madeline had never known anyone like Anthony. He would not be manipulated. Intimidated. Goaded. Or nagged. He was a gentleman in the truest meaning of the word. None of the usual games applied. He was not after sex. Even if he were, Madeline doubted he would indulge in the usual platitudes to get it. His word was his bond. No seeming truths or false *I'll call you* would drip like venom from his tongue.

And yet he wanted her. Of that she was certain. But he would never break his vow of celibacy. Madeline was equally certain of that.

Anthony could make me a better woman. I could make him

a better man. Maybe all these years of work haven't been about hiding. Or running. Maybe they were about waiting. For someone like Anthony. If only–

Madeline stopped herself. She knew *if onlys* were dangerous territory.

There's no future with Anthony Lamberti. The man is a monk. He might want me. Flirt with me. Love me, even. But his love for God and for Saint Valentine's was more than she could ever compete with.

She sighed.

So, for tonight, I can just be–myself. Not a CEO. Not someone's wife. Not someone's girlfriend. Just Madeline.

It did not occur to her that, in spite of everything–and like it or not–she was still someone's sister.

* * * *

Jonathan scurried about making dinner preparations. His family was reunited for dinner. It had been years since his mother, father, and aunt would be dining together. He had arranged for a table to be placed outside in the courtyard. Tonight was a special occasion for him and he wanted everything to be perfect.

The table could have been a photograph in a gourmet magazine. The white tablecloth was pressed crisp. Fresh flowers were placed in small bud vases at each place setting. Hand-dipped red candles, made by the nuns at Veronica's abbey, illuminated the scene, while lanterns cast a soft golden glow on Saint Valentine's ivy-covered travertine walls. The silverware and plain white china glistened, waiting for their culinary adornment.

Madeline was the first to arrive.

Jonathan was in the midst of examining a basket of rolls. "No –no! Don't we have something a little more–" The plain wicker container was in question.

"Jonathan. This isn't The Vatican." The other novice replied, and hastily set the basket down on the table and hurried off.

"Fine, then." Jonathan muttered under his breath.

An amused Madeline had watched the exchange. She walked over to Jonathan and placed a gentle hand on his shoulder.

"Aunt Maddie!"

She loved it when he called her that.

"Everything is perfect."

"Well, not quite what you and Dad are used to, I'm afraid."

Jonathan's tone was apologetic.

Madeline bristled at Jonathan calling David – "Dad". But that was the truth of it. David was Jonathan's father. Until now, it had been a vague concept–an idea she had been able to store away in the farthest reaches of her mind. Yet here was Jonathan and David would be arriving soon.

So would Carrie.

Madeline remembered how happy the three of them looked when they were huddled together earlier in the day. She wondered how Carrie had been able to forgive David so easily.

Jonathan broke into her thoughts. "Aunt Maddie?"

Her mood was pensive. "Hmmm?"

"You looked so far away."

She changed the subject. "Jonathan, it's perfect. Maybe what your fa-" She couldn't bring herself to say it. "David and I are used to isn't really all that special."

Jonathan pondered for a moment. "You're very kind. I just hope Dad feels the same way."

Madeline was at a loss for words. She certainly couldn't speak for David, and, she realized, she didn't want to. She was incapable of understanding him. Or, it occurred to her, understanding Carrie.

"Where's Anthony?" The question rose, unbidden, from Madeline's throat.

"I don't know. The winery, probably. Now that I think of it, he said he was going to get a special bottle–" Jonathan smiled and added, "or two."

The winery. She had completely neglected her promise to Father Marco about helping Anthony with the winery. At least with the marketing part of it. She wondered if Anthony had a business plan. Probably not. She could at least sketch one out for him. Point him in the direction of some resources.

Could a little winery in an Italian monastery actually be profitable?

"I think I'll take a walk down there and see what he's up to." Madeline said.

"Don't be long...dinner's almost ready." Jonathan prompted.

Madeline put an affectionate arm around his shoulder. "I won't," she smiled.

He smiled back at her with a smile that she had seen a thousand times on David's face. How like his father Jonathan was. Yet their personalities were like Jekell and Hyde.

You'd think there would be some virtue in David to have fathered a son like Jonathan, Madeline thought.

Somewhere.

Madeline found Anthony seated at a wooden table. She stopped and stood quietly in the doorway to watch him. With an elbow on the table, he cupped his face in one hand and a glass of red wine in the other. He wore a contented smile and gazed downward, lost in thought. The flicker of a candle shadowed and defined his face–the face–that Michelangelo could have carved.

How could someone be so simple and so complicated at the same time? There was such strength in his simplicity. Such power in being so comfortable in one's own skin. And such freedom.

I'm becoming that way. Imagine, Madeline O'Connor not having to worry about what anyone thought. She felt something lift and somehow, she was lighter than a moment ago.

"Hello," she said finally.

Anthony's eyes drifted up, his face still cupped in his hand. His smile remained. "*Buona sera*."

Standing in the doorway, Madeline herself was a study in simplicity. She had loosely pulled her auburn hair back into a ponytail with a wayward black scarf. The dress she had decided upon was a short black jersey shift with black sandals to match. A brush of mascara, a dusting of powder, and a sweep of lipstick were her only make-up.

The fashion editors in New York would have been surprised; this was not the Madeline O'Connor they knew.

"You look positively radiant."

"Thank you," she beamed. "You look happy."

His lips parted into a smile that disarmed Madeline. In some ways Anthony was so open, almost like a child. Someone not yet jaded by the world. Yet, in other ways, so mysterious. She smiled too and shook her head in disbelief.

How can this be happening?

"I am happy. Content, really." He got up and retrieved a wine glass from the counter. "Care to try this?" He motioned to the bottle on the table. "It's one of our very best vintages. I wanted to try a blend of cabernet and merlot."

"Please."

Anthony poured a glass of wine. Madeline pulled herself away from the safety of the doorway and walked over to the table, pulled out a chair, and sat down.

Too close to Anthony was a dangerous place. She felt her heart start to pound in her chest at the nearness of him.

"Here you are." He held out the wine, and more. It was as though his eyes reached into her and offered his heart. His soul.

It would be so easy to fall completely in love with him, Madeline thought, and wondered if this was how Adam felt when Eve tempted him with the apple.

Madeline could barely speak as she reached out and accepted his offering. "Thank you."

He nodded a silent you're welcome.

"Anthony, what made you become a monk?" Madeline asked him.

His eyebrows rose at the question. "You get right to the point, don't you?"

Madeline smiled. Nodded. She loved his accent. And knew that at any moment, he would rub his chin as he considered her question.

He thought for a moment. Rubbed his chin.

Madeline's heart swelled.

"When I was a little boy, an infant actually, my mother left me here. I guess–how would you say? – she abandoned me here."

"And your father?"

"I don't know anything about him."

They shared a long look. Sipped their wine.

Anthony continued, "The orphanage had no room for me, and so Father Marco and the brothers took me in. I had nowhere else to go, I suppose."

"So you've been here...your whole life?" Madeline was incredulous.

"No–I served in other monasteries. Father Marco thought travel would be a good education for me. I've spent time in France, England, Switzerland. Learned English. French. But ... I have lived all my life in monasteries." His eyes were fixed on Madeline. He trailed the tip of his index finger lazily along the rim of his glass.

Madeline watched him and wanted to be that glass. She took a sip of wine.

"What about school?" Madeline struggled to keep talking to him instead of touching him.

"The monks taught me. Home school." He shrugged as though to apologize. "I went to the University of Rome on a scholarship. Studied theology and languages. Later I studied for a summer at Oxford. More theology."

He surprised her. A worldly monk.

Not worldly exactly. A man isn't worldly until he's been to New York.

She had to stifle a smile at her snobbery. Not worldly perhaps, but educated. Anthony was definitely educated. Articulate. Attractive.

"There must have been women at the university." Madeline teased.

Anthony laughed. "Yes. There were women at the university, but I lived here. Back then, I wore my robe."

"Ah. So you managed to avoid the girls." Madeline persisted.

"They didn't interest me."

"Not at all?"

Oh God, what if he's gay? Then again, he's a monk. What would it matter?

Anthony shook his head. "Sex, Madeline, in general, didn't interest me. Souls are not male or female so at that level, it becomes irrelevant. How can I say–romantic love and spiritual–ecstasy–are the same thing–the same feeling–just expressed differently. I never missed it. Until now." Candlelight flickered in Anthony's eyes and illuminated his wanting.

His words hung almost tangibly in the air. They rippled through Madeline until they finally came to rest at her core.

Romantic love and spiritual ecstasy. Her mind devoured the idea. Her body ached with desire for Anthony. And her soul yearned to mate with his.

She stood up and went to him. He pressed his face below her breasts. She stroked his head. Drew him closer to her. Madeline was certain he could hear and feel the thunderous beating of her heart.

Her moan echoed through the stillness of the candlelit room.

His hands found her bare legs and he stroked them. Lifted her dress up to her waist. He stood now, and pulled her dress up over her head.

Madeline's black lace lingerie was all that concealed her bare body. She stepped back so Anthony could see her entirely, then reached behind her back and undid the delicate clasp of her bra. Madeline slipped it off and revealed her breasts to him. Her nipples hardened in the cool night air. Her chest rose and fell with the quickening of her breath.

Anthony's rapt expression weakened her. No man had ever looked at her with such pure appreciation. As though she were a work of art. She closed her eyes. Slid off her panties and gave Anthony the gift of her nakedness.

He stepped to her and knelt. Wrapped one arm around her waist. She felt his fingers tremble when he gently placed the other on her breast. Caressed the hardness of her nipple.

He gasped.

"Anthony..." Madeline breathed his name. She had never known such passionate tenderness.

She dropped to her knees now too and kissed him. Their tongues mingled and blended. Madeline pulled away and they looked deeply into each other's eyes. She slowly lowered and lay on the rug beneath them. Pulled Anthony to her.

He followed her lead and, fully clothed, rested on top of her. He pressed his cheek gently but ardently against hers, and Madeline felt, for the first time in her life, cherished.

They kissed. His mouth pressed hard on her and she was engulfed by his hunger. Madeline's skin burned as she felt Anthony's hands stroke her neck. Her cheeks. He pulled away and looked down at her, wonder and appreciation in his eyes.

She took his hand and placed it on her breast, arching her body to him. He kissed her breasts. Let the tip of his tongue travel down her stomach and then to her thighs. He explored her. Slowly. Tentatively.

Anthony paused and looked up at her and it seemed to Madeline he was unsure of what to do next. She wondered if he might be regretting this, if guilt were setting in.

"It's okay," she whispered. "We're not going to do anything either one of us is going to regret."

She opened her legs and exposed herself completely to him. He touched her and moaned at the inviting warm pool of her wanting.

She trembled beneath him, barely able to speak. "Kiss me, Anthony. Taste me, like wine."

And he did. He kissed her. Explored her. Stroked her until her body quaked in complete surrender to him and she finally melted into the floor.

Selflessly Anthony moved to lie beside her and held her to him. Madeline lay naked, wrapped in his arms, nestled against him, spent.

There they stayed, motionless. Speechless. Rested from the exhaustion of their rapture. Madeline felt him hard against her and she marveled at his self-control. Her body was limp but questions started to flash through her mind. How had he managed to resist? Why hadn't he torn off his clothes and –

Madeline's thoughts were cut when the door opened. "Anthony? Madeline? Dinner's—" Carrie's voice trailed off when she saw them.

Madeline was shocked into reality. She looked up and saw her sister in her red dress standing in the doorway, Carrie's eyes wide and jaw dropped in shock.

"Carrie!" Madeline was too bewildered to move.

"Oh! *Dio*! Oh, my God!" Carrie shook her head, spun around to leave, and slammed the door behind her.

Leaving naked Madeline and fully clothed Anthony sitting stunned on the floor.

* * * *

1944

The ticking of the clock in Father Delatorre's office made young Marco even more nervous than he already was. He sat in the uncomfortable chair, motionless except for the twiddling of his thumbs, and awaited the priest's arrival. His eyes took in the shelves and shelves of books. The neatly arranged papers on the desk. The half finished cup of tea. He had no idea why he had been summoned to see the head of the monastery. One did not question a summons from Father Delatorre. One simply showed up at the requested time, listened to the agonizing tick tock of the clock, and waited.

Twenty minutes had passed when the priest arrived. By then, Marco had begun to pray silently to God. Thy will be done. He jumped at Father Delatorre's booming voice.

"Marco! *Ciao!*"

At the greeting, Marco rose and bowed his head slightly. "Father Delatorre."

The priest took his seat behind his desk. Then Marco sat back down. He looked in awe at the older man and at how he had led his life. Totally devoted to God. In service to God.

"I shall get directly to the point," Father Delatorre said. "It is time for you to return to Saint Valentine's."

Marco blinked. "But–"

"Your work here is finished, Marco. I'm told your studies have gone very well. Three of the brothers have left Saint Valentine's and gone to Africa. The monastery needs you now and you will go. Soon Lorenzo will, too."

Marco opened his mouth to speak but the old man raised a hand to silence him.

"You have no choice in the matter if you wish to continue on to priesthood. That is what you want, isn't it Marco?"

"Yes. More than anything. But here in Venice I can–" He stopped.

"You could what?"

Marco could not possibly tell the priest the truth. That he could continue to see Isabella if he stayed in Venice. "Nothing, Father."

"Good. Then the matter is settled. Go on and pack your things."

"Pack my things?"

"Yes. One of the brothers will drive you. You can leave right away."

Marco was stunned into silence. Things were out of his hands. It was all happening so quickly. Is this how life was? Did things boil down to these minutes, seconds, when choices were made and everything changed? Could this be God's will for him? It must have been. But then why did he feel like he was being expelled instead of being asked to serve God?

He did have a choice. He could refuse to go. He could tell Father Delatorre everything about Isabella and turn his back on the life he thought he wanted to be with her. But what would he do? What did he have to offer? She needed to stay at the abbey to be safe from the Germans. He could not possibly protect her from them. She was safer where she was. His heart ached with yearning for her. How could he leave her? He loved her so much. But what was the best thing to do? The best thing for everyone? He remembered Sister Francesca's fear about others in the church finding out about Isabella. Maybe it would be safer if he left. For everyone.

"Go on, son. Pack your things. A car is waiting."

Maybe that was the answer, after all. Marco nodded. "Thank you, Father Delatorre."

The priest nodded and turned to the papers on his desk. Marco left the office, his heart shattered. He walked along the hallway and down the stairs. Through the courtyard. There was indeed a car waiting for him. Then something–God perhaps–compelled him to glance back up at the building behind him. At first, he did not believe his eyes. So he looked again and there was Sister Francesca in the window. With Father Delatorre. The two of them were in his office. Looking down at him. Watching him.

Watching him leave Isabella. Without even saying good-bye.

Could she ever forgive him?

Could he ever forgive himself?

* * * *

Present Day

Seated at the luminous dinner table in Saint Valentine's courtyard, Madeline was certain that everyone there knew that she and Anthony had just had sex. Not intercourse, admittedly, but sex just the same. Or was it?

Madeline was not so sure. She had never known anything like what she had experienced with Anthony. Nothing had ever been so tenderly passionate. So purely loving. So...pure. Yet her physical desire had been completely fulfilled. To call it sex diminished it somehow.

Madeline knew she glowed.

How had Anthony known what to do?

There at the table with Father Marco, Jonathan, David, Carrie and Anthony, she did not want to think about it. She could not look any of them in the eye. Particularly Carrie.

What a relief that she did not have to, since Carrie, as she always had, dominated the conversation and all Madeline had to do was laugh occasionally and eat. She felt Anthony's eyes on her and glanced up from her plate.

Yes. Anthony was looking at her. It did not seem to Madeline that he was the least bit embarrassed or out of sorts.

Or guilty.

What if this was his modus operandi? What if he's done this kind of thing before with other women; hovered at the edge of breaking his vows but never really quite crossing it?

Maybe with Veronica?

Madeline's wild imagination ran rampant. Scenes of Anthony with women of all kinds, guests at Saint Valentine's, ran through her mind like an adult video. Madeline wondered just how much sex had gone on behind the aged walls of Saint Valentine's. She'd heard stories about the hypocrisy of the church. Of religion in general. But had never given them much thought.

But now–

She glanced at Anthony. He was fully engaged in a dialog with Jonathan and Father Marco about his plans for spring's planting season.

Perhaps he did not realize the gravity of what had happened, but it was not lost upon Madeline.

What must Carrie think of me now, Madeline wondered. Her

gaze drifted over to David and Carrie who were also deep in conversation.

Then it occurred to her that Carrie was in absolutely no position to judge Madeline. Carrie, her sister who slept with her husband for years. Carrie who had borne her husband's child.

Madeline's eyes drifted over to David.

How had they borne it? Spent all those years as lovers? And lied about it? Every meal. Every family occasion had been a mockery.

My entire marriage was a mockery, Madeline thought bitterly.

Yet here she was, guilty, in her mind, of almost the same violation. Worse, even, Madeline thought.

Anthony cheated on God with me.

Yet, it had not felt that way. If anything, it had felt to Madeline as though their physical bonding had been a human expression of God's magnificence. A celebration of the bodies that God had created. It did not seem to Madeline that a loving God would ask His most devoted children to forgo the ecstatic physical demonstration of loving.

Romantic love and spiritual ecstasy are the same thing, the same feeling, only expressed differently. Anthony's words echoed in Madeline's memory.

What if passion, in its purest essence, is prayer?

She wondered what storms raged beneath the placid surface of Anthony's demeanor. It was he, after all, who had taken vows of celibacy.

Madeline felt she was free to do exactly as she pleased. But was she? Wouldn't she be an accomplice in the betrayal of his vows?

Is that who I want to be? How I want to think of myself?

"What do you think?" Carrie's question rang through the courtyard.

Madeline stared blankly at Carrie. She hadn't been listening to a word her sister had said.

"You were thousands of miles away just now."

I wish I were a thousand miles away. Anywhere but here.

A flutter of wings caught her attention and she watched a pair of pigeons fly toward the bell tower. They reminded Madeline of how the winged rats, as she thought of them, annoyed her in New York. Here, though, they were somehow beautiful. Graceful.

Creations of God. Then again, isn't everything? Even New York?

A torrent of homesickness rushed through her veins and pumped through her heart. She missed her penthouseand her officeand her work. Things were clearer in New York. Safer.

"I guess some things never change." Carrie said and smiled. She looked straight at Anthony and continued. "When we were girls, I could go on and on about school, or boys, or something. Or maybe Mom or Dad would be talking about their days. But not Madeline. She was always so quiet. We never quite knew what was going on in that red head of hers."

"I really don't remember anyone ever asking." Madeline's tone was flat.

Silence thundered between the two sisters and they looked hard at each other. The shell that had encased itself around Madeline's heart over the years held her gaze steady.

Carrie glanced away. "I was saying that the tumor is shrinking. I'm getting better. I'm going to make it, Madeline," she said into thin air.

The words pierced through Madeline. Through the protective shell around her heart. It wasn't until she gasped that she realized she had been holding her breath.

"Carrie, that's wonderful," she said, tears of relief and happiness welling up in her eyes. "That's so wonderful."

Madeline felt an unexpected joy soar in her heart. As much as she despised her sister over the years, she knew she was not ready to lose Carrie. Her sister was the only family Madeline had, the only person she was really connected to.

"So, you do care," Carrie said quietly.

Madeline softened. "Of course I care."

Carrie rose and walked to Madeline. Hugged her. "*Grazie*," Carrie whispered into Madeline's ear.

The sensation of Carrie's arms around her was strange to Madeline. When had they last embraced?

Madeline struggled to remember but failed. In that same moment, Madeline realized that she was now free to leave. Carrie would have her health and her life in Italy. Nothing was keeping Madeline here now. All she wanted to do was return to her life–her real life–in New York.

Carrie released Madeline. Let her go. And Madeline thought about Anthony.

But how can I possibly leave Anthony?

Her heart, her body, longed for him and she lifted her eyes to his place at the table. But his chair was empty.

He was gone.

* * * *

The bed was cold as Madeline, empty and drained, collapsed onto it.

She had looked for Anthony everywhere. In the chapel. In the winery. She had knocked and knocked on his door but to no avail. It eventually occurred to Madeline that Anthony did not want her to find him. He wanted to be left alone. Maybe even needed to be alone.

But that was the last thing that Madeline needed after they had shared such intimacy. Lying there, on the bed, she remembered the look on his face when he had seen her disrobed body. She wanted to be in his arms again. To feel his warmth.

What had made him leave?

Guilt?

Madeline was overwhelmed with certainty and confusion. Every cell in her body told her that Anthony loved her. Her heart felt it. Knew it. She had seen it in his eyes. Yet, he was gone. He could never truly be with her. His disappearance confirmed it.

Madeline wanted to cry but found she was too exhausted by her conflicting emotions. Restless, she rolled over in bed. Something thudded loudly to the floor.

The Fedex package that Tyler had sent. Madeline had tossed it on the bed earlier in the day and forgotten all about it.

Tyler Reed. What could he possibly have sent?

It must be preliminary paperwork for the sale of Felicity. Probably an initial proposal. Madeline was certain it was an unacceptable offer of some kind.

How could he be so relentless? So mercenary?

A cynical inner voice sliced her thoughts. *I'll bet he slept with me thinking I would melt like a twenty year old. Well, he's in for a surprise.*

She opened the package.

Inside, neatly rolled into tight cylinders, was a week of the New York Times. With a note. Handwritten. On expensive stationery. In Tyler's impeccable handwriting.

> *I picked up a paper and remembered you said you missed them. So...here you go. Online news really isn't the same, is it?*
>
> *Happy reading. When you get back home, let's have dinner again? I'll call you.*

Madeline was overcome with emotion. Too much had happened

too quickly. Tyler was proving to be quite a surprise. She had not expected to hear from him. Not so soon anyway.

She set his note on the nightstand beside the bed and picked up one of the newspapers. It transported her back home to New York. Her mind's eye could see the traffic-filled streets and blocks of skyscrapers of the city that was home. She could almost hear the honking horns, the people clamoring, the buzz of deals being made. Central Park. The theater. French toast at Bettie's diner.

Her heart quickened and she decided.

Madeline O'Connor was going back to New York.

Back home where I belong.

* * * *

Madeline's packed bags were lined up beside her bed like warriors ready for battle. She had dressed quickly in faded blue jeans, a black cotton turtleneck and a favorite old pair of black loafers. Her hair was pulled tightly back in a sleek ponytail fastened with a black clasp. The bed was neatly made. Satisfied, she stood and glanced around the now familiar room and thought that it looked exactly as it had on the day she arrived.

Except for seven editions of The New York *Times* from Tyler. They were in the trash. Old news. She had missed some good sales.

She walked over to the window to take one last look at the Italian countryside she had come to love. The hills and vineyards shimmered as the sun heralded the beginning of a new day. She now understood with her entire being why Carrie loved it here. Why she had stayed even after David had left her.

Madeline thought of Anthony and sighed.

She had not seen him since their passionate exchange at the winery. The next morning she had called Eric and asked him to get her on a flight out of Rome the next day. Within minutes, he had emailed her an itinerary for a business class non-stop flight to New York. Now here she was, packed and ready to go. Jonathan would be here any minute and they would go to Rome so she could say good-bye to Carrie. But what she wanted was to say good-bye to Anthony.

Yet she did not want to say good-bye to Anthony. Madeline hated good-byes. She always had.

It felt strange, though, leaving without saying anything at all. It seemed like the very least she should do.

Questions gnawed at Madeline's heart. What had made

Anthony disappear? Was it guilt? Was he scared? *Will I ever see him again?*

The final vestiges of her encrusted heart broke wide open for want of him. For need of him. Her lips quivered. She wanted to cry but could not. The sorrow that veiled her heart was too profound even for tears. Madeline was overcome with a yearning for Anthony that reached into the infinite fathoms of her soul. She felt a lump in her throat.

There was a quiet knock at the door.

Could it be him? Madeline raced to the door. Flung it open breathlessly.

"Aunt Maddie. Good morning." Jonathan whispered because of the early hour.

Madeline smiled to hide her disappointment. "Good morning Jonathan."

Her nephew caught sight of her luggage. "You're ready to go, I see."

Madeline nodded uncomfortably. "Yeah."

Jonathan took a deep breath and sighed. "Shall we, then?"

Madeline nodded. "Okay." She bit her lower lip and reached down and picked up one of her bags.

Jonathan walked into the room and grasped the remaining two. Silently, he walked out.

With one last look around the small room, Madeline followed her young nephew into the quiet corridor and closed the door behind her. They chatted easily as they walked through Saint Valentine's courtyard. Madeline was distracted, though, looking for Anthony. Hoping he would appear as they turned each corner of the monastery.

Madeline's rented Mercedes waited for them in the parking lot. Jonathan loaded her luggage into the trunk and slid into the passenger seat beside Madeline.

"So, this is it," he said quietly as Madeline turned on the ignition.

"Yeah. I guess so," she said, and pressed back tears.

"Too bad you can't say good-bye to Anthony."

Madeline's breath caught at the mention of him. "What do you mean?"

"He went into seclusion. Sometimes he does that." Jonathan thought for a moment. "But, you'll be back to visit, right?"

"Of course I'll be back." She shifted the car into gear and pulled out of the parking lot.

Seclusion. I wish I could go into seclusion. To think. To escape. From what?

"When?" Jonathan asked, anxious to know when his Aunt would return.

"I don't know," she said, and watched Saint Valentine's disappear in the rear view mirror.

* * * *

Breakfast was ready when Jonathan and Madeline arrived at Carrie's apartment in Rome. Madeline's flight departed in three hours. She had just enough time to eat and get to the airport.

Carrie had not once mentioned what she had seen at the winery. Madeline was surprised at her sister's discretion and sensitivity. She had not even given Madeline a sidelong glance. Madeline felt grateful and watched Carrie as she dished out eggs and toast.

"Here you go," she smiled at Madeline and set down a plate filled with food.

"Thank you." Madeline was not hungry but started to eat anyway.

"This is wonderful, Mom," Jonathan said.

"Yes, delicious," Madeline quickly agreed.

"Thank you," Carrie said. "It feels strange, that you're leaving already. I feel like we haven't really spent any time together."

"I know. It's hard to believe I've only been here for a few weeks." She sighed.

Everything that had happened felt like a dream to Madeline. She wondered if Anthony even existed.

Was he real? Or was it all a dream?

"When will you be back?" Carrie sat down across from Madeline and looked at her.

Madeline took a sip of coffee. "I really have no idea. I probably shouldn't have been away this long. It feels like I've completely lost touch with Felicity."

"I'm sure everything's fine," Carrie said. Truffles the cat jumped into her lap and curled up.

Madeline marveled at how simple Carrie could be. Her sister had no idea what it was like to run a company.

Then again, Madeline had no idea what it was like to be a mother.

Or have cancer.

"You're probably right," Madeline answered. "Still, it makes me nervous to be away for so long."

"I can't imagine living life that way," Jonathan said. "Always feeling stressed."

Madeline protested. "It's not stressful, really. I've always thought of it as exhilarating."

Quiet fell among them for a moment.

"Are you happy?" Carrie asked.

The question caught Madeline off guard and she responded too quickly. "Of course I'm happy."

Carrie regarded her sister. "Then I am, too. Coffee?"

The phone rang.

"That'll be David." Carrie said to herself and got up to answer, carrying Truffles.

David. Madeline had forgotten all about David. She realized she had not seen him since the dinner at Saint Valentine's, either.

"Hello." Carrie's voice was animated.

Madeline wondered if David had stayed with Carrie after dinner. That would certainly explain Carrie's high spirits.

What if they really are in love with each other?

The thought was new for Madeline. But the idea of Carrie and David loving each other came as a relief. It would have made everything worth it somehow.

But why would they have divorced if they loved each other?

Probably the guilt, Madeline thought. How could any marriage survive the guilt of what Carrie and David had done?

"Jonathan," Carrie held out the phone to her son. "Your father wants to talk to you."

Jonathan looked excited as he got up from the table and took the receiver. In a motherly gesture, Carrie stroked Jonathan's glossy dark hair. They exchanged an affectionate smile.

Of course, Madeline realized. Jonathan would have been the connection Carrie and David shared all these years. The bond that was powerful enough to overcome the guilt of what they had done. Of all the lies they had told to Madeline and to Bobby. And to Jonathan.

Madeline felt a sharp unexpected envy rise in her heart.

Motherhood. The relationship that Carrie had with Jonathan was something that Madeline might never have.

But did a child really factor into Madeline's plan for herself? She smiled and imagined a playpen in her Manhattan office. Pictured a line of nursing bras right alongside designs of fishnet stockings and garters.

Get over it. You're almost 40 years old. It's just the ticking of your biological clock, Madeline told herself and played with the eggs on her plate.

How she had loved the years when Jonathan was a little boy. He had found such joy in simple pleasures. On weekends, she had often taken Jonathan to play in Central Park, and his small face would light up when she bought him some candy or an ice cream cone. His life had changed so much. Yet, in many ways, he was still young and childlike and found joy in simple pleasures. She thought of Anthony and was grateful for his presence in Jonathan's life. David had turned out to be quite a disappointment as a father to Jonathan, and Anthony was proving to be a good influence on Jonathan. It occurred to Madeline that Anthony would be a wonderful father. He would be–

"Madeline?" Carrie broke in. "You're not eating."

Madeline blinked. "I'm sorry. I guess I'm just anxious to get back to New York," Madeline said and took a bite of eggs to placate her sister. "Carrie?"

"Hmm?"

"Do you and David still..." She couldn't quite find the words to finish.

Carrie looked surprised. "You mean, do David and I still ..." She let the question trail off, too. They were, after all, sisters.

I should have been asking the hard questions all along, Madeline thought. *It could have saved us all a lot of grief.*

Carrie paused, looked down at her plate, thinking. "David and I are, after everything–maybe because of everything–good friends. He's Jonathan's father, after all."

Madeline felt the lie. They were more than friends. Weren't they? "One of us should have had a happy marriage," she said.

"It's not too late for you, Madeline. It's never too late. You haven't given up, have you?" Carrie looked genuinely concerned for her younger sister.

"Maybe I'm just not the white picket fence type."

Carrie accepted Madeline's answer. "I really am glad you came. It means a lot to me." Carrie reached over and squeezed Madeline's hand for emphasis.

"Me too," Madeline said, but pulled her hand out from under Carrie's and glanced at her watch. "We should go."

Carrie walked over to Madeline and gave her a hug. "Good-bye, Madeline," she said, and pulled away. "I'm so glad you came. Have a good trip home."

Madeline was at an uncharacteristic loss for words. She hated good-byes. Had always been terrible at them. The possibility always loomed that a good-bye would be for good. That a person she cared about would be snatched from her life as her parents had been. But by whom?

Death? God?

Following his mother's lead, Jonathan, too, embraced Madeline.

"I love you, Aunt Maddie. Come back again, soon."

"I love you, too, Jonathan," she pulled away from her nephew, tears in her eyes.

"Okay, then. Let's go."

* * * *

1944

Marco stood on the terrace at Saint Valentine's holding the letter he had written to Isabella. The envelope was marked "Return to Sender" and the writing was not Isabella's. His hunch was that Sister Francesca had redirected it. Unopened and unread. A long lonely month had passed since he left Venice and he had written her every day. Now he understood why there had been no answer. She was not receiving his letters.

The peacefulness of the valley that Saint Valentine's overlooked did little to soothe the ache in Marco's heart. It was clear that somehow Sister Francesca and Father Delatorre had found out about his relationship with Isabella. But how? They must have slipped up somewhere. Been seen by someone. But when? And who?

Did it matter? The damage was done and could not be undone. All the prayers in heaven could not change what had passed between them. His mind puzzled and struggled to find a reason for why she had come into his life. So they could share a few months together and then never see each other again? So they could find love only to lose it? None of it made any sense. Only a cruel God would divine such a plan. A God capable of creating such beauty, such love, could not possibly be cruel.

A gust of wind rustled through the bare trees below and snapped a branch, putting a small flock of birds to sudden flight. Marco watched them alight into the crisp blue sky, longing to join them in their travels. He sighed, resigned. The truth was there was nowhere else he wanted to be. Except with Isabella.

He looked down at the envelope. Impulsively, he began tearing it into small pieces, tossing them into the air. They drifted with the wind as he watched through tear-filled eyes until the last piece had blown away.

He turned and made his way to the chapel. He would pray. Again. For Isabella. And a way for them to be together.

After all, prayers, he knew, were always answered.

* * * *

Present Day

Madeline stood in the short line at the business class counter, checking in her baggage for the long flight ahead. Alone and listless, her mind drifted. Back to Saint Valentine's. To the valley that she had come to love. To Jonathan. The vineyard. Anthony. Always, Anthony. Somehow she had come to love him, too. Yet she barely knew him. Not the details of him. Of his day-to-day life. But him. His essence.

His soul.

Confusion possessed her.

How is it possible to love someone I barely know? I don't know. All I know is that I just...do.

"Madeline."

It was his voice.

God! Now I'm hearing things.

She felt a warm hand take hers.

"Madeline."

She looked up into the mystery of Anthony's dark eyes.

"I had to see you before you left. It didn't feel right to let you go without at least saying good-bye."

The pretty attendant behind the counter cut in. "Can I help you?"

Madeline was grateful for the interruption. It gave her a few moments to collect her thoughts.

Why is he here? To say good-bye? Then he should not have come. Not if it was only to say good-bye.

Madeline stepped forward and Anthony helped with her bags. She handed her itinerary to the woman, and looked at Anthony.

"How many bags?"

"Three."

A moment passed while the attendant processed the ticket. "Here's your boarding pass. Your flight leaves from Gate Seven."

"Thank you." Madeline took the papers, and turned to Anthony.

"I know a quieter place. Let's go," she said.

Anthony nodded. They made their way to the airline lounge. In contrast to the bustling terminal, it was quiet, elegant, and private.

Like Anthony.

There were a thousand things Madeline wanted to say. Not among them was what she finally said. "Jonathan told me you were in seclusion."

"I was. But I had to see you."

"Why?" Madeline asked, her heart hopeful.

He replied, "Because ever since I met you, I haven't been able to think of anything but you. Seclusion only made it worse."

"Worse?" More hope.

"I'm sorry about what happened between us ... in the winery," he said.

Madeline's heart sank into her somersaulting stomach. How could Anthony be sorry? Sorry for what?

For loving?

It took effort for Madeline to speak. "What do you mean?"

"Madeline, it should not have happened."

He looked at her with soulful eyes that found places in Madeline's heart that she thought had been lost.

How easy it would have been for the tempest of her emotions to explode into anger. But somehow, it did not. What she was feeling was more complicated than anger.

"How can you say that?" she asked.

"I am a monk, Madeline. My life is with God."

How am I supposed to compete with that? With God? Why should I have to?

The loudspeaker announced the boarding call for Madeline's flight. She fought to regain focus. To find some kernel of hope to hold onto in these last moments with him.

"Help me understand, Anthony. I know your mother left you at Saint Valentine's...but why did you become a monk?"

"It's different for everyone."

"I'm not asking everyone. I'm asking you."

Anthony pulled his eyes away from hers and stared at the floor. Together, they sat in silence for a few moments. Until he replied, "I wanted to live differently. To commit my life to something higher. To something that mattered."

"You had to become a monk to do that?"

He lifted his eyes back to hers. She saw in them a vulnerability that she had somehow missed before. Or perhaps, he had not revealed it to her until now.

"At the time, Madeline, it was all that I knew." His answer was simple. "Saint Valentine's was all I ever knew."

Her heart burst open with a flood of compassion for him. In this moment, he seemed to her a boy. Not a man. Not a monk. Just an abandoned little boy. She reached over and grasped his hand.

"Oh, but Anthony. It doesn't have to be that way. There are other choices. Other ways to live a life that matters. I don't think it was God who demanded a solitary celibate life."

"No. You're right. It was something that I chose. Voluntarily. But in some ways, this life chose me." He watched her face intently as she listened. He sighed and ran a hand through his hair. "I don't know what the other choices are." A slight pause. Then, "Are you living a life that matters?" He turned the tables.

"I–"

She was interrupted by the loudspeaker that announced the final boarding call for her flight.

"You have to go," Anthony said.

Spent in every way, Madeline surrendered. She had to leave. Just as he had to stay. They lived completely different lives. In completely different worlds. "Yes. Yes I do. I'm sorry, too, Anthony. Not for what happened between us. But for what isn't going to." She stood up. "I'm sorry that what exists between us holds no meaning for you. Good-bye, Anthony."

"Madeline, it isn't that simple. I–"

She shook her head and interrupted him. "Please. Don't. There are no explanations that would make any sense. There never are."

She picked up her carry-on bag. Turned. Walked away from him. Just in time. She did not want him to see the tears that began streaming down her face. Tears that, if he saw them, would betray her by revealing too much.

Part II

New York's nighttime glitter surrounded Madeline as the taxi pulled up in front of her apartment building. The four thousand mile trans-Atlantic flight had been long and turbulent. She was exhausted. She tipped the driver and emerged from the cab onto the hard sidewalk. Weary, she bumped into a young man who passed by wearing a headset.

"Watch where you're going, lady," the teenager shouted without even a glance at Madeline.

Yes. Madeline was back in New York. She breathed the city in and felt her heart beat faster. Everything moved more quickly here. Including her metabolism.

The morning shimmer of the Italian countryside flashed across the screen of Madeline's mind. She already missed Saint Valentine's.

She already missed Anthony. Missed him the moment she left him at the airport. For a fleeting moment, felt his presence wrapped around her. Palpable. Real. As if just thinking about him beckoned him near.

I wonder what he's doing right now.

Madeline pushed the thought of him away. A resigned road warrior, she took her bags from the curb and wheeled them into the gleaming marble and brass lobby of the Murray Hill building that was home.

"Welcome back, Miss O'Connor," Mike, the doorman, greeted her. He helped with her bags. "How was Italy?"

"Great. Thanks. But it's good to be home." Madeline somehow smiled.

"Well, someone's been waiting for you." Mike's look was conspiratorial but playful.

"What?" Madeline was confused. Beyond all rational thought she hoped it would be Anthony. But that couldn't be, could it? Anthony Lamberti was now thousands of miles away. A world away.

"Who?" Madeline's tone was crisp. She was back in New York.

"I promised I wouldn't say." Mike was pleased with himself. He smiled.

The elevator arrived and she stepped anxiously inside. Pressed the button to the penthouse. The ride up took forever, or so it seemed.

The doors parted and Madeline saw him sitting on the foyer's expensive black leather chair. Tyler Reed. What did *he* want? As tired as she was, his good looks were not lost upon her. His blonde hair and blue eyes were strikingly set off by a gray turtleneck and black wool trousers. Not to mention his brilliant smile. His easy-going charm that was at once inviting and irritating.

"Welcome home."

"Tyler!" Madeline was annoyed. "This is quite a surprise." What right did he have to show up this way? They'd slept together once. That did not entitle him to show up unannounced. She swept past him like a cool breeze. Still, in spite of herself, she was flattered. This was, after all, *the* Tyler Reed. She opened the door.

"Here, let me help you." He took a bag and followed her through the door.

"How did you know I'd be here?" Madeline tossed her purse on a chair and looked at him.

"You don't seem very happy to see me. I'm sorry–maybe I shouldn't have intruded this way."

His insight surprised Madeline and she softened. "No. It's all right. I'm just tired, that's all. It was a long flight."

"Heather told me," he finally explained.

"Ah. Heather." Madeline thought it was strange that she had not missed her friend.

"Things just felt unfinished in Rome. I woke up and you were–gone." He gestured to emphasize his confusion. "No call. No note. Nothing. Just–gone."

Madeline wondered if anything like that had ever happened to him. Women were usually circling him like vultures, of that she was certain.

"I'm sorry. That was rude."

"If a man behaved that way, I'm sure you'd have a few choice things to say about him."

"Well...thank God for double standards." She smiled.

He laughed.

She laughed.

Madeline looked at him. What would she ever do with someone like Tyler?

Her mother's voice echoed in her memory, "*A bird in the hand is worth two in the bush.*"

"So...you'll have dinner with me?" He tilted his head to one side. Smiled.

"I don't know, I–"

He regarded her thoughtfully. Seriously. "Did something happen in Italy?"

"No." Madeline lied. More to herself than to Tyler.

"Then?"

"I'm not selling Felicity." Madeline was serious now, too.

"That's another subject altogether."

She shot him a yellow light look.

"Okay. Okay. I wasn't going to bring it up." Tyler raised his hands in mock surrender.

"Oh, you weren't."

He changed the subject. "You look terrific."

Madeline laughed in spite of herself. He charmed her.

"Okay. Well, I'll let you get settled. I just wanted to see you and make sure everything was okay." He walked over to her. Placed his hands gently on either side of her waist.

"Everything's okay," she whispered, surprised at how easy it was to let him touch her.

"I'll call you tomorrow." His voice was rich.

Maybe. Maybe not. She'd heard that before.

"Okay." She shrugged.

He reached out and lifted her chin to gaze at her face.

"You really are beautiful." His voice was just above a whisper.

She looked up at him and felt his breath moist and warm against her skin.

His lips brushed gently against hers and he sprinkled Madeline with the tenderest of kisses.

"Bye," he said and pressed his cheek against hers.

"Bye."

A domani. Until tomorrow.

* * * *

Thousands of miles away, Anthony opened the door to what had been Madeline's room. He stood in the same place that Madeline had stood and glanced about. Everything was in perfect order. He noticed that Madeline had left the small book of *The Rule of Benedict* on the nightstand. Then something caught his eye and he reached down into the trash can and picked out the newspapers. *The New York Times.*

Moving slowly and deliberately, he placed them gently on the bed. The bed where Madeline had slept for the past several weeks. He ran his hand slowly across the bedspread. A small piece of paper drifted to the floor.

Tyler's note. Anthony retrieved it and with no hesitation skimmed the neatly written words. He crumpled it into a tiny ball and tossed it into the trash.

He took one of the papers and unrolled it. Flicked it open.

And began to read.

Father Marco appeared in the doorway. "Anthony!" he said, looking surprised.

"Father," Anthony said calmly. He bowed his head in a gesture of respect.

The old man slowly entered the room and sat on the small wooden chair across from Anthony. He picked up a paper, scanned it with his still alert eyes, and tossed it on the bed.

"I don't think I would like New York very much," he said. Then added, "I was in love with a woman once."

The two men's eyes met and held. They were silent for a moment.

Father Marco nodded and smiled. "Come, let's talk."

* * * *

They sat together, priest and monk, on a bench in the small chapel. The afternoon air was heavy and Anthony watched tiny particles of dust drift in and out of sunbeams that streamed through the windows. He waited for Father Marco to speak. Finally, in Italian, he did.

"She was living a cloistered life. Although she should not have been. But, then, that isn't really for me to say. She'd been brought to the abbey, Santo Spirito, in Venice... *Venezia.*" He sighed. "I was there for six months or so during the war. I was seventeen. She was barely sixteen."

Anthony watched Father Marco pause, the old man's blue eyes distant, traveling back into his life, into himself, as he thought of things he thought of every day. Yet hadn't really thought of in years.

"Her name was Isabella. The first time I saw her, she was lighting candles. Dozens of them. It was the most beautiful thing I'd ever seen. She was luminous. She looked at me with eyes so brown, so unreadable, that I could see in them anything I wanted.

I felt things for her that I'd never felt before. Things that made me question priesthood. Question my love for God. But she was a woman. Just a woman. A girl, really."

He broke into sobs then. Gentle sobs. "I was with her, Anthony. We spent months together. Stealing hours. Making love. It was like something took us over. We couldn't help ourselves." Softly, he wept. "Then I had to leave Venice. Just leave. I told myself that when the war ended, I would go back to find her. But I never did. I never knew what really happened to her. But then, one day–" he broke off. Collected himself. "And so I became a priest. And tried not to think of her again."

"One day, what?"

Father Marco shook his head and pulled a handkerchief from his pocket. Dabbed away his tears. "She was a Jew, Anthony. A Jew. It's cruel, son, the way we have to make choices." He looked straight at Anthony and, without apology, said, "I've never spoken of this to anyone. And I've never stopped loving her."

* * * *

Nothing was the same. Yet nothing had changed.

Or had it?

It was eight thirty in the morning when Madeline waved her access card across the security panel of Felicity's 49th floor Manhattan offices. The light blinked green and bade her entry. She opened one of the double glass doors and passed through. Made her way through the lobby, down the hall greeting staff along the way, and walked into her office.

Her assistant's desk was, as usual, neatly organized. She reached into her purse and pulled out the small gift she'd purchased in Italy for Eric. Whenever she traveled, she brought back a little something for him. This time it was a small Murano glass sculpture of Venice's fabled winged lion.

The phone rang. She scrambled over to her desk to check the caller identification screen. She did not recognize the number but answered anyway.

"Madeline O'Connor."

"Madeline, it's Veronica."

Madeline smiled. "Hi! How are you?"

"I'm fine." She sighed. "No. I'm not fine."

"Veronica, what is it?"

"I feel like an idiot. I shouldn't have called you."

"Oh, Veronica. What is it?"

"I'd rather discuss it in person. Could we have dinner?"

Madeline clicked her computer to her calendar. "Of course."

The two women worked out the details of their evening and Madeline hung up the phone. Dialed Eric, who had just arrived.

"Yes," he said.

"Cancel my dinner meeting tonight. Reschedule it, please, with my apologies. Something's come up."

"You got it."

She hung up again and remembered how anxious Veronica had sounded.

What if something had happened to Anthony?

She looked at her desk. A neat pile of file folders awaited her attention; mail, invitations, magazines to read. She had somehow managed to stay reasonably current on email while she had been in Italy. Heather and her other managers had done an excellent job keeping Madeline updated on important developments.

She spent some time going through the folders. Her mail. Memos from staff with reports and sales summaries.

I have such wonderful staff. She looked forward to seeing everyone in person at the management meeting scheduled later in the morning. It was strange Heather had not called her last night, but Madeline shrugged it off.

It was even stranger, Madeline realized, that she had not particularly missed her friend.

She walked over to the window and looked at the view of the awakening city. Everything was the same as it had been just a few weeks ago.

Yet everything looked different to Madeline. Felt different. The steel and glass metropolis was missing–something. Something graceful and peaceful and beautiful.

Soulful.

Madeline pressed her palms against the smooth cool glass and imagined the stone of the ancient buildings of Saint Valentine's. She missed her morning walk along its labyrinth of pathways. She could almost see the first golden mauves of sunlight as dawn broke over the dew kissed olive groves. Almost hear the tolling of the bells announcing the beginning of the day.

Almost.

She pictured Anthony burying a grape tendril in that certain way he had. So it would shoot out new growth. She saw his hands as they moved the dirt to cover the delicate vine.

His hands.

A red and white streak of lights below caught Madeline's eye. A police car. It jarred her back to the cold expanse of awakening New York.

She took a deep breath of the office building's recirculated air. Let it out.

Nothing's changed.

Everything's the same.

Except me.

* * * *

Madeline glanced at her watch. It had been a gift from Heather to celebrate Felicity's first $100 million in sales. Despite repeated repairs, the second hand had stopped. Again.

Madeline sighed and thought of Italy. Time hadn't mattered there. Madeline had not even worn her watch during her stay at the monastery. Time had been told by the resonant tones that cascaded from Saint Valentine's aged bell tower. By the sunrise. Sunset. Life had a different rhythm in Italy.

The clock on her phone read seven forty-five. Her first day back at Felicity had ended. She was due to meet Veronica for dinner at eight.

Hearing from Anthony's friend had come as a surprise. That Veronica had left her abbey and intended to move to New York was not news to Madeline, but it was a surprise that the former nun actually called. Especially so soon.

Madeline wondered again what had upset Veronica. Had Anthony contacted her? Given her a message for Madeline? It thrilled Madeline to think of it.

What else could Veronica possibly want?

Madeline started to pack up her briefcase. Reports. Magazines. A tangle of power cords. She glanced around at the lingerie samples that were strewn on the sofa. Sketches of passionate scarlet and fuchsia nighties, bras, panties, and garters were scattered everywhere, ideas for the Valentine's Day line a year and a half away.

Valentine's Day.

Saint Valentine's.

Anthony.

How was Anthony?

Who was Anthony?

Veronica, Madeline thought, would have some answers.

Anthony and Veronica had known each other for years. They knew each other well. *How* well was the question foremost in Madeline's mind. She zipped up her briefcase and thought about what it would be like to have dinner with a nun.

Ex-nun.

Questions consumed Madeline.

Had Veronica ever lain naked in Anthony's arms? No. She was a nun. He's a monk. But he was with me. But–not really.

What did *Veronica want?*

"This should be an interesting evening," Madeline said to herself.

"Really?" Heather poked her head in Madeline's door. "*How* interesting?" Heather leaned on the doorframe with her arms crossed. Her Cheshire cat grin accessorized her impeccable designer suit. "With Tyler?"

Heather's question levitated. Madeline thought she detected something more than friendly curiosity. Exactly what was Heather's interest in Tyler?

"No," Madeline answered. Funny. She had not thought of him all day.

"Someone else then?" Heather sashayed into Madeline's office and sat down.

Funny. Madeline had never noticed the sashay before.

"Veronica," Madeline answered and watched Heather try to place the name.

"Who's Veronica?" Heather finally asked.

"Heather, I really have to go."

"Okay. Okay!" Heather sighed and got up out of the chair. "Are you all right, hon'? We haven't even had time to catch up on anything."

"I thought our meetings went well today." Madeline was matter-of-fact. She suddenly minded that Heather called her "hon'".

"No. You know, girl talk."

Madeline struggled for a moment to think of something to say. She wasn't the same anymore. If it were any man other than Anthony, she would have shared all the graphic details with Heather. But it *was* Anthony, and she wasn't going to diminish him or the intimacy of their experience by gossiping with Heather. Or anyone.

"Oh Heather–you know me. All work and no play." Madeline shrugged and glanced at her stopped watch, a habit now. "I really do have to go."

"Okay, then you won't mind if I call Tyler and have a drink with him."

Madeline's stomach lurched. She was unsure of whether Heather had asked a question, made a statement, or issued a challenge.

She was, however, sure that she minded.

"Well, I–" Madeline stammered. She had no claim on Tyler. "He stopped by my place yesterday. We'll be having dinner soon."

Heather grinned. "Business–or pleasure?"

"Heather!" Madeline started out of the office. "What exactly happened between the two of you in Italy?" Heather followed Madeline.

"Nothing."

"Oh, come on. Something must have. I had lunch with him last week and he seemed very interested," Heather said.

"Interested? In what?" Madeline turned to look at Heather.

"In Felicity...and me." Heather raised her eyebrows and smiled triumphantly.

For the first time, Madeline noticed the cattiness about her friend and wondered if it had always been there. Or if she had been blind to it all these years.

The way I was blind to Carrie and David.

A chill glided down Madeline's spine. Her body shivered.

What of Tyler? He had seemed so–so–*interested*. Maybe men really were all the same. Untrustworthy cowards. Still, to sleep with two supposed best friends seemed particularly unconscionable.

But David had slept with two sisters.

Two sisters!

Even Anthony had–

She stopped herself. Anthony was all that was decent and real and honest. She would not malign him by including him with the likes of David and Tyler.

"Heather, there's not a woman in New York who wouldn't want Tyler. Go for it." She forced a smile at her vice president and chief financial officer. "I just hope that it's you he's interested in, and not Felicity. Neither one of you is going to convince me to sell."

"Of course not. What on earth would you do without Felicity?"

Madeline ignored the question. "I'm late. I have to go. See you tomorrow."

"See you tomorrow."

A domani.

Madeline turned and walked down the hall to the elevator she had ridden for years. As she descended, she wondered just how much time she had spent in elevators. Going up. Going down.

Going nowhere.

Madeline reached into her purse and pulled out her compact and lipstick. Powdered her nose and applied red lipstick that perfectly matched her nails.

She caught the reflection of her own green eyes in the mirror. Looked long and hard into her eyes. Into herself.

She knew, with all her heart, all she wanted was Anthony.

* * * *

1944

Everything in the valley below Saint Valentine's seemed to hold its breath. It was more serene in winter than at any other time of year. The trees were bare and the wind slipped through the branches in silence, absent the rustling of leaves. Marco stood outside on the terrace, angry with God for leaving his prayers unanswered. He, too, felt like he was holding his breath. Waiting for word of Isabella. Words from Isabella. But it was January and there had been nothing. His heart ached unceasingly.

The war kept pounding. The Red Army advanced into Poland. Had broken the nine hundred day siege of Leningrad. More Allies landed in Italy. At Anzio. Marco found it hard to believe that a place like Saint Valentine's could exist while such violence was being executed in other places. That bombs were being dropped and people were killing each other and here he was, overlooking a valley that was so still it hardly seemed alive. Yet it was. All he wanted was for the war to be over so he could -so he could–what?

What?

In the winter stillness his heart decided. He knew what he would do. His days of waiting for God to answer his prayers would be over with the war. He would go to Isabella. He would leave Saint Valentine's. Leave the Order. Live his life with her. Marry her. He could see everything so clearly now, in his mind's eye. Once the war was over and life returned to normal, maybe they could open a store. Or a restaurant. Something. Anything. Anything that would keep them together. This separation had taught him one thing. He never wanted to be apart from her again.

Marco thought of his brother, Arturo. Who had given his life in the war. How Marco had promised that he would become a priest.

He imagined his brother was there, beside him. That he could explain how much he loved Isabella and wanted to be with her. It occurred to him for the first time that what Arturo really wanted was for him to be safe. That he simply wanted Marco to be at Saint Valentine's instead of the battlefield. He knew then that all Arturo wanted was for Marco to live. That was a promise he could keep. Live he would. A beautiful life with his beautiful Isabella.

He saw the valley now through new eyes. *After winter,* he thought, *spring always comes.*

The war will be over soon, he thought. *I just know it.*

* * * *

Present Day

When Madeline arrived at Amista she was fifteen minutes late. She had been pleasantly surprised at Veronica's choice of restaurant. It was luxurious and expensive. Not the kind of place she expected a nun to choose.

Ex-nun. God, I hate being late. What will she think?

Veronica looked composed and graceful seated at the table, but stood up when Madeline arrived. They greeted each other with a fleeting hug and Madeline quickly surveyed Veronica. Her smooth dark hair gleamed in the candlelight. She had intelligent cornflower blue eyes that were set off by a pale blue sweater with a sexy plunging neckline. Pale pink lipstick and a faint sweep of eye shadow on the canvas of Veronica's milky complexion reminded Madeline of an Impressionist painting. Her nails wore a demure French manicure. Veronica was a natural beauty perfectly placed in elegant surroundings.

She seemed to Madeline a woman at home anywhere. Who carried within her a sense of peace. Of belonging.

Just like Anthony.

"God, I'm sorry I'm late," Madeline said.

"Are you apologizing to me, or to God?" Veronica teased.

Madeline's felt her face flush. Her stomach tighten.

Veronica smiled warmly. "Sorry. I guess you can take the nun out of the abbey..." She shrugged.

A waiter appeared instantly to take their order. That accomplished, Veronica launched into a series of questions about life in New York. Gone was her reserved demeanor and in its place was a sparkling *joie de vivre.*

Madeline humored Veronica, but was anxious to ask a question or two of her own about Anthony. But that would have to wait until just the right moment. Meanwhile, during dinner, Madeline found that she enjoyed Veronica's company. She was refreshingly uncomplicated. Something about Veronica brought out a protective feeling in Madeline, as though Veronica were a younger sister.

An overwhelmingly bitter thought swept through Madeline. *Older sisters were supposed to protect younger sisters, not screw their husbands.*

Madeline was despondent. How would she ever find her way to forgiving Carrie?

"What is it?" Veronica asked.

Madeline shook her head. "Nothing."

Veronica gave Madeline a disbelieving look.

Madeline wanted to end the suspense. "Really. It's nothing. I'm more concerned about you. You sounded upset on the phone."

What kind of a message did Anthony give to Veronica?

"Well," Veronica blushed. "I've met someone."

Madeline was momentarily silenced, then managed, "You've met someone. I'm not sure I–"

Veronica nodded and smiled. Reminded Madeline of an innocent schoolgirl.

"A man. I'm afraid I don't know what to do at all," Veronica confessed.

Madeline quickly assessed Veronica's predicament.

You want my advice about men?

Veronica had been a nun. She had absolutely no experience with men. Except Anthony. And that had been strictly platonic. That didn't count. Of *course* she wouldn't know what to do.

"Would you, you know, fill me in a little about men? Nothing personal, of course. Just general things. I mean, when do I let him kiss me? Does he pay for dinner? And Madeline," she leaned over conspiratorially and whispered, "What I really want to know is–" she paused shyly. Leaned forward and lowered her voice. "Sex. I don't know anything about it."

The natural elegant beauty that Veronica had been just an hour or so before was gone. Seated across from Madeline now was a young virginal girl who hovered on the brink of womanhood.

Was *this* what Veronica wanted? To befriend Madeline? Seek her advice? About men, of all things?

There was no message from Anthony?

Madeline's heart turned to lead but her face revealed nothing. She regarded Veronica. "How long were you at the abbey?"

"Right after high school...so it was...fifteen years or so."

Fifteen years!

"I went to Catholic schools all my life. The nuns always seemed so..." Veronica trailed off thoughtfully. "At peace with themselves. I wanted that. I thought the only way to find it would be to become a nun."

"And did you find it?" Madeline asked quietly.

"Yes...and no. A part of me always wondered about life outside the abbey. I was always a little restless, I guess. Curious."

"Now you're curious about men. And sex."

Veronica looked down at the table. "Oh, I'm sorry. It's not appropriate that I should have come to you. It's just that–I don't know many people here yet." Veronica leaned back into her chair. She sighed.

Madeline softened. Veronica's vulnerability touched her.

"No. It's not that. It's just that you're asking me questions that women, *experienced* women, ask themselves all the time. I'm no expert on the subject of men. There just aren't any rules."

Madeline remembered Anthony's words. "You know, Anthony told me that romantic love and spiritual ecstasy are the same thing, the same feeling, just expressed differently."

Veronica looked at Madeline thoughtfully. "Anthony said that?"

Madeline nodded. "You seem surprised."

"Well, it never occurred to me that Anthony thought about–well, *eros*."

"The two of you never talked about it?"

Veronica winced, "No. Madeline. He's a monk. I was a nun. We never discussed such things. But you talked about it with him?"

The knot in Madeline's stomach vanished. She had not even noticed it had been there.

"In theory."

Veronica glanced down. Nodded. "In theory."

Madeline blushed.

Graciously, Veronica rescued her. "You know, when I told Anthony I was leaving the abbey, he was not so surprised.I know there have been times when he has wanted to leave Saint Valentine's. A life devoted to God is not easy."

"A life devoted to anything is not easy," Madeline philosophized.

Veronica regarded Madeline for a moment. "Has your life been devoted to your work?"

Madeline considered the question. "Yes. I suppose it has. It wasn't my choice really. It just turned out that way."

"I like to think we always have choices," Veronica said. "God granted us free will, after all. Maybe you were making a choice, but didn't know it." She smiled.

Something deep inside Madeline clicked perfectly into place. Like a piece of a puzzle. Free will. Choices. Did she really have choices?

"You made a choice to leave God. That couldn't have been easy."

"Oh, Madeline. I haven't left God. God is everywhere. In everything. I just decided that I could serve God just as well living in the world, instead of hiding from it."

God is everywhere. That was something Mom used to say.

Madeline marveled at Veronica and at their conversation. When had she discussed such things? What had begun as a conversation about men had turned to a dialog about God.

"What do you think Anthony really meant? About spiritual ecstasy and romantic love?"

Veronica thought for a moment. "There are moments, in prayer, or deep contemplation. Or even gazing at the stars, when your heart breaks open with such joy that it brings tears to your eyes. When you are so connected to yourself and to everyone and to God that everything is truly and deeply perfect. Ecstatic. Maybe in those moments, God is like a lover. I suppose making love feels that way. Like ecstasy."

Madeline was stupefied. Had she ever felt ecstasy? Ecstasy! She had never wondered about it. That, she supposed, was her answer. In all her years at Felicity. All the awards she had won. Her marriage to David. She had never felt the thrill of ecstasy. Yet Veronica had clearly experienced it.

Anthony had experienced it.

What is it that brings about ecstasy?

Veronica smiled. Her eyes sparkled.

Madeline looked at her untouched new friend and hoped Veronica would not be disappointed by sex. By love. By men. The way she had been.

She thought of Anthony. Of all that she wanted to know about him. All the questions she had.

Those would have to wait. For another day.

Tonight, Madeline was tired and wanted to go home.

Alone.

"Let's get our check," Madeline said.

"Oh, there's no check," Veronica said. "My parents own the place."

Madeline was startled. "Your parents?"

Veronica laughed. "I *do* have parents."

Madeline laughed too. Mostly at herself. Of course Veronica had parents. Obviously well-off ones. Veronica was full of surprises.

"Okay. Well. Next time, it'll be my treat," Madeline said.

Veronica smiled. "Fair enough. Let's get together again soon."

"The sooner the better." Madeline said.

Next time, she thought, she *would* ask about Anthony.

* * * *

Madeline walked out of the restaurant into the cool autumn evening. A few well-suited businessmen lingered on the street and talked about their latest victories. Defeats. Here and there a couple walked arm-in-arm.

Then Madeline saw him turn the corner. Her eyes widened. Her heart opened. He was taller and more handsome than she remembered in a grey cashmere turtleneck that perfectly set off his graying-at-the-temples dark hair. Black trousers draped his lower body perfectly as he walked toward her.

Anthony.

God, how she wanted him. Her heart opened in a rush of love that only he could inspire. Everything around Madeline disappeared except for him. Anthony was all that mattered. All that ever would matter.

He walked toward her in that slow deliberate way of his. And turned into someone else. Her eyes had deceived her. This was a stranger. Just someone who reminded Madeline of Anthony. He passed by and despite herself, she turned to watch him.

How could I have thought it was him. Here. In New York.

Anthony is thousands of miles away.

Madeline wondered if she had lost her mind.

She knew she had lost her heart. *Or maybe I've found it. Maybe Anthony has shown me my heart again.*

How could that have happened after so many years? How had the walls she had so carefully constructed crumbled so easily? After just weeks of knowing Anthony?

Resignation consumed her. Resignation to a life of reminders of Anthony. To memories of him. Of how it felt to be with him. Painful reminiscences of what *could* be, but never actually, *would* be. Or so it seemed to Madeline.

The thought of going home to her empty penthouse became

unbearable. Unacceptable. Loneliness had been her companion for too long. For the first time in years, she had begun to recognize her own needs. It was time for a change. Anthony was miles away, but Tyler. Tyler was only blocks away. She reached into her bag and took out her cell phone. The small screen told her she had message. How had she missed a call? Within seconds, she was listening to a message from Tyler. He had called to just check in. Had been thinking about her.

She took a breath and dialed his number. She heard one ring. Had second thoughts. Hung up. Laughed at herself. Hesitated. Dialed again.

Another ring. Then two. Then, "Hello?" Tyler's voice was deep and resonant.

Her tone was expectant. "Hi. It's me. Madeline."

"Hi." He waited.

A short awkward silence passed. Madeline felt like a high school girl. What to say?

"Well...I just happen to be in your neighborhood and–" She could not quite bring herself to say the words.

"You thought you'd stop by?" Tyler sounded surprised. He laughed.

Nervously, Madeline laughed too. "I got your message. And-well, yes. Would that be okay?" Madeline's cool tone masked the vulnerability she felt.

He laughed again. It was a full contagious laugh and Madeline joined in.

Madeline caught her breath and asked, "What's so funny?" A smile remained on her lips.

"Well, Heather was just here. It's like a Felicity road show."

Madeline's smile faded. She paced on the sidewalk.

"Heather was just there?" Madeline's anger flared. "What did she want?" In the cool evening air she could see her breath as she spoke.

"She just dropped off a press kit. The pictures of you are great."

"A press kit! What for? Why was she dropping it off at your place?"

Madeline's stomach churned. How long had Heather been sneaking around behind her back with Tyler? Giving him company information?

"Madeline, it's just a press kit. It's harmless. Nothing our research department couldn't find online."

"What do you want it for? How many times have I told you

Felicity's not for sale?"

"Madeline, I know Felicity's not for sale. My niece is doing some research on the fashion industry for a high school project. When I told her I knew you, she got all excited. I guess she wears all your bras and panties and things. Well, not *yours*," he paused. "Anyway, I offered to get it for her and we were hoping you might, well, spend half an hour or so with her. Maybe all have lunch?"

"Why didn't you ask me for it?"

"You never return my calls. Not until just now. So finally, Eric suggested that I talk to Heather. She *is* second in command."

"For a press kit? She's my CFO. Why didn't you just talk to marketing?"

"I have a relationship with Heather, Madeline, you know that. We did do several financings together, remember?" he paused. "You know, you actually sound jealous."

"That's ridiculous." Madeline laughed uncomfortably but admitted to herself that Tyler was on target. He and Heather had worked together. It was entirely appropriate for him to call her. Like it or not, she was jealous.

"So, let's start over. Where were we? Where are you?" His voice was quiet. Calm.

Madeline matched his tone. "Just outside Amista."

"Amista. I love Amista. Did you have dinner there?"

"Yes." Madeline's heels clicked as she walked back and forth on the sidewalk. Her arms started to ache under the weight of her briefcase and she stopped to set it down.

"With who?"

"Just a friend." As she spoke, she realized it was true. She wanted Veronica to be her friend.

"Just a friend. That's an interesting expression, isn't it? I mean, aren't friends important? To me, there isn't a just about it."

That was something Anthony would say.

Madeline considered for a moment. Tyler surprised her. Pleasantly. Maybe there was more to him than she originally thought.

Yet, her heart ached at the reminder of Anthony. "You're right, you know," she said quietly.

"So...would you like to meet for a drink? Some coffee, maybe?"

Surprised again. Madeline had been sure he would invite her up to his place. It intrigued her that he had not. "Coffee sounds good."

"Great. How about Café Lalo?"

Madeline smiled. It was a perfect choice, very Westside, not far from Lincoln Center. She loved the café's charming interior and its menu read like an encyclopedia of desserts. "Sounds perfect. I'll grab a cab and stop by your place. We can ride over together," she said.

"I'll be waiting downstairs."

* * * *

Tyler was standing on the curb when Madeline arrived in the taxi. She noticed immediately how handsome he looked in jeans, a navy cotton turtleneck, and a black sports coat. How was it that a man so perfect was available in a city like New York? Lonely single women were everywhere.

He must be constantly approached by them. There must be some reason he's not married. Something ... maybe he's just buried himself in his work. Buried himself alive. Like me.

He opened the door to the cab and slid in the back seat beside her. Looked at her.

"Hi. You look great." He smiled at her. A warm open genuine smile.

Madeline smiled back at him. "Hi. So do you."

"Café Lalo." Tyler said to the cabbie. They drove off and Tyler turned his undivided attention to Madeline. "So, how are you? How was your day?"

Madeline fixed her eyes on his and thought of Anthony. Chaste sequestered Anthony. She tried to imagine him in New York. Tried to imagine him getting into a cab and asking about her day. Tried. But could not.

An expression she had once heard came to mind. She struggled to remember it. *Something about how a bird could love a fish, but where would they live?*

A long slow sigh escaped her. When and how had life become a confused tangled web? All she wanted was Anthony. All she wanted was to forget about Anthony. Forget that she had ever met him. That she had ever wanted him.

Tyler cupped her chin in his hand. "That bad?"

She remembered that Heather had been with him only moments before. "Tyler, you and Heather have never..." she stammered. "I mean...your relationship has always been strictly professional, hasn't it?"

Madeline was through with tangled webs. Things with Tyler

had to be clear. Honest. True. Right from the start. Her breath held, waiting for his answer.

The cab stopped at a red light and Tyler turned to face Madeline. She felt his hand cup the other side of her face and he gazed steadily into her eyes. He leaned toward her and pressed his lips gently against hers. Kissed her softly. Tenderly. He whispered, "No, Madeline, Heather and I have never been involved. Ever."

"I want to go home." Madeline said quietly. "Will you just take me home?" She could breathe again.

Tyler did not hesitate to recite Madeline's Murray Hill address to the driver.

He gathered her into his arms and she nuzzled into his shoulders. His neck. The smell of his cologne was subtle and sexy. Tyler held her. Stroked her hair.

"Shhhh," he murmured. "It's okay. It's all okay."

It was just what Madeline needed to hear and she melted into him.

She imagined that somewhere in Saint Valentine's, on the other side of the globe, Anthony was praying.

* * * *

Madeline curled up on her living room sofa and waited for Tyler. He had left her sitting there to sip a glass of red wine and listen to the radio play sultry jazz. He had issued a stern command that she stay in the living room, smiled, then disappeared to the bedroom to do God knows what.

God knows what. A strange expression, really. Of course God knows.

She closed her eyes and let her head sink back into the soft cushions. Her mind's eye drifted to the cobbled courtyard of Saint Valentine's–to Anthony–and she could see him as clearly as if he lingered near. She felt his cheek as it pressed against hers.

She wondered, again, how he could have let her go. How could he not know how rare and special what they have is? She was filled with a thought, a knowing, that Anthony understood completely. It was that understanding that made him push her away. That made him deny his feelings. He did love her!

She knew in her heart of hearts that she would see him again. There was too much left unsaid—and undone—between them. It was as though just the thought of him reunited them. As if he were right there beside her. Her breath caught.

I can feel you. All around me.

Serenity overwhelmed her and her entire being felt at perfect peace. The moment merged into forever and was instantly imprinted on Madeline's heart. Her soul. Her lips volunteered a contented smile.

"You look happy." Madeline could hear Tyler pad into the living room.

The moment evaporated. Replaced by the now familiar doubt and confusion about Anthony. About whether she would ever see him again. About what it all meant.

If it had meant anything at all. A moment ago I was so sure. And now-

Madeline felt Tyler's hands on hers and he coaxed her off the sofa. He stood behind her and kissed the back of her neck. Unzipped her dress. The fabric slipped off her body easily and fell into a pile on the living room floor. Tyler stood back and looked at her and she shivered from the combination of his desire and her near nakedness.

"You really are lovely," his said simply. "Come."

His outstretched hand invited her to take it. And she did, surprised at how easily and naturally their hands meshed together. He collected the glass of wine she had been drinking and led her out of the living room. They walked silently down the hallway and into the bedroom. Past the bed.

"Ummm...Tyler?"

"Shh...you'll see." He glanced back at her and smiled.

Madeline could see the faint glow from the doorway of the en suite bathroom as they made their way toward it. "So this is what you were up to." Madeline grinned.

He opened the bathroom door and stood aside so she could enter. She was met with the warm glow of candlelight and a bath brimming with bubbles. The fragrance of jasmine drifted in the air and reminded Madeline of the first breaths of spring. With the brush of his fingertips on her shoulders, he slipped off her bra. He stood behind her and unfastened the clasp. Ran his hands down her sides and glided her panties off.

Gently, he nudged her toward the bath. Helped her get in.

The warmth of the water enveloped her and she felt the frozen tension in her body begin to thaw. Tyler replenished her glass of wine. She inhaled the cherry and oak and vanilla of the burgundy and the bouquet once again triggered thoughts of Anthony. How he had taught her to experience the subtle layers of wine.

Madeline watched Tyler take off his shoes and pour himself a glass of wine. He sat down on the thick mat beside the tub and gazed at her.

He smiled and raised his glass. “Cheers.”

Madeline laughed. His lightness of heart was like a breath of fresh air after her long day. “Cheers,” she said, smiling back at him.

“To us,” he said.

Madeline took his face in. His tender smile. His gentle eyes.

Had he always looked like this? How had she missed it? All she had noticed before were his handsome features. As though his face was a puzzle made up of disparate pieces. A broad smile. Unnervingly intense blue eyes. A perfectly cleft chin.

It was as though now, here, in the soft glow of her bathroom, Madeline saw Tyler Reed for the first time. How had she missed the kindness he displayed? Was that a glimmer of vulnerability in his eyes?

She met his eyes. And his heart.

“To us,” she replied.

In unison, they took a sip of wine.

“So, Madeline O’Connor. Tell me about yourself.”

She laughed. “Well, what is that you want to know?”

He looked directly at her. “Everything.”

Surprised again. Or was this some elaborate seduction scene that Tyler played out with countless other women?

The question flashed in Madeline’s mind. *When did I become so cynical?*

He reached across the bath for a sponge. Soaked it in the water and began rubbing her shoulders.

Madeline looked up at him. “Well, that could take a long time. To know everything about me.”

“Then let’s get started.”

Madeline smiled and took another sip of wine. She did not want to surrender to Tyler. That would somehow betray what she felt for Anthony.

But Tyler was here. Now. Not thousands of miles away in a monastery. She sunk back in the tub with Tyler sitting on the floor beside it. He looked so at ease with an elbow propped on one knee holding his glass of wine, his faced relaxed and handsome in the candlelight.

She surprised herself with the seductive tone of her voice. “Well...you’ve seen the press kit,” she said.

"Ah, but that's Madeline O'Connor, CEO." Tyler touched her nose with a fingertip. "I want to know about Maddie. The woman. May I call you Maddie?"

She had never allowed anyone but Jonathan to call her Maddie. She considered the idea for a moment. "You may." An unbidden smile crept onto her lips.

"When was the last vacation you were on?"

"Well, I was just in Italy."

"Visits to family are never vacations. I've been wondering how your sister is. Haven't been quite sure how or when to ask." Tyler's expression was concerned. He soaked the sponge and squeezed the water out on her neck and shoulders.

The warmth of the water reached into Madeline's body and she relaxed more deeply into herself. "She seems better. We're all expecting a full recovery."

"Do you feel closer to her after having spent some time with her?"

Madeline was warmed as much by his attention as the wine and the bathwater.

She considered the question. "No–I mean–not really."

"Any reason in particular?"

Madeline gazed into the bubbles that shimmered in the candlelight and thought of Carrie. The usual image of her sister and husband together leapt into Madeline's mind. Followed immediately by the shock on Carrie's face at finding Anthony and Madeline together in the winery at Saint Valentine's. It occurred to Madeline that there was much unsaid between them.

It's better that way.

She took a deep breath and lifted her eyes to Tyler's. He had been watching her patiently.

"It's a long story," Madeline managed.

"They always are, aren't they?" Tyler's face was pensive.

Madeline wondered about Tyler. What was his story? Here she was in the bath with a man she barely knew. About to have sex with him. And she knew next to nothing about him.

"What about you, Tyler? What about your family?"

He grinned. "It's a long story. One day, we'll exchange our tall tales." He leaned over and kissed her. "Now is not the time or place," he whispered.

He was right. Madeline was not ready to tell him about Carrie. Nor was she ready to hear about his past.

Tyler stood up and reached for a towel. Held it open for her.

She stood up. Water sheeted over her skin and reflected the golden light of the candles. The air was a cool shock after the warm bath. Tyler wrapped the towel around her and helped her step out of the tub.

Tenderly, slowly, he dried and kissed her body. Madeline felt herself respond. She moaned and a warm pool of wanting began to stir inside the core of her being. He pressed the side of his cheek against hers and pulled her into him.

"Oh, Tyler..."

He stood back and gazed at her. "You have to promise me one thing."

Promises. It was too soon to talk of promises. Vows that would only be broken. Her brows furrowed and her eyes cast downward.

Before Madeline could speak, Tyler lifted her chin so she would look at him and continued. "You *have* to be here in the morning when I wake up." He smiled.

Madeline laughed and remembered how she had left him sound asleep in his hotel room in Rome. Snoring.

The memory made her smile. This was a promise she could keep. "It's my place, Tyler. Of course I'll be here in the morning."

She surprised herself at how much she looked forward to waking up with him. Things were different here in New York than they had been in Italy. Somehow he just naturally seemed to belong in her penthouse. In her world. In her bed. In her heart?

It had been a long time since a man had slept in her bed.

Too long.

Tyler took her hand and led her to the bedroom. Pulled back the covers to let Madeline slide inside. Lit some candles. Madeline smiled and watched while he quickly undressed. She quivered at the thought of his skin next to hers. A moment later, it was.

Tyler's lips met Madeline's. His arms drew her to him. With hearts and bodies pressed together, they made love to each other. Passionately. Sweetly.

Exhausted with pleasure, Madeline nestled into the length of Tyler's body. He cradled her tenderly and she looked up at him. His face was warm and loving in the soft glow of the room. They exchanged a smile.

Was that love in his eyes? Madeline's heart wondered. She thought of Anthony.

Love was always in Anthony's eyes.

Love for life. Love for God.

She kissed Tyler quickly on the lips and got up to blow out the candles. The room was dark except for the glimmer of the city that filtered through the windows. Red digits gleamed on the LCD display of the clock on the nightstand and caught her eye. It was almost midnight. The alarm would go off in five hours.

Madeline drowsily nestled back into bed with Tyler. Felt her body engulfed in his arms while her mind wandered to Italy.

At Saint Valentine's, birds would be serenading the morning sun accompanied by the echo of bells from the tower. The monks would have completed their morning prayers and be enjoying breakfast.

Anthony would be in the simple dining room silently spreading his favorite marmalade on crisply toasted bread. Or perhaps he would be lifting a coffee cup to his lips and taking a sip of the steaming hot tonic. Maybe he just finished pouring freshly squeezed juice into a glass.

Or maybe...he's thinking of me. Missing me.

Madeline sighed and Tyler pulled her closer into his arms.

"Good night Maddie," he whispered.

"Good night, Tyler."

Good morning, Anthony.

* * * *

1945

The war created shortages of many things, but wine was not one of them. At least, not at Saint Valentine's. Last fall's harvest of grapes had been bountiful, and the barrels of wine in the monastery's cellar needed constant monitoring. Marco enthusiastically volunteered to tend to the tasks in the winery, hoping to learn all he could about the art and science of winemaking. He decided that once the war was over, he would find a job at a vineyard. It was something he could learn while still at Saint Valentine's. It occupied his time between his studies and his prayers. And it was a way he could work at the monastery while he stayed there. Winemaking would be a beginning for his life with Isabella.

He thought about his future with her as he walked down the aisles of the wine cellar, turning the bottles, one by one, a quarter turn. It had been eighteen months since he had left Venice and he had not heard from her. Or of her. Nor had he written to her. But he thought of her every day. With every breath. She would be waiting for him to return to her in Venice. She would be waiting for him.

He sighed and turned yet another bottle, his fingers leaving an impression in the thin film of dust that had formed on the green glass. The process of winemaking awed him. That grapes and time could yield such a tonic.

Sometimes he imagined owning a winery one day. How beautiful Isabella would look in the vineyard, helping him inspect the rows of vines. He could see the summer sun kissing her face, her complexion radiant. Those eyes that he swam in sparkling with happiness and love.

Lorenzo's voice sliced through the silence. "Marco!"

Marco turned to see his friend running toward him in a panic. "What is it?"

As Lorenzo approached, Marco saw tears streaming down his friend's face.

"The Americans have dropped a bomb on Hiroshima. An atomic bomb."

"An atomic bomb?"

"Come quickly. We're listening to reports on the radio in the dining room."

"An atomic bomb. The world has gone mad."

Lorenzo looked seriously at his friend. "The world will never be the same again, Marco. It will never be the same."

Marco chastised himself for being so selfish. There he was, turning wine bottles, thinking about Isabella, while a war was being waged. A war that made no sense to him. No sense at all.

As though Lorenzo read Marco's mind, he said, "It can't go on much longer now, Marco."

"I've been telling myself that for months."

"This is different. Come on, let's go."

"No. I don't want to listen. I'll finish my work here," Marco said. He did not need to hear any more news.

Lorenzo nodded. "Suit yourself." He turned, leaving Marco in the wine cellar.

Marco went back to turning the wine bottles. A quarter turn. One by one. As though a bomb had not been dropped on Hiroshima. As though nothing changed.

But everything had. Even if he did not know it yet.

* * * *

Present Day

The following week, Madeline found herself having lunch on

the balcony of the Bryant Park Grill with Tyler and his niece, Trudy. She had arranged for the high school girl to spend the day at Felicity's offices with various departments, shadowing a day in the life of the company.

Trudy was an awkward girl in her teens. Nothing like the stunning young models that Madeline was used to meeting. She was overweight, her clothes were tawdry in a failed attempt at hip rebellion, and her dark hair was badly streaked with platinum blonde. More than one staff person had raised an eyebrow when they saw Madeline arrive with the teen in tow. It was hard for Madeline to believe this was the girl who had an interest in the fashion industry. It was harder still for Madeline to believe that a man as polished as Tyler could have a niece like Trudy.

That girl needs a complete makeover.

"So how was your morning?" Tyler asked his niece.

"It was okay."

Okay. Just okay?

Tyler regarded Trudy for a moment. Pursed his lips. "Well, what kinds of things have you been doing?"

"Well, I sat in on some meetings. Watched a graphic artist lay out some pages for the catalog. Saw a photo shoot." She lowered her eyes to the table. "The models were thin and beautiful of course."

The waiter arrived and offered the discordant trio a reprieve. Madeline quickly ordered some coffee and let her eyes wander over the treetops and picturesque green of Bryant Park. She retreated into thought while Trudy and Tyler negotiated dessert.

Madeline's heart lamented. She asked Eric to arrange a day filled with glamour and excitement for Trudy, and he had done a wonderful job. She'd seen a photo shoot. Sat in on interviews with models. Spoken with designers. Another girl would be having the time of her life.

But Trudy. Well, she must be feeling out of place. Self-conscious. Or she should be.

"You know, Trudy. Every woman is beautiful. Sometimes it's just a matter of bringing it out."

Trudy nodded and continued to stare down at the table. "Then why are all the models in your catalogs skinny? No one past a size six can properly fit into any of your things."

"Trudy, that's not true."

The girl raised her eyes to glare coldly at Madeline. "Yes it is. I went to one of your stores to try on some things. I couldn't fit into anything. I didn't even want to come today."

Anger flared inside Madeline. She glared at Tyler who uncomfortably in his chair.

"Your catalogs and advertising are socially irresponsible. Do you know what happens to most women who read fashion magazines? Their self-esteem goes down after looking at them. All you do is make women feel worse about themselves, not better. Your models probably throw up after they eat."

Maybe you should. Madeline immediately hated herself for the thought. In her heart, she could only try to understand this young woman. Madeline had always been beautiful, although she had not always known it. She simply thought of herself as pretty, and had no idea what it was to be unhappy with how she looked.

Except at Saint Valentine's. My red nails...

She remembered how deeply shamed she had felt. How isolated. How easy it had been to remove the polish. How *freeing* it had been to remove the polish.

"You know, you're right. Some models do throw up after they eat. But–"

"What about that is okay?"

"Nothing. Nothing about that is okay. But not all models do that. Most girls work very hard to take care of themselves. It's not a crime to be beautiful, Trudy. But it's not the answer to life's woes, either. If you tried–"

"It's not a crime to be fat and ugly, either. I don't want to try. To be what? Some totally unattainable standard of beauty? It's too much work. Always painting yourself and primping."

Madeline regarded the young woman thoughtfully for a moment. "Trudy, what kind of a report are you writing?" she asked.

"It's on how fashion contributes to the erosion of women's self-esteem in our commercial culture," Trudy spat her reply.

Out of her corner of her eye, Madeline saw Tyler shift in his chair. But he said nothing. Her heart went out to Trudy.

What happened to make her so angry?

Madeline recognized herself. Saw in Trudy her own anger and feelings of worthlessness after she found out about Carrie and David. How she felt Carrie had something she didn't, just as the models have something that Trudy lacks. Perhaps the two of them were not so different after all.

"Trudy, fashion can't do that. You're giving it far too much power. Who we are is on the inside. Not our jobs or what we wear. Fashion is fun, but nothing more than that. By the time a woman

agazine, her self-esteem has already been
some of the most beautiful and well-dressed
lf-esteem. But yes, it is work. Being your best.
too. Maybe we could–"
ner fork down and stood up. "Is that what you call
est?"
inced. Not the right choice of words. She had meant
to say ... g. Looking your best.

Trudy turned to Tyler. "I'm not going back this afternoon. I'm taking a cab to school." She picked up her knapsack and stormed out of the restaurant.

Tyler sighed. "Well, that went well."

Madeline took in a breath and realized her heart was racing. With little to no experience dealing with teenagers, she had been completely unprepared for Trudy's hostility.

"I thought the models we work with are difficult." She smiled weakly in a feeble attempt to lift the tension. "Is your whole family like that?" She had forgotten what it was like to deal with families. Mothers. Fathers. Children.

"Maddie, you live in your own little world...your little ivory tower of fashion. Believe it or not, there is more to life."

Madeline's body tensed in a fight-or-flight response. "Really? What, exactly, would that be?"

Tyler set his jaw and ignored her question. "She had a point," he said in defense of his niece.

"About?"

"It's true. Women's self-esteem does go down after they look at a fashion magazine."

Madeline sighed. She read the studies. "Then they should stop buying the magazines. Or buy different ones. It seems to me that as long as women are buying the products that pay for the ads, companies will continue to advertise and make the products."

"The advertising creates the demand," Tyler said almost condescendingly. *Almost*.

"No. Tyler. I don't really think that's how it works."

Tyler raised his eyebrows and looked quizzically at her.

She explained, "Women want to feel good about themselves, so they focus on their looks. It's never enough. Because there's always someone prettier. Younger. And they focus on pleasing men. Being beautiful for men. Because we're all so terrified of losing a man to someone younger. Prettier. Of being alone.

"And men? When they want to feel good about themselves,

they compete against each other. Bigger cars. Bigger companies. Bigger accomplishments. But there's always someone richer. More accomplished."

She thought of Anthony and the other monks at Saint Valentine's. How detached they were from these kinds of concerns. How they got up each morning wondering how they could best serve God. How they could see beauty in everything. And everyone. Even if they had to look for it.

Tears trembled on her eyelids and she continued. Softly. Quietly. "Maybe we should all just focus on being beautiful on the inside. Think beautiful thoughts about ourselves and each other. That's more work than putting on make-up and conquering commerce. It's a lot harder to make choices and be responsible for ourselves and our thinking." She glanced at her watch. Composed herself. "I have to go. I have a busy day ahead of me making women feel terrible about themselves."

"Madeline–"

She raised her hand and stood up. Enough had been said. "Never mind, Tyler. It's okay. We're not going to fix society's ills right here and right now. I'm sorry for upsetting Trudy."

"No. Thank you. For everything that you did for her. She's a handful."

Madeline nodded. Collected her handbag. "See you later."

Tyler nodded. "See you later."

She bent down and kissed him lightly on the cheek, and then began to walk out of the restaurant.

Contemplating beauty and what it really was.

* * * *

Time in New York passed quickly. Madeline barely noticed the leaves in Central Park were more abundant on the ground than in the trees. She was like most CEO's. Every moment of her time was filled. Meetings. Email. Phone calls. Reports.

Tyler.

Several weeks went by in a blur of time spent with him. Midday walks in Central Park. Sleepovers at their respective apartments. Quick little I'm-thinking-about-you emails to each other during seemingly endless meetings.

It was a Saturday morning and, in a rare quiet moment, Madeline stood at the edge of her terrace and took in the city view. The leaves *had* fallen off the trees.

Everything's so different. Everything's changed. She remembered how only a few short weeks ago she had stood on the terrace at Saint Valentine's and gazed upon the sun drenched valley that the monastery overlooked.

Despite all that had changed, she had thought of Saint Valentine's and Anthony every day. Wondered what he was doing at any given moment. Her remembrances of him were vivid and real.

There were moments when guilt stirred in the confused cauldron her emotions had become. Was it wrong to be with Tyler when she felt so strongly about Anthony?

She sighed and the approaching winter exhaled a cold early wind. A chill reached all the way to her bones.

She went inside and felt lonely in the silence. She had become used to Tyler's presence in her life. He fit in seamlessly. It was as though a magician had said abracadabra and pulled Tyler out of a black silk hat.

Magic. Tyler had appeared magically in her life, and yet that was exactly what she missed between them. Their time together was always romantic. Walks in Central Park. Candlelit dinners. Saturday morning breakfasts at Bettie's Coffee Shop. Yet, somehow, it lacked romance. Madeline stood in the middle of her immaculate living room with her arms folded across her chest in a failed attempt to warm her heart.

She wondered if being used to Tyler's presence in her life was the same as loving him. Sometimes being with him felt too perfect, almost orchestrated.

How do you know if you really love someone? If you really even know him?

What hidden realities lurked below the surface of Tyler's perfectly polished veneer? The question floated along the stream of Madeline's thoughts.

A cup of hot tea would help clear her mind, and she started toward the kitchen but stopped when the phone rang. A quick glance at her watch told her it was eleven. She gasped and realized that she was supposed to have met Heather at the office at ten-thirty for a couple of hours followed by lunch. Heather had left her a voicemail and asked to see her.

How had she forgotten?

"Damn!" She darted to the phone. "Hello?"

Heather's tone was angry. "Where are you?"

"God, I'm so sorry. Look, I'll be out the door in five minutes. I'll be there in fifteen."

"You know, Madeline, what has come over you? I hardly see you anymore, except here."

Madeline knew she meant at the office.

Heather continued, "You just haven't been the same since you got back from Italy."

It was true but Madeline could not admit it. "I'm on my way."

She hung up the phone and scrambled into the bedroom where, like a model backstage in a fashion show, she put herself together and was out the door in less than two minutes.

* * * *

Heather's tone was matter-of-fact. "I'm leaving Felicity."

Nothing prepared Madeline for this news. She stared at Heather in shock and disbelief. For a moment, neither woman spoke.

"I'm sorry, Madeline. Things just aren't the same. They haven't been for a while. I don't really know what to say." Heather shrugged. "It's just no fun anymore."

"I see." Madeline's tone was even.

"I've accepted a position at Saks. Chief Operating Officer. They approached me about four months ago with a terrific offer. I'll be starting in a month."

"A month!"

"They wanted me to start right away. A month was the best I could do."

"Four months ago. Heather! Why didn't you talk to me about this?" The too familiar feelings of betrayal and abandonment began to wrap their frozen sinewy fingers around Madeline's heart. Squeezed.

"What would I have said? That I'm tired of shivering in the great Madeline O'Connor's shadow? I need more than this. While you're here, I'll always be second in command."

"Being first in command isn't all it's cracked up to be, Heather. I didn't know you felt that way. I wish you'd said something."

"I can't imagine what you could have done to fix it."

Heather was right. Felicity was Madeline's empire. Madeline had never thought about it in those terms. There was no higher rung at Felicity. She had underestimated Heather's ambition.

"Tyler thought it would be a good career move." Heather said.

"What?"

Heather's tone was sarcastic. "Your new boyfriend didn't tell you?"

Madeline hated to think that Heather was enjoying herself but she certainly appeared to be.

"You discussed this with Tyler." Madeline's head throbbed. That these discussions and machinations had occurred covertly was beyond the furthest reaches of her mind. She could not conceive of such treachery and so could not imagine those closest to her capable of it. The wounds inflicted by Carrie and David began to emerge from remission.

"Yes. And he–"

Madeline interrupted, "You're leaving just before the end of the fiscal year. That– " Madeline was about to say was unprofessional of Heather but changed her mind and continued, "leaves me in quite a bind."

Heather softened. "It won't be hard to replace me, Madeline. I'll help with the transition however I can. There are even a few names I can give you."

"Well, I'd like to postpone our work today until Monday. I need to make some calls."

Heather folded her arms across her chest and sank back into her chair. "Fine."

Without another word, Madeline gathered her briefcase, stood up, and walked regally out of Heather's office.

Madeline failed to notice the glorious Indian summer day when she emerged from Felicity's offices. She needed to think. To let off steam. To be alone amidst the pulsing throngs of the city. Feeling crushed by Heather's announcement, she began to walk toward her apartment.

How had she not seen Heather's departure coming? How had things between them eroded so quickly?

What changed?

It was a familiar question. All too familiar.

Does everything always have to change? Do relationships always have to end?

What about Tyler? Madeline had trusted him. Trusted him!

How could he have advised Heather to leave Felicity–to leave me*–without ever mentioning it?*

Madeline swallowed hard and blinked back the beginnings of tears. She walked on.

Did everything always have to be a struggle? A battle? Couldn't things ever, just once, be easy?

Madeline continued.

She walked up Fifth Avenue. It was a path she had t times en route to lunch or dinner meetings, or on the when she decided to walk instead of taking a cab. Madeline w so accustomed to the sights along the way that usually they disappeared into the background, eclipsed by her thoughts.

Today, Saint Patrick's Cathedral shined. Maybe it was the way the arched stained glass windows gleamed in the mid-day sun. It might have been the young woman on the steps wearing a bright red jacket that caught Madeline's eye. Or perhaps it was the movement of a door as it opened and a priest emerged and stood at the entrance, taking in a breath of fresh air. He leaned against the doorframe, folded his arms across his chest, closed his eyes, and lifted his face toward the sky.

Madeline watched him, mesmerized.

Anthony. Thoughts of him always lingered around the edges of her mind. How could she ever escape him? Escape her own heart?

The priest enjoyed his respite for a moment more, then slipped back through the door and out of Madeline's sight.

A quiet urging rose up inside of Madeline and beckoned her to follow him.

Was it her intuition? Her heart?

God?

"This is nuts," Madeline said aloud.

No.

Go.

How often had Madeline ignored the quiet prompting that surfaced from the depths of her being? Not trusted the guidance of her soul?

Not trusted herself.

She crossed the street.

Madeline reluctantly started up the steps of the old building. The young woman in the red jacket looked up at her and smiled. Encouraged, Madeline went on. She opened the heavy door where a moment before the priest had stood, and passed through.

* * * *

The cathedral's stillness enshrouded Madeline and drew her inside. Her feet fell silently upon freshly polished floors as she slowly passed row upon row of gleaming wooden pews. There were people seated in several of therows. Some were homeless.

thers prayed. Others cried. Perfuming the air was the delicate fragrance of incense and she inhaled it deeply. Finally, she reached the first row and sat down.

She looked up at the altar. At a crucified Jesus. Candlelight married the afternoon sunlight that filtered through the stained glass windows and cast a faint light upon the suffering figure.

Madeline contemplated God and Jesus. Wondered if her life mattered to them. If Heather's resignation played any part in the grander scheme of life.

If there was a grander scheme of life.

A potent exhaustion overcame her.

She sighed, closed her eyes, and leaned back into the hard bench.

What would Anthony have said? How would he have advised her? He might not have said anything all.

Maybe he would have just pulled me into his arms and held me. Cradled my head against his chest so I could hear his heart beating. Stroked my hair. Stayed like that until the rest of the world just faded away.

Madeline's lips barely moved. "Oh Anthony," she breathed.

"Madeline?" A voice next to her whispered.

She opened her eyes to see Veronica seated on the bench beside her.

"Veronica!" Madeline said aloud, and wondered if she had heard her mention Anthony.

"Madeline. It's so good to see you. I've been meaning to call. I'm so sorry I haven't." Veronica smiled.

It occurred to Madeline that it was a genuine smile. One that traveled from Veronica's lips into her eyes. A kind sincere smile.

You don't see smiles like that very often anymore, Madeline thought. At least not in the circles I travel in. People are too worried about ruining their latest collagen injections.

Veronica continued, "I've begun to do some volunteer work here, and between that and helping my parents with Amista, I'm busier than I like to be."

Madeline sat upright on the bench and smiled back at Veronica. A real smile. "You're a New Yorker already. It's all right. I'm sorry I haven't called you, too. How's that new romance coming along?"

Veronica grimaced playfully. "After a few more dates, I realized he just wasn't...I don't know...evolved enough for me."

"Evolved enough for you?"

Veronica's eyes fell to the floor. "The truth is, I slept with him,

Madeline. We had sex. He never called me after that. I must have been terrible."

"What?" Madeline shook her head. "No! No! No!"

Veronica looked back up at Madeline with tears in her eyes.

Oh my poor sweet friend. Men! Cowards! All of them!

Veronica shook her head. "I must have been. Why didn't he call me? Or return any of my calls?"

Madeline pursed her lips in frustration while she thought of something to say. "Veronica, that happens sometimes. It had nothing to do with you. Or how you were with him."

"I don't understand how people can share such...such intimacy ...and then never see each other again."

Madeline nodded. "Sometimes things just–" She shook her head, not knowing how to respond to the truth of what Veronica had said. She continued, "Are you okay?"

Veronica nodded. "It was okay. Not what I expected. It just doesn't seem possible I won't see him again. He told me we would."

The vulnerability Madeline saw in Veronica's eyes mirrored her own.

How fragile we all are. How confusing it all is.

Veronica's tone suddenly became matter-of-fact. "He lied so I would sleep with him. He can't like himself very much if he has to do that. As if ... as if ... if he told me the truth, I wouldn't be with him. He must be terribly wounded to behave that way."

Madeline shrugged and sighed. "Aren't we all?"

Veronica looked carefully at Madeline. "Oh, I'm sorry. Going on about myself that way. Are you all right?"

"I've been better."

"Is it your sister?"

Funny. Madeline hadn't thought of Carrie today, she had become so preoccupied with Heather's resignation. Guilt stabbed her heart and a question Madeline had never asked herself before flashed across her mind.

What kind of a sister have I been to Carrie?

It had become an old habit for Madeline to tell herself that Carrie had been disloyal. Had betrayed her.

But maybe I betrayed myself, too. I knew that something was wrong with my marriage. I never confronted it. I have to admit that to myself. Take responsibility for it.

"Madeline?" Veronica prompted.

"No, it isn't Carrie. A key member of my staff, a friend, actually, resigned." Madeline explained. "At least I thought a friend."

"Can't you replace him?"

"Her. Yes, eventually. The CFO part. Not necessarily the friend part."

Veronica nodded. "I'm sorry if I interrupted."

"Interrupted what?"

"Your prayers."

Madeline looked at Veronica, surprised. She had not been praying when Veronica appeared. She had been missing Anthony.

"I can't remember the last time I prayed."

Veronica looked surprised now.

Madeline was suddenly sheepish. "I'll bet you can't imagine someone not praying."

Veronica softened and shook her head. "We all have our own way of relating to God. For some of us, it's not at all. The beautiful thing, though, is that God is always relating to us, whether we know it or not." She paused. Smiled. Then added, "It's better, though, if it's not quite so one-sided."

Madeline felt comforted somehow by Veronica's words and smiled. "Like any relationship, I suppose," Madeline said.

"You know, I have something for you."

"Oh?"

Veronica reached into her bag and pulled out a small envelope. "I've been carrying it around for days. I wanted to call you...but time just got away from me. Anthony sent it to me."

Madeline shouted, "Anthony!"

Veronica regarded Madeline carefully.

It occurred to Madeline that Veronica suspected she was in love with Anthony. She looked around the cathedral, embarrassed, and regained her composure. Her voice was a whisper now. "Anthony sent me something?"

Veronica spoke quietly. "No. He sent it to me. I just thought you might like to have it." She held out a photograph.

Madeline tentatively reached for it. It was a photograph of Carrie, Anthony, Jonathan, and Madeline. Father Marco had taken it on the evening of the dinner at Saint Valentine's. Madeline had forgotten all about it. Until now.

The floodgates that fortified Madeline's heart swung open as she took in the image of Anthony. His broad smile. His eyes. His hand that held the glass of wine. The hand that only a few moments before had held Madeline.

The image began to blur as tears welled in Madeline's eyes and her lips quivered.

Veronica reached out to Madeline and gently touched her forearm. "It's all right, Madeline."

The gesture touched Madeline deeply. When was the last time someone had cared about Madeline's feelings? She was overcome now and surrendered to the sobs that rose up within her.

"Oh, Madeline." Veronica put an arm around Madeline's shoulders and kept it there.

Madeline cried.

Veronica prayed. For Madeline. For herself. For everyone.

* * * *

When Madeline arrived home an hour later, there were four distraught messages from Tyler on her answering machine. Madeline surmised that Heather told him about her resignation because he wanted to see Madeline right away. To explain about what had happened with Heather.

Madeline was still standing in her home office listening to the end of the last recording when she heard knocking at the door. She shook her head and sighed. Building security was obviously getting sloppy. She made a mental note to look into it.

Then she realized it might be Tyler. Of course the doorman would have let him up. He had practically lived there lately. She heard his voice through the door.

"Madeline. It's me. Please let me in." Tyler kept knocking.

Madeline set her jaw firmly. "This should be good," she said. She strode to the door, and yanked it open.

"Tyler really!" Madeline's patience with men had long evaporated. "Must we do this?"

Were they all so easily led astray? Did honor and loyalty mean nothing to them? Were they such outdated ideals?

Still, Madeline knew it would be necessary to play out this scene. To indulge Tyler in his self-serving cathartic apologies. Then she could be rid of him.

His tone was fervent. "Madeline. Please let me explain."

She stepped aside and he surprised Madeline by taking her hand and leading her into the living room. He sat her down on the sofa. She glared out the window, arms folded across her heart.

"Now, please just listen," he said.

Madeline was quiet.

"Would you at least look at me?"

Madeline blinked. He was not making this easy. She looked

hard at him. Could see what seemed like genuine pain in his eyes.

"Thank you. Look, I don't know exactly what Heather told you. She called me this morning and told me she met with you. I can understand that you'd be angry with me for not telling you, but –"

Madeline stood up now, enraged. "Angry? Angry! Tyler, that's the least of it. How could you have been sleeping with me and telling her to resign!"

"Madeline, I told her nothing of the sort." Tyler stepped toward Madeline. Reached out to touch her.

She pulled back. "Don't."

"I did not tell her to leave Felicity. You have to believe me."

"That's what she said. I don't *have to* anything."

He looked straight into Madeline's eyes. "Then she lied."

"I don't believe you."

"No. I don't believe *you*. Heather has been angling to go out with me for ages. Haven't you seen that? I'm not interested in her. She just said that I told her to resign to come between us. And it's working. It's got to be hard for her to know we're together."

"Oh. It's hard on Heather. Well, what about me? I'm the one who's got to run Felicity without her."

"No you don't, Madeline. You have choices."

Madeline's eyes narrowed. "So that's what this is about. You haven't given up on my selling. How many times have I told you? Felicity is not for sale. Even now."

Tyler shook his head, frustrated. "Madeline, there's no master conspiracy here. I'm just pointing out that maybe it's time you did something else with your life. Moved on."

"To what?"

"Well, this wasn't exactly how I was thinking of broaching the subject, but, well. To us. To me. I thought maybe we could think about getting, well, married."

Madeline's stomach somersaulted. Married! She had sworn she would never remarry. Ever. No more marriage. No children. Nothing that could break her heart.

Yet a fragile voice inside Madeline surfaced, a seedling thrusting itself through the soil toward the sun. What if?

Maybe...

"No. Tyler. I don't think so." Madeline's voice was cold. "We're past that, don't you think?"

"Think about it, Madeline. We could be good together. I'll help you find a new CFO, if that's what you want. It shouldn't be too hard."

Madeline's head spun. Too much had happened. Heather resigning. Tyler practically proposing.

What could possibly happen next?

"I don't know what I want, Tyler. Right now, I really just want to be alone." Madeline looked at him.

Tyler bit his lower lip until it turned white. "Okay. I'll call you tomorrow," he finally said.

He bent down, kissed her gently on the cheek and whispered, "Madeline, believe it or not, I love you. God help me. But I do. I only want what's best for you. Whatever you think that is."

Madeline lifted her eyes to meet Tyler's and saw the unmistakable look of love in them. She felt as though his heart reached out through his eyes to caress hers.

She knew, now, that there was love between them.

Love, she knew, is not always enough. She had learned long ago that it did not conquer all. It only–

The phone rang.

Tyler looked at it as though to curse the interruption. He sighed in surrender and bent to kiss her softly on the cheek again. Then picked up the cordless handset from the coffee table and handed it to her.

"Hello," Madeline said and watched Tyler let himself out.

"Aunt Maddie! It's Jonathan." He sounded as though he were calling from the next room.

Madeline's heart lifted and she smiled. She could picture him calling from the small office at Saint Valentine's. There, it was almost the middle of the night.

There, it was almost the middle of the night.

A cold wave of worry rushed through Madeline. "Is something wrong?"

"Aunt Maddie, it's Mom. We took her to the hospital today. It's back. The cancer's back..." his voice trailed off and all Madeline could hear were the muffled sobs of her seventeen year old nephew.

"Jona–"

The deep resonance of Anthony's voice came across the line and interrupted her. "Madeline."

"Anthony."

"I'm here at the hospital with Jonathan. Carrie's not been well for the last week, but she absolutely forbade us to call you. I think it would be best if–well–if you came back."

Madeline's mind struggled to grasp the news. "Is it that serious?"

"I think so. I'm so sorry to have to tell you."

His voice was a much needed balm for Madeline's spirits. "No," she protested. "If I needed to be told, I would rather hear it from you than anyone."

"So will you come, then?" Something in his voice told Madeline that he wanted to see her.

"Yes, Anthony. I'll be there just as soon as I can."

"Good. *Ciao*."

"*Ciao*."

Madeline hung up the phone and collapsed into the sofa. Her heart was riot of conflicting emotions.

She knew she loved Anthony. Could she ever have him? Did he love her? Only a moment ago she had been so sure he did.

Yet, she could not deny that she had feelings for Tyler, even if she still could not bring herself to trust him entirely. Marriage to him was, in Madeline's mind, out of the question. He was still young. Her age, in fact. In all probability he was a player. At the very least, Madeline felt certain an illustrious bachelor like Tyler Reed would be incapable of fidelity.

She could not endure another infidelity.

Then there was Carrie who now, it seemed, was succumbing to the final ravages of cancer. Their parents' deaths had been excruciatingly painful for both sisters, and Madeline wondered how she would ever find the strength to be there for Carrie. Especially after everything that passed between them.

She found herself wishing she could talk to her mother. Wishing she could ask her what to do. She knew what her mother's answer would be.

She could almost hear her mother's voice, "What I think isn't important, Madeline. You have to figure it out for yourself."

It was what her mother always said. Madeline was exhausted by the answer even now. Sometimes she just wanted someone to tell her what to do. To tell her that everything would be okay. That *she* would be okay.

She picked up the phone and called her usual airline. Booked the next available flight to Rome. Her heart was beating quickly as she finalized the reservation and hung up the handset.

In two days, she would be back in Italy.

With Carrie.

And Anthony.

* * * *

1945

Three days after the atom bomb was dropped on Hiroshima, another annihilated Nagasaki. Five days after that, the Japanese surrendered unconditionally. Now, it was August 15 and the war was declared over. It was the day that Marco had been waiting for, for what seemed to him like forever. It was a day that he would, forever, remember.

He was in his room, packing his things, when Lorenzo arrived at his door.

"What are you doing?" Lorenzo asked.

Marco looked up at his friend but did not answer.

"You're going back to Venice, aren't you?"

Marco tossed a sweater onto the top of the things in his suitcase and turned to his friend.

"I have to. I can't go on like this, without Isabella. It's been almost two years since I've seen her. I still think about her every day. I'm going to marry her, Lorenzo. If she'll have me, that is."

"Marco, I-"

"My mind is made up, Lorenzo. I'm leaving Saint Valentine's."

Lorenzo sighed. "Father Giovanni wants to see you. In his office. Now."

"What for?"

"How am I supposed to know? You're the one with all the answers."

Marco glanced around the room. At his few belongings that were still left to pack.

"Now, Marco," Lorenzo said. "Come on. Let's go."

Lorenzo accompanied Marco through the grounds to the small building that housed Saint Valentine's offices. When he entered the priest's office, he was startled to see Sister Francesca seated across from Father Giovanni.

"Sister Francesca!"

"Marco," the old woman said quietly, not taking her eyes off Father Giovanni.

The priest was in his sixties, which, to Marco, seemed ancient. But Marco knew him to be a kind man who had always treated him well. Marco began to feel a darkness fall over the room. Something was wrong. Something was terribly wrong.

"What's going on?" Marco asked.

The priest pursed his lips and looked at the young novice.

Marco's heart started to pound.

"Marco, I'm going to leave you to talk with Sister Francesca.

She has some news for you – some news from Venice." Father Giovanni got up and left the old woman and the young man alone in his office.

Marco sat down across from the nun and looked at her. "Tell me. Tell me what has happened to Isabella."

* * * *

Present Day

Monday morning arrived before Madeline was ready. Even though she had worked all weekend, there were a thousand details that needed her attention. She had solicited Eric, her assistant's, help. As always, he had been there. Interviews needed rescheduling. Meetings needed postponing. How would she ever find a new CFO while she was in Europe? Heather's departure from Felicity now was an extreme hardship to the company.

It was six in the morning and she sat at her desk. The phone rang. Tyler's number floated on the caller ID display. He was already at the office, too.

She managed to avoid his calls the previous day. All she wanted was to take refuge in the comfort her work provided. Stay on the solid ground of her intellect and off the unpredictable waters of her emotions.

Now she shook her head in disbelief at his tenacity. At once annoyed and flattered, she picked up the phone.

"You don't give up, do you?"

"Wall Street is hardly the place for someone who gives up."

Madeline's heart responded to the familiar sound of his masculine voice. In spite of herself, she admired him. Everything about Tyler Reed was likeable. Lovable.

Why is it that I can't surrender to him?

"I'm leaving for Italy today." Madeline stated matter-of-factly.

Tyler was quiet for a moment. "Is it Carrie?"

"Yes. She's taken a bad turn, I'm afraid."

"I want to come with you."

His offer blindsided Madeline. She shrieked, "What?"

He would not work his way that deeply into Madeline's life. *He can't be serious.*

There was a short silence between them. "Madeline. I love you. Let someone be there for you for once. Let *me* be there for you."

She thought of Anthony. Anthony would be there.

Wouldn't he?

"Tyler, please. I need to be alone...with my sister. Please try to understand that."

The silence of Tyler's pause said more than words. "That's all? That's all there is to it?"

"Yes, of course. What else would there be?" If he was going to accuse her of something, she wanted him come out with it. But what would she say? There was someone else. There was Anthony. *Or was there? Was there really Anthony?*

She held her breath waiting for Tyler's reply.

"Okay. Then you'll call me?"

His persistence was flattering. God, she *wanted* to love him. Yet, there was something holding her back. Was it something about him?

Or is it something about me? Or is it Anthony?

"Yes, I'll call you."

"You promise?"

"Yes, Tyler. I promise." Madeline smiled at his boyishness. Men could be so adorable. Sometimes. Damn them.

"You mean it?"

She could hear the smile in his voice and she smiled, too. Damn him! He was being so lovable. So very lovable. Her other line rang. "Look, I've got to go. Conference call."

"Go rule your empire. Bye."

"Bye."

Without skipping a beat, Madeline punched the button on her phone. "Madeline O'Connor," she answered.

So began a string of phone calls that tied Madeline to her desk for another two hours.

Finally, at eight o'clock, Eric poked his head into her office to say good morning and to pass her a note.

Madeline reached for it.

Your car's here.

It was time to go. How did the time pass so quickly? She scowled. Nodded.

Eric scurried around her, packing up her laptop while she finished the call. She was just hanging up when Heather appeared in her door.

What could she want?

"Hi Madeline."

Madeline glanced up at her. "Good morning, Heather," she said formally, and busied herself stuffing a few last minute reports and magazines into her attaché.

"I heard about Carrie." Heather said tentatively. "I'm sorry."

"Thanks." Madeline reached for her laptop from Eric and collected her briefcase, purse.

"Look. I'll take care of things while you're gone. It's the least I can do." She paused. Then, "Any idea how long you'll be?"

Madeline looked hard at Heather. "Sorry. Carrie's death isn't scheduled on my calendar."

Heather broke away from Madeline's glare and looked down. "I really am sorry." She pursed her lips.

Eric stood awkwardly between them. "Madeline, your car's waiting."

Madeline looked at her handsome assistant. "Thanks...for everything."

"No problem. I'll keep you posted." The phone rang and Eric answered, waving at Madeline.

Madeline smiled weakly at him. Nodded. Weighed down with a laptop case on one shoulder, her attaché and purse slung about the other, Madeline wheeled her suitcase behind her and made her way out of Felicity's offices.

* * * *

The black Town Car cocooned Madeline from the bustling city streets. John F. Kennedy airport was fifteen miles from the offices, and the drive offered Madeline a respite from the fast pace of her morning.

Madeline looked out the tinted window at all the people crowding the sidewalks. How was it that there, in the middle of thousands of people, a person felt so alone? *So...lonely.*

Madeline's lower lip quivered and she forced back an uprising of tears.

She would not cry now.

There will be plenty of time for tears later. I'll cry tomorrow.

Instead, Madeline pulled her cell phone from her purse. Dialed.

"Hello?" Veronica's voice was like a warm Italian breeze.

"Veronica, it's Madeline."

"Madeline! *Bon giorno*! How are you?"

"I'm good. Actually, I'm on my way back to Italy."

"Really?" Veronica paused, "Oh, Madeline. Is it your sister?"

"I'm afraid so."

Veronica's tone was quiet. "Oh, I wish I could go back with you. It isn't easy facing these things alone. But Anthony will be there. For Carrie and Jonathan...and for you. Are you going to be all right?"

Madeline's thirsty heart drank in the compassion that Veronica poured. The tears she had been thwarting began to flow freely now.

"I don't know, Veronica. I just don't know. I'm so tired of it all... I'm just so tired. Carrie's dying. And I'm in love with–"

"Anthony." Veronica spoke his name quietly.

"Yes. I'm in love with Anthony," Madeline confessed to Veronica as much as to herself. "You must think I'm terrible."

"No. I knew there was something between you. Anthony wasn't the same after you arrived. Are you going to tell him?"

"Do you think I should?" Madeline's tears subsided.

"Yes, Madeline. I think you should. Love...the real thing...is rare. It should be expressed."

"How can it possibly be the real thing. I barely know him."

"That's what makes love so wonderful...its mysteries. Sometimes just the way someone's voice sounds can make you love him. Just because you don't know what brand of toothpaste Anthony uses doesn't mean your feelings for him aren't real."

Madeline laughed and wondered what kind of toothpaste Anthony used. Wondered what kind of toothpaste Tyler used.

"So you'll tell him?" Veronica pressed.

"Why are you supporting this?"

There was a pause before Veronica answered. "Because I think that love, and life, denied is an affront to God. I believe that God's will for us is to live and to love. It's why I left the abbey. I've often thought that Anthony is hiding at Saint Valentine's. Maybe you're just what he needs to make him leave." Madeline's pulse quickened at the idea of Anthony leaving the monastery.

"Do you think he would?"

"It's a big decision, Madeline. I don't know."

"I'm scared." Madeline admitted.

"It wouldn't be courage if you weren't afraid. You're one of the most courageous people I've ever met. I've lived my life hidden away with nuns. You've been out here in the world. Making things happen. Making mistakes, sure. But you're alive. Vibrant. Passionate. God only gives you what you can handle."

Madeline was soothed by Veronica's words. She sighed. "Thank you, Veronica. I'm lucky to know you."

"Call me anytime. I could use a friend here."

"Me too. Well. I have some other calls to make before my plane leaves. We'll talk soon?" Madeline was glad she had called Veronica.

"I'd like that. Take care. Bye for now."

"Bye." Madeline pressed the "end" button on her phone and reflected on her conversation with Veronica.

God only gives you what you can handle. The thought gave Madeline strength. Maybe she *could* deal with all the challenges she faced.

The Town Car approached the airport and she looked up at the departing planes. Soon, she too would be on her way. To Italy. To Anthony.

To tell him that she loved him.

Part III

Madeline struggled through the crowd at Leonardo da Vinci airport. She had expected to see Anthony and Jonathan at the gate when she arrived, but they had not been there.

How could they have missed each other?

Madeline scanned the blur of faces that passed by. Businessmen. Some beautiful young women, models probably. Some handsome young men. There was something different about Europeans. To Madeline, they seemed more at ease with themselves than Americans.

Or was it that they were more at ease with themselves than she felt with herself? Where *were* Jonathan and Anthony? *Had* they missed each other? Panic began a riot of emotions in her heart. Anxiety. Confusion. Fear.

"Madeline." It was Anthony's resonant voice.

She felt the firm grasp of his hand on her arm and she turned around to see his eyes pouring into hers. At the sight of him, her only feeling was relief. Gently, he slipped the bags from her shoulder and pulled her into his arms. Cloaked her in his gentle strength. Madeline's face burrowed naturally against his shoulder. She let out a long deep breath that she had not realized she'd been holding. In that moment, all was right in the world.

"Anthony," she whispered.

The only thing she wanted was to be alone with him. To tell him how she felt. To *show* him how she felt.

He pulled her close and whispered, "We must go directly to the hospital."

An avalanche of confusion smothered Madeline. Had his embrace been meant to comfort her? Had he intended it as a gesture of friendship? Not a romantic reunion? She pulled away and gazed up at him.

"Carrie is back in the hospital. Jonathan is with her. We really should go." Anthony's expression was serious as he explained.

"What happened?" The confusion and panic were back like boomerangs. Except this time, they brought guilt along. Guilt for desiring Anthony while her sister was back in the hospital.

"She collapsed this morning. The cancer is spreading and her heart is getting weaker. Things aren't good, Madeline."

Her heart is getting weaker.

Madeline furrowed her brow. Set her jaw. Nodded. "Okay. Let's go."

She bent down and wearily started to pick up her bags. Anthony stopped her and took them, leaving Madeline with just her purse to carry. Feeling as though she carried the weight of the world on her shoulders, she looked at him with an unspoken thank you in her eyes.

Understanding, Anthony reached out and took her hand in his as if to say you're welcome. Squeezed gently. "Okay. Let's go."

Their eyes met and held. Anthony's quiet strength reassured Madeline as he took a step toward the exit.

Madeline followed him and, hand in hand, they made their way out of the airport and into the bustling chaos that was Rome.

* * * *

The antiseptic smell of the medical center struck Madeline's nostrils and she was instantly reminded of how much she hated hospitals. Of how much she hated the memories of time spent in them.

Jonathan's accident.

Her mother's death. Her father's death.

Hospitals are places that rob you of everyone that matters. Where you leave behind pieces of your life. Of your heart.

The click of her heels echoed throughout the corridor as she and Anthony made their way to Carrie's room without speaking.

As they approached the doorway, Anthony placed a hand gently, reassuringly, on the small of Madeline's back and ushered her through.

She was completely unprepared for the sight of her sister lying motionless on her side, her back to the door. A clear tube had been carved into a small hole just beneath her shoulder and drained brownish fluid from her lungs into a container beneath the bed. Madeline's stomach churned violently. Bile erupted in her throat. Her hand flew to her mouth. She had never seen a hole carved into a body before.

Carved into her sister's body.

She would have lost her balance were it not for Anthony standing behind her, silently strong and supportive. She swallowed. Struggled to regain her physical and emotional composure.

"Jonathan, is that you?" Carrie's voice was quiet and hoarse.

Madeline opened her mouth to speak but words would not come.

Anthony answered, "No, Carrie. It's me." He paused. "And Madeline."

"Madeline," Carrie said quietly.

"Hello Carrie," Madeline said.

"Come. Sit where I can see you." Carrie gestured to the chair placed in the corner beside her bed.

Madeline looked up at Anthony. He nodded in the chair's direction. Madeline slowly walked toward it.

"Where's Jonathan?" Anthony asked.

"I remember now. He's at home, looking in on Truffles," Carrie answered.

Carrie's cat. Madeline had forgotten all about Truffles. Her spirits were heavy as she moved her exhausted body into the chair and looked at her frail sister lying in the hospital bed.

Self-loathing dripped into Madeline's heart like the I-V that she watched. What kind of a sister had she been to Carrie? She had not even remembered that Carrie had a cat. Then again, Carrie had never known how Madeline took her tea. And when Madeline remembered Carrie and David's betrayal, her guilt was blustered away by a gust of anger.

With empty eyes that already had the vacant stare of a soul departed, Carrie looked at Madeline.

"Jonathan has been such a wonderful son to me," Carrie said.

I've been such a terrible sister...

"Jonathan is wonderful," Madeline managed through her conflicted emotions.

"And I've been such a terrible mother," Carrie said and held out a limp hand to Madeline. "And a terrible sister." She voiced Madeline's thoughts.

Madeline looked at it, not knowing what to say. She looked up at Anthony who stood leaning against a wall and watched them. His eyes met Madeline's and, unable to hold them, his gaze dropped to the floor. Madeline looked back at Carrie. Took her hand and held it.

Carrie smiled faintly and sunk deeply into her pillow. "I'm glad you came. But I'm tired now. Could I have a sip of water?"

Madeline stared at her sister and inwardly shuddered. This time she had come to Italy to watch Carrie die. All she had been able to think of was seeing Anthony again. While Carrie was dying.

Unshed tears of shame began to sting Madeline's eyes. Gently, she placed Carrie's hand back on the bed. Her own trembled as she reached for the small carafe of water and poured. It took all Carrie's strength to lift her head to receive the water. Madeline held the glass to Carrie's parched lips while her sister took a sip and let her head fall back on the pillow.

Madeline watched as Carrie closed her eyes and slipped into sleep. She collapsed back into the chair and looked up for Anthony.

He was gone.

Madeline's whole body ached with fatigue and her eyelids were leaden with want of sleep.

"Anthony, where are you?" Madeline sighed.

The next moment, she was asleep.

* * * *

For the next week, Madeline visited Carrie in the hospital every day. She reserved a small suite in a nearby hotel to be close to the medical center. Quickly, her routine became one of working evenings to make calls to New York, sometimes staying up until midnight in order to reach associates, then rising early to spend the day at the hospital with Carrie.

She had seen Anthony at the hospital every day, too. He and Jonathan drove into Rome from Saint Valentine's. It was obvious they were close, closer even than Madeline had initially thought. It had become a practice for them to smuggle gelato into the hospital for Carrie. It was not long before they started bringing it for Madeline, too, and the four of them would sit in Carrie's room and talk and laugh and eat their gelato.

There were times, during a moment of laughter, when Madeline would look at Anthony and catch him looking at her, too. Carrie would pretend not to notice. Somehow, in the midst of death, those simple moments of shared laughter became messengers of life. Reminders of its eternal essence. Of what really mattered. Sometimes it hurt Carrie to laugh. Those moments became reminders of death. That life and death are married. That one cannot be—cannot *be*—without the other.

It had been a long emotional week and Madeline felt exhausted and overwhelmed. Desperate to find a new CFO, she was working fervently with an executive search firm. The recruiters were doing an excellent job of prescreening candidates. Tyler had been right; there were plenty of talented finance professionals very interested in the position. Still, the search ultimately required Madeline to meet with candidates. She had no idea when she would be able to return to New York.

Finally it was Saturday morning. Madeline was still asleep in bed when the clamor of her ringing phone jolted her awake.

"*Buon giorno*. This is your wake up call," Madeline said to herself groggily as she reached over to pick up the phone.

"Thank you," she moaned into the receiver, and hung up.

It rang again. She picked it up again.

"Madeline. Don't hang up. It's me."

Tyler.

He had tried to reach her unsuccessfully for the last three days. Between the nine hour time difference and their respective schedules, it had been difficult for them to connect with each other.

Madeline sat up. "Hi," she said.

"Hi. How's Carrie?"

Madeline raked a hand through her hair. Sighed. "Touch and go." She pictured Carrie lying in the hospital bed, her body connected to sensors and tubes and toxic with drugs. "God, Tyler. Is this what we all have to look forward to?"

There was a short pause. Madeline imagined Tyler, handsome in a crisp white shirt. Platinum cufflinks. Silk tie. Contemplating death in his investment banker's office.

"I suppose so," he finally said. "I suppose that's why we're supposed to be living. Have you thought about...things?"

Madeline knew he was referring to his proposal and anger swelled in the pit of her stomach. How could he be so selfish? She was a world away watching Carrie die and all he cared about was roping her into a commitment.

"Tyler, I'm sorry. I just–so much has been going on."

"Be careful, Madeline. That's when life happens. When so much else is going on."

"Be careful? Of what?" Was he threatening her?

"That you don't let life pass you by."

"Life isn't passing me by, Tyler. This is it. I'm living my life."

"Are you? You haven't been in a successful relationship in years."

"And is that it, Tyler? Is that what life is about? A successful relationship? What is that, anyway?" She sighed, "I don't even know."

"Exactly." His tone was cold. Sharp.

He cut her to the quick. The strain caught up with her. The

stress of dealing with nurses. Doctors. Even good ones. The exhaustion. Felicity. The smell of the hospital. The smell of sickness and death. And now Tyler.

She threw back the covers. Hurled out of bed. Paced. "Cut the pop psychology crap. Have you been talking to a shrink? This is life, Tyler. This is *it*. Companies fail. People lie. People die. You're sitting there thousands of miles away in your ivory tower trying to tell me it can be different. It can. But it isn't. This is it, Tyler. Right here. Right now!"

"It's about choices, Madeline. You do have them."

"Choices Tyler? Choices! Just what am I supposed to do? Shop for wedding dresses while Carrie's in the hospital? What do you want from me?"

There was tension in the wordless pause before Tyler spoke. "The question, Madeline, is what do you have to give?"

His words sliced through Madeline's anger and it collapsed like a house of cards. She was silenced.

What *did* she have to give?

She did not know. Nothing, maybe.

"If you need an answer now, in this moment, it's no." The words were out before she could take them back. She held her breath. Regretted having said them.

There was a long silence.

"Look, I've got a call I've got to take. I've got to go." Tyler said.

Just as Madeline said, "Good bye," he hung up.

Madeline's mind whirled with conflicting thoughts as she placed the receiver back in its cradle. She had told him no. Her mind was racing. How could she have told him no? Was it because she was in love with a monk she could never have?

Everything was happening so quickly. Changing so quickly. Tyler had everything a woman could want. And he loved her. But he wasn't Anthony. Was her answer really no? Was there a part of her that wanted to say yes?

I don't know. I just don't know!

The phone rang again. Maybe it was Tyler. Somehow Madeline wanted it to be. Saying he loved her and she could take her time. Apologizing for pressuring her.

"Hello?"

"Madeline. It's Anthony. You need to get here. Now."

The sound of his voice was a beacon of light in the storm that battered the shores of Madeline's soul. "What is it?" she asked, already knowing the answer.

"Madeline," Anthony said simply. "It's time."

* * * *

When Madeline arrived at Carrie's hospital room, the bed was empty.

"Oh, my God," Madeline gasped and leaned against the door-frame, staring in disbelief at the bed where Carrie had been just the night before.

How could I have missed her?

A collage of memories played in Madeline's mind. Fleeting scenes of happy childhood days at the beach building sandcastles. Carrie playing with her kittens. Ice cream sundaes at the local parlor.

Her thoughts finally settled upon a time when the two of them had gone shopping with their mother. They were looking for Madeline's prom dress, and she had fallen in love with a rich forest green taffeta gown. It was strapless and showed off her long neck and stunning young figure. Her mother had found a white satin dress that was also beautiful but that Madeline hated. Madeline had tearfully begged her mother for the green gown. But it wasn't until Carrie took their mother by the hand, led her away and talked to her privately, that their mother allowed Madeline to have the green dress. Madeline never knew what it was that Carrie had said.

And I never will, Madeline thought.

"Oh, my God. Oh, my God. Oh, my God." Madeline repeated the phrase over and over and over and slid to the floor, hugging her knees.

"Madeline!" Anthony dropped to the floor and clutched her shoulders firmly. Shook her gently.

Madeline, dazed, looked at him. Then fell into his arms. "I've missed her!" she cried. "I've missed her."

Anthony pressed her away and cupped her face in his hands. "No! No! She was moved to another room, Madeline. That's all. She was moved to another room." His eyes clung to hers. He stroked her cheek.

Madeline was overcome with relief. And by the nearness of Anthony. By his voice. By his touch. Her skin melted beneath his fingertips.

"Another room?" she whispered, her eyes gazing into Anthony's.

He pulled her into his arms. Buried his face in her hair. They sat on the cold hospital floor in the doorway of Carrie's old room. Clinging to each other. Clinging to life.

* * * *

Madeline was grateful for the guiding hand that Anthony placed reassuringly on her elbow as she walked into Carrie's room. Carrie was lying on her back, staring at the ceiling, but turned her head when she heard them. Her complexion had taken on a yellow pall. Her hair seemed dull and lifeless. But it was Carrie's eyes that startled Madeline. They were distant. Empty. No. They were full. But of what? Death? Truth? Fear? Madeline could not tell. Anthony's gentle pressure on her elbow urged her on.

"Hello," Carrie said with a strange grin on her face. "You two."

You two. As though Madeline and Anthony were a couple.

"The doctors are giving her morphine," Anthony whispered, placing a hand on Madeline's shoulder.

Carrie snapped, "Don't talk about me as if I'm not here. As if I were already gone."

Morphine. It had come to that. Madeline stood and looked at Carrie. Took a deep breath.

This was at once a strange and familiar place. She could see their dying mother in Carrie. Their father's death had been different. A sudden fatal accident. But death had lingered with their mother like a long lost friend sipping lemonade on the front porch. It had been an endless battle with cancer.

It struck Madeline that her parents were dying again along with Carrie. Her sister was all that was left of her immediate family. And they had wasted so much time. Seven years. Estranged. Angry. Hurt. And Carrie was already gone. The drugs had taken her.

Madeline swallowed the hard lump that had formed in her throat.

What Carrie had done was unforgivable.

Wasn't it?

Anthony squeezed Madeline's shoulder softly.

"Hi," Madeline greeted Carrie.

Carrie smiled and stared back at the ceiling. Madeline looked at Anthony. Into his dark eyes.

"Maybe you should just sit down a while," Anthony said. "I'm going to pick Jonathan up from Saint Valentine's."

He pulled the small chair out for Madeline and she reluctantly sat. She reached for his hand. Begged him to stay with her eyes.

He shook his head slightly. "I won't be long."

He squeezed her hand reassuringly and was gone, leaving Madeline alone with her sister.

Carrie moaned quietly. A slight sound that belied the depth of pain Madeline could see she was in. Carrie looked around the hospital room. At the sage green walls. Out the small window at the clear blue sky. Then directly at Madeline.

"So this is the room where I will die," Carrie said with surprising clarity.

Tears swam in Madeline's eyes. She reached out to take Carrie's hand in her own. It was cold. Weak. Small. Madeline was overcome with an unfamiliar feeling of powerlessness as Carrie's words hung heavily in the air.

What could she say? This *was* the room where Carrie would die.

"It's okay, Maddie. It's okay," Carrie spoke quietly. "I'm so tired of this world."

So am I, Madeline thought, tears streaming down her face openly.

"You know, Maddie, I would never ask you to forgive me. Because the truth is, I'm not sorry for how I've lived my life. I'm not sorry for loving David. But I am deeply sorry that I hurt you."

Madeline struggled to find the right words. What were they? That it was okay? Because it wasn't. Or was it? Nothing seemed to make sense any more. Or matter. What really mattered? Here. Now. While Carrie was dying.

Until finally, "You did hurt me, Carrie." It was the truth, and after saying it aloud, Madeline felt better. Lighter.

"I know. I spent the last seven years hating myself for it. It was why things didn't work out with David, I think. I hated myself so how could I possibly have loved him? I wonder sometimes if it's why I got sick."

Madeline's lips quivered. All these years she imagined Carrie and David living happily ever after together. How irrational that belief had been. She tried to make herself forget. With work. With Felicity. But she had not forgotten. She only buried her pain and hurt.

What had it all been for? What had been the cost?

She looked down at her sister and saw the young girl that Carrie once had been. Memories of their shared childhood flooded back.

"Carrie?" Madeline asked through her tears.

"What is it?"

"Do you remember the day you and Mom and I went shopping for my prom dress?"

Carrie smiled faintly. Nodded slowly. "Mom wanted that horrible white thing."

"What was it you said to her that made her change her mind?"

Carrie's eyes filled with tears of her own now, and the two sisters looked at each other through the eyes of teenage girls. "I told her that if she got you the green one, I'd keep my room clean for a month."

Madeline laughed. Carrie's room had never been clean while her own had always been impeccable.

Carrie laughed too, but had to stop when it began to hurt.

"I remember Mom just looked at me and said 'You must love your sister after all'".

Tears cascaded from Carrie's eyes and she nodded, unable to speak.

Madeline moved to sit on the side of Carrie's bed and pulled her sister into her arms. Started to cry, too. They sat like that for a long time. Two sisters. Holding each other, and crying.

It was Carrie who pulled away first, and looked seriously at Madeline. "You love Anthony, don't you?" she asked. The morphine made her brave.

Madeline avoided answering and reached for a tissue to dab the wetness from Carrie's face. Then did the same for her own eyes and cheeks.

"It's okay, you know, to love him. He is one of the most beautiful souls I have ever known."

"But I'll never have him," Madeline said.

"Oh, Madeline. It isn't about having him. Just love him. The rest will fall place into place. Or not. But either way, the love will stay with you forever. Love doesn't need a reason, Madeline."

"That's a beautiful thought," Madeline said. It reminded her of something Veronica would say. Or Anthony.

Madeline watched the corners of Carrie's lips curl upward in a small smile. Secretly she marveled at her sister. Her courage now in the face of death. Her love of life. Her love of love.

A tentative knock on the door broke the moment.

"Hello," a familiar male voice said.

Both women looked up and Madeline's breath caught when she saw him.

David.

Of course she should have expected him to come, yet somehow it was a surprise. Jonathan appeared behind him. Then Anthony.

Well the gang's all here, Madeline thought wryly and for a moment felt like the New Yorker that she was. She watched her ex-husband.

David looked at her. Then at Carrie. He walked quietly toward them, his expression serious.

Madeline saw him through new eyes now. Saw past the designer clothes and polished demeanor to see the small boy underneath it all who, more than anything, needed to be loved. Even if he himself didn't know it.

"Madeline, hello," he said, and bent down to give her a kiss on the cheek that was no more than a breath.

"Carrie," he said.

Madeline stood up and David took her place on the bed beside Carrie. His eyes were glistening with tears and he took Carrie's hand and they shared a long look.

Jonathan moved past Madeline and sat with his parents.

Madeline turned and looked at Anthony. He held out a hand to her. He gestured toward the door.

Relieved, Madeline walked to him and took his hand. It was strong. Warm.

"We'll be back," he said.

Madeline turned to look back at her sister, who only smiled.

* * * *

"Where are we going?" Madeline asked.

"Shh...it is a secret," Anthony answered with a boyish grin.

Madeline shook her head and laughed easily. Anthony was like a tonic. The perfect remedy for Madeline's ailing spirit. It surprised her how easily he could make her laugh. For just a moment, he reminded her of Tyler. Not in the way he looked. But in the way he looked at her. With such affection.

Such love.

Something was different about being with Anthony. Madeline felt a connection with him that was missing with Tyler. It was almost as though they had known each other all their lives. All of many lives, perhaps.

It will always be this way, Madeline thought.

"I hate secrets," she teased. Anthony smiled directly at her with such innocent abandon that she had no reply save a shy smile.

Together they strolled through Rome's chaotic but charmed streets. Stopped to browse in a shop or two. Rome was a magical city. Not unlike New York with its millions of people and urban sprawl. But it seemed to Madeline to have more heart. As though all the people throughout all the ages who had lived there left an imprint of their lives. Their stories.

The thought flickered across Madeline's mind that perhaps what she felt for Anthony had more to do with Italy than with him. Even the Italian air caressed her with the intoxicating whisper of a fall wind. Except one look at him. At his dark eyes. His strong jaw. But there was more to him than his handsome features. Carrie was right. Anthony was a beautiful soul. Madeline was convinced yet again that she loved him.

He led her down some steps and into a Metro station. They chatted casually about Rome. Saint Valentine's. Veronica. Anything that had nothing to do with Carrie. Or Felicity. Or real life.

Why is it that we think of real life as our troubles? Our responsibilities. Why isn't real life moments like this? Moments of such simple...joy?

Madeline allowed herself the unfamiliar indulgence of forgetting all her troubles. She wanted to simply enjoy being in Rome. Of riding the train. With Anthony. The warmth of his palm pressed against hers was reassuring. Inviting. It gave her permission to be herself.

"Where are we going, Anthony?" Madeline looked into the depths of Anthony's eyes with an open smile.

"Shh...we're almost there."

"Where?"

"Must you always have an answer?" He smiled back at her now.

Yes. "No," she answered.

"We're almost there. Have a little faith." He grinned. Squeezed her hand.

Where? Madeline refrained from asking him again and instead pondered his question. Did she always need to have an answer?

Have a little faith. *Faith.*

I don't have faith.

It was a painful revelation. One that surprised Madeline. But something in her mind clicked into place and everything was all so clear now. Why she needed to be in control at Felicity. Why she had buried herself in her work. Why she had not allowed herself to fall in love again. She saw now that her whole view of the world was based on her need to control.

The truth was that she had none. Even now, in this moment, she was a passenger on a subway. Just a passenger on a subway. Someone else was driving. Anything could happen. Even her destination was not in her control. But if she didn't have control, who did? Was everything a question of trust? Was life itself the ultimate act of faith? Just living?

Anthony had been watching her think.

"We're here," he said quietly.

Madeline looked at him.

"Come on, let's go." Anthony stood up and pulled her off her seat.

They emerged from the train at The Vatican station. People milled about everywhere. And the line! It was the longest line Madeline had ever seen.

"Don't worry about the line...I have connections." Anthony winked. Laughed. "I used to give tours here and have friends in high places." He laughed again.

Madeline laughed, too. How good it felt to laugh. How young. Free. Light.

Here Madeline was at The Vatican. It was a place she had always wanted to see but had never made the time. She stopped walking and Anthony turned around to look at her.

"Are you all right?" he asked.

"I've always wanted to see The Vatican. I've always come to Rome alone. So I've never gone. Thank you. It's a wonderful surprise."

"Madeline, you're never alone. Wherever you are. Remember that." Anthony was earnest when he spoke. He pulled her to him and kissed her gently on the cheek. "You're welcome."

Of course. Someone like Anthony was never alone. He lives close to God. He lives *in* God. The way a fish lives in water. God was in the very air that Anthony breathed.

But we breathe the same air, Madeline thought. *We breathe the same air.*

* * * *

Reverence washed through Madeline as she stepped into the building's stillness. Reverence. Awe. Humility. She could not help but marvel at the history that was steeped within its walls. And the art. Michelangelo himself had walked these floors. Perhaps where Madeline and Anthony now stood. She took in the scenes on the walls and ceilings of the Sistine Chapel with childlike wonder.

"It's funny, isn't it?" she whispered.

"What's funny?" Anthony squeezed her hand.

"How fleeting life is."

"Fleeting?"

"I mean, people come and go. We're born and we die. And for what? What is it all for?" Madeline looked at Anthony for an answer.

He responded with a question. "Does it have to be for something?"

"Yes...otherwise it's all so meaningless," Madeline replied.

"What if we're simply here to love and to learn?"

"To love and to learn?" Madeline looked vulnerable as she looked up at Anthony.

"Shhhhhhhh!" A Vatican staff member admonished them. Silence was to be observed in the Chapel.

Anthony nodded. He took Madeline's hand and led her underneath the scene of the Delphic Sibyl and pointed upward at the ceiling.

Madeline took a quick breath at the painting of a young woman with an undeniable resemblance to herself. The image was striking, with radiant skin, wide eyes and tendrils of red hair blown by a soft wind. She was unwinding a scroll with her left hand and seemed to be turning to look right at Madeline.

Anthony smiled. "See the resemblance. What is most beautiful, about both of you, is that you are both essentially feminine. You both embody womanhood at its very best. Strong. Powerful. Vulnerable. It is hard to imagine either of you in bondage to a male."

Madeline dropped her eyes to the floor. "I'm not so strong and powerful."

Anthony gently lifted her chin until she met his eyes with hers.

"You are stronger and more powerful than you know. But not because you run a company. Because of who you are. Because of your strength of heart. Because you strive for high ideals, even if you don't always reach them. It is the striving that matters."

"Oh, Anthony," Madeline smiled an embarrassed smile and looked away.

He pulled her eyes to his again. "I love you Madeline. More than I can possibly tell you. I've made a decision. To leave Saint Valentine's. I can no longer honor my vows in good faith. I want you Madeline, more than I've ever wanted anything."

Madeline felt as though her heart had broken with joy. "Anthony, I love you, too."

"Shhh!"

Anthony smiled. He took her into his arms then and kissed her. Fully. Passionately. Tenderly. With Michelangelo's Adam and Eve and angels bearing witness to his declaration.

* * * *

By the time Madeline and Anthony returned to the hospital, she was at once elated and exhausted. Joy and grief exchanged places in her heart with the abandon of children playing musical chairs. Everything in her life had careened out of her control. But strangely, it was all perfectly orchestrated in a random sort of way. All Madeline could do was respond. Resist or surrender. To events. And to herself. *How* she would respond was her choice. Hers and hers alone.

The door to Carrie's room was closed when they reached it and David and Jonathan were standing outside in the hall. Jonathan was clearly shaken and David looked serious.

"What's happening?" Madeline asked.

"The doctor is in there with Mom," Jonathan answered.

Madeline nodded. She liked Carrie's doctor and had come to trust him. He was, after all, one of the best in his field. But even the finest doctor could only do so much, and despite all the recent advances in treating cancer, it still remained a fatal disease for many. Carrie had fought bravely. But it was clear she was losing. Maybe even wanted to lose.

Madeline leaned against the wall and folded her arms across her chest. Her body was suddenly heavy with fatigue and it was an effort to stand. She closed her eyes. The smell of death hung heavily in the air.

I wonder how I will die, Madeline thought.

The idea of her own death had never crossed Madeline's mind and she found that she did not feel afraid.

I suppose how we die isn't as important as how we live.

The thought reminded her of Tyler's words. *I suppose that's why we're supposed to be living*. His face appeared vividly in her mind's eye. His blue eyes dancing with life. His lips always at the ready for a kiss or a smile. Tyler made things happen with thought followed by decisive action. He made mistakes of course. But learned from them. Yet he wasn't pushy or aggressive. He had his own way of being in the world. Like a sailboat navigating a course and leaving behind its wake.

Madeline respected him. He had a zeal for life and went after what he wanted fully expecting to get it. She knew he wanted her.

A hand placed gently on her shoulder drew her back to the hospital corridor. She opened her eyes and saw that Adam, Carrie's doctor, had emerged from Carrie's room.

"Why don't you all come with me for a moment," he said in a soft voice.

The foursome followed him to a small waiting area. They were silent as they each took seats, except for Adam, who remained standing. The lump in Madeline's throat prevented her from speaking.

"News like this is never easy," he paused before continuing.

"Carrie has lost consciousness. Her body is simply shutting itself off and she has slipped into a coma. I don't expect that she will come out of it. She left specific instructions that if this happened, she did not want to be kept alive artificially. She wanted to be allowed to die," he said. "Gracefully."

Madeline took in the doctor's words. So that was it then.

"But just a few hours ago..." Madeline trailed off. A brief silence. "What happens next?"

"Right now, we're keeping her alive with glucose and a respirator. Whenever you're ready, I'd like to remove them."

"What does that mean, exactly?" Madeline's heart started racing.

"Madeline, you're her only relative. It seems like something you should decide," Adam said.

"It's what Carrie wants, isn't it?" Madeline's eyes burned with tears.

"I can show you the papers."

"No. I think I'd like to see her," Madeline said. She stood up and Anthony rose with her.

"I understand," the doctor said.

Madeline nodded and looked at Anthony. "I need to see her. Jonathan, will you come with me?"

The young novice's eyes were wet, too, but he nodded. He stood up and walked over to Madeline. They left the waiting room together and made their way back to Carrie's room in silence.

"I'd like a minute alone with her. Is that okay?" Madeline asked.

Again Jonathan simply nodded in response. Madeline pressed her palm to his cheek and smiled. More for herself than for him.

She pushed open the door to Carrie's room. Nothing prepared her for the sight of her sister. Tubes and wires were connected to Carrie's motionless body and Madeline had the sense that she walked onto a movie set instead of her sister's hospital room. This could not be real. But it was.

"Oh, Carrie," Madeline inhaled the words through a sob.

She walked over to the bed and sank down on the small chair. Only this morning, Carrie had been talking. Smiling. But now she was perfectly still. The only signs of what life remained were the faint rise and fall of her chest and the blinking of the monitors.

Everything had changed in the last few hours. Anthony was leaving Saint Valentine's. And Carrie was leaving this world.

Madeline was suddenly overcome with grief for all that she had lost. And was losing. Her life would never be the same after today. She could no longer be angry at her sister.

If anything, it's Carrie who should be angry with me, Madeline thought.

"I wish I had forgiven you long ago. We lost so much time. I'm so sorry, Carrie. I'm so sorry," Madeline whispered.

She wanted to cry but found she could not.

I have had enough of tears.

The long slow hiss of the respirator was the only sound in the room. It seemed to Madeline that the machine mocked life, instead of supporting it. Artificial respiration. This was not life.

A calm clarity spread throughout Madeline. Enough with half lived lives. She understood Carrie's decision now. Artificial life was not living. Whether it be in a hospital room or a Manhattan high rise. It was not good enough.

Madeline looked down at Carrie through new eyes. Carrie had lived a happy life. She had made her own choices and had followed her heart. Carrie had been true to herself. For that, Madeline found she respected her sister.

She heard Carrie's words again. "I am tired of this world," she had said.

So now, Madeline listened to her heart and knew that the right thing to do was to let Carrie go. She wanted to go, it was clear. It was time. Enough of this lingering between worlds. Between life and death. Between life and *life*.

Madeline stood up and bent over to gently kiss Carrie on both cheeks. She squeezed Carrie's hand one final time.

"I love you, Carrie," Madeline said, smiling peacefully. "You can go now."

She walked out the room into the hallway where Adam, Anthony, Jonathan, and David were waiting. Her eyes met Adam's and she nodded.

"After it's done, how much time is there?" Madeline asked Adam.

"A day or two. Maybe less. Maybe more. It's hard to say."

Madeline looked at Jonathan who was standing beside his father. David had placed a hand reassuringly on Jonathan's shoulder. It occurred to Madeline that with Carrie's departure, perhaps David would be more involved in Jonathan's life. As involved in a monk's life as was possible.

"Okay then," Madeline said. "Go ahead."

"Why don't you all get some rest. There's nothing more you can do here."

"I'd want to stay, if that's okay," Jonathan said.

David squeezed his son's shoulder. "I'll stay, too."

"That's fine. You're welcome to. I'll send the nurses in and once they're done, you can stay as long as you like."

Madeline watched Adam leave them and walk over to the nurses' station. She assumed he was telling them to remove Carrie's life support.

"Madeline?" Anthony asked.

"Adam's right. Let's go." Carrie was with her family, her son and his father. *They should have their time.* "I think I'd like to get some rest," she said. She walked over to Jonathan and took him into her arms. "I'll see you later," she whispered to him.

She pulled away from Jonathan and walked over to David. He took her hand in his and looked deeply into her eyes. "I'm so sorry, Madeline."

Madeline wondered for a moment if he meant he was sorry about Carrie. Or about everything. But it didn't matter anymore. There had been a time when an apology from David would have meant everything to her. But now, there was truly nothing to be sorry for.

"Thank you, David," was all she said.

She turned to Anthony now and reached for his hand and as they had done earlier that day, they walked out of the hospital together.

Hand in hand.

* * * *

Madeline awkwardly opened the door to her hotel suite.

"You must be exhausted," Anthony said.

Madeline turned and gazed into the depths of his dark eyes and wanted with all her heart to understand the mysteries she saw. It occurred to her that there were things about Anthony she would never quite understand. A part of him would always be a mystery. That was, in part, why she loved him.

"Actually, no. The truth is, I really don't know how I feel. Everything is changing," Madeline's tone was quiet.

They stood at the threshold of Madeline's room, neither of them quite sure of what would happen next.

"Stay with me tonight." The words were out before Madeline could stop them. She could not take them back. Nor did she want to. She was through with thoughts of death and dying. She wanted to live. To feel alive. To love.

"Madeline, I'm not so sure that would be–"

"Just come in," she said holding his eyes with hers. She wanted him. She had wanted him from the first moment she saw him. And he was here. Now. And she loved him. "Just come in. Don't leave me alone tonight. Please." She had not felt so vulnerable in years. All she knew was that they had to be together. But what if he refused? She held her breath and looked up at him.

They shared a long look. Madeline stepped inside the room and Anthony followed.

"Would you like a glass of wine?" she asked. "I could certainly use one." She was nervous suddenly and smiled awkwardly. As she walked to the wet bar, she tried to imagine how he must be feeling. Was he anxious? Afraid? Consumed with wanting?

Like me.

"Please." His voice was just above a whisper.

He watched as she poured the glistening red liquid into glasses and held one out to him. Raised her own.

"I'd like to propose a toast," she said. She wanted to forget that her sister was dying just a few blocks away. Yes by God, tonight she would forget. She would forget all the years that had been filled with pain and loneliness. She would be with Anthony. He loved her. He would leave Saint Valentine's and they would sort everything out later. But tonight, all she wanted was to be with him. She thought of Carrie. Of how her sister had followed her heart. Broken the rules. Lived life without regrets.

Yes. Carrie would approve. Celebrate, even.

Madeline clinked her glass lightly against Anthony's. "To life.

To life and to living it. Living it to the fullest."

He smiled at her. "You're a strong woman, Madeline. To life and to living it."

In concert they raised their glasses to their lips and drank. Madeline felt the warmth of the wine as it seductively caressed her throat.

"I love you, Anthony." Tears sprang to her eyes as she said the words. "I love you so very very much. I could not have made it through this without you."

"Oh Madeline. Yes...you could have. But I'm glad that I was here," Anthony's voice was rich with wanting her. His accent, as always, enchanting.

He pulled her to him and kissed her with such passionate tenderness that Madeline thought her heart would break from the love she felt for him. She pressed her body against his and felt how much he wanted her.

She pulled away from him to look into his eyes. The feelings she saw there were unmistakable. He did love her. Every fiber of her body knew it. Madeline had never been more sure of anything in her life.

She slid her hand down his arm and clasped his hand. Led him into the bedroom. She turned the lights on dimly and a warm glow cast about the room. He stood and watched as she undressed. Slowly slipping off her silk blouse and skirt to reveal the lingerie that had made her who she was. She reached behind her back and unclasped her bra, letting it float to the floor and revealing her breasts to him.

She could see the rise and fall of his chest quicken with his heightened desire. They held each other's eyes in what felt like a spell cast upon Madeline's soul. Misty remembrances of loving Anthony lifetimes ago sealed Madeline's fate. She felt as though they were both rendered powerless against some kind of preordained agreement. A sacred contract. It was done before it had even begun. Madeline felt her own chest rising and falling rapidly now.

She was breathless as Anthony walked to her. He collected her into his arms and a moment later she was lying on the bed before him. With deliberate hands he slid off her panties and she was naked. She watched, mesmerized, as his hungry eyes took her in as he towered over her.

Anthony ripped his shirt over his head revealing his chiseled upper body. Deftly he slipped off his pants and revealed his full desire. They were both naked now. He rushed to her. Cupped her breasts with both hands and moaned softly at the hardness of her nipples. He pressed the side of his face against her stomach and wrapped his hands around her hips. Nothing existed for Madeline but this moment. The electric feeling of Anthony's hands exploring her body. She raked her fingers through his dark hair. Pulled him to her for a long deep kiss. A kiss that reawakened her sleeping soul.

"Madeline." Anthony said her name quietly and gazed into her eyes.

For the next hour, they discovered each other's bodies. Licking here. Lingering there. Kissing. Touching. Stroking. Caressing. Madeline savored every second as Anthony smelled and sipped her body like a vintage wine, drinking her in with his eyes, nose, and lips.

Finally Madeline was engulfed by her need for him. She rolled onto her back and pulled her to him and they kissed gently. Then more passionately. Opening herself fully to him she guided him inside her and they surrendered to each other fully. Completely. Madeline thrilled at the sensation of having him inside her. He moved slowly at first. Then more quickly.

Too quickly.

It was over almost as soon as it had begun. Madeline cradled Anthony to her breasts and smiled. His inexperience had revealed itself and she found it charming and much more attractive than the alternative. She had never been with a virgin before. *Tonight was a first for both of us.* And it had been at once satisfying. And unsatisfying.

They tried again. And again. And again. Until they both wilted with pleasure. Madeline took in a long slow satisfied breath. Released it with a quiet moan. She felt a warmth–a sweetness–in her body that she had never experienced before. Her heart, her soul, was filled with a feeling of love that was so tender and so precious that she thought she would break. But she did not break. Instead, she smiled peacefully. Contentedly.

A moment later, they were both asleep, Madeline cupped perfectly against Anthony, enveloped by his arms.

* * * *

Someone is in the room, Madeline thought. She opened her eyes. Then dismissed the idea. Then opened her eyes again. The room was dark. Quiet. Cold. She wanted to move but could not. She felt paralyzed, frozen in place. With all her strength, she rolled over in bed. Carrie stood at her side, illuminated by a soft warm glow. Anthony? Where is Anthony?

Carrie?

Madeline stared up at her sister who was looking down at her with love-filled eyes.

"Carrie? What are you doing here?" Madeline asked, afraid but not afraid. Filled with panic. And peace.

Carrie simply smiled in response. A happy joyful smile.

For a long moment, the two sisters gazed into each other's eyes.

Finally, Carrie faded away. Into nothingness.

Madeline tossed and turned in bed. "Carrie?"

She was cold. The air in the room was ice. Yet she was sweaty. Had she been sleeping? Or dreaming?

It seemed so...so...real.

The phone rang and startled her. Her heart raced. She looked at the time. Five thirty.

Who would call at this hour?

And she knew.

She reached over to the nightstand and picked up the receiver and heard a familiar but unfamiliar voice.

"Madeline, it's David. Carrie. She's...she's gone, Madeline. She's gone."

"No–she was just–oh, my God," Madeline said, sitting up in bed. She turned to look at Anthony.

But she was alone. His clothes were missing. Had he left? Certainly he could not have. Could he? Anger rushed into her heart as she wrestled with the idea that Anthony was gone. How could he? How could he have left her after the intimacy they had just shared?

"Madeline?" David jarred Madeline back.

She shook her head sharply as though trying to shake off the memory of Anthony. "Where's Jonathan?" she finally asked.

"He's here with me. I'll drive him back to Saint Valentine's later today. We spent the night at the hospital. We were sleeping when it happened. It was peaceful, Madeline. She died in her sleep."

"When?"

"A few hours ago."

Madeline and Anthony had been making love when Carrie died. A sickening sense of guilt washed over Madeline.

I should have been at the hospital. I should have been there.

Silent tears ran down her face. "I wish I'd been there. It was good of you to be with Jonathan," Madeline acknowledged David.

"He's my son. It's about time I was there for him, don't you think? We all have regrets, Madeline. Don't worry. There was nothing you could have done."

Madeline was surprised at David. Empathy had not come so easily to him in the past. Maybe he had learned there was more to life than fast cars, expensive clothes, and easy women. Maybe he'd had enough of the fast lane. Of caviar and martinis.

I have, she thought, surprising herself.

"I want to come with you to Saint Valentine's," Madeline said. *I need to see Anthony.*

"Sure. Why don't we pick you up in a few hours. Nine?" David sounded surprised.

"Perfect. I'll see you then," Madeline answered.

She hung up the phone and sunk deeply into the pillow. Knowing that Carrie was going to die was much different than knowing she had. Her sister was gone. Nothing had quite prepared her for the reality of it. Except for Jonathan, she was alone now. Alone.

Sobs rose in her throat and she tried to bury them. But regret and sorrow and grief would not be dissuaded. They demanded release. She did not have the will left to deny them.

So she cried. A long hard cry that was physically exhausting but cleansing. The kind of cry that every woman needs once in a while. Madeline was in its final throes when the phone rang.

She blinked the last of her tears from her eyes and reached for a tissue. Blew her red swollen nose.

"Hello?" Her voice was nasal, as though she had a cold.

"Madeline?" Tyler asked. "Are you okay?"

Madeline closed her eyes. Tyler always had a way of knowing when she needed someone. He was always there.

"Carrie died last night." Tyler was the first person she told.

"Oh, God, Madeline. I'm sorry. I'll be right there."

Madeline smiled at his eager support. "Tyler, you don't need to fly all the way here."

"Maddie, I'm already here. I'm calling from the lobby."

Madeline needed a moment to wrap her mind around his words. "You're here? In the lobby?" She repeated, bewildered.

"Umm hmm. I'll be right there."

Click. He hung up.

He's here. He really came!

Madeline sat back against her pillow and blew her nose again. She was just gathering herself to get out of bed when there was a knock on the door. She walked through the suite and, on the way, caught her passing reflection in a mirror. Her face was pale. Her eyes swollen. Her nose red. But there was something different. A look in her eyes beyond the scarlet. A kind of peace. Somehow she had...softened. Opened.

Madeline wondered if making love with Anthony had done that.

There was another small knock and Madeline took one last look at herself. It was as good as it was going to get.

She continued to the door and opened it.

Tyler stood there. He had actually flown all the way from New York to be with her. And she loved him for it in spite of everything. Maybe even because of everything.

Without a word, Tyler stepped through the door. Closed it behind him. And took Madeline in his arms and held her close. Madeline found herself grateful that he was there. That she was in his arms. Because as much as she hated to admit it, she needed him. Needed someone to be there if not to share her pain, but to be a strong witness to it. To tell her that she would be okay even though now, she knew she would be.

"Maddie, you cry all you want," Tyler said in a low voice. "Cry all you want. You're going to be just fine. It's all going to be okay."

Madeline pressed closer to him. "Thank you, Tyler," she said. "I'm so glad that you're here. Thank you for coming."

It surprised her to find that she was truly happy to see him. It crossed her mind as she stood there with Tyler, that somehow it was best that Anthony had left.

It crossed her heart that maybe–maybe–loving Anthony could be simply that. Loving Anthony. That she could love him and not be with him. That love was enough and not enough–at the same time. After so much anger and hurt and loss, Madeline's heart yearned to create a life that she loved. A life of loving.

She slowly drew away from Tyler and looked up at him as if searching for the answer to an unknown question. The love she saw in his eyes embraced her in its warmth. Tyler was a good man. She wondered if, after all these years, he was a man she could, at last, be with. Love. And be loved.

* * * *

The morning drive through the Italian countryside to Saint Valentine's was strangely slow and silent. David and Jonathan arrived at the hotel at exactly nine o'clock, and they had started out right away.

Tyler graciously suggested that he sit in the front of the black sedan with David. At first, Madeline hesitated at the suggestion. Introducing Tyler to her ex-husband had been awkward enough. David was clearly surprised at Tyler's sudden presence. But Tyler had persisted. Madeline finally acquiesced. And he had been right.

Now, Madeline sat in the back of the car with Jonathan. Holding his hand. Both of them stared out the window at the passing hills, each lost in their own selves. Every few minutes, words they could not find were spoken in the reassuring squeeze of the other's hand. They would turn and look at each other as if to say "I'm still here". Then turn to stare back out the window and travel again to the oasis of their thoughts.

Occasionally, Madeline would glance up at the rear view mirror and catch David's reflection looking back at them. Their eyes would meet and hold for a moment, then one of them would look away. David looked tired. Of course, sleeping at the hospital would not have been restful. But he had been there for Carrie and Jonathan, and Madeline felt a tender gratitude to him. He was a good man in his own way.

Then there was Tyler. Sitting quietly in the front passenger seat. Looking out the window. Thinking his own thoughts. Madeline wanted to reach out and touch the familiar nape of his neck. To know what was occupying his mind.

The only person missing was Anthony. Madeline sighed and watched the pavement blur by. It was hard to believe that just a few hours ago they had been together. Kissing. Holding each other. Making love. A part of her was angry with him for having left her alone afterwards. What would she say to him at Saint Valentine's? Why had he left? Why was he leaving the monastery? Where would he go? All Madeline had were questions.

They ascended the cypress-lined drive and pulled into Saint Valentine's parking lot. Madeline felt her heartbeat quicken in anticipation of seeing Anthony. And getting some answers.

Tyler held Madeline's hand as they walked through the centuries old courtyard. The fall air felt cool against Madeline's face but the sun warmed her body. Tyler's palm warmed hers. What if Anthony saw them? Holding hands? How would she explain? Would she need to? Would it even matter?

"It's so beautiful here," Tyler said, taking in his unfamiliar surroundings.

Madeline looked at him. Here, in the peace and calm of Saint Valentine's, he seemed completely at ease with himself. Totally self-assured. Tyler would be at home anywhere, Madeline thought.

Sometimes he reminds me of Anthony.

Could it be this place? Madeline asked herself. Was there something about Saint Valentine's that made everyone who passed through its gates settle deeply into themselves? Into, perhaps, God?

Tyler looked at her. "I've missed you, Maddie," he said simply. Honestly.

"I've missed you too," she said. It was true, she realized. She *had* missed Tyler.

"Madeline!"

She turned in the direction of the call. It was Father Marco. He seemed to glide toward them as he crossed the courtyard.

"Father Marco! Hello," she greeted him.

"I'm deeply sorry to hear about your sister. God bless her."

"Thank you," Madeline responded.

The priest regarded Tyler and Madeline remembered they had never met.

"Father Marco, this is a friend of mine from New York. Tyler Reed."

Tyler let go of Madeline's hand and reached out to shake Father Marco's. The old man looked curiously at the two of them. He smiled at Tyler openly.

"Welcome to Saint Valentine's. Please make yourself at home here. Will you be staying with us for a few days?"

"Oh, no," Madeline responded. "I have a room in Rome. I wanted to be close to..." Her words trailed off. With Carrie gone, there was no real reason to be in Rome. After the funeral, Madeline was free to go back to her life in New York.

New York.

Why had it not occurred to her before? She had been so wrapped up in all that happened with Anthony that it had not occurred to her that she would be leaving Italy in a few days. To go back home. That her life would return to normal. It would go on. Without her sister. Just like it had before. A spring of fresh tears overflowed in Madeline's eyes and silently streamed down her face.

How could it go on as before? Everything had changed. Things were exactly the same. But totally different.

"I'm so sorry," Father Marco repeated kindly.

Madeline nodded. Unable to resist, she asked, "Is Anthony here?"

Father Marco looked into her eyes and into her soul.

He knows, Madeline thought. *He knows all about Anthony and me.*

"Yes, he's here," Father Marco answered. "Where else would he be?"

Anywhere but here, Madeline thought. But he *was* here. Still.

Father Marco turned to Tyler. "Anthony is one of our monks. He and Jonathan are very close. He was good friends with Madeline's sister."

"And a friend of yours?" Tyler asked Madeline.

"Yes," Madeline replied simply.

Tyler nodded, "I would very much like to meet him."

"I'm afraid that won't be possible. Anthony is in seclusion," Father Marco explained.

Silence sulked in the courtyard like an unhappy child who would–this time–not have its way. Madeline looked away from Tyler and watched a bird peck at the ground, searching for seeds just as Madeline was searching for answers. Why was Anthony in seclusion? *Again.* A sick feeling settled in the core of her stomach. It was so easy for Anthony. He could escape into the sanctuary of seclusion whenever it suited him. Madeline had to face life. Head on.

"Seclusion?" Tyler asked.

"A retreat of sorts. Into silence. To reflect. Pray."

"Run away," Madeline said aloud, a flicker of disdain seeping into her voice.

Father Marco looked at her.

"Run away," Father Marco challenged. "From what?"

"From life," Madeline accused.

Another sulking silence.

"We all do that, in different ways." Tyler finally said.

Madeline looked back up at him, surprised. He sometimes revealed a depth of wisdom that completely contradicted his sharp Wall Street demeanor. She understood what he meant. Understood *him.*

I have been running. From life. From love. From myself.

"Yes, well," Father Marco said, "I must get back to work. Please stay as long as you like. *Arrivederci.*"

"Thank you," Tyler said and watched as the priest floated away in the folds of his black gown. He turned to Madeline. "What would you like to do now?" he asked.

She looked at him thoughtfully a moment. "There's something I'd like to show you," she said. "It's one of my favorite places here."

She took Tyler's hand and led him slowly and silently through the courtyard until they reached the terrace. Before them, the valley basked in the golden fall sun, perfectly still except for the whisper of a cool breeze. Tyler stood close behind Madeline and wrapped his arms around her waist. She leaned back into him and breathed in the peaceful surroundings.

In the stillness, a slow movement caught her eye. Anthony. Her stomach tightened. They had played out this scene before when Anthony had walked in the valley with Veronica. But this time, it was Madeline standing on the terrace with Tyler. Now it was Anthony who was alone. Wearing his black robe. She had never seen him wear it before. Cloaked in the dark fabric, he looked somber. Serious. Like the monk that he was. *The like monk that he is. And always will be.*

He walked deliberately and gazed downward, focused on the path before him.

The pull of Madeline's eyes must have reached him because he suddenly lifted his own to meet them. Breathless, she watched him stand motionless for a long moment and look up at them.

At her.

Eye to eye, they held each other's souls across the divide of time and space and destiny, and in that moment, Madeline knew it was over between them. No words would be spoken. There would be no explanations. No confrontations. No good-byes. It was Anthony who peeled his eyes away from hers first. He looked straight ahead, and walked on, his eyes once again on the path. Through a misty veil of unshed tears, Madeline watched his solitary figure walk away.

Until he simply disappeared.

* * * *

The morning sunlight gleamed on Carrie's mahogany coffin as it was lowered into her grave in the small cemetery at Saint Valentine's. Madeline looked on. She had buried her mother. Her father. And now her sister. She felt as though a piece of her heart had been buried along with each. Into the cold dark earth, never to be recovered.

Madeline's face was pale, almost translucent, against the blackness of the suit and hat she wore. Tyler was at her side, holding her hand. She looked at him, grateful for his presence. Her eyes moved to rest on Jonathan. His face, too, was drawn. She understood how alone he must have felt. David stood beside him. At least he had his father.

And God.

Anthony's words came back to Madeline.

You are never alone.

His words echoed in Madeline's memory. That was all she had left of Anthony. Memories. She had not been surprised that he chose not come to Carrie's service. She was disappointed. But not surprised. She had wanted to say good-bye to him. Then again, Madeline hated good-byes.

It's better this way, she thought.

Father Marco's words broke the silence. "As we close this service today, there is one thing left. Brother Anthony, who could not be here today, left this letter and asked that I read it." He looked at Madeline. Then at Jonathan. Then began reading.

> *The first time I met Carrie, she was crying. Not weeping. But crying. She was leaving Jonathan here to begin his journey as a novice, and it was then that I first began to understand what it must be like for a mother to leave her child. Over time, I came to know Carrie and learned what a truly courageous woman she was. Her life had been filled with difficult choices. And each one had defined the course of her life. She had no regrets, but felt great remorse over the pain her decisions had caused others. She expected–no–demanded the best from life. For herself. And for others. She took risks in life. For life.*
>
> *She often said that life was a series of defining moments, and that when she died, she wanted to look back on her life and know that in each one, she would have been true to the call of her own soul.*
>
> *That is what I most want you to know and remember about Carrie. That she was someone whose deepest desire in life was to be true to her own soul. For Carrie, I want to ask each of you to*

look deeply within yourselves and ask, what is it that your soul craves? What is it that your soul wants to express? What is your soul's calling?

Carrie asked herself those questions, and, like most of us, answered them as best she could. But the point is, she asked.

Whenever you remember Carrie, remember the way she lived.

Blessings,
Anthony

Madeline watched as Father Marco finished reading and folded the letter carefully. He walked toward her, reached for her free hand, and pressed Anthony's words into her palm, gently folding her fingers over them.

"He wanted you to have it," Father Marco said. "God bless you."

Madeline searched the priest's blue eyes. For answers. For questions. For anything.

"God bless you," he said again, squeezing her hand gently. He leaned close to her and whispered, "All you need to know, Madeline, is your own heart." He looked at her. Then at Tyler.

Finally, Madeline watched him walk over to Jonathan and embrace her nephew. Jonathan, she knew, would be just fine here at Saint Valentine's.

As she looked down at Carrie's grave, she was less sure about herself. She squeezed Anthony's letter in her hand. He was right. Carrie had lived a life true to her own heart. Even at the expense of betraying Madeline.

Which is the greater betrayal, Madeline wondered. *Betraying your sister? Or betraying yourself? Maybe it was the same.*

Madeline wanted to cry but found she had no tears left. How little she had known her sister. Known her thoughts and dreams. Her sorrows and joys. How little, really, she knew anyone.

Including myself.

She felt the squeeze of Tyler's hand and realized she had forgotten he had been holding hers. She lifted her eyes to his.

"Hello," he said, the tenderest of expressions on his face.

"Hello," Madeline replied.

"I've been thinking," he started.

Madeline caught her breath, wondering what he was going to say.

Is he about to leave me, too?

He continued, "That while we're here, we should take a few days just to ourselves. Maybe go to Sardinia. Take long walks along the beach. Talk." He put an arm around her waist and pulled her close to him. "Make love," he whispered. "I know this isn't really the time or place. But we're here. Now. It sounds like Carrie might have understood."

He surprised her. Carrie *would* have understood.

Encouraged, even.

"Then we can go back to Rome and take care of things. Then get back to New York."

Take care of things. Tyler meant pack up Carrie's apartment. Donate her clothes. Truffles. Someone needed to adopt Truffles. *Maybe Saint Valentine's could adopt Truffles.*

Then it would be time to get back to New York and its crowded streets and skyscraper lined skies. Madeline's gaze drifted to the still hillsides surrounding the monastery.

Once again, Tyler was right. Madeline was not yet ready to take care of the necessary things. He understood her.

I don't think anyone has ever been there, really been there, to help me take care of things. Been that big a part of my life.

"You're very good to me," she said.

"Get used to it," he replied, a smile in his eyes.

Get used to it. Get used to being loved. Standing there, looking at the warmth in Tyler's eyes, a still small part of her soul said yes. Yes. She would allow herself to be loved.

And to love.

"I think maybe I will," she said, the first tear of the morning winding its way down her cheek. "You're a good man, Tyler. A very good man."

So, on a fall morning in Italy, thousands of miles from home in the small cemetery at Saint Valentine's, Madeline looked into Tyler's eyes as though for the first time and fell deeply, truly, and simply in love. And he was there to catch her.

* * * *

Madeline closed her eyes and deeply inhaled the fresh sea air. The ocean breezes combed through her coppery hair and she lifted her face to the soothing warmth of the sun. In fall, the beach was almost deserted with only the occasional wayward soul drifting along its empty shores. This was the kind of day that Madeline had not allowed herself in – how long? She could not remember.

An aimless lazy day with nothing to do but dream and think and dream some more. It was the first day in almost two weeks that Madeline had not smelled the stale perfume of death lingering in the air. She inhaled deeply again, wanting to breathe in the life giving water, air, and sun. Grains of sand roughly caressed her bare feet. She opened her eyes to watch her toes wriggle into the beach with the delight of a young girl.

She looked at Tyler who had been watching her, wearing a grin that would turn any woman's heart to–to–mush. Sometimes he seemed like such a boy. Yet, in so many ways, he was very much a man. Still, Madeline could not dismiss the feeling that there was something...something. No. It was nothing. She would allow herself this moment of pure innocence. She was ready to be innocent. To forget all her worries and sorrows and losses. For just a day.

She felt a smile of her own lift her face and she watched Tyler walk toward her. Handsome in a favorite pair of old faded jeans, a white T-shirt and windswept blonde hair, he looked like Sardinia itself. A shining island wearing blue and gold and tan.

Carrie will never have this again. Never again see the sea. Never again feel the sun warm her face or wriggle her toes in the sand. Never feel the anticipation of a lover's touch. His kiss.

The image of Carrie lying in the hospital bed flashed in Madeline's mind. Her body failing her. Frail. And Madeline wondered again how death would claim her.

When death would claim her.

Because it would. One day. Tomorrow? The tomorrow after that? The tomorrow after *that*?

How many tomorrows do I have left? How do I want to live them?

Joy for being alive, and guilt for being alive, dueled for a place in Madeline's heart. Tyler reached her and she felt the strength of his arms encircle her waist and pull her to him. She buried her face in his neck and breathed in the smell of him. He was here. Now. And so was she.

Maybe that was all that mattered. Maybe that was enough. In that moment, Madeline decided to reclaim her life. She was here. Alive. Now. Life was hers to be lived. Until she died.

She wrapped her arms around Tyler's neck and shoulders and pulled him close. His chest felt strong against the softness of her breasts. Gratitude filled her heart now. For Tyler. For his presence in her life. For her life. The salty sting of tears filled her eyes.

"I love you, Tyler," Madeline said.

"I love you, too," Tyler replied.

He gently pushed her away and looked down into her face. Tenderly, he brushed away the tears that had settled in the corners of Madeline's eyes. His thumb traced its way across her cheek and down to her lips. He kissed her then. So tenderly that Madeline's breath caught in a moment of perfect...peace.

Abruptly, nervously, he stepped back and Madeline watched while he dug deeply into the pocket of his jeans.

"I've been carrying this around, waiting for the right moment. But who ever knows when the right moment ever really is. Maybe sometimes we need to create the right moment." The way he spoke reminded her of Anthony. Of how she loved his gentle strength.

They really are alike sometimes.

Madeline watched Tyler gingerly hold up a solitaire diamond ring set in gleaming platinum.

Madeline gasped. Her mouth fell slightly open. Her heart raced. Time paused. *Oh my God!*

Sunlight rushed to the stone and even the glittering sea was not as worthy a partner when the jewel reached out to accept the light's invitation to dance. Together they sparkled and shimmered, the light and the diamond, each more brilliant in each other's company.

"I want to marry you, Madeline. I can't promise it will always be easy. It won't always be perfect. And it certainly won't always be like this." He waved an arm across the sea's expanse.

"I can promise you, that as best I can, I will love you. I'll be there with you. I'm sure I'll screw up. And maybe you'll forgive me. Maybe you won't. But I hope you will."

Emotions raced through Madeline. Love. Hope. Fear. "I–"

Tyler interrupted her. "Before you answer, there's something I need to tell you. Something you should know."

Madeline held her breath. Here it was. The inevitable bomb. Just when she was ready to believe. To hope. To give in to love, Tyler was going to shatter her reverie. She looked at the eternally glittering diamond. No matter what the ads said, nothing, not even a diamond, was perfect. There was always a flaw, however small.

Tyler raked a hand through his hair. "This is harder than I thought. I guess I should just be out with it. There was never a buyer for Felicity."

Madeline furrowed her brows. "What?"

"I wanted to meet you, Madeline. Get to know you. But you made it so damned impossible."

"So, you made up a story about there being a buyer for Felicity?"

"Yup." He smiled.

Madeline laughed. "You're such a liar! What if I'd taken you up on it?"

He looked at her. Raised his eyebrows. "And the chances of that were? You love what you do. It's one of the things I love about you." Madeline smiled. He knew her well. Even when he had not known her. "It's true. Felicity is like my family. I could never let it go."

"So?" He held up the ring. Smiled.

She smiled. Shook her head. "Tyler, I–"

"Just say yes."

"Don't you think there are some things we should talk about?"

"Like what?"

"Like I want to keep doing what I'm doing. Maybe I don't want to settle down. Have children. I like my life."

"Maddie, I'm not asking you to change your life. Settle down. Maybe for us, settling down looks like having careers and traveling. Supporting worthy causes. Having good friends. But sharing all that together. I could be perfectly happy without children."

"You could?" Somehow the idea surprised her.

She pictured him with children. A family. Married to a woman who sent Christmas cards displaying family portraits with everyone wearing red and green plaid and a Santa hat.

"Maddie, we can make our life together whatever we want it to be. Unless you really want children?"

Something in his tone made Madeline take pause. She looked down. Gingerly drew a circle in the sand with her big toe. After David, she had not seen another marriage in her future, let alone children. Oh, there had been wistful moments when she saw a couple with a beautiful little boy or girl. But the day-to-day reality of raising a child was something she had never envisioned for herself. Felicity had been her husband. Her child. Her family.

She shook her head. "No, Tyler. Having a baby is something I gave up on long ago." She grinned and, tongue-in-cheek, said, "We'll just be yuppies. Rich. Shallow. Materialistic. We could always just leave things to chance. See what happens..."

"So, it's yes?"

Madeline nodded. "Yes, Tyler Reed. I will marry you."

"Madeline Reed. I like the sound of that."

Madeline scowled. "Madeline O'Connor. Tyler, I changed my name once, and it didn't work out. After my divorce, I promised myself I'd never change my name again," she explained. "I never thought I'd get married again. Would it bother you if didn't change it?"

Tyler smiled. "This is exactly why I love you. You're clear about things. You know what you want. There's nothing about you I would change."

It was what Anthony had loved about her, too. And what she had loved about him. That he had loved her exactly as she was. For who she was. Not who he wanted her to be. Or to become.

"Wait. There's something I need to know," Madeline said.

Concern deposited on Tyler's face. "What is it?"

"What brand of toothpaste do you use?"

"What?"

She laughed. "Just answer!"

"*Tom's of Maine*. Peppermint."

She smiled and nodded. "I never really paid attention, and I just wanted to know."

Tyler laughed and shook his head.

As if it was happening to someone else, Madeline watched Tyler take her hand and slip the ring on her left hand.

So it was. Madeline O'Connor was now officially engaged. The thought of Anthony flickered again in her mind. It was just a few days ago that they had made love. Now, she had no idea when or even if she would ever see him again. Looking down at the ring on her finger and up at Tyler's beaming face, she realized it truly did not matter. Brother Anthony Lamberti was out of her life forever.

* * * *

Tyler and Madeline laughed as the bed beneath them creaked. Their room at the small inn was charming and comfortable, but luxurious it was not. There were two wing chairs, a dresser, a small table where they could eat. It was the window, though, with its spectacular view of the water that gave the room its appeal.

Lying on the bed with Tyler pressed up against the entire length of her body, Madeline gazed out at the sea, aglow with the amber and pink of the setting sun.

"Beautiful, isn't it?" Tyler said.

"It is...absolutely beautiful," Madeline smiled and looked at Tyler.

Their twilight lovemaking had left her feeling completely fulfilled. She wondered if it had something to do with knowing that Tyler would be there tomorrow. The tomorrow after that. And the tomorrow after that. He would be there for all the tomorrows they had left together. She surrendered to the richness of the quiet joy that filled her heart. To the peace. The ecstasy.

From the depths of her memory, Anthony's words floated in her mind. *Romantic love and spiritual ecstasy are the same thing, the same feeling, just expressed differently.*

So this was it. This was how it felt to love. And be loved. *How it felt to love God. To surrender to God.*

Tyler smiled at her and stroked her hair. Lazily traced the outline of her cheek with his index finger. "You look so happy," he said.

"That's because I am. I love you, Tyler."

"I love you, too, Madeline."

He kissed her. A kiss that was long and rich and full of love. Pulling back slowly, his gaze drifted slowly along the entire length of Madeline's body, as though he were looking at her for the first time. He reached for a small silver packet. Started to unroll its latex contents.

"Tyler?"

"Hmmm?"

"Let's not. Just this once. I don't want anything between us. I'm almost forty. What are the chances that..." All she wanted to feel was him inside her. Just him. Flesh to flesh.

He smiled. Dropped the condom without hesitation. "One in a million."

So, with nothing at all between them, they made love again. While the sun set over the sea and Sardinia.

* * * *

1945

The old woman began.

"They found Isabella."

Marco swallowed. "The Germans."

"Yes," Sister Francesca replied.

He could not breathe. "What happened?"

Sister Francesca continued. "She left the abbey."

"What? But I made her promise. I made her promise me not to ever leave."

"Marco. We had to take Isabella to see a doctor."

"A doctor. Why?" His Isabella was sick.

"She had a baby, Marco. A baby boy."

He felt as though everything in the world stopped. He stared at the old woman, silent.

"She had a baby boy, Marco. Your baby."

He could not imagine it. Could not imagine that Isabella had a baby. He had not been there. Had not been there for her. He hated himself. Hated himself for what he had done to her. Hated himself for how he failed her. Hated himself for how he had failed God.

He swallowed. "How did the Nazis find her?"

Sister Francesca looked directly into Marco's eyes. "There were some complications with the delivery, so we called a doctor we thought we could trust. It was the middle of the night. He came and helped with the delivery. The baby was perfectly healthy. But Isabella– she was weak after the delivery. She wouldn't stop bleeding and the doctor insisted she be taken to the hospital. He promised us that she would be safe. But on the way, his car got a flat tire and two Germans stopped to see what the trouble was. They saw Isabella and..."

The old nun's eyes filled with tears and her voice trembled as she continued. "We watched the Nazis take them both away. There was nothing we could do. No one knows where they went. Or what happened to them. No one's heard anything from them or of them ever since." She swallowed.

Marco's mind raced with horrifying possibilities. What if they raped her? Shot her? Sent her away to one of those torturous camps? He heard of the atrocities that went on—what if—no! This could not be. God would not have allowed it. She had to be alive. Somewhere. Somehow. Isabella had to be alive! He knew it! He felt it!

"Marco," Sister Francesca went on. "Jews captured by Nazis never return." She swallowed. "I'm afraid Isabella is dead."

Rage surged through Marco and he stood, knocking the chair onto the floor.

"Marco!" Sister Francesca rushed after him and grabbed his shoulders. "Stop!"

"No! I must find her!" Tears poured from his eyes.

"Marco! No! You're forgetting something!"

He glared at the old woman, his fury unleashed. "What? Nothing matters except Isabella. She can't be dead. She isn't dead. I know it."

Marco's anger was no match for the force of Sister Francesca's whisper. "Oh, you're wrong Marco. There is something that matters. That matters very much. The baby, Marco. Your baby."

He stopped. The baby.

Our baby!

* * * *

Present Day

The engagement made headlines in the social columns of all the right publications. Much to the dismay of more than one charitable organization, Tyler was no longer one of New York's most eligible bachelors and available to bid upon as a date at silent auctions. Tongues also wagged at Felicity. Not out of malice, but out of curiosity, and, in most cases, pleasant surprise.

Eric, Madeline's assistant, had beamed. "You're getting married! When?"

It was the question on everyone's mind.

Including Madeline's. She stood at her favorite spot by her office window, arms crossed, and looked out at the sparkling New York night. It was eight o'clock and she was still working. Or trying to.

She wanted to have a long engagement. Her relationship with Tyler had, after all, been a whirlwind of just several months. It seemed appropriate to Madeline to wait at least a year. Planning a wedding would take at least that long.

A wedding. She had just been at her sister's funeral in Italy and now was here in New York about to plan her own wedding. David had been so gracious and offered to pack up Carrie's apartment.

"So many of the things were ours. It would mean a lot to me if you would let me do it," he had told Madeline.

After her time in Sardinia, she had been too exhausted and anxious to return home to argue. David had said he would send a few things to Madeline if there was anything he thought she might want. Clothes and furniture would be donated or sold. Any money would be given to a worthy cause. Saint Valentine's, most likely.

Saint Valentine's. She could almost smell the fragrant air that floated in the hills surrounding the monastery. Feel the peace of the place. She remembered Anthony. She thought of him every day and when she did, she felt either love for him or anger toward him. Sometimes, she simply felt grateful for having known him. She often wondered how he was doing. Jonathan told her that

Anthony remained in seclusion for weeks after Carrie died. After that night they had made love.

She felt a familiar throb of guilt at the memory. Had making love with Anthony been wrong? A terrible mistake? But she had loved him. A kind of unexplainable heart-opening love that she had never known. Being with him had felt so right. So real. So true. Still, she felt guilty about Tyler.

Was it possible to truly love two men? Love them differently, perhaps. But truly nonetheless. And not without ultimately making a choice. She had chosen Tyler. Perhaps if circumstances had been different. If Anthony had not been a monk. Then again, perhaps she had not made a choice after all. Life had chosen for her. Or had it been God? Either way, Anthony was a monk. That, she knew now, would never change.

David sprang to mind and a swell of compassion and understanding unexpectedly filled her heart. Maybe he had, in his own way, loved her after all. Loved her *and* her sister. Both. Differently, but truly.

Maybe he had loved us both.

Rhe last traces of hurt and anger floated away from Madeline. In their place, peace rinsed through her whole being like a warm summer rain. Its healing balm cleansed and caressed and soothed every cell of her body. In the depths of her soul, she knew that this was the essence of forgiveness. *So this is how forgiveness feels.*

Through tear-filled eyes, she glanced down at her engagement ring that played with the lights of the city below.

She thought about her night of lovemaking with Anthony but this time, banished the memory from her mind. It was time to let go of Anthony. To say good-bye to him, in her heart.

Tyler would never have to know about her night with Anthony. It would be a private reminiscence she would carry in her heart forever. And so, it seemed, would Anthony. The remembrance of it would be a bond between them. Between time. Between distance. Between lifetimes.

She pressed her lips together and let out a long breath through her nostrils that fogged the window. She watched the moisture disappear and brushed away a tear.

No, she thought.

Tyler would never have to know.

* * * *

"I think we should elope," Tyler teased, folding his arms across his chest and grinning broadly.

Three women glared at him. His mother, Gloria, his niece, Trudy, and Madeline. The four of them were having dinner at The Pierre.

It was the first time Madeline had met her future mother-in-law and she liked the older woman tremendously. With chic grey hair that she wore in a short bob and warm blue eyes that missed nothing, it was easy to see where Tyler got his handsome features. Gloria was a socialite through and through, living for parties and fundraisers. She was glamorous and intelligent, with a marvelous sense of humor and a heart to match. As a wealthy widow, she could afford the lifestyle she so obviously enjoyed. Still, there was not a snobbish bone in her body.

"It's not a bad idea," Gloria beamed at her son. "Then you could start on some grandchildren right away."

Madeline's eyes darted quizzically at Tyler who glanced sheepishly down at his exquisitely prepared grilled salmon entrée.

For the first time in the evening, Trudy lit up. "Maybe you could create a line of maternity lingerie."

Madeline looked at Trudy and wondered if this was an apology of sorts. For Trudy's behavior the last time they had seen each other. She started to reply but her train of thought was interrupted.

"You do want children, don't you Madeline?" Gloria placed her perfectly manicured hand on Madeline's forearm and looked at her with kind hopeful eyes. "It's the most wonderful thing."

Madeline turned to Gloria. How long had it been since she'd had dinner with someone's mother? Even her own. Gloria was so full of delightful expectation and so perfect herself, Madeline could suddenly understand how Tyler would want to please her. Something pulled softly and tenderly at Madeline's heartstrings.

I miss my own mother. I miss her.

"I think mothers are the most wonderful people in the world. To be honest, Gloria, I don't know if I have the courage," Madeline confessed.

"Oh, my dear, it will come to you. Something tells me that you're stronger than you think."

It was what Anthony had said. *You're stronger than you know.*

Maybe. Maybe not.

"I still think you should start a line of maternity lingerie," Trudy said again, unwilling to be unheard.

"You know, it's not a bad idea," Tyler agreed.

"It never occurred to me. But you might be onto something there. Pregnant women want to feel sexy. Pretty lingerie helps."

"Well, you be sure to take some sexy things along on your honeymoon and start working on some grandchildren," Gloria instructed Madeline.

Madeline smiled and took a bite of her pasta. She liked Gloria and Trudy. Somehow, until actually meeting Tyler's mother and liking her so much, it hadn't occurred to Madeline that she would gain a mother in the marriage. Gloria had just been a faceless name. Someone she'd seen in photographs.

"You know, I just couldn't imagine my life without Tyler," Gloria said, a distant look in her eyes.

Madeline looked over at him. "Neither can I," she said and reached out to hold Tyler's hand. They shared a look that only lovers could.

"Neither can I," Madeline repeated.

It was true. Madeline could not imagine her life without Tyler.

Thank God, she thought.

Nothing can come between us now.

* * * *

The next day was a flurry of phone calls and meetings. Madeline finally had to make a decision concerning Heather's replacement. She had narrowed the field down to three candidates. She sat at her desk staring at the three resumés before her.

Her management team had already met with the applicants. They were all qualified. Likeable. Talented. But none of them were Heather. None of them shared her room with her in college. Or been maid of honor at her wedding. Or been there during her divorce. Somehow they managed to avoid each other over the last week since she had returned from Italy. Their only conversations had been during regularly scheduled group meetings. About business.

Madeline's gaze drifted up from the resumés to the clear blue fall sky just beyond her window. She frowned, remembering what Heather had said about why she had resigned from Felicity. That she had grown weary of shivering in Madeline's shadow. Madeline wished with all her heart that she had only known how Heather had felt. Maybe there was something she could have done.

Her phone rang and Madeline looked at it. Like a heavy black velvet cloak, weariness draped itself over Madeline. She sighed and let the phone ring. The caller could wait. What was it about being back in New York that Madeline suddenly found overwhelming? Or was it being back at Felicity with its chaotic pace and constant demands?

Madeline rose from her desk and walked down the hall to Heather's office. Heather was on the phone, but waved a hand to signal that Madeline should come in. Madeline walked in and sat down in one of the guest chairs opposite her.

"No. No. That's not right," Heather was saying to the person on the other end of the phone. "Look at it again. There's a mistake somewhere. That can't be right," she pressed another button on the phone to end the conversation and immediately began another one.

"This is Heather," she said, an edge in her voice.

She raised her index finger to Madeline indicating that she would need another minute and continued talking.

Madeline watched her old friend as she worked, turning to respond to email even while she was on the phone. As if looking in a mirror, instead of seeing Heather, Madeline saw herself. Was this how she had been living her life? Was this was mattered to her? Profits and losses and email and phone calls. Meetings to discuss new designs. New products. Cutting costs.

Was this all there was?

Was this all there would ever be?

She remembered Carrie's funeral and Anthony's letter. His words.

Look deeply within yourselves and ask, what is it that your soul craves? What is it that your soul wants to express? What is your soul's calling?

Is this *my soul's calling?*

Heather hung up the phone and turned abruptly to face Madeline.

"Hi. Sorry about that. What's up?" Heather asked.

Madeline looked at the stranger sitting across from her, suddenly not sure of what to say or why she was there.

"Are you happy, Heather?" was what came out of Madeline's mouth.

Heather laughed and said, "What do you mean? Of course I'm happy." She shook her head as if confused by Madeline's question.

Averting her eyes downward to hide the tears she felt rising, Madeline shakily replied, "I don't know. Are you happy that you're leaving Felicity? I mean, is that what you really want? To work somewhere with people you hardly know?"

She felt herself engulfed by a tidal wave of grief and could do nothing but be swept up in it. The loss of her sister was more painful than she expected. Now she was losing Heather, too. Was life just a succession of loss after loss?

She heard Heather sigh a long slow sigh.

"Madeline. I've signed a contract with Saks. You know that."

The cold tone of Heather's words sobered Madeline and she looked back up at her.

"I know. I was just wondering if maybe – if you'd interviewed the three candidates that the rest of the team met."

Heather glanced at her watch.

"No, I haven't. It doesn't really seem appropriate, does it?" Of course it was not appropriate for Heather to interview her possible successor. But Madeline had to think of something to say. She had been on the brink of asking Heather to change her mind. She decided to take the chance.

"Heather, is there any possible way you might consider changing your mind...and stay?"

Madeline watched Heather glance at her watch again. Heather opened her mouth in the beginnings of a response, but stopped herself and instead sighed.

"I really don't know what to say, Madeline. I'm sorry this is so hard for you."

It was Madeline who sighed now. She thought for a moment.

"I'm sorry that this *isn't* harder for you," Madeline replied. Then added, "I'll miss you."

She turned and left Heather's office and walked back down the hall into her own. The resumés were on her desk where she left them. She picked them up and strode over to Eric's desk.

He continued typing an email but looked up from his computer screen and saw the resumés in Madeline's hand.

"Narrowing the field?"

She held the papers out to him. "Call them, please, and set up dinners this week."

The phone rang and Eric answered with one hand and took the resumés with the other.

"Madeline O'Connor's office," he said while Madeline looked on.

"Yes, I was just about to call you. Madeline would like to have dinner with you this week. Are you available?" he asked the caller and pulled up Madeline's calendar on his computer. "Tomorrow it is. Seven o'clock. At..." he looked up at Madeline.

Madeline mouthed, "Amista."

"Amista...good, then...yes, thank you," Eric finished and hung up the phone. "That was Jeff Straus," Eric waved Mister Straus' résumé in the air triumphantly. "See, you'll have a new CFO before you know it."

She raised her eyebrows and nodded slightly. "Any idea where I can hire a new friend?" she asked.

Eric gave her a sympathetic look, and handed her some messages.

"Business goes on, Madeline."

Madeline snatched the messages from Eric and replied, "You're all heart, Eric. All heart." She managed a smile and continued on to her office.

She dropped into her chair and leafed through the slips of paper. One caught her eye. Veronica had called.

Of course. Veronica. It would be so good to see her.

Madeline picked up the phone and dialed.

* * * *

The last time Madeline had seen Veronica was when they met coincidentally weeks ago at Saint Patrick's. So much had happened since then. They were having sushi at Jewel Baka, and, as always, Veronica looked fresh and pretty.

"I got a letter from Anthony." Veronica looked serious as she reported the news.

Madeline's breath caught. It had, of course, occurred to her that Veronica might have heard from him. But the truth was it had lifted her spirits to hear from Veronica. Just for Veronica. But news of Anthony. Just the mention of his name quickened her heartbeat. Of course Madeline was anxious to hear what his letter said.

"What did he say?" Madeline asked.

"Well, he's left Saint Valentine's. I always knew he would," Veronica closed her eyes and took in a deep breath of her red wine.

Something about the gesture reminded Madeline of Anthony. How he breathed in wine. Breathed in life. Maybe it was an Italian thing.

He left Saint Valentine's.

Madeline swallowed. "What do you mean?"

"Well, I've always felt that he needed to move beyond the

monastery. Do more with his life. I hoped that meeting you ..." Veronica paused. "I'm so sorry, Madeline. That just wasn't meant to be. Anthony must follow another path."

"I know," Madeline said. "It's okay, really." She did not want to dwell on the subject. "So where is he?"

Veronica's eyes fell to the table. "He decided to go to Africa. To do some missionary work there. He's in the Congo."

Madeline's face turned white. "The Congo! But the civil unrest –it's so dangerous! What is he doing there?"

"Bible translation. Bringing literacy to remote groups. He'll be all right. Whatever happens, he's with God."

He's certainly not with me, Madeline thought.

"And with you," Veronica added. "Madeline, love doesn't end when someone's gone."

It was as though her new friend had read her mind. Their eyes held and Veronica reached out and placed her hand upon Madeline's.

"He's in your heart, Madeline. The love that the two of you felt for one another was real and can never be destroyed. Keep it. It's yours. And always will be," she smiled tenderly at Madeline.

Madeline wanted to believe Veronica. A small part of her knew it was true. The love that she felt for Anthony was still in her heart. Somehow he had been able to reach into her very depths and open her heart.

Veronica continued, "You know, it's even there for you to give away. Because the supply...is endless."

Madeline had to laugh.

"What is so funny?" Veronica smiled.

"You. You are such an optimist," Madeline was smiling too.

"Maybe just a romantic."

"What about you? Any romance in your life?" Madeline asked.

"Well...that brings me to another point," Veronica seemed serious. "There's something else I wanted to tell you."

"What is it?"

"I'm going back to Italy."

No! Don't move away. I don't want to lose another friend...

"What? Why?" Madeline was surprised and disappointed. They were just becoming friends, and now Veronica was leaving.

"I miss Italy...and there's someone there."

Madeline managed a smile and nodded. "Of course. Is that why you really left the abbey?"

Madeline could not help wondering if it was Anthony. But he

was in Africa. Still, the thought nagged.

"What's his name?"

"Christina," Veronica answered.

Madeline managed her best poker face to conceal her shock. Her surprise, even, at being surprised. Nothing should surprise her anymore and she chided herself for her naiveté. Maybe she wasn't the sophisticated New Yorker she liked to think of herself as. "Good for you," Madeline smiled.

Veronica smiled, too. "Well, I suppose I needed to leave to find out that what I had, was what I really wanted."

"Hmmm." Madeline considered what Veronica had said. Marveled at how universal the human condition is. How other lives always seem better than one's own. How, whether male, female, straight, gay, single, married, young, old, everyone wants what someone else has. Yearns to be happy. Thinks that something or someone can provide that. The right relationship. The right career. The right clothes.

What causes happiness?

Veronica glanced down at the table and noticed Madeline's ring. Reached out for her left hand. "Madeline, my God! You're engaged!" Veronica leaned forward to examine the brilliant stone on Madeline's finger.

Madeline laughed at her friend's excitement, "I am indeed."

Veronica looked up at her. "So...who? When?"

"Tyler Reed. And we don't know yet."

"Well, what are you waiting for?"

Madeline looked down at the table and gave a slight shrug.

"Do you love him?" Veronica asked seriously.

Madeline raised her eyes to Veronica's. "I do, Veronica. I do. But not the way I love Anthony. Sometimes I don't feel like ... Tyler really knows me. All Anthony had to do was look at me and I felt as though we'd known each other all our lives. And then some. But with Tyler, it's different somehow."

Veronica regarded Madeline thoughtfully. "Maybe Anthony knew your soul. Because the truth of it is, Madeline, he hardly knows *you*. The day in and day out Madeline who gets to the office early and runs a corporation and comes home tired and stressed."

Madeline sighed. Veronica was right. She remembered going to Tyler's apartment one night after work and finding him in the kitchen unpacking some Chinese food he picked up on the way home. He had set out some Harvard sweats for her so she could change into the cozy fleece. He was wearing a pair of old jeans and a sweatshirt himself. They had curled up on the couch together and talked and laughed and caught up on each other's days.

"I do love him, Veronica."

"Then set a date. Make it sooner rather than later. Love deserves an appointment in your daybook, too."

* * * *

Time seemed to pass more quickly in the fall. Maybe it was because the days were getting shorter with night falling earlier and earlier each day. There was a chill in the air most mornings, and this Sunday morning was no different.

Madeline was curled up in bed with Tyler, their bodies nestled together like spoons. Tyler's body covered the entire length of hers. She wriggled her toes against his. He moaned softly and wriggled his toes in response. Pulled her closer. A contented smile drew itself on Madeline's face.

Two weeks had passed since Madeline's conversation with Veronica but she thought of it every day. And asked herself why it was that she wanted to wait to marry Tyler. She had known him for years, albeit in a business context. But she knew him to be successful and ethical in business. Here he was, lying beside her, a wonderful man, lover, and friend. She would be happy with him.

"Tyler?"

"Hmmmm?"

"I've been thinking..."

"Always a dangerous thing," he said, half-asleep.

Madeline elbowed him and they laughed.

"Why don't we get married in February?" There, she said it.

Tyler was quiet for a moment, and then turned her to face him. "Why the change of heart?"

"Because I love you, Tyler." Tears swam in her eyes as she spoke the sacred words. "I really love you. And I don't want to wait for happiness anymore."

Tyler cupped her face in his hand and said, "I love you, too. Okay then, February it is. The first Saturday."

Madeline nodded, "The first Saturday. It's perfect, really. After the holidays. We'll celebrate Valentine's Day as newlyweds."

Tyler smiled. Kissed her. She surrendered to it. To him. And returned a kiss that was long and rich and filled with all her love. When they finished, their eyes, and souls, met. Madeline knew that she had, at last, found her home. Within herself. And within

Tyler.

"Coffee?" she asked her soon to be husband.

"Mmmm...please."

Madeline slid out from under the covers, wrapped herself in a thick terry robe and nestled her feet in cushiony slippers. She walked, yawning, into the kitchen and began making a pot of her favorite French roast coffee.

Holding the coffeepot under the faucet, she watched the water flow into the glass container. From nowhere, weakness swept over her and a sick feeling rose from the depths of her stomach. She almost dropped the carafe but managed to set it down in the sink at the same as she wretched.

As quickly as it had risen, Madeline's queasiness vanished. She shook her head in bewilderment and carried on with the task of making the morning brew.

Must have been something I ate, she thought, and tried to recall what she and Tyler had eaten for dinner the night before.

The shrimp, Madeline decided. It must have been the shrimp.

* * * *

Gloria was thrilled with the news that Tyler and Madeline had set a date. The first Saturday in February. It would be February 1. Madeline liked the idea of being married on the first of February. The first of any month seemed like a good day to be celebrating a wedding anniversary. To Madeline, it heralded a new beginning. A new life.

To Gloria, it meant sending out invitations and making announcements. The guest list was small–they wanted to keep it under one hundred–but impressive. Gloria maintained friendships with all her late husband's influential friends. Business leaders. Academics. Politicians. Then there were a select few of Tyler's associates.

Madeline's list was the shortest. She wanted to invite Heather despite what had transpired between them. A few key members of her executive team. Reviewing the list of names, her heart ached and she lapsed into a spell of grief for Carrie. For her mother. And father. None of them would be there to witness her marriage vows. But, she told herself, they would be there in spirit. Although that was not the same as actually having them there. In person.

Madeline felt Gloria's eyes on her as she reviewed the list. They were seated at Tyler's dining room table. Gloria with a cup of a tea.

Madeline with a cup of coffee.

"It's a good list," Gloria said, beaming.

Madeline looked up at Tyler's mother, who reached her hand out for the names. Madeline handed them to her. "It is a good list," she said.

She watched as Gloria perused the names for what was probably the thousandth time. A thousand and one. A swell of affection for her future mother-in-law rose up in Madeline. It was met with a rush of gratitude. Gratitude for what was going to be her new family. A husband. A mother. In-law. And for a breeze of a moment, Madeline wondered what it would be like to have a baby. Tyler's baby.

Tyler would be a wonderful father, she thought. *What kind of a mother would I be?*

Count your blessings, Madeline told herself. But thought of Anthony. Wondered where he was. What he was doing. Wondered if she would spend the rest of her life wondering where Anthony was and what he was doing.

Letting go is a process.

Finally, Gloria lifted her blue eyes, eyes that were identical to Tyler's, to meet Madeline's. They were almost moist with tears.

"Gloria?" Madeline reached out to place her hand on Gloria's. "What is it?"

Gloria shook her head. "I don't know." She looked deeply into Madeline's eyes and Madeline felt their hearts connect. "I feel like I'm losing him," she said, tears flowing freely down her face.

Madeline's heart filled with compassion for Gloria. She knew what it was like to lose a loved one. Knew how painful it was to endure the endless loss and loneliness.

"Oh, Gloria. You're not losing Tyler," she said.

Gloria nodded and laughed, embarrassed, through her tears.

"I know. I know. I guess I'm finally realizing that one day, he'll lose me. And you'll be with him then. You'll be his family."

Madeline let out a long slow breath.

Life is full of love and loss, isn't it?

"You know, a very dear friend of mine told me once that love is never lost. That when it's real, it's forever."

Gloria stared down at the table, a thousand miles away. Madeline wondered what she was thinking. Maybe about her late husband. Maybe about someone else. After all, who really knows what memories people keep buried like long lost treasure in the fathoms of their hearts. The way memories of Anthony would always be buried in hers. Finally, Gloria nodded and wiped her eyes with the back of her hand. Sniffled and smiled. Then waved the list of names in the air with bravado.

"Tomorrow," she said, "the invitations will be in the mail."

* * * *

It was the third time in five days that Madeline found herself kneeling before the toilet, sick to her stomach.

What's going on? she asked herself. She felt fine otherwise, but the nausea she was experiencing was unusual. She was always so healthy. How could she have gotten so sick? What could it be? Terror sliced through her like a guillotine. She thought of her sister.

What if she had cancer? Like Carrie. She wretched again.

OhmyGodohmyGodohmyGod!

Her heart started racing and her head throbbed. Panic gripped her. What if she was going to die?

She stood up and stumbled with bare feet across the cold marble floor to the basin. With trembling hands she splashed cold water on her face and looked up at herself in the mirror. Her face was white.

Okay, get a hold of yourself.

It can't be cancer. But if it wasn't cancer, then what was it? It was more than just eating some bad shrimp.

What is it?

From somewhere deep within the core of her being, a voice told her.

"Oh, my God," she said, to no one but herself.

* * * *

Madeline hurried into her office and started up her computer. Pulled up her calendar. Looked at the dates. Counted.

Twenty-eight. Twenty-nine. Thirty. Thirty-one. Thirty-two.

Thirty-three.

She was late. Not for work. Or for a meeting.

But late. Five days late!

She was pregnant. Every cell of her body told her it was true.

Her mind flew back to Italy. To that night with Anthony. That night filled with kisses and caresses. Passion. Love. Death.

And now, life.

Images of Anthony rushed back to her. She could see his dark eyes gazing into hers. Feel the tender touch of his hand upon her cheek. The warmth of his breath. She had wanted to forget him. Had pushed the memories of him from her mind. And her heart.

Oh, Anthony.

As though she beckoned him, he was there. Beside her.

Behind her. She felt his love pouring over her like a warm shower. It surrounded her. Was within her.

Then she remembered the time with Tyler. In Sardinia. When they had made love without protection. That one time.

What if Tyler were the father?

"Madeline, I've got–" Eric's voice jarred her back into the room. He stood in the doorway.

She swung around in her chair and cut him off, "Not now."

"But it's–"

"I said not now. Close the door please."

Eric looked at her, surprised. She was never short with him. Quietly, he turned and pulled the door shut.

Madeline sunk deeply into her chair and placed a hand on her belly. Felt Anthony. Felt Tyler. And Tyler's engagement ring.

Oh my God.

How could she marry Tyler if the baby was Anthony's?

* * * *

The waiting room was filled with pregnant women. Well, not all the women were pregnant, but many of them were. Some of them were accompanied by their husbands or boyfriends. The woman seated beside Madeline looked at least eight months pregnant. She was an attractive brunette, Madeline guessed she was in her late thirties, and was leafing absently through a magazine. As if she felt eyes upon her, she glanced up at Madeline and smiled warmly.

"How much longer will it be before you look like me?" she patted her enormous stomach.

Madeline stammered, "I–uh–ummm..."

"Oh," the woman glanced at Madeline's engagement ring. "You're trying. We had to try for two years. But now, here I am, forty-two and pregnant with my first. It's a little girl. We're naming her Charlotte," the woman glowed. "Oh," she placed her hand on her belly. "The baby just moved. Here..."

She reached over for Madeline's hand and placed it underneath hers. “Feel that?”

Madeline was speechless. Underneath her hand, inside this woman she did not even know, was a baby. A new life squirming and kicking. She had to smile and the two women exchanged a look that can only be shared between women. Women who know the secret mysteries of what it is to be a woman. To be in a body that changes from moment to moment, month to month. With all its sacred rhythms and beauty and life-giving gifts.

The door to the hall of exam rooms opened and a nurse stood holding it open.

“Doris Carter?” the nurse shouted.

“Oh, that’s me,” the woman said to Madeline with a smile. With effort, she heaved out of the chair, stood up and straightened her expensive suit. Hesitating, she lowered herself close to Madeline’s face and placed a hand on Madeline’s arm. “Keep trying. It can happen. Look at me, I’m proof. It’s the best thing that could have ever happened. A real blessing.” She looked deeply into Madeline’s eyes, then turned and walked over to the nurse and disappeared through the door.

Madeline sighed a long defeated sigh. A blessing. A blessing. The words repeated themselves over and over. She thought of Anthony. That is exactly what he would have said. Somehow this pregnancy was a blessing. How could she keep it, not knowing who the father was? How could she explain to Tyler the need for a paternity test?

The door opened again and this time the nurse called Madeline’s name. She got up from her chair with another long sigh and gathered up her purse and briefcase and followed the nurse through the door.

“How are you, Madeline?”

“Fine,” she answered.

I’m not fine. Not fine at all. I hate the smell of doctors and medicine and hospitals. I just want this over.

Madeline was led to a small exam room and sat down. She went through the rigors of her temperature and blood pressure being taken. Of being weighed. Finally, she had answered all the young nurse’s questions and was left to change into the flimsy paper towel that imitated a gown.

“Doctor Simon will be right with you,” the nurse said.

Madeline could only manage a nod. She had been seeing Doctor Simon for years. She was an excellent physician whose reputation had only improved over time. Madeline wondered if she would try to talk her out of having an abortion.

It was the decision Madeline had reached. What else could she do? How could she ever explain to Tyler that she slept with Anthony? Gotten herself pregnant without knowing who the father is? How could she have been so careless? So irresponsible?

She was almost forty. Women that age who wanted to get pregnant had to *try* to get pregnant. Madeline had only been with Anthony for one night. One beautiful memorable night.

What were the chances that the baby was Anthony's?

She and Tyler had only lapsed with protection that one time. Maybe the pregnancy wasn't a blessing. Maybe it was a miracle.

There was no way she could follow it through. It had taken her all her life to find someone like Tyler. She was finally happy. Truly happy for the first time in her life. There was no way she could tell Tyler she might be pregnant with someone else's child. So, there was no way she could keep the baby. No way at all.

Was there?

* * * *

Monday mornings had always been one of Madeline's favorite times. Unlike most people who worked Monday through Friday, week after week, Mondays signaled, to Madeline, the beginning of a new week of possibilities. But this Monday was the commencement of Heather's last week at Felicity. And the first that Jeff Straus, her successor, would be aboard. So, this particular Monday was one that Madeline was not particularly looking forward to.

Riding up the crowded elevator to the office, she tried to forget that on Friday, she would have the abortion that Doctor Simon had reluctantly agreed to perform. Reluctantly not on any moral or ethical grounds, but because she feared that Madeline would regret the decision. She had told Madeline as much. But Madeline was a skilled negotiator when she chose to be and managed to convince the doctor that she was making the right choice. But the more she tried to forget, the more she remembered.

She rubbed her engagement ring and smiled. Tyler loved her and the thought of him warmed her heart. She had been distant with him ever since learning of her pregnancy, and he had responded with love and reassurance. Teased her that she was getting cold feet. But he let her be. Tyler, she knew, was her future. Anthony was the past. And on Friday, he would finally be out of her life.

The doors opened and Madeline stepped into Felicity's offices as she had done for years. Walked down the hall to her office. And, as usual, her phone was ringing. She hurried to pick it up.

"Hello, this is Madeline," she answered.

"Aunt Maddie, it's Jonathan."

"Jonathan," she said and plopped herself into her chair, smiling. "What a wonderful surprise! How are you?"

"I'm fine. What about you?"

Madeline brought him up to date about her February first wedding date. She had been keeping current with news of her engagement via letters. She cherished her time spent with pen and paper to write them. Enjoyed the more personal touch and feel of them instead of sending an email for him to read on a cold computer screen.

"I have some news myself," Jonathan said.

"Oh?" Madeline was instantly wary of his tone.

"I'm going to the Congo to be with Anthony."

What? No! Don't go!

She remembered a headline in the *Times* about the civil war in the Congo. How it was still dangerous there. Vertebra by vertebra a shiver crawled down the length of Madeline's spine. Her heart raced. Every cell in her body screamed that he should not go. She stood up and started pacing.

"The Congo with Anthony! Oh, Jonathan. I wish you wouldn't," she pleaded and paced. "It's just too dangerous."

"That's exactly why I need to go. To help bring peace." He sighed. "Besides, Saint Valentine's just isn't the same without Anthony. Father Marco thinks it's a wonderful idea for me to get out beyond the monastery's walls. Experience some of the world."

"Then come to New York. There's so much you could do here, too."

"It wouldn't be the same. You know that. And I...I miss Anthony."

Her heart skipped a beat at the mention of his name.

So do I. I miss him, too. God, how I miss him...

"I know. But, Jonathan–"

"Aunt Maddie, I want to do some good for a change. I'm starting to feel like I'm locked away at Saint Valentine's." His voice implored her. "This is why I became a monk. To serve God. To serve humanity."

Anger at God rushed into Madeline. God was always taking

the people she loved away. Was that what God demand

Isn't there some other way to serve God? Do you h come a monk and run off to Africa to serve God?

"Can't you serve God and humanity in New York?"

There was a short silence before Jonathan replied. "Aunt Maddie, in my heart, I know I need to go to Africa."

How could she argue with that? How could she ask him to deny his heart? She sighed. Defeated. Powerless.

"Are you sure? What if something happens to you?"

There was a short pause before he answered, "Then it will be God's will."

God's will. What about free will?

She sighed again as she realized that Jonathan was exercising just that. Free will.

What if the things we most want are *God's will? What if the deepest desires of our heart are what God wants most for us?*

Madeline fell into her chair. Surrendered. "Does Anthony know?" she asked.

"I talked with him yesterday. He's happy that I'll be joining him."

Madeline nodded her head slowly while tears floated in her eyes. "How is he?"

"He sounded happy. And excited about the work that he's doing there," Jonathan's voice lifted. "I've never heard him this way."

Madeline nodded to herself again and held the back of her hand to her lips. "When are you leaving?"

"Next week."

"Next week! So soon?"

"Why wait?" he responded.

Why wait indeed.

* * * *

Somehow the week rushed by and, before Madeline knew it, Thursday was upon her. Friday would be Heather's last day at Felicity. But Friday, Madeline would be out of the office, having an abortion.

So, for me today is Heather's last day. And then tomorrow...

She pushed the idea of tomorrow and the abortion out of her mind. Instead, she turned her thoughts to Heather's successor, Jeff. In spite of herself, she had to admit that she liked him. He seemed to be navigating the ins and outs of Felicity well. He was right. Personable. She was satisfied she had made the right choice. Heather had also said good things about him, and, in spite of their personal differences, Madeline trusted her professional opinion.

Their personal differences. Madeline took a sip of her decaf and pursed her lips at the demise of their friendship. But what was she to do? Heather had made up her mind and, in Madeline's heart, she resigned herself to the truth that if a staff member really did not want to be at Felicity, then it was in everyone's best interest that they leave. Heather was no exception. Still, it would feel strange to say good-bye to Heather.

Good-bye. Madeline felt her lips tremble at the word. She always hated good-byes. The more of them she said, the more painful the next one was.

Oh, God...please let me get through this day without crying.

She checked herself.

Was that a prayer?

Oh, what the hell, it couldn't hurt.

She smiled to herself at the irony of her thoughts. Wondered if maybe she shouldn't pray more. Somehow, it did make her feel better. Maybe, mysteriously, it would all turn out well.

She lifted her coffee mug to her lips for another sip and Heather appeared in the door. She set the mug down.

"Hi," Heather said.

"Hi," Madeline answered.

Heather leaned against the doorframe. "I thought I would stop in and, well...since you're not going to be here tomorrow... "

"Check out?" Madeline said.

Heather smiled.

Madeline smiled.

It was the first time they had exchanged a smile in weeks.

Madeline regarded Heather. Oh, how she wanted to tell her she was pregnant. Ask her to go with her to the clinic tomorrow. Heather had always been there to help Madeline weather the stormiest of storms. But things were different now. As much as she wished Heather could be there for her, it simply was not to be.

"Well, yeah," Heather shrugged. "I'll come in tomorrow to pack up. But that's about it. Jeff has caught onto things really well. He'll do a good job. He's got my number at Saks. I've left it with Eric, too. So call me if you need anything."

"Thanks. So...no lunch?"

Heather shook her head. "No, thanks. I have some loose ends

to clean up. So..." She winced, shrugged.

Madeline started to get up.

"Oh–no–" Heather held out her hands in a gesture to stop Madeline.

She sat back down.

"I know how much you hate good-byes," Heather said, her eyes beginning to moisten.

Madeline looked down at the carpet for a moment, not knowing what to say.

When she looked up, Heather was gone.

* * * *

"Mom says the RSVPs are coming in. Everyone's coming. We haven't had any no's so far," Tyler took Madeline's overnight bag and helped her off with her black wool coat. It was nine o'clock and she was just arriving, having stayed late at Felicity.

His apartment had become like a second home to Madeline. They were struggling with the decision of whose place they should live in. Tyler loved his apartment overlooking the park. Madeline loved her place overlooking the harbor.

She wrapped her arms around his neck and kissed him lightly on the lips. "That's wonderful news."

They shared a deep close embrace and Madeline allowed herself to relax fully into Tyler's arms.

"Hmmmm...," he moaned. "This is nice."

"Ummm hmmm...it is nice," she responded.

"Do you really have to travel tomorrow?"

Madeline lied to him. Told him she was flying to Montreal to see about some business in Canada.

"I'm afraid so," she hated the deception. "I'll be back on Saturday morning."

He pulled away from her and smiled. "It's too long," he teased, and started down the hall to the kitchen with Madeline in tow.

"It's one night. It's nothing."

"It's nothing...it's nothing," he mimicked. "So, what should we do about dinner?"

"You haven't eaten? It's so late,"

"I actually just got in about half an hour ago," he started to open a bottle of wine and began to pour a glass. A second glass.

"Oh, no thank you," Madeline said.

"No?"

Madeline shook her head. "No...I'm suddenly really really tired. I think I'll just take a bath and go to bed."

"Nothing to eat?"

"I had such big lunch." Another lie.

"Anything wrong?"

"It was a strange day, that's all."

"Oh, that's right. You won't be seeing Heather at work again. How'd that go?"

Madeline shrugged. "Okay, I guess. I wonder if she'll be coming to the wedding."

"We'll know soon enough," Tyler said.

She went to him and gave him a brush of a kiss on the cheek.

"I'm going to take that bath and turn in," she said quietly. "I have an early day tomorrow." That much was true.

"Okay, I'll join you later."

Madeline nodded and left him in the kitchen to reheat some leftover Chinese food.

She ran a hot bath and added a gel fragranced with lavender. Lit some candles. Exhausted, she sank her naked body into the soothing water. Closed her eyes and inhaled the scent of the bubbles that floated all around her.

By tomorrow night at this time, it would all be over. She would not be pregnant any more. She thought of Anthony.

What if the baby was his? She could not marry Tyler if there was even the remotest possibility that she was carrying Anthony's baby. No. She would resolve the matter. Tomorrow, Anthony would be nothing more than a pleasant memory. Still, she wondered what he was doing in Africa. Where he was sleeping. If he was sleeping.

With only the thought of him she felt him all around her, as if he had somehow become the very water she soaked in. She felt him touch her. Kiss her. Sense his body against hers. *In* hers.

A voice inside told her. *This baby is Anthony's. This baby is Anthony's.*

She knew it was true. A deep certain soul-knowing.

She opened her eyes. Reminded herself that Anthony was a part of her past. Someone she had loved. And lost.

Yes. She rested a hand on her belly. Tomorrow, it would all be over. She would never have to lie to Tyler again.

There was no question in Madeline's mind that she was doing the right thing. What she wondered, though, was why she was crying.

* * * *

Madeline sat nervously in Doctor Simon's waiting room. And, well, waited. She glanced around the room which was again filled with impatient looking women and uncomfortable looking men. Were gynecologists' offices *always* crowded?

The door to the suite opened and in walked the woman who had encouraged Madeline so lovingly to keep trying to get pregnant. What was her name? Madeline struggled to recall. Doris... Doris Carter. Madeline looked down, not wanting to catch Doris' eye. Held the New York Times up in front of her face. Crossed her legs.

"Madeline O'Connor," it was the nurse calling her name.

Thank God, Madeline thought.

She gathered her purse, rose from the chair, and followed the nurse into Doctor Simon's office.

"Can't we just get started?" Madeline asked impatiently.

The nurse nodded. "We're prepping the room. It won't be long. Doctor Simon will be right with you." With that, the nurse left Madeline alone with the door open.

So, Madeline was left to wait. Again.

Doctors. Damn them. They're never on time.

Movement outside the doorway caught Madeline's attention. It was the nurse leading Doris Carter to an exam room. She watched Doris waddle along, ripe with life.

What was it that Doris had said? Madeline's mind struggled to recall.

"It's the best thing that could have ever happened. A real blessing." That was it.

A real blessing.

Doubts overflowed in Madeline's mind.

No.

The truth was, they poured from her heart.

All the memories of Anthony that she had held at bay flooded through her as if a dam had broken. The looks they had shared. His quiet strength. Laughter in the hospital room with Carrie. The caresses. The kisses.

The love.

Carrie. Madeline had thought that when Carrie died, so had almost the last of her family. Of course there was Jonathan, but he was so far away. And he wasn't...hers.

This baby is my family. My son or daughter. Anthony's yes.

But mine, too. Mine.

So, unbidden, from the very soul of the universe, love for the baby that she carried inside her pierced her heart. A precious tender love that Madeline had never known.

She tried to blink back tears. But could not. They streamed freely down Madeline's face and Madeline was powerless to stop them. She wanted this baby. She wanted it. With all her heart.

"How are you this morning?" Doctor Simon blew into the room carrying Madeline's file.

Madeline looked up at her.

"Oh," the doctor stopped. Retraced her steps and closed the door behind her. Walked behind Madeline and sat in the chair beside her. "Tell me all about it," she said quietly, and waited.

Like her tears, her story poured from Madeline. How Carrie had betrayed her. How she worked so long and hard at Felicity, trying to forget. How she traveled to Italy. To fall in love with Anthony. To watch Carrie die. And now, how she was engaged to a wonderful man who she loved. But was pregnant with a monk's child.

For the first time in Madeline's life, someone sat with her. And listened. Just listened.

"I really don't know what to do,"

Madeline finally concluded. "I really don't."

Doctor Simon shook her head. "Oh, I think you do, Madeline. I think you do."

Relief rushed though Madeline and she found herself laughing and crying at the same time. Doctor Simon was right. In her heart, Madeline knew exactly what she was going to do.

She looked at her physician and smiled.

Maybe doctors aren't so bad after all.

* * * *

1945

The first time Marco saw Anthony he was sleeping, wrapped in a blanket Isabella had knit.

When Anthony finally opened his eyes and looked up at his father, all Marco could see was Isabella.

Marco turned and smiled at Sister Francesca through his tears. "He has his mother's eyes, doesn't he?"

"Yes, he does." Sister Francesca replied.

"Every time I look at him, I will see her."

Sister Francesca smiled. "That is how she will live on, Marco. As long as you remember her, she'll never die."

"What will I tell him, when he asks about his parents."

"That you don't know. That the orphanage was full, so an old nun brought him to you one day after the war ended."

"He'll never know his mother or his father."

"No. But he will know God. That's more than most people ever have."

It was the truth. Marco looked down at his son, who was sitting up and clapping his hands as though he just discovered he had them.

Marco knelt down toward his little boy and clapped too.

Anthony laughed outrageously, and Marco smiled proudly at his son. It was the first smile that father and son exchanged, and Marco's heart filled with love for his little boy, for Isabella, and for God. He felt a bittersweet gratitude for the miracle of life. For its mystery. And for its infinite beauty, even in the midst of tragedy.

Anthony reached out his arms to his father, and Marco picked him up. He smiled at Sister Francesca, and then it occurred to him. He had no idea how to take care of a baby.

"Sister Francesca, what do I do? How will I raise him?"

"You'll do what most parents do, Marco. You'll figure it out as you go along." She smiled. "I'll stay for a day or two to help you get started."

"Thank you, Sister Francesca. For everything."

"Isabella would have wanted him here with you."

Marco smiled and looked down at Anthony. He knew in that moment he could never love another woman. That there would never be another Isabella in his life. He would love his son. Love God. And be the best priest he could be. His life was here, at Saint Valentine's.

So was Anthony's.

* * * *

Present Day

"I can't marry you, Tyler," Madeline said quietly.

They were sitting on a bench in Central Park. Madeline called him after leaving Doctor Simon's office. She had made up her heart. She was going to have her baby and be its mother. Be a good mother. There was no room in that decision for Tyler. Canceling the engagement was the fair thing to do.

"What?" Tyler was incredulous.

"I can't marry you," she repeated.

So this is what it feels like to be the one doing the hurting.

"Madeline! What are you saying? You're not making any sense!"

He looked at her. Confused.

"Tyler, this has all happened so fast. We rushed into things. I just–I just can't do it,"

"Madeline. You wanted to set the wedding date. The first week in February." He shook his head and raked his fingers through his hair.

Madeline's heart ached. He was right, of course. She remembered the morning they had decided on their wedding date. How happy they had been. She sighed.

"Is there someone else?" he asked.

Her brows furrowed in confusion. "No. Yes. No. I–"

"No! Yes! No? Which is it?"

Madeline closed her eyes. The last week had wrought havoc with her emotions and they were raw. She rubbed her forehead, feeling the beginning of a headache.

"No! There was. But there isn't anymore."

"What is that supposed to mean?"

Angry at herself, Madeline could not find words. She shook her head. This was too painful.

Too painful.

Tyler grabbed her shoulders. Shook her. Caught off guard, Madeline felt scared. Vulnerable.

"Stop it!" she shouted. "Stop it, Tyler."

"No! Not until you tell me what this is about. You love me. I know you do!" He shook harder.

Madeline burst into tears. "All right! All right! I'm pregnant. I'm pregnant, okay!"

Struck speechless, he stopped shaking her. Looked at her.

"While I was in Italy. The night Carrie died. I was with Anthony."

She watched Tyler absorb the news. Watched him think.

"Anthony...Anthony...the monk!"

Madeline pursed her lips. Nodded while tears flowed down her cheeks. Tyler sat beside her. Stunned.

She told her story for the second time that day. Of how she traveled to Italy and fell in love. How somehow, in ways that she did not and perhaps would never know, Anthony had been able to hold out a hand and reach into her heart in a way no one ever had before. Or ever would again. How he had been a source of strength for both Carrie and herself. She explained that they had been together only once and that now, as unlikely as it was, she was pregnant. And how she somehow knew the baby was Anthony's. Like Doctor Simon, Tyler sat, and listened.

"Of course, there is the possibility that the baby is yours. But somehow, in my heart, I just know it's Anthony's." Finally, she finished. Her heart pounded in her chest. Breaking. She watched the fallen leaves at her feet swirl in a sudden cold gust of wind and be whisked away.

Everything changes, she thought. One minute everything is fine and the next minute someone comes along and nothing is ever the same.

I'm one of those breezes in Tyler's life. Just like Anthony was to me.

She fought back tears. Waited for Tyler to erupt in anger. Whatever he was going to say, she deserved it.

"No, Madeline. You're right. The baby is Anthony's."

She looked up at him.

"I was going to tell you. I wanted to tell you. But you didn't want children so I didn't think it would matter."

He bit his lower lip. "I'm sterile."

"Sterile!"

"In high school, a girlfriend claimed I had gotten her pregnant. I knew she had been sleeping around, but back then...anyway, I was scared to death. I, so I denied the baby was mine. Had some tests. And it turned out it was true. I'm sterile."

"But your mother wants grandchildren."

"I never told her."

The both sat quietly. Thinking.

Tyler spoke first. "That day on the terrace. The way he looked up at us. At you... "

"I know. That's when I knew he'd stay a monk. He doesn't know any of this. Nor will he." Madeline stared at the leaves at her feet.

"Do you love him?" Tyler asked.

"Yes, Tyler, I do. Which is why I can't marry you." She slipped the engagement ring off her hand and pressed it into Tyler's palm. She rose from the bench and walked away.

Leaving is just as hard as being left, she thought. And started the walk home. Her heart broke for Tyler. And for herself.

"Madeline?" he called her.

She spun around to look at him.

"I need to ask you something," he said.

"What is it?"

"If he left Saint Valentine's, would you be with him?"

It was a question Madeline had not considered. There had been a time when it was what she would have wanted. But now a deep peacefulness descended upon her and she knew the answer.

She shook her head. "No. It would never have worked with him. We're from two different worlds. Being a monk made Anthony who he is. And that is who I fell in love with. If he left for me, he'd only resent me, and himself. It's better this way."

"Will you tell him about the baby?"

"No."

Tyler nodded slowly, but said nothing.

There was nothing left to say.

So Madeline turned and continued to walk. Less than twenty feet away, she started to miss him.

She glanced back. Tyler still sat on the bench. Motionless. His face was in his hands. She wanted to go back to him and hold him. Make his pain disappear.

Instead, with tears streaming down her face, she turned and walked away.

* * * *

Saturday mornings with Tyler had typically meant a walk to Bettie's, the local coffee shop, for breakfast and running errands. *This* Saturday morning, Madeline was exhausted. The events of the week had taken their toll. She wanted to stay in bed. Under the comfort of the warm covers where it was safe.

But she was hungry. *Eating for two now.* The thought unleashed an avalanche of sadness, joy, fear, and love that pounded her heart. How was it possible to feel so many things at once? She missed Tyler. Wished he were there curled up in bed with her. But she was so...so...grateful for the life growing inside her own body that her heart ached and soared at the same time.

Her stomach growled, a reminder to return to the practical matter of breakfast. She rubbed her belly, slid back the covers and got up out of bed. A few minutes later she was dressed in jeans and a gray cashmere sweater, heading out the door.

A cloudy November day cast a somber spell on Manhattan and drew Madeline in to its gloomy mood. Feeling melancholy, she walked a few blocks to Bettie's Diner where she and Tyler had become regulars. She wondered if she would find him there. Hoped she would find him there. But knew that she would not. But...then again.

She opened the door and glanced around expectantly. No Tyler.

"Hi Madeline," the owner, Bettie, said with a cheerful tone. She was an older woman, in her fifties, who had come to New York to be an actress but whose only career had been waiting tables. With dyed blonde hair and ruby lips, she belonged to another time. In spite of her smile, there was a sadness that resided in her brown eyes. "Alone today?" The smile slowly faded.

Madeline nodded and Bettie became quiet, almost melancholy. As though she felt Madeline's frame of heart. A bell chimed and the waitress turned and hurried toward the pick-up counter, leaving Madeline to take a seat.

The usual booth was empty and she slid onto the brown vinyl upholstery. Magically a cup of hot chocolate appeared before her.

Bettie smiled down at Madeline. "Chocolate always makes a girl feel better. Drink up."

Another diner shouted, "Bettie. Where're my eggs?"

Bettie rolled her eyes. "I'll be right back," she told Madeline and went to attend to the other table.

Madeline wrapped cold hands around the warm mug. Tendrils of steam wafted from the rich brown liquid and caught Madeline's eye. She watched them rise up until finally they disappeared.

God is in that cup, Madeline thought, and took a sip.

Now, God is within me. The idea filled her with a sense of peace.

She reached for a menu and opened it. Tyler would have teased her had he been there. "Why do you read the menu? You always order the same thing," Madeline imagined him saying.

As promised, Bettie appeared at her side. "The usual?"

Madeline smiled and nodded. "The usual."

Madeline put the menu away and picked up the business section of *The New York Times* that had been left on the seat by the previous patron. She glanced at it absently, uninterested in the headlines that usually said the same things over and over again but about different people and companies. But one captured her attention. Saks was being bought out by a huge retail conglomerate.

That's strange, Madeline thought. *Why would Heather have gone to a company that was on the market? Maybe she hadn't known it was for sale,* Madeline speculated. Companies do those kinds of things. Hire people knowing that in a few months they would be back out on the street, looking for work.

Bettie appeared and Madeline turned her attention to the perfectly prepared French toast with hot maple syrup that was set on the table.

"Here you go," Bettie said and quickly left.

"Thanks," Madeline said to herself. She thought there was something strange in Bettie's manner this morning, but Madeline attributed the perception to her own misty mood. She folded up the newspaper and put it away, then began to devour her breakfast.

Shortly, Bettie returned to silently replace Madeline's finished mug of hot chocolate with a second cup. She placed the handwritten check face down on the table.

Madeline finished her meal quickly and left a generous tip. She picked up the check and went over to the cash register where Bettie quickly met her.

Madeline looked carefully at Bettie as the waitress rung up the sale. "You seem a little quiet today, Bettie. Everything okay?"

The waitress pursed her red lips and looked up at Madeline.

"No. Everything isn't okay, is it?"

Madeline furrowed her brows. "What do you mean?"

"Well...he'd be angry if I told you. He said not to."

Madeline shook her head. "What are you talking about?"

"Your boyfriend was here for three hours this morning. Got here at seven and waited until ten. Drank about eight cups of coffee. Left about fifteen minutes before you got here. He'd never admit it, but he was hoping you'd turn up. You should go and straighten out whatever it is that's goin' on. I can't figure out which one of you looks more miserable."

"Tyler was here?" Madeline's heart leapt at the news.

"Sure was." Bettie reached for the twenty dollar bill that Madeline held out, slapped it in the drawer, and hastily counted up change. "That was his paper you were reading."

Madeline took the money that Bettie held out. "You go and patch things up. You two were one of the happiest couples I've ever seen. Gave me hope, seeing the two of you. That it can still happen in this crazy world."

Madeline was at a loss for words. "Bye, Bettie. Thank you," was all she managed to say.

Madeline left the diner without any particular destination in mind. Life was strange. How fifteen minutes or just one could make all the difference in a person's life. In living or dying. Or meeting the love of one's life. Or just missing him.

Not ready yet to go home, she started to walk.

Was it all just random fate? The events that took place? The people who drifted in and out of one's life? The ones who stayed? She thought of Anthony and what he might have said.

Grace. He would have said nothing was fate. Seeming chance was really the grace of God. His faith in God was unshakable, Madeline thought, and felt a familiar swell of love for him.

As she walked, she remembered Saint Valentine's and the peace and serenity she had felt there. The hills and the blue skies and the stillness. The chapel.

Of course! Why hadn't she thought of it sooner. Madeline quickened her pace as she thought of Saint Patrick's. She would go there and sit for a while.

Pray.

* * * *

When Madeline arrived home, Tyler was waiting outside her door. He was unshaved. Uncombed. Disheveled. Sexy. There was an F.A.O. Schwarz bag at his feet. Something for the baby. Madeline felt a rush of love for him. And for her unborn child.

"Hi," she said tentatively.

"Hi."

She opened her purse and took out her keys. "Come in?"

Tyler nodded and followed her through the door. Madeline remembered all the times they had walked down her hallway. Once they had been in such a hurry to make love that they peeled off their clothes and fell to the rug just inside the door. She smiled to herself at the memory.

"Coffee?" she asked as she walked into the kitchen.

"That would be great. I could sure use some. Madeline, we need to talk."

"Okay. I've only got decaf." She began the ritual of brewing some coffee, opening drawers and running water and grinding beans.

"That's fine. Madeline. I was up all night. Thinking. Just thinking. About you and me. And Anthony. And the baby."

He walked over to her and took a pitcher of water out of her hands and set it on the counter. Held her by the shoulders. Looked deeply into her eyes.

"Madeline, I want to marry you. I love you. I love the idea of being a father. Let's get married. Have this baby and raise it together."

Madeline burst into tears of joy. Could this really be happening? Did he really still want her in spite of everything? She threw herself into Tyler's arms.

"Oh, Tyler, really?"

He squeezed her close to him. Lifted her up off the floor. "Yes, sweetheart. Really." He set her down and she pulled far enough away to look at him.

"It's such a big commitment. Are you really sure?"

Their eyes met and held and Madeline knew Tyler was going to share something important with her.

"Madeline, when I found out I couldn't have children, I was devastated. I'd always wanted to be a father. Somehow, I felt like less of a man. So, I never got serious with anyone. I just never felt good enough. Never felt like I had enough to offer. But then I met you. And you were such a mystery. So successful and yet so...so vulnerable. All you needed was to be loved. And I knew I could do that. I knew I could love you the way you needed to be loved. And I do. The baby, well, the baby is a real blessing. I'd be honored to be its father. So, yes, Madeline, I've never been more sure of anything in my life," he beamed. "Oh-I just remembered. Wait right here."

Madeline wiped her eyes and nodded. She leaned against the counter, exhausted by the emotional storms of the last two days. Everyone, it seemed, agreed that this baby was a real blessing. Madeline rested a hand on her stomach.

If only Anthony...

Tyler returned with the F.A.O. Schwarz bag. "This is for you. And the baby."

Madeline bit her lower lip. "Oh, Tyler...what is it?"

"Well open it," he smiled expectantly.

She removed the sparkling tissue paper and pulled out a snow white teddy bear. He had dark brown eyes and a precious pink nose. One of his paws was encircled with her engagement ring.

"Oh, Tyler," Madeline looked up at him.

"Here." Tyler reached for the bear's paw and slid off the ring. "Let's put this back where it belongs."

He reached out for her left hand and held the ring at the tip of her finger. "Madeline, will you marry me?"

"Yes, I will. I will marry you, Tyler," she said through tear-filled eyes.

Tyler slipped the ring up onto her finger. "Now, don't take it off again."

Madeline shook her head and smiled. "I won't. I promise. Are you really sure? I'm so...so flawed."

Tyler smiled. "So am I. That's what makes us so right for each other. Our flaws are a perfect fit."

He pulled her to him. Kissed her deeply and passionately. A love passed between them that Madeline had never known. It was the kind of love that reached into the core of her being with such warmth and tenderness that every cell in her body was filled with radiance.

It was the kind of love that wrapped itself around her heart and mended every place where it had ever been broken.

So there, in Tyler's arms, with Anthony's baby in her belly, Madeline was filled with a deep feeling of peace and gratitude. For her life. For all its losses. And its loves. For every betrayal and heartache. Because they had all led her to this place. This moment.

And returned her home.

To love.

* * * *

The next few months passed in a blur of holidays and wedding plans. Gloria was thrilled at the news of Madeline's pregnancy and had suggested that the couple elope in Las Vegas.

Madeline had wanted to go through with their wedding as planned. It was important to her that she become a part of Tyler's family with all the people who were important to him present.

It saddened her that Jonathan would not be at her wedding. While she offered to pay for his travel, he was reluctant to leave the work he was doing. To leave Africa. *It's so beautiful here. I can't imagine ever leaving. Even to go back to Saint Valentine's.* His note had been the only correspondence Madeline received from Jonathan since he had left the monastery, and she resigned herself to his absence at her wedding. But Heather accepted the invitation. It seemed that she met someone and would be bringing him to the wedding. Madeline hoped it might be the beginning of the renewal of their friendship. It could never be the same, she knew. But it could be something different. And good.

* * * *

It was the morning of February first and the soaring steeple of All Souls Church glistened in the winter sun. Madeline was inside, already wearing her wedding gown. It was a simple strapless dress with a full tulle skirt that concealed her now showing pregnancy. Not everyone knew that she was pregnant. They would, of course, eventually find out, but that was for another day.

She and Gloria were surveying her reflection in the mirror. Her auburn hair was swept up into a French twist with white baby's breath sprinkled here and there. A dusting of powder, a brush of mascara over her green eyes, and a sweep of lipstick were all that she needed to transform her into a naturally beautiful bride. The only jewelry she wore was her engagement ring and the brilliant diamond studs on her ears.

"You look absolutely radiant," Gloria said.

Madeline turned away from the mirror to look in Gloria's eyes. "I've never been happier," she said.

"Well, it shows."

Madeline's cell phone rang.

She smiled easily. "It's probably Tyler," she said to her almost mother-in-law.

"He shouldn't be calling you, it's bad luck," Gloria responded.

Madeline grinned at the superstitious thought, reached into her handbag for the phone, and answered it.

"Hello?"

"Is this Madeline?" the male voice was vaguely familiar.

"Yes."

"Madeline, it's Father Marco. At Saint Valentine's."

"Father Marco! Hello!" Madeline was happy to hear his voice. She had always liked him. But why would he be calling?

Her blood ran cold.

"My dear. Oh my dear. I'm afraid I have some terrible news. I wish I could tell you in person."

Madeline sat down.

"What is it?" Gloria whispered, sitting down beside Madeline.

Madeline shook her head and continued her conversation.

"Is it Jonathan?"

"I'm afraid so. He and Anthony were flying into a small village. Something went wrong with the engine...and the plane...and the plane crashed."

"What?" Madeline could not grasp the news.

"I'm so sorry."

"Jonathan *and* Anthony? When?"

"I just got the news. The crash happened two days ago."

"They're both..."

"I'm so sorry," the priest repeated.

"Is there going to be..." she could not finish.

"Local missionaries found the bodies. They were buried at the mission there."

"In Africa?" Madeline froze at the news. Numb. "I see." *Anthony and Jonathan are buried...somewhere in Africa...*

"Yes. We'll have a memorial of some kind...here at Saint Valentine's. Let us know when you're ready."

A memorial service. Madeline's stomach churned and her heart was in her throat while her mind wrestled with the news.

Jonathan and Anthony! Both gone! It could not be. But it was.

"My dear, how are you?" He spoke slowly.

"It's my wedding day, Father Marco," Madeline said in despair.

There was a pause on the other end of the line. "Your wedding day. A sacred day. Get married, my dear. Live your life. Jonathan would have wanted that."

Madeline made a heroic effort and fought back tears. Father Marco was right. It was what they all would have wanted. Her parents. Carrie. Jonathan.

Anthony.

She wondered if they were together...somewhere. Remembered Jonathan's wisdom that was beyond his age. How he had said that if something happened to him, it would have been God's will. He knew the risks he had taken. Had followed the call of his soul.

"They'll be with you, you know. All of them." Father Marco said.

"I know," Madeline's voice quivered.

"God is with you, my dear. Be happy."

"Thank you, Father Marco. For everything."

"Good-bye, my dear."

"Good-bye."

Madeline hung up the phone and set it down. Sat down.

"Darling, you're white as a ghost. What happened?" Gloria asked.

Madeline was overcome by a monsoon of tears. Gloria rushed to Madeline's side and pulled her son's fiancée into her mothering arms. "Madeline, my God! What is it?"

"They're gone! They're both gone!" Madeline cried, her body convulsing with pain.

"Who is? Who is, darling?"

"Jonathan. My Jonathan!"

And Anthony. My Anthony!

Madeline had never known such anguish. She had lost everyone. Everyone she ever loved. Who had ever loved her. Gone. Just gone. In one breath of an instant.

She sobbed. Deeply. Wholly. For Jonathan. Anthony. Carrie. For all her losses. And for herself.

Because with every loss, a part of her was taken. A part of her heart. Her love. She felt empty. Bereft. Like nothing was left. Nothing left but an abyss. An unfathomable dark abyss.

"Ohhhh!" Gloria was crying too, now. And she started rocking. Rocking Madeline back and forth in her arms.

"Shhh...it's all right, my dear. It's all right. I'm here. I'm here." For a time. That's how they stayed. Madeline rocking in Gloria's arms. Gloria holding Madeline. Rocking. Rocking.

Eventually, Madeline became aware of the arms that held her. Then, even in the immeasurable sea of her sorrow, she felt it. There was something left after all. Something. Emptiness. Space. That would be filled again.

Then, finally, from deep beneath the waves of her own tears, Madeline surfaced. And found she could breathe. Her tears subsided. She slowly moved away from Gloria and looked into the older woman's wise eyes. Saw Tyler's eyes looking back at her. Tyler. She had been keeping him waiting.

"Oh..." Madeline murmured.

"It's all right, dear," Gloria said. And brushed away the last of Madeline's tears. "Weddings never start on time."

* * * *

Madeline waited in the church's foyer to make her entrance. A young altar boy stood at the doorway, waiting for her to give him the cue to open the door. Beyond it, the guests waited. Gloria waited.

Tyler waited.

Madeline wondered how many other brides had waited anxiously right there. With their fathers. Or brothers. Or whoever it was that was giving them away.

That no one was giving Madeline away felt right to her, in a strange sort of way. She was giving herself away. Freely. Happily. Sacredly.

Jonathan's memory came to mind. How she would have loved

for him to have been at her wedding. Now, she would never see him again. Or Anthony. She took solace knowing that, if she had to lose Jonathan, he was with Anthony in his final moments. They had been there for each other when–

She pushed the image of the crashing plane from her mind and remembered Anthony. Remembered how the love she felt for him was woven into the tapestry of who she was. He had been right. Love survived even death. In a way, today, she was marrying him, too. He would be a part of her forever. While they never exchanged vows, they had exchanged love. True love. Their hearts were forever tied by the indestructible golden thread of that love and by the child that she carried.

Now, she was about to begin a new journey. Weave into her life's tapestry new colors. New threads. New love. And share the love that Anthony had shown her with Tyler. With the new little soul they would raise and love together.

She remembered the day on the terrace at Saint Valentine's. How she had stood there with Tyler and watched Anthony walk with such dignity and intention along the vineyard path. How he had looked up at her with such love, such understanding, such reverence. It was the first time she had seen him in his monk's robe. And the last time she had seen him at all. Walking along the path, beginning the journey that led him away from her.

Oh, Anthony. I wish you were here.

In an instant, it felt as if he was.

As if she felt him breathe. Like he was standing next to her. She knew it was him. She felt him. Feel his love all around her. In her. She closed her eyes and breathed him in. Held him. Felt his soul caress hers. Reunited. Beyond time. Beyond space. Beyond death.

She could hardly breathe.

"I'll never be very far from you...listen to your heart...I'm there...I'll always be there... I'll always be a part of you," he whispered to her heart.

Her soul heard him.

"Anthony," she breathed. "You're here..."

Oh, Anthony...

The young boy at the door coughed. The sound echoed throughout the foyer and beckoned Madeline back to the present moment. To her wedding. To the new life that would begin with a walk down the aisle just beyond the door.

She inhaled deeply. Smiled and nodded at the altar boy.

Exhaled. He smiled back at her and slowly opened the door.

Madeline could see all the guests stand up to bid her enter. Watched Tyler turn his head and look at her. Their eyes met and held in a moment they would each remember all their lives. And longer.

Madeline took a step. Then another. And another. With dignity and intention.

And began. Again.

Epilogue

Madeline had just put Jonathan down for his morning nap when there was a knock at the front door of the Tudor house in upstate New York that she and Tyler had made their home. A fluffy tan and white collie bounded through the house barking.

"Coco. Quiet," Madeline said. "You'll wake the baby." She caught up with the dog and held its collar. In spite of herself, she smiled. The pace at Felicity was leisurely compared to being a wife and mother. But the company was in good hands with Heather at the helm.

Funny how things always seem to work out in the end. God must be everywhere. Even if we don't always believe it.

She accurately predicted that Heather would be unhappy with the sale of Saks and Madeline had offered her the position of President at Felicity. Mothering year-old Jonathan was a full time job and Madeline loved it. She happily held a part-time position consulting at Felicity, and while her relationship with Heather had never fully recovered, it was on its way. With a last look over her shoulder to make sure Jonathan was resting soundly, she hurried to the door with Coco at her side.

The postman was waiting patiently for her arrival. Madeline was radiant as she smiled at the old man.

"G'morning, Madeline," he said.

"Hi Art," Madeline said.

"Not outside today?"

Madeline, Coco, and Jonathan were often outside in the yard when Art arrived with the mail.

Madeline shook her head and smiled. "Not today."

"I wanted to deliver this letter to you personally. Make sure you got it okay." He handed Madeline a letter stamped with African postage. "It was in a bag of air mail that got lost. Sorry it took so long to get it to you."

She knew without looking at the envelope that the letter was from Anthony. The moment she touched it, she felt his presence. Almost as though he was standing right beside her. The way he had so many times when she needed him.

Madeline looked up at Art's wise old face. He seemed to know the letter was important.

"I'm sorry for any inconvenience," he said.

Madeline shook her head slightly and said, simply, "Thank you."

The old man nodded and left her.

She turned back inside and gently closed the door behind her. Leaned her back against it. With trembling hands, she opened the envelope and slid the letter out. It was dated seven months earlier.

Bella Madeline,

How many times have I asked myself what it is that you have done to me? I am not the same man I was before I met you and I am not the same monk. I am better.

But before I tell you about these things, I want to tell you that I am very sorry. It was wrong of me to disappear the way I did and not tell you what I was thinking. But I was thinking so many things that I did not make sense, even to myself. I hope and pray you can forgive me.

It is important that you know I do not regret loving you. And I do not regret that I am a monk. I do regret that I cannot be both a man to you and a monk to God and that is where painful choices must be made. It is important to me that you know that I was not lying to you in Saint Peter's when I told you that I was going to leave Saint Valentine's. In that moment, it was the truth.

I see now how the truth can change. The greater truth is that I am a monk and I am a more compassionate and understanding monk because of you. I studied many years to learn that I am divine, but you reminded me that I am also human and better able now to serve humanity.

And so it is that I love you and must choose not to be with you. It is better this way. I could not have made you happy. In your heart, you must know that.

Jonathan tells me you are married now. Your husband must be the man I saw you with on the terrace at Saint Valentine's that day. You looked well together. Jonathan also tells me that you are to have a baby. I am very happy for you. You will be a wonderful mother.

If there is any sadness I feel about my choice it is that I cannot leave behind a son or daughter. The rules do not allow such things and it is those choices that make this way of life so difficult. I often ask myself if this is what God truly would have us do. Are these in fact God's rules or man's? It seems that it could be time for change, but change is slow and it is too late for us. While the rules are the rules, I must strive to honor them as best I can. Just as my father did.

You see, Madeline, because of you, I learned that Father Marco is my father. He never came right out and said so. Not in so many words, but he told me a story of how he'd been with a young woman in Venice during World War II. A young Jewish girl. And how one day she just disappeared from his life. And how one day, I just appeared at Saint Valentine's. I like to imagine that she was not able to keep me and so she did the best she could. That she left me at Saint Valentine's. More likely she was killed along with all the other Jews. But however it came to be, I was left with my father. And the whole time, my whole life, I never knew my father. And yet, the whole time, I did. So it has taken me all my life to learn that nothing is ever black or white. Just heartbreakingly infinite shades of gray.

And so, Madeline, I sit here looking at the plains of Africa. I am in the middle of skies that never end and am surrounded by God's creatures. The people I work with are good. They know God in their own way and I believe more strongly now that God truly is everywhere. You should be very proud of Jonathan. He is already a big help to me. He is truly steadfast in his devotion to God and will be a better monk than I.

Now I fear it is time for me to say the goodbye I should have said to you in Italy. I do wonder if we will see each other again, maybe one day back at Saint Valentine's. I will return to Italy. It is my home and my heart. The sun shines in a different way there. And my father is there.

In truth, my dear Madeline, I had to leave Saint Valentine's because at every corner there was a reminder of you. Time, and God, heal all things and when I return, I hope to remember you and not feel the terrible hurt that I cannot have you, but feel my heart filled with love for you.

So I thank you for teaching me how love can change hearts and lives. I will never be the same and I would not, for anything, go back to being the man who had never known you.

It was signed, simply, Anthony.

Oh, Anthony.

Anthony was Father Marco's son! *His son!*

Madeline cried as she folded the letter and returned it to its place in the weathered envelope.

Cried for herself and for Anthony. Never again would they see each other among the ancient buildings of Saint Valentine's. He would never return to the Italy he loved. To his father. *Or maybe he will. Or has.*

Coco followed as Madeline slowly walked upstairs to Jonathan's nursery and found her baby sleeping soundly. How easy it would be to spend hours just watching the miraculous rise and fall of his breath as he slept.

Placing the letter gently beside his small body, Madeline looked at her son. Anthony's son. He would never know Anthony. Never even know *of* him. Tyler was his father in every way. Every way that mattered, really.

Oh, Anthony.

She closed her eyes and felt him again. In her and around her. Felt herself encircled in his arms. Felt his heart beating against her breasts. His breath warm and alive against the skin of her cheek.

He seemed to say, *"I'll always be here, Madeline. I'll always be a part of you."*

"Oh, Anthony."

I'll always love you.

Madeline stood, her arms resting on the rails of the crib, and watched little Jonathan sleep. She smiled through her tears, not certain if she was feeling great sadness or great joy.

Finally, she picked up Anthony's letter and walked over to the rocking chair and sat and rocked. And read the letter again. And again. Until she could not read it any more. Once more she folded it up and returned it to its envelope.

Rising from the chair, she walked into her and Tyler's bedroom. To her walk-in closet and a set of drawers. She pulled out the second from the bottom drawer, moved away some folded sweaters, and found a small box.

Lifting the lid, she found the letter from Jonathan. The one he had written from Italy that started it all. She remembered the day she had read it at her desk in Felicity's offices.

How life has changed since then.

Underneath it was the letter Anthony had written for Carrie's funeral. Madeline set Anthony's last letter on top of Jonathan's and replaced the lid. Covered the box again with her sweaters and closed the drawer.

With the back of her hand, she wiped away the last of her tears and walked back to little Jonathan.

"Maybe one day, we'll go to Italy. And you can meet your grandfather," she said, knowing it would never be.

She thought of Father Marco. Of how he and Anthony had spent all those years together as father and son. And Anthony never knew. *He never knew.* Now, Anthony's son would grow up never knowing *his* father.

She marveled at the irony of it. At the tangled web of it all. At how if any of it, any of it at all, had happened any differently, she would not be standing there. As Tyler's wife. Jonathan's mother. If her sister and husband had not fallen in love. If the car had not struck Jonathan. If Carrie had not gotten sick. She would never have traveled to Italy.

Would never have met Anthony.

Would never have loved him.

Fresh tears burned her eyes and she knew – she knew–she would not change a thing. Not a single moment. Not one.

Because loving Anthony had, after all, been enough. Had made her more of herself. More of who she is.

Yes. Carrie had been right. Loving Anthony had been enough. *Just loving him.*

And so all of it, *all* of it, had been perfect.

Just the way it was.

She looked down at her son. Stroked her wedding ring. Smiled through tears.

Yes. All of it is perfect. Somehow. Just the way it is.

About the Author:

Monica Marlowe divides her time between North Carolina and California. A lifelong reader and writer, Finding Felicity is her debut novel.

Her blog, Monica's Musings, can be found at http://www.monicamarlowe.blogspot.com

Also from Eternal Press:

Slam Sisters of Serendipity
by Terry Campbell

eBook ISBN: 9781615724215
Print ISBN: 9781615724222

Contemporary Humor
Novel of 66,625 words

The South rises again as the Slam Sisters of Serendipity come unleashed to investigate crime in their small community of Serendipity, South Carolina. After savoring the sweet taste of victory solving the murder of their locker room attendant at Magnolia Blossom Country Club, they search for more mysteries. The key to their success: their sex lives improve dramatically with each one they solve. In their first year of sleuthin', the team tennis sisters, aged thirty-eight to sixty-two, fall upon crime, murder, family lies and secrets, not to mention extreme adversity. While villains may score in a game of crime, not to worry, for the Slam Sisters serve aces with each toss of fate.

Also from Eternal Press:

Taking Back His Widow
by Kerri Williams

eBook ISBN: 9781615722983
Print ISBN: 9781615722990

Contemporary Paranormal
Novel of 55,460 words

Livinia Jacobs grudgingly ran from the love of her life with his child in her womb and into the arms of another man. She never thought she'd see Dean Stone again.

Eleven years later, she finds herself widowed in a picturesque little coastal town and her past has come back to haunt her.

Livinia was completely aware of her lack of control in Dean's presence. Heck, that was half the attraction in the first place, but her secret kept her feet firmly on the ground and her heart guarded from the once youthful dream of a future with him.

Dean forgot the most important thing of all about Livinia—she was his addiction. Ten minutes with her and he craved her touch again, wanted to hold her, to feel her soft naked skin against his, to kiss those supple, pink lips. Hell, he wanted her period.

Can he forgive her and prove he's no longer the scared boy he once was, but the man she needed him to be—a man she could trust with her heart, no matter the sacrifice?

Eternal Press

Official Website:
www.eternalpress.biz

Blog:
http://eternalpressauthors.blogspot.com/

Reader Chat Group:
http://groups.yahoo.com/group/EternalPressReaders

MySpace:
http://www.myspace.com/eternalpress

Twitter:
http://twitter.com/EternalPress

Facebook:
http://www.facebook.com/profile.php?id=1364272754

Good Reads:
http://www.goodreads.com/profile/EternalPress

Shelfari:
http://www.shelfari.com/eternalpress

Library Thing:
http://www.librarything.com/catalog/EternalPress

We invite you to drop in, visit with our authors and stay in touch for the latest news, releases and more!

CPSIA information can be obtained at www.ICGtesting.com
Printed in the USA
268683BV00001B/1/P